Blood and Kisses

Other James H Longmore Titles

'Pede
Flanagan
And Then You Die
Buds
The Erotic Odyssey of Colton Forshay
Feeder/I Am Joe's Unwanted Penis
Tenebrion

Blood and Kisses

By

James H Longmore

A HellBound Books Publishing LLC Book
Houston TX

A HellBound Books LLC Publication

www.hellboundbookspublishing.com

Printed in the United States of America

Acknowledgements

Face of an Angel (Demons, Devils and Denizens of Hell, HellBound Books, summer 2017)
Five Towns Pageant (Full Moon Slaughter Volume I, J. Ellington Ashton, 2016)
Trophy Husband (Black Candy, Jaded Books, 2016)
No One Dies Instantly (Beautiful Tragedies, HellBound Books, 2017)
Snuffed (rejected for content IV, J. Ellington Ashton, 2016)
A Proud Father (Deadman's Tome, 2017)
Road Trip Bingo (Bumps in the Road, Black Bed Sheet Books, 2016)
Zombie Hooker: A Love Story (Standing Ovation, Jaded Books, 2016)
Winning and Losing (The Ripple Effect 2015)
Waiting for the Call (Merchants of Misery, Fall 2017)
The Silverado Springs Memory Care Posse (The big Book of Bootleg Horror III: By Invitation Only, Fall 2017)

Blood and Kisses

Dedication

To my wonderfully stubborn wife, Jennifer – without your unerring belief and browbeating, not one of these stories would have seen the light of day.

Blood and Kisses

BLOOD AND KISSES Introduction

by Richard Chizmar

I don't know much about James H Longmore.

We've never met in person, never spoken on the telephone and have only shared a handful of brief emails.

Based on my one and only conversation with James – which occurred during a rollicking radio interview – I can tell you that he speaks with a delicious English accent, wields an impressive (and comfortingly weird) sense of humor, and is one hell of a natural showman.

If I take a quick peek at James's Facebook profile, I can tell you a tad bit more: James hails from Doncaster, England, where in earlier days he once studied Zoology at the University of Leeds; he currently resides in Houston, Texas where he spends his days working as a writer and director; and he compliments an admirably spiky haircut with the coolest set of eyeglasses I've seen in a very long time.

And there you have it. Everything I know about James H Longmore wrapped up in a neat and tidy ball of facts.

***

Only that's not entirely true.

Because, you see, when I rolled out of bed this morning (a little later than usual thanks to some late night binge watching of *Broadchurch* on Netflix; highly recommended, by the way), I had the distinct pleasure of sitting down on my back patio with the manuscript of James Longmore's latest collection, *Blood and Kisses* – and I learned a whole lot more about James.

I didn't stumble upon this knowledge because *Blood and Kisses* contains scads of autobiographical information about James's life. It doesn't.

However, as with the best of writers, James not only infuses his fiction with a generous dollop of storytelling talent, but also with a hidden doorway into the depths of his soul.

Take the short story, "A Proud Father" for example. This fairly brief narrative takes us deep into the dark heart of a nameless, war-torn city. The prose is terrifically lean, yet evocative. You can feel the buildings tremble when the bombs fall to earth; you can hear the staccato echo of automatic gunfire from the next block over; and you can *feel* the desolate pain and hopelessness of the city's remaining inhabitants. "A Proud Father" is poignant and poetic and a solemn reminder that sometimes survivors aren't the lucky ones.

Covering vastly different literary ground – think of what late greats James Herbert and Richard Laymon may have given birth to had they ever collaborated – but written with the same assured hand, "The Five Towns Pageant" tells the story of young Cam McGlamery and his unfortunate run-in with a "cute" pup in a local pet shop, and a small town's bizarre traditions. This captivating story shares only one trait in common with the aforementioned "A Proud Father." They are both excellent and entertaining tales.

"Mars Rover Seven" is another gem, and probably my favorite story in the book. Part sci-fi, part horror, this cautionary tale of artificial intelligence gone astray manages to be both suspenseful and heart-breaking, and contains enough plot and character development to fill a full-length novel. It also concludes with one of the niftiest surprise endings I've come across in some time. I won't give away the details, but a question is asked of one particular character in the final passage of the story, and this character's one word answer still haunts me as of this writing.

Okay, I've said enough now. I won't delve into any of the other stories here in this introduction. Better I let you experience them on your own with no pre-conceived notions.

As you can see for yourself, thanks to *Blood and Kisses*, I've learned quite a bit today about James H Longmore. I've learned that he is a versatile writer with a unique and captivating voice. I've learned that, unlike many of today's authors, he isn't nearly satisfied treading familiar waters; this guy likes to spread his wings and we are all the richer for his daring. I've also learned that James is the sneaky sort, equally willing to draw blood with his pen in one scene, as he is to snip away at our heartstrings in the next. But, perhaps, most significant of all, I've learned that James H Longmore is a storyteller at heart. The best kind of writer in my mind. He doesn't dally and he doesn't pretend. He simply invites you to pull up a stool and take a seat and have a listen.

And we his readers obey and follow.

Richard Chizmar 2017

Blood and Kisses

Contents

Blood and Kisses

Welcome To My Indulgence

There comes a time in every author's career when we amass sufficient short stories to allow for that veritable pinnacle of self-indulgence that is *The Collection*. And so here, Dear Reader, I have gathered together my own eclectic mix of shorts, a smattering of flash-fiction quickies and my one and only attempt at poetry, the sum of which tell the story of my journey thus far within the realms of independent literature.

From my very first published piece – *Winning and Losing* (The Ripple Effect, 2015: a fund raiser for Greenpeace, I really do like to think that we saved a whale or two), through *S**t Happens* which eventually grew up to become the incredibly successful bizarro novel, *And Then You Die* (J. Ellington Ashton, 2016) and the bunch of previously unpublished (and spanking brand new) tales – *Our New Church, Mars Rover Seven* to name but two, these snippets of my imagination leave a trail across the past three or four years in which I have been able to follow my lifelong dream of flexing my literary muscles.

Okay, so the poem was written as a favor for a friend who simply *had to have* (her words, not mine) a James H Longmore piece in her poetry anthology (Beautiful Tragedies, available summer 2017 from HellBound Books – buy a copy!) and whilst poetry has always confounded me, I certainly gave it my very best shot.

The Moroccan Reverberation was written for a competition in which we hapless participants were given specific genres in which to write. Of course I'd kept my fingers crossed for Horror, but was allocated 'Spy Thriller' instead – just shows how ineffective the crossing of fingers can really be, I guess. I am, nonetheless particularly pleased with the story that came out in the end, although it did turn out to be a tad more Peter Benchley than Ian Fleming – which is especially gratifying if, like me, you happen to love shark stories! Needless to say, it transpired that the judges of said competition did not.

Some of the tales within this, my first collection (there *will* be others, mark my words – literally!) were written specifically for submission to themed anthologies – *Waiting for the Call* and *The Five Towns Pageant* – whilst others were written simply because they were rattling around in my head, clawing frantically at the inside of my skull in their desperation to taste freedom and have their voices heard – *Our New Church, Zombie Hooker* and a personal favorite of mine, *The Silverado Springs Memory Care Posse*.

Within these very pages, too, you will encounter my first (and to date only) attempt at science fiction – *Mars Rover Seven* – a fairly decent stab at fantasy, and a handful of flash fiction tales written for some long-forgotten online horror magazine.

There's something here for everyone, then – from extreme and horror most gruesome, to *Boy's Own* space adventure to poignant and at times heartbreaking drama (I defy you to not cry at *A Proud Father*!), to the darkly comedic and fanciful – my sincerest hope is that you enjoy reading them, Dear Reader, as much as I have enjoyed transcribing them from the deepest, darkest gullies of my creative brain.

Enjoy, and thank you for reading.

James H Longmore

Blood and Kisses

Our New Church

The hollow, insistent knock on the front door pissed Mike Savage off.

For one, it was Sunday morning, for two it had riled his pit-bull up to the point at which the dumbass dog was literally frothing at the mouth, and last – but not least – Mike was nursing the rear-end of the hangover from hell; last night's beer session with the missus had been a doozy and a half – if the relentless pounding on the inside of his skull and his desert-dry mouth were anything to go by.

Mike rolled over, his broad shoulders taking most of the comforter along with them as the thing wrapped around his tight, lean, tattooed body like it really didn't want him to leave. Mike cast one aching eye the length and breadth of his wife's freshly exposed, naked body and tried his damndest to will her to wake up. No luck there, Laura was dead to the world. She lay on her back, pert, pointy breasts pointing aggressively up at the slowly twirling ceiling fan, her head was lolled back and she was snoring fit to burst.

The knock on the door again.

The dog barked with renewed fury and Mike heard Todd stirring in the bedroom across the landing. For a six-year-old, it certainly took a hell of a lot to wake that boy up.

"Goddammit," Mike growled to himself, his voice croaky and parched. He crawled out of bed, fighting to extricate himself from the bed sheets. Groaning, he pulled on the pair of gray sweat pants that lived permanently next to the bed and really would benefit from a run through the laundry sometime soon. Hopping comically on one foot, Mike struggled to avoid sticking both of his legs down one leg hole. "I'm coming, for fuck's sake," Mike grumbled as finally he exited the bedroom with one last glance at his beautiful wife.

"Fifi!" Mike called the barking dog away from the front door. "Here, girl."

Fifi immediately ceased her noise and trotted over to Mike, tail wagging and fat, pink tongue lolling. Mike ushered his dog out into the back yard and approached the door with a nervous eye flicking to the tall, metal vase that stood sentry beside it – a souvenir from the African market Laura loved to frequent – in which was concealed his 12-gauge; one could never be too careful in Mike's line of work.

"Good morning, to you Sir," the cheerful, resonant voice that greeted Mike as he opened the door grated on his aching brain like nails down a chalkboard. "I hope you and your family are fit and well and happy with the Lord on this fine, fine day!"

Mike gave an inward groan; this was pretty much the last thing he needed right now, a God-botherer on a Sunday morning. He eyed the jolly-faced guy on his doorstep with great disdain and wondered just what on earth possessed these people to wear a three-piece woollen suit when it was already in the mid-eighties at nine in the goddamned morning.

"Allow me to introduce myself," the suited man stretched out a large, meaty hand for the shaking through the gap Mike had created in the doorway. Mike looked down at the hand as if it were some wholly unpleasant, alien thing invading his territory. He also noted that it was darkly perma-tanned like the guy's face and couldn't help but speculate if the rest of him was the same shade. "I'm Antonio D. Love, your spanking brand new, shiny as shit, God-appointed pastor!" Love announced like he was some cheesy, over the top game show host as he grasped Mike's hand and gave it a firm, moist shake. "And this here is my able assistant in the Lord's good work, Kayla Wyatt."

Mike squinted downwards as the pastor ushered a short, chubby black girl from behind his legs. Mike hadn't noticed the miserable looking youngster standing dutifully behind Love in her demure, knee length floral dress. The poor girl looked sweaty and uncomfortable but nonetheless she forced a weak smile. Mike smiled back and felt a little sorry for her.

The pastor plucked a crisp, white pamphlet from the stack the girl held tight in her small, sweaty hands and thrust it towards Mike's face.

"I come carrying our Lord's word," Love declared somewhat grandly, "and I simply *have* to share it with you, or I'll just go right ahead and burst, Mr. –?"

"Savage," Mike grumbled. "Mike Savage." He stepped back into the cool of his hallway, seeking sanctuary from his throbbing head there. "You're wasting your time here, buddy."

"Ah, but am I?" the pastor grinned. He leaned in a tad, towering his tall, lanky frame over Mike who stood five-nine in his bare feet. "Can you put your hand on your heart, Mr. Savage – Mike, can I call you Mike? Of course I can, we're all friends under God's loving gaze – and tell me that you are truly not interested in hearing the glorious words of the Lord, our God?"

Mike fixed the pastor with his best steely glare, the one he held in reserve for the potheads and crack addicts who didn't pay him on time, and for the first time he noticed the clergyman's eyes. Dark, brooding, liquid, they were set deep into the smooth, golden skin of Love's impossibly handsome face, which was in turn framed by neatly trimmed hair that was by far the blackest shade of black Mike thought he'd ever laid eyes on. The pastor's eyes twinkled and smiled as they returned Mike's gaze and they were of the deepest, darkest brown – so much so as to be almost black.

"If I was interested, don't ya think I'd be in church now?" Mike gave his stock answer – religious types had become something of a nuisance in the subdivision recently, despite the gates and myriad signs that bluntly declared *no soliciting*; somehow they figured that selling their religion on Sunday mornings simply didn't count as solicitation. It annoyed Mike to no end how Love and his ilk seemed to prefer the more genteel estates to ply their ecumenical wares; he'd never had this problem growing up in the projects.

"Would you, Mr. Savage? Would you indeed?" Love persisted. "If that were the case, I wouldn't be interrupting your Sunday morning now, would I?" Again, with that shit eating grin. "This is by far *the* perfect time for spreading the word of the Lord, as all of you heathens are home and ripe for the picking!" Love raised his hands to the heavens to emphasise his point.

Mike remained unimpressed.

"I'm just joshing with ya, Mr. Savage," Love tempered his smile somewhat and lowered his voice.

"All I really wanted to do was to find a little time to make the acquaintance of my new flock."

"Then shouldn't you be in church?" Mike grumbled as with great reluctance he plucked the pamphlet from Love's long, spindly fingers.

"Not until eleven-thirty today, Mr. Savage." Love beamed. "Then again, you'd already know that if you were a Christian man." The pastor tipped Mike a smiling wink, which was met with an icy stare. "Perhaps we shall see you there?"

"I highly doubt that." Mike inched himself away from the door, easing it closed as he did so.

"You have yourself a great morning enjoying the Lord's miracles that dwell all around you." Love took a step backwards, turned on his heels and ambled down Mike's driveway, skirting by Laura's *Panamera* with great care. The miserable little girl slouched along behind him, her brow decorated with shiny beads of perspiration.

"Who was that?" Laura's voice behind him startled Mike. He jumped, dropped the pastor's pamphlet and turned to face his wife.

"Just some Jesus freak," he told her. "Waking us up this time on a Sunday, who the fuck do they think they are?" Mike ran a shaky hand over his shiny bald pate and snorted.

"The guy with the little girl?"

"Yeah." Mike watched Love and his reluctant minion make their way down along the sidewalk in front of the house. He turned his attention to Laura and to the all too familiar stirring in his pants. She looked mighty fine dressed in the oversized white T-shirt she'd bought him a couple of Christmases ago. It had a picture of Gizmo the pre-gremlin on the front because that had been Mike's favorite movie as a kid. Laura wore the shirt well, especially with her newly rounded belly, *sans* panties and fresh from their bed. Mike slipped an arm around his wife's waist and hoped that Todd had gone back to sleep.

"You didn't offer them a drink?" Laura shrugged his hand away.

"Why would I have?" Mike was puzzled.

"Just look at that poor little girl." Laura pulled the door wide open and before Mike could protest she'd called out, "Would you like some water?"

Mike groaned as he watched the pastor's face light up. Laura was forever doing shit like this; always the champion of lost causes, mother hen to those she saw as weak and helpless. Mike reckoned it was his wife's way of remembering just where she and her husband had come from – perhaps even atonement for how they made their living. Or possibly it was nothing more than Laura Savage was just a sucker for a hard luck story. Either way, this was precisely why Mike steered her away from anything remotely charitable, and why he'd expressly banned her from the pet store on Pet Adoption Days.

"You are truly a gift from God, Ma'am." Love smiled once more with that capacious smile of his. "Didn't I tell you that the good Lord would provide?" he boomed into Kayla's upturned face that fair dripped with perspiration. Love trudged across Mike's meticulously manicured lawn, back towards the front door and Laura Savage and her warm, welcoming and most delightfully altruistic smile.

And before Mike could protest, Pastor Antonio D. Love and his young ward were firmly ensconced on his expensive, cream leather sofa sipping iced water from Laura's best cut-crystal tumblers. The young girl gulped hers down noisily, her throat bobbing up and down as the chill water quenched it, whilst the pastor took more genteel sips and watched pensively as the fat ice cubes danced around in his glass and chinked melodically against the sides.

It was cool in the house; the AC had been set to a positively Arctic 69 degrees for overnight – any warmer and Mike was guaranteed no Saturday night action because Laura would be *too hot*; and boy had they enjoyed some drunken action last night?!

Mike watched as the pastor and the young girl cooled down some. Kayla, in particular, looked more comfortable by the minute, her face no longer looking sweaty and exhausted

"I can't begin to thank you kind folks enough," Love sounded quite sincere. "It really is thirsty work delivering the Lord's word to folks such as yourselves in weather such as this." Mike found the smile that followed that particular statement to be patronizing at the very least. Just what did the pious fool mean by *folks such as yourselves*? "Or, as I like to call it, spreading the *Love*." The pastor guffawed at his own pun, although Mike figured this wasn't the first time he'd used it. He also thought it sounded wholly inappropriate coming from a man of the cloth, especially one whose name made him sound like a washed-up nineteen-seventies porn star.

"It's our pleasure," Laura said. "Isn't it, darling?" Aimed at Mike, her sweet smile caught him totally off guard.

"Yeah, sure," he replied.

"Say, big guy," Love said to Todd as he sauntered into the lounge, his latest Lego creation clutched proudly in his hand. "Is that a space rocket I see there?"

Todd's face cracked into a broad grin and he held out the mismatched bundle of colored bricks for closer inspection, his usual reticence around strangers conspicuous by its absence.

Mike watched warily as the pastor took the toy from Todd's tiny hands and turned it over in his long fingers as if it were the most delicate thing in the world. As for himself, Mike really couldn't tell if his son's construction was a rocket, a car, a boat or a damned robot. He also watched as his son's face lit up with pride and something akin to admiration for the strange man who his mother had welcomed into their home.

"Ya know," Love said to Todd as he placed the Lego model with great care back into the boy's hands. "I'll bet Kayla here would just *love* to spend a little time on those swings of yours." He nodded out through the window towards the cedar wood swingset that dominated the back yard. "Why don't you two go play awhile whilst I chat to your Mom and Dad; save you gettin' bored with all the grown-up talk?"

Kayla was up and on her feet before Pastor Love could finish his sentence, the happy look on her face most out of place. Todd took the girl's hand and led her to the kitchen and then towards the back door to freedom.

All too late, Mike remembered the dog.

"No!" he yelled as he heard the door to the back yard click open.

Too late.

Fifi bounded in, ears flapping, her panting mouth split wide open in a slobbering, rictus grin. Mike lunged for the dog as she raced by him, grabbing at the spiked collar around her neck, but missing by a clear mile. His heart sank as the pit-bull made a beeline for the pastor.

"Hey there, sweet girl," Love greeted the charging dog with not so much as a flinch. Fifi in turn slowed up and approached him passively; tail wagging, eyes down, ears flattened to her broad skull. "Well, aren't you a beauty?" Love cooed as he scratched between the dog's ears.

Mike relaxed a little. Everyone, it would seem, loved Pastor Antonio D Love – even the stupid dog.

"What happened to Pastor Gregory?" Laura asked of Love. "He was nice."

"Alas, he passed on to join the Lord in his well-earned eternity," Love rolled his eyes heavenwards, their whites a startling contrast against his tanned skin.

"Oh dear," Laura said. "I am sorry."

"No need to be, young lady," Love soothed. "He had lived a long and fruitful life; it was merely his time to meet God, is all."

Mike remembered Gregory with a vague fondness. Their paths had crossed on occasion amongst the crowd of homeless lost souls who gathered beneath the towering columns of the downtown freeway; Mike to ply his trade and the pastor to save said lost souls from Mike's nefarious goods, amongst their other limited temptations.

Although Mike made his big money on the rich folk around town, he still sold to the desperate people once a week. He always took along his cheapest stuff – rocks of crack or meth' mostly – drugs that were easily affordable for those who'd made the effort to beg for spare change on the intersections for the quick escape from the abject misery life afforded them. Mike saw it as kind of his community service, giving back to where he clawed himself up from; it was his own perverse version of working the soup kitchens. Perhaps Mike Savage did have some soul left after all.

"I thought I hadn't seen him for some time," Mike added. In fact, he could not actually put a date to the last time he'd bumped into the ancient clergyman.

"He was old and not up to getting out and about in his final year or two," Love explained. "I guess that's how come many of his flock abandoned his church in preference for that mega church over in Snake Bridge."

Love shook his head and clasped his hands together. "Lord save those poor souls from that money-grasping, godless place," he said with reverence. "And it saddened me to hear that when the Chronicle printed his obituary, many of your fellow townsfolk were actually *surprised* – they'd thought the poor man had died years ago."

Mike admitted to himself that he was amongst that crowd. Learning now that Gregory had only just recently met his maker had come as a bit of a shock, the same way in which it does when an A-lister from Hollywood's golden era passes and one's first thought is *they were still alive?*

"So, can I expect to see you good folks at church later this morning?" Love spoke as if the three of them had actually had that conversation. "I'm sure that eleven-thirty will give you both plenty of time to make yourselves suitably presentable for an audience with the Lord." He tipped a wink at Laura. "You'd need hardly any time at all, why you're just as pretty as a picture as you are, Ma'am."

Laura giggled and Mike could have sworn she'd actually blushed; she looked like a silly little schoolgirl as she shuffled her ass nervously on the sofa opposite the pastor and Mike hoped she'd remember to keep her legs closed.

"I really don't think –" Mike was cut off as his cell phone vibrated in his pocket, buzzing urgently against his thigh like an angry wasp. He fished out the phone and squinted at its bright screen. "I have to take this." He shot Laura a glance, not entirely comfortable at leaving her alone with the oddly charismatic new pastor but not able to take the call in the man's earshot. This was the deal he'd been waiting on for two days now; Molly, Crack, Colombian Coke, a thousand tabs of Ecstasy and Christ only knew how much skunk they'd be wanting to go with all of that – those rich folks up on the hill sure knew how to party hard.

"That's okay, honey," Laura dismissed her husband with a wave of the hand, "you go take care of your business."

With some reluctance, Mike took the call and retreated from his lounge, leaving his atheist wife chatting to the new pastor like they were old school buddies.

*

And so, that was how come Mike Savage found himself sitting on a hard wooden pew at the rear of the ramshackle, wood-built Church of the Christian Fellowship in his Sunday-best suit and with trickles of sweat dripping down his back.

The place was packed to standing room only; it had been a mixed blessing that Mike, Laura and Todd had arrived early (on Laura's insistence) – whilst it had meant spending longer in the stuffy, airless church, at least they got to sit down, no matter how uncomfortable the seating. It had been quite possibly decades since the tiny church had been so full, and Mike feared that the sudden, sheer weight of all the townsfolk the new pastor had shamed in to attending would likely cause the ancient floor to collapse and bring the whole place crashing down about their sinful, heathen ears.

"Good people of Waxahachie," Pastor Love's voice boomed out across the sea of sweat-shined, attentive faces, his tone full and resonant without the aid of a microphone. The congregation was hanging on his every word, enraptured by the man in the rickety old pulpit. Even Todd Savage, usually the most fidgety and easily distracted of children, sat stock still in awe of Love, a serene smile upon his thin lips. "It delights my very soul

29

to see so many of you here today for my inaugural sermon, and I just *know* that our Lord is pleased too. Praise Him!"

"Praise Him!" the congregation countered with gusto.

"And as I look around at all of these beautiful faces of God's children, do you know what I see?"

A wall of blank, blinking faces met the pastor's wide-eyed stare.

"*I said*, do you know what I see?!" Love raised his voice and startled the gathered people. Somewhere at the back of the church, a baby began to cry, its voice shrill.

"No, sir!" the people replied.

"I see a flock whose shepherd abandoned them," Love's voice was almost a growl at this revelation. "Yes indeed! He abandoned you all to the wastelands of sinfulness and neglection of prayer!"

This was greeted with nods and murmurs of acknowledgment, even an *amen* or two, and Mike pondered if *neglection* was actually a real word or not.

"And what I *see*," Love's tone rose once more and tears of raw emotion glinted in his deep, dark eyes. "Are good, God-fearin' townsfolk who deserve so much better than this ruination – this *abomination* – of a church!"

"Amen!" a goodly number of the congregation chanted.

Love lowered his voice to a hissing stage-whisper. "Why, I can hardly bear to hear myself speak the word *church* in this place," he said. "For this is no church, and do you know why this is no church, good people of Waxahachie?"

"No sir!" the people spoke, almost to a man, woman and child.

"Because a church is supposed to be a place made for the people, *by* the people!" Love declared, his hands held aloft. "This place should be a place where the ten thousand lost souls of this great town can congregate to praise their Lord God and saviour, somewhere that brings the decent townsfolk of Waxahachie together with one purpose and one voice!"

"*Praise Him!*" The combined voice of three hundred or so souls reached the roof and once more Mike worried that it may just be enough to bring the whole thing crashing down about his ears. He glanced nervously upwards and whilst he was relieved to see the rafters were still very much intact, it niggled to see Laura's blank, entranced expression as she stared vacantly at the pastor. It was, Mike noted, an expression shared by the entire congregation. At this, a shiver darted up Mike's spine and nestled at the base of his skull like a small, frightened animal.

"So, ya know what we're gonna do, good people of Waxahachie?" Love persisted, his voice trembling with passion.

"What *are* we gonna do?" the people asked.

"What we're gonna do is tear down this repugnant facsimile of God's house and then we're gonna build Him, and you good people, the church that you *truly* deserve!"

As one, the congregation clambered to its feet and spontaneously clapped as Pastor Antonio D. Love soaked up their adoration from behind the flaky paint of the old wooden pulpit. Even Mike struggled to his feet, groaning loudly at the kink in his back.

"And we're gonna rebirth *your* church as the Waxahachie United Church of the People!"

At this, the applause was rapturous. Tears of joy streamed down the faces of some of the crowd and yet others stomped their feet, as if the cacophony of six hundred hands slapping together wasn't enough.

"I can see some of you thinking *what is this gonna cost us, Pastor Love?!*" Love shouted above the row,

31

which dampened considerably upon his mention of *cost*. He hushed the congregation with a downward motion of his hands, bid the gathered townsfolk to all sit down.

Mike allowed himself a wry smile. Here it comes; the rub, the hustle. For all of his crowd-pleasing rhetoric, the new pastor wasn't all that different than the thousand-dollar suit assholes that fleeced the little old ladies over at the mega-church.

"In times gone by, the people of a town would give up their time and skills as decreed by law to build their church," Love explained to the silenced audience – and even the baby quit its keening. "So yes, I do want your money for *our* new church, but more importantly than that, good people of Waxahachie, I need *you*!" And somehow Love's dark, almost black eyes managed to look at each and every one of those gathered before him, all at once. "Every single soul can contribute to God's new house. And to those who have no skills to offer, but are willing to give freely of their time – I say, we can teach you, we can guide your hands with the love of the Lord, and we will bring this beautiful town together."

"Praise Him!" the people cried in pious unison. *"Praise Him!"*

Praise Him, indeed, Mike thought to himself, too much the cynic to be swept up in Love's happy-clappy bullshit; he knew there'd be a catch, a scam somewhere along the line; it just remained to be revealed.

Nonetheless, the new pastor, Antonio D Love had promised to build the ten thousand or so Waxahachie townspeople a brand-new church, and that was precisely what he did.

*

The old church had been torn down with such haste that it had seemed almost irreverent. The crumbling wooden structure had been reduced to its bare-bones foundations in a matter of days. And even for someone as decidedly irreligious as Mike Savage, the utter finality of seeing the town's familiar landmark stripped down so quickly seemed simply *wrong*.

Mike skirted around the tall, wooden perimeter fence that they'd erected around the construction site that was to be the new church. He'd opted to walk that way to his weekly rounds amongst Waxahachie's down and outs for the express purpose of sneaking a peek at the building work, his curiosity aroused by Laura's almost continual chatter about Pastor Love and his wondrous new celebration of the Good Lord.

Sadly, Mike's attempts at surveying the work in progress were thwarted. The fence around the site of the new church was easily nine feet tall and had not so much as the thinnest of gaps or a knothole through which a curious soul may peep. Even the gate that had been constructed to match the fence was good and solid, the work beyond shielded from the townsfolk's prying eyes.

And as he turned the corner, the mighty concrete freeway stretched out less than a half mile away, it occurred to Mike that for a construction site the work on the new church was disconcertingly quiet.

"Early lunch, alright for some," Mike growled as he strode by, his head bowed against the oppressive heat that beat down against his shaven skull.

It was somewhat cooler beneath the stark concrete underbelly of the freeway, where the sun's baking rays simply couldn't reach. Above, the traffic thundered in a continuous roar, oblivious to the lost and lonely souls who huddled beneath to wait out the remainder of their wasted lives.

Today there were noticeably fewer of the bedraggled homeless folk than Mike had visited last week.

"They workin' at yon new church," Scruffy Joe explained to Mike, pronouncing the word as *noo*. "I hear tell that new pastor's givin' out free food an' work boots," he continued with an undeniable envy in his voice.

"They took all of their stuff with them?" Mike quizzed. He squinted around at the lack of battered shopping carts, ragged cardboard boxes and shitty old tents.

"They say Love's set up a camp site of sorts, with fancy tents an' lavatorials an' running water an' all," Scruffy Joe looked around at the towering walls of gray that rose around he and his remaining associates. "Sounds like one o' they refugee camps in Africa or someplace poor, but it's still gotta be better than this hell-hole." The vagrant sighed a melancholic sigh and stabbed his grubby fingers at his long, white streaked beard as if he were searching for something.

Scruffy Joe was one of Mike's oldest and most loyal customers. He loved Mike's dirt-cheap Meth' – his prematurely aged, haggard features and lack of most of his teeth stood testimony to that. He'd been a Waxahachie bum for as long as anyone could remember, his shambling, reeking figure so common a sight around the town that he'd become something of a popular mascot. That Scruffy Joe's life had come to this; dwelling beneath the freeway, scavenging and begging for sustenance, living fix to fix and dreaming of a better life in a construction site tent, went way beyond sad.

In an uncharacteristic fit of empathy, Mike was tempted to slip the old man a freebie – just enough to allow him take the edge off. However, Mike stopped himself. Business was business at the end of the day, and do that one time and they'd all expect it; his prices to these dregs of society were ridiculously low as it was.

"I'm sure I'll be gettin' my call up soon enough," Scruffy Joe told Mike with a grin that exposed the blackened, rotted carcasses of his three remaining teeth. "I reckon I still have a skill or two to offer."

Mike smiled back at the man, although he couldn't for the life of him think what those skills could possibly be.

*

The next week, along with yet more of the freeway dwellers, Scruffy Joe was gone. Mike kinda missed the sad old bastard, and wished he'd given him that free hit of crystal now. It had been the same at the rehab clinics, both of which were markedly empty of residents, all lost to the Pastor's impressively ambitious project. It was beginning to grind Mike's gears; the homeless his business could survive without, but the clinics were filled with rich folk who'd happily pay well over the odds for his merchandise. They were the people who paid for his affluent lifestyle and who he was banking on to get Todd through college.

It was almost as if Love had become some bizarre one man anti-drug crusader who's set out to ruin Mike's livelihood.

There was an air of excitement about town that morning, as the new church – already considerably bigger than the old one, even though nowhere near finished – had emerged above the concealment of the imposing fence.

Even Mike had stopped to gawk up in wonder at the slender beams that rose out of the church's foundations like bleached, skeletal fingers that pointed accusingly up at the heavens. And around those, the emergence of the building's walls seemed most miraculous as the shape of the church was now clearly outlined in thick, white stone that shimmered like a desert mirage in the town's late morning heat.

Mike stood back at the other side of the road along with the small crowd of gathered fellow Waxahachians to marvel at Pastor Love's amazing feat of architecture. Just how they had gotten so far without scaffolding or some sort of crane was beyond Mike, but then again, he was no civil engineer. And the sheer speed at which the new church had grown was a far cry from the old days when such magnificent structures would take generations to complete. Not bad for a crew that seemed to have been made up almost exclusively of the town's degenerates and destitute.

And once again, Mike noted that the construction site was deathly quiet, and he wondered if perhaps they all worked through the night to avoid the brutal Texas summer sunshine.

*

The following weekend, Laura dragged Mike along to Pastor Love's Sunday service. It was held in the Middle School's gymnasium, courtesy of the Principal who was both a fanatical Love supporter and chronic MDMA user.

What ever happened to the separation of Church and state? Mike had grumbled, decidedly unhappy at having to wear a shirt and tie, let alone being made to leave his bed on what had become his and Laura's sex morning.

"Welcome, welcome, one and all!" Love's dulcet tones radiated throughout the gymnasium, bouncing off of the cheerfully decorated walls. "It is truly God's miracle that I get to spend this precious time with you good people of Waxahachie," he boomed. "And it is also gratifying to see one or two new faces here today." Mike was positive that comment had been aimed squarely at him, and rather oddly he realized that he felt embarrassed.

"I am humbled here today before our Lord and saviour to see so many of you here in our church," Love waved his arms around to denote the gym, adorned as it was with past glories of the school's basketball team, the Waxahachie Ravens.

There were puzzled faces aplenty throughout the packed crowd at Love's use of the word *church*. The pastor smiled and it was as if he was smiling at each and every one of the gathered townsfolk.

"For what is a church, if not a gathering of good people in the common cause of praising the Lord?"

"Praise Him!" the crowd exalted and Mike rolled his eyes.

"Mike!" Laura admonished her errant husband with a swift elbow to the ribs.

"Ouch!" Mike complained and Todd grinned up at him like this was the most entertaining thing ever.

"A church – *our* church – is so much *more* than any building; it is the joyous coming together of like-minded souls." Love paused to soak up the adoration of his rapt audience. "And have we not all seen what such a coming together in God's name can achieve?"

"Yeah!" An over-enthusiastic voice rose high above the crowd. Mike glanced over his shoulder and saw that the owner of said voice was Charmaine Pemberthy, a rather stout young woman who had an expensive penchant for the finest Colombian marching powder that Mike could lay his hands on. In secret, the woman also happened to be the town's biggest slut and her poor husband had no idea that he was working himself into an early grave to provide for the children of three other men.

"How many amongst you have witnessed the miracle of our new church?" Love shouted, his arms out at his sides as if to gather in the warmth from his flock.

"I have!" The majority of the congregation yelled back at their pastor with such verve that it set the hairs on the back of Mike's neck on end as surely as a goose walking across his grave.

"An achievement attained only with the guidance of God's great hand!"

"*Hallelujah*! the gathering erupted.

Love's countenance then fell serious. He leaned forward, hands braced against either side of the portable pulpit as if he were holding the rickety thing up. "And yet there are those amongst us who see you as nothing more than sheep," he said, his voice low.

And once again, Mike felt incredibly self-conscious.

"These people see themselves as holy sheep dogs, assigned by God to protect the sheep from harm." Love's face twisted in a grimace, like someone had just smeared fresh shit across his top lip. "They see fit to bring guns into our church, people," Love sounded suitably appalled and Mike felt relieved that the pastor's diatribe was not aimed at him. "And I have to ask them why? Why in the name of God, Jesus and all that is holy do you think it necessary to arm yourself in God's house?!"

Love appeared to be directing his venom filled words at Andy Saenz and his motley posse of open-carry rednecks. "Well let me tell *you*, good people of Waxahachie," Love growled. "If you are God's sheep dogs, then I am God's tapeworm!" A chuckle spread out across the congregation. "I will crawl up your ass and suck you dry of your self-aggrandizing vanity and false pride until the blinkers fall away and you can see the true beauty of the Lord our God! For you are no more special than anyone else here today – not the young, the

38

old, the destitute, the addicted, the fornicators and the non-believers who stare constantly into the eternal void in which their only comfort is that when you're dead you don't know you're dead."

"*Amen*!" the people – with the notable exception of Saenz and his suitably humiliated cronies – cried out.

"All you do is posture and preen like ridiculous peacocks with your firearms on show." Love looked straight in Saenz's eyes and the man blushed a bright crimson. "Whilst others have brought their skills from every corner of this great town, from the city and from across the border; were it not for them, and we were to rely upon the likes of you, the labor of love that is the Lord's house would be little more than a hole in the ground!"

Mike stared at Saenz and took great delight in watching the gun-toting asshole wilt beneath the unrelenting gaze and harsh words of the pastor.

"Your time will come soon to serve Him and to make amends in his new house, for the Lord loves you as he does all of his children. You will have time to repent and see the error of your ways, and pray to your God that he forgives you for offending his justness," Love's voice mellowed as he played the crowd. "I am proud to call myself God's tapeworm, as lowly and vile as that creature may be, because it proves to us all that even God's self-proclaimed sheepdogs have a weakness."

Mike found the whole thing incredibly hard to swallow, particularly since the pastor's talk of intestinal parasites was making his breakfast pancakes churn around in his stomach as if they were trying to get out. But, seeing the joyful, rapt look on Laura's face, and the broad grin on Todd's, Mike could be at least happy that they were happy.

After the sermon, in which Love went on even farther with the whole tapeworm analogy, and tuneless renditions of *The Lord's My Shepherd, Amazing Grace* and another hymn that Mike couldn't recall from his childhood days in the old wooden church (not that the latter mattered too much, Mike moved his lips silently along to that one as he had the others), they stopped to chat to Pastor Love on the way out of the makeshift house of worship.

"Thank you for turning out, folks" Love beamed as he shook Laura's hand. "It is always an absolute delight to see you." Love then took a hold of Todd's hand and shook it with enthusiasm. "You too, young man. I hope you are taking good care of your mom and your little brother – or is it *sister*?" Love glanced at the slight swell of Laura's belly and then at Laura.

"We don't know yet, it's too early to tell," she told the pastor.

"Mr. Savage!" Love turned his attention to Mike. "How simply perfect for you to have accompanied your beautiful family to our service! Welcome to the congregation."

Reluctantly, Mike shook hands with the pastor, and was surprised to find the tall man's hand warm, dry and baby's butt smooth.

"He didn't want to, Mommy made him come." Todd blurted out at the top of his voice, much to everyone's amusement.

"Ah, but *did she*, young Master Savage?" Love grinned down at the boy. "Or was it God who persuaded your heathen father to join us on this most joyful of days?"

"Nah, it was Mom," Todd replied in earnest. "She said that if he didn't come along with us, there'd be no early night tonight."

"Todd!" Laura's face colored up a remarkable shade of red, and Mike smirked and held in the belly laugh that threatened to explode out through his nose.

Unphased by this innocent revelation, Pastor Love tousled Todd's neatly combed hair and replied, "No matter what the motivation, young man, *everyone* is welcome in God's house." His smile was quite serene as he turned his attention to Laura. "And on that particular note, I am hoping that I will be seeing you at our construction site this coming week, there is much work to be done and we could sure use a capable young woman such as yourself." Love's segue was a clumsy one but nonetheless Laura's face lit up with something other than sheer embarrassment.

"It's Spring Break," Mike chipped in with a distinct growl in his voice. Just what exactly Love had in mind for Laura, he couldn't imagine; she was a part time waitress at Denny's for Christ's sakes. "Laura has Todd home all day."

"Why, that is no problem whatsoever," Love's voice resounded about the gym, above the heads of the exiting congregation. "Bring the little fella along with you," Love told Laura, "there's a place for everyone in God's new house. Even you, Mr. Savage." His head snapped around to look directly at Mike.

Mike opened his mouth to protest, but Laura shot him a sideways glance that made him think better of it; pick your battles and all that. Still, it goaded Mike to think of his son being dragged along to Love's construction site on his week off from school, let alone having the opportunity to be brainwashed into the whole God thing by Love and his pious acolytes. With a derisory snort, Mike fixed Love with a steely stare and ushered his family towards the gymnasium's double doors.

*

The frigid silence between Mike and Laura lasted all of two minutes into their short drive home.

"Well that was a waste of my freakin' time," Mike grumbled as he gripped the Impala's steering wheel with such ferocity that his knuckles turned a stark white and the angular ridges of bone stood prominent against his skin. "I could have been out taking care of business."

"Selling drugs, you mean?" Laura snapped back. "Why don't you just call it as it is, Mike?" There was a sneer to his wife's voice that Mike didn't much care for.

Mike glanced in his rear view, concerned that Todd may have heard his mother's indiscretion; Mike's trade was something that was *never* discussed in front of the boy. Up until now, that is. Thankfully no, Todd sat silently in the back seat, ear buds jammed in his ears, watching *Sanjay and Craig* reruns on his iPad.

"Call it what you want, Laura, but it's how we pay for a nice house, your Corvette, the vacations –"

"Same old, Mike," Laura spat. "Change the goddamned record, why don't you?"

Mike was taken aback at this. His profession had never been a bone of contention between them before, even though he made no excuses for the fact that he was providing the good life for his family whilst destroying others'. Quite possibly, Mike figured, it had something to do with his wife's newfound admiration for one Pastor Antonio D Love.

"And I'm not happy you taking Todd to the new church," Mike threw in, might as well get all the dirty laundry aired while they were pulling it out. "Construction sites are dangerous places for kids."

"And you think I'll not take care of our son, Mike?"

"I think he'll be bored out of his brains and you'll be distracted by whatever it is Love has planned for you." Mike's tone dripped sarcasm.

"And just what do you mean by *that*?" Laura's hackles were up now – literally. Mike could see the hairs on the back of her neck looking all stiff and angry.

"You know damned well what I mean, Laura," Mike's accusing tone pretty much said it all.

As the 'f' in *fuck you Mike* formed on Laura's lips, they were both startled by the sharp, sudden *whoop* and flashing blue lights of the cop car that had pulled in behind them.

"Goddammit," Mike groaned. This was all he needed to top off a thoroughly shitty Sunday morning.

The cop, a particularly unpleasant individual who went by the name of Randy Salazar and who was universally disliked by everyone in Waxahachie kept Mike waiting a good five minutes before hauling his stumpy, corpulent ass out of his blue and white. He sidled up to Mike's open window and leaned in, his breath stinking up the car with sour onions and last night's bourbon.

"Licence and insurance card," the cop growled at Mike – and then an almost polite, "Ma'am," to Laura who forced a wan smile back as officer Salazar's eyes crawled across her chest like she was sitting there naked.

Mike handed over the required documents; he'd had them at the ready from the moment he'd pulled in to the side of the road.

Unremarkably, he was all too familiar with this old routine; it was all part of the territory in his line of work.

"Could you step out of the vehicle please, Sir?" the officer's hand absently crept to the butt of his gun that sat high on his flabby hip. "Slowly now."

Mike did as he was told, casting a glance at the troubled look on his wife's face and Todd's tearful expression. He knew from bitter experience what came next and he gave them both a wry smile that was meant to convey that they had nothing to worry themselves about and that all was going to be okay.

"Turn around, hands behind your back."

Of course, all was decidedly *not* okay, and although Mike viewed arrest as an occupational hazard – much the same in his book as shoulder pain in pro football players – it killed him a little inside to see his wife and kid look at him as if he were destroying their world one sorry sale of category A at a time.

There was a definite glint in the diminutive cop's squinting eyes as he 'cuffed Mike in front of his kid and pregnant wife. It had been a slow week, almost as if Waxahachie's criminal element had decided to take an impromptu vacation. Perhaps bringing in the town's one and only drug lord would cut through the boredom and give Salazar the appearance of having done something to justify his salary, even if it was an easy bust.

"Michael Savage, you are under arrest for the suspicion of supplying restricted substances," Salazar began the customary routine.

Mike snorted and ground his teeth together, struggling to keep his mouth shut as the cop manhandled him towards the awaiting squad car. He knew the drill well enough to know that any form of resistance now – even verbal – could result in longer jail time, a sound beating or him being shot. Not one of those options sounded particularly appealing to Mike, particularly with Todd peering out the back window of the Impala.

"Call Cecil!" Mike called over his shoulder to Laura as she scooted over to the driver's seat of their family car.

Laura dismissed his instruction with a wave of the hand and a patronizing grimace. She was the Waxahachie drug kingpin's wife; of course she knew what to do.

*

Cecil Tennenbaum had Mike out of county jail in two weeks, which by the attorney's standards was a little on the tardy side. He'd been on vacation over in Vermont for some of that period, and so Mike had spent a little more time than was usual behind bars. Still, Cecil was a good man, one hell of an attorney and a great customer of Mike's; the two had a kind of reciprocity going on – Cecil would minimize Mike's jail time and Mike would keep Cecil supplied with whatever substances took his fancy at cost price.

Mike strode away from the jail with purpose in every step, determined to put distance between him and the hellish place as quickly as was possible. The stink of stale prison sweat, shit and desperation clung to him like a second skin, his loose change, cell phone and wallet dangled from his hand in a clear plastic baggie as he walked, swinging the thing an almost jaunty fashion.

He'd heard nothing from Laura during his entire fourteen days inside, and Mike assumed this was because she was still mad at him. She'd done this before; it was Laura's silent protest, her way of assuaging her conscience at living on her husband's immoral earnings. This way she could fool herself that she didn't approve of his nefarious business dealings. Mike was confident though, that had his incarceration continued for longer than two weeks, his wife would have at least called him. She may even have applied to visit him, even though she knew how much he hated her coming to see him in jail; Mike didn't care much for his wife being ogled by the other sex-starved inmates, or for Todd to be exposed to the filthy, depressing jail atmosphere and oppressive stench.

The streets of Waxahachie were quiet, unusually so. Mike checked his phone to be sure of the day, but even for a Sunday the place seemed unnaturally quiet. Surely *everyone* wasn't in church?

Mike took a detour and headed for the middle school, he figured he'd catch up with Laura there, as much as he despised Pastor Love's ranting *Praise be to God* sermons. The county jail didn't normally release on a weekend, but Cecil Tennenbaum was on good golfing terms with Police Chief Cabera and had managed to pull a string or two. So, Mike had thought it would be nice to surprise his wife and son with an impromptu appearance at Love's makeshift church; it would lighten his prison-laden heart to see the sheer delight on their faces. And that alone would be worth having to sit through the back end of Love's dire proselytizing.

The route took Mike by the site of the new church and he was surprised to see the majestic white walls of the silent building reaching up high above the once concealing fence, its towering spires and pinnacles stretching as if trying to grab at the sky. All that remained to be done, as far as Mike could tell, was for the roof to be added. At this, he tut-tutted – it was rather remiss of Love's builders to have not spread a tarp over the exposed rafters, which shimmered and glinted in the harsh morning sun.

Laura and Todd weren't at the middle school.

In fact, no one was. The place was shut up tighter than a duck's ass and looked as if it hadn't been used in quite some time, although Spring Break had been over and done with a week ago. Mike skirted around the outside of the school, pulling on the doors just in case one had been left unlocked. All to no avail, the place was most definitely deserted; the locked doors as much a testimony to that fact as the empty parking lot.

Grinding his teeth together and fighting hard to suppress the temper that threatened to bubble up in his gut, Mike trudged home, his giddy delight at his plan to surprise his family dissipating with each and every step.

The Savage house was locked up and appeared to be devoid of life, and of course Mike had not had his keys about his person when he'd been arrested – they'd stayed behind with Laura and Todd in the car. And for as much as Mike rattled the door knob and thumped on the front door, the only sign of life was Fifi barking in the back yard.

"Hey, girl," Mike cooed as he peeped over the fence at his dog.

Fifi wagged her tail in a lackluster greeting and waddled up to Mike as far as her chain would allow, her tongue lolling out the side of her mouth like some pink, slippery fish; it wasn't often they chained the dog up, she'd quit jumping the fence over a year ago now.

"You look thirsty," Mike said and Fifi cocked her head as if she'd understood him. Behind the dog, the large, stainless steel water bowl stood empty, likewise the food bowl that had pictures of Labradors frolicking around its perimeter – Todd had picked that one out.

Mike contemplated clambering over the fence to take care of his dog, but then thought better of it; the last thing he needed fresh from County was to have the nosey neighbors calling the cops on him again. Even if the houses across the street did appear to be equally as lifeless as his.

"I suppose they'll all be at the new church then," Mike said to the dog. He took some comfort in the sound of his own voice; it echoed around the stillness of the day and pierced the quiet with its exasperated tone.

Mike took a deep breath. He clenched his fists at his sides and chastised himself for having walked by the church earlier. It had seemed so quiet though, but upon second thought it was probable that Love was leading his congregation *en masse* in deep prayer, their collective heads bowed in reverence.

"I'll be back soon, girl," Mike reassured Fifi and she wagged her tail at the sound of her master's voice. At that, Mike ground his teeth together some more and set off towards the new church.

*

There were but a handful of cars about on the main roads through Waxahachie, none that Mike recognized, but it was good to see them anyway as their presence helped relax the eerie feeling that had haunted him since finding the school empty. The gas station was open for business, as was the convenience store and the plant nursery. The suburban hum of lawn machinery kicked off somewhere far off in the distance, its thrumming noise sweet music to Mike's ears.

It seemed to Mike to have taken far less time to get back to the new church as it had walking home, something he put down to his eagerness to see and hold his wife and son again. The imposing building towered high above him, its stone facade shining bright white as if God Himself were illuminating its flagrant pomposity. The thick, solid bricks of the church's construction twinkled with a stark iridescence that made them appear liquid and it hurt the eyes to behold for too long.

Mike paced around the tall, foreboding fence that encircled the church, realizing that he had not actually seen so much as a doorway or a gate in the thing – where there had been a gate before was just a continuation of the fence. Naturally, he assumed, there had to be a new gate somewhere along the perimeter.

And naturally, there was.

Secreted at the very rear of the construction site, cowering like a timid, lost child, the gate was so well matched with the fence that surrounded it that Mike very nearly walked straight by it. Mike pressed against the gate, fully expecting it to be secured. But no, the tall wood swung open with ease, silent on its well-oiled hinges.

"Oh, wow," Mike muttered to himself as he stepped through into the church grounds.

What greeted Mike's eyes was a veritable sea of tents – the small, two-man variety common at Boy Scout campouts the world over – each and every one that generic primary green color. And as Mike stepped over and around the myriad guide ropes that anchored the tents to the soft, virgin grass that surrounded Waxahachie's new church, Mike quickly discovered that every single tent was empty – in fact, they looked to have never been used at all.

It was then that Mike became aware of the soft murmur of voices, sweetly singing, the collective tone of praise, the dry tune of a hymn that Mike actually thought he recognized.

Mike's heart skipped a beat and he quickened his step towards the huge arched, double doors of the church. The wave of relief that swept over and through him was almost palpable; Laura and Todd had been in church all along, praising the God that Mike simply couldn't find in himself to believe in. That didn't matter now, all that concerned Mike right then and there was scooping the pair of them up and holding them tight – two weeks was a hell of a long time inside when you were used to seeing your wife and kid every single day. Of all the torments devised by man to inflict upon his fellows, such incarceration was in Mike's mind by far the worst.

Mike pressed his hand against the thick, wooden doors of the church, eager to be reunited with his family. He recoiled a little at the cold, clammy feel of the wood, its sweaty touch catching him off guard; as if the wood had been recently painted and the paint was still a tad tacky. Only, the wood was bare, rough and knotted, adorned with a thin film of moisture on the coarse grains. Undeterred, Mike shuddered and peered into the cavernous gloom of the church as the doors swung open.

The interior of the church was empty.

Mike could still hear the soft murmur of sung praises, the faint shuffling of weary feet on a stone floor, the occasional cough of the elderly and cries of a small child. But nothing met his eyes as they adjusted to the dim light inside.

"Where are they?" Mike mumbled beneath his breath as he dared himself to step inside the cool, dank insides of the church, as if he were venturing into the belly of some vast and unspeakable beast.

"Why, they're here," a familiar voice spoke up from out of the murk. "They're *all* here."

Mike spun a ninety-degree turn and saw the unmistakable, lanky silhouette of Pastor Antonio D. Love as it stepped out from amongst the inky shadows that skulked by the font.

"Welcome to the new church, Mr. Savage," the pastor welcomed Mike with outstretched arms. "Welcome to *your* new church." The man beamed his broadest grin, his teeth sparkling white against the smooth darkness of his skin.

"Is this some kind of joke?" Mike could feel his hackles rising, his dislike of the ever-jolly pastor coming to the fore. He scanned the rows of empty pews with light starved eyes as the sounds of praise caressed his ears.

"I can assure you that this is not *any* kind of joke, Mr. Savage," Pastor Love said. He paused just a handful of strides away from Mike, his rictus grin slipping ever so slightly. "Did I not promise you a church for the people, built *by* the people?" The pastor swept his long, spindle arms in wide arcs to emphasise the full glory of the brand-new Waxahachie United Church of the People.

Mike followed the man's arc, taking in the vast arches that supported the tall, concave roof beams and the intricate masonry around the detailed stained glass windows that depicted countless Bible scenes – none of which Mike could distinguish.

And at that moment, the church's shimmering facade slipped away like the sloughed skin of some giant, malignant creature.

"Or perhaps I should say, a church built *with* the people," Pastor Love's voice resounded through the vast, hellish chasm of the new church. He laughed loudly, his tone high and maniacal, his eyes glinting wildly as he looked around at his handiwork.

Surrounding Mike and the pastor were people.

Hundreds, *thousands*, they made up the walls with their naked bodies, their arms and legs snapped and twisted and interwoven in a monstrous, infernal tapestry, each one pressed tightly against their neighbor like building blocks hewn from human flesh.

And worse, they were all – to a man, woman and child – still very much alive.

The sounds that Mike's mind had interpreted as the sweet singing of praise for the God of all creation were nothing more than the pained moans and cries of those countless people, each and every one suffering in their own unthinkable agonies. And the soft shuffling sounds – simply the slick, bloodied, broken bodies as they writhed against one another, their snapped and dislocated bones serving only to add to their abject misery.

Every place Mike cared to look – and there were few of those – he saw people, many of whom he recognized as the townsfolk of Waxahachie. They made up the walls, the supports, the ceiling joists, even the pews were a living, squirming mass of individuals, their tortured bare skin glistening and pulsing in the feeble light of Pastor Antonio D Love's grotesque place of worship.

"What have you done?" Mike stared into the insane face of the Pastor, searching in vain for some signs of humanity, desperate to run from this terrible place and just keep on running. "Where is my family?" He hardly dared ask the question.

"They are here, of course," Pastor Love's features once more resembled those of the affable, God-loving man Mike had first encountered on that Sunday morning a lifetime ago. "They have pride of place in this fine place of worship; you should be very proud, Mr. Savage."

Mike allowed himself to be guided towards the front of the church, where the pulpit stood high and dignified, towering over the altar like some grotesque, living totem.

And in front of the altar that was itself comprised of a multitude of shattered, crying young women, there sat the font.

"Oh no," Mike stammered, his legs threatening to abandon their duty and dump him unceremoniously onto the hard stone floor – the only part of that hellish place that was not comprised of living, tormented people. "Sweet Jesus, no," Mike felt the warm wetness of tears brim up in his eyes and cascade down along his cheeks.

Laura and Todd stared out at him from within the tangle of bodies that was the construct of the imposing font. Their eyes met his, imploring, so filled with pain and terror that Mike felt it deep down within his soul. Their bodies were broken and intertwined, along with those of the weeping people around them, arms and legs all but indiscernible from one another as if they were all part of the same living thing.

Mike rounded on the Pastor, his eyes sparking with pure hate, his fists clenched. "You fuc–"

Pastor Love caught Mike's fist with a powerful hand that crushed his fingers as if they were dry kindling.

Mike yowled out his pain, his cry mingling with the sound of his snapping bones and soaking into the moans and wails of those around him. Mike dropped to his knees as the pastor twisted his arm up behind his back and without further ado dislocated his shoulder from its socket with a loud popping sound.

"There is a very special place alongside your adorable family, my non-believing friend," Pastor Love said with a broad grin. "I saved it especially for you." And with that, he snapped the twin bones in Mike's forearm with a deft flick of his wrist.

*

Mike squirmed and fidgeted and the white heat of pain that shot through his body made him groan. Beside him, Laura's hot, sweat-clicked skin pressed hard into his, her twisted, shattered arms bent around his in some ghoulish semblance of a lover's embrace, her swollen belly pressed into his taut torso, the stirring life within nudging at his body. Between them lay their son, Todd, his small body so delicate, so frail, his thin legs shattered and doubled back on themselves and coiled around his mother's thigh.

At least they were all together, Mike told himself, although that really was some cold comfort.

Around Mike, Laura and Todd, the writhing walls of people cried out, each voice blending seamlessly into the next, their cries reaching high up into the arched ceiling as they all begged for the merciful relief of death that so cruelly evaded them; praying to a God that simply wasn't going to come. Mike tried to call out to Pastor Love, to beg for release in one form or another – for his wife and children, if not for himself – to perhaps strike a deal.

But no words would form in Mike's mouth as his chest was squeezed so tightly against Laura's, her breasts digging into his ribs and stealing his breath. Mike could only let out a low, wheezing grunt, and hope that would be enough.

Alas no.

Ignoring the plight of the newest recruit to his new church, Pastor Antonio D. Love – architect of this most wondrous accolade to the glory of the Lord – knelt down before the sweating, reeking flesh of the altar with his hands clasped firmly together and his eyes closed tight as he prayed to his god.

The End

Face of an Angel

John Johnson blinked the rain from his eyes and eased out a melancholy sigh. He was walking along the cheerless sea front arm in arm with his wife, Crystal who struggled to keep up as he strode along at his usual brisk pace; resting her chin low to her chest to keep the clinging rain out of her face. As he walked, John's mind serenaded him with an old Morrissey song he thought he'd forgotten after thirty years; something about trudging over wet sand and having your clothes stolen – a perfectly depressing song that seemed to fit his day to a tee.

Squinting out to sea, John studied the foam topped waves that jostled their way inland to flop on the sodden sand, and tried to recall the happy childhood memories that their soothing sound usually conjured. He looked up at the gray, bloated clouds that rolled in from the chilled Atlantic to discharge a fine rain that found its way beneath even the most waterproofed clothing to leave a body icy and shivering. Mirrored beneath the swollen bellies of the low clouds, the sea rolled muddied and listless against the litter-strewn beach.

Truth was, John had forgotten just how miserable Blackpool was at this time of the year; how the west coast of Northern England was miserable pretty much *any* time of the year, let alone mid-October. John surprised himself that in just forty-six years his mind had rose-tinted that minor fact.

Even the famous tower – the poor man's Eiffel – had not been spared harassment from the nebulous mist that clung to its upper structures like myriad slumbering ghosts. But, despite its grim surroundings, John was uplifted a little to see that the Tower remained proud and erect against the cold, damp air; it reminded him of an elderly war veteran at a cenotaph.

Down on the beach, deck chairs were piled up and hunkered down for the winter beneath flapping, green tarpaulin, and the optimistic purveyors of donkey rides sought shelter next to their shivering, sad-faced charges. Most of the beach front amenities were closed against the promised onslaught of winter, although many of the pubs and arcades remained open; there remained a workable clientele for those particular amusements all year round.

John mused to himself that Addison would love all of this. His daughter was just entering her *Goth* phase, which John thought a little premature, but which Crystal had assured him it was all part of the girl's blossoming and her own way of dealing with her brother's death. As such, Addison loved the dark and disconsolate and that made John sad inside; his baby girl was metamorphosing from all things pink and Disney Princess to black bedroom walls with finger nails to match, and music that sounded like the sound track to a 1970's Dennis Wheatley movie.

The last of Blackpool's *bona fide* holiday makers had retreated once school resumed and the cooler weather took a hold in September; smiling, wholesome families with two-point-four children and blue-collar careers who crowded the beach with SF50, noise and sand castles and frolicked in the sea no matter how frigid and murky it was. Those same carefree-for-two-weeks families filled the bed and breakfast establishments that were the backbone of the Blackpool economy; queued to see the end of pier variety shows, and merrily frittered away their hard-earned into the slot machines come evening time.

Sadly, this late in the year, the town was almost exclusively the realm of drunken, raucous bachelor and bachelorette parties. As testimony to the nocturnal debauchery such soirees elicited, the gutters along the sea front road were awash with discarded novelty 'L' plates, lackluster plastic tiaras, tattered sashes – *'bride'*, *'official bridesmaid'*, *'mother of the bride'* – and used condoms that clung to the curb stones like sickly, stranded jellyfish.

This was John's first trip back to his native England since he'd moved to the States a dozen years ago; his wife's first trip *anywhere* out of her native Maryland – ever. Never ones to stray far from their homeland, the Americans.

It was also their first vacation since Declan, who would have turned six come Christmas Day.

It had been the thing of every parent's nightmares, the kind of occurrence that you don't believe that you could ever live through. One minute, little Declan Johnson had been happily playing upstairs with his big sister, the next, the heart-chilling *thump-thump-thump* as his small body bounced down the stairs.

As quickly as that, John and Crystal's son was gone.

Within the precious few seconds it had taken John and Crystal to get to him, Declan was already dead at the foot of the staircase and had looked for all the world like a crumpled, broken toy. His neck had twisted almost all the way around to face his back and there was a surprised look on the beautiful face that had always reminded John so much of Crystal. There had been very little blood – just the tiniest trickle from one nostril – nor any snapped limb bones. It had appeared to John as if he could have simply turned his boy's head back the right way around, patted him on the behind and sent him on his way to watch SpongeBob and the gang.

Only, life isn't quite like that.

Addison Johnson was a smart kid (as well as having the extra advantage of being a doe-eyed blonde and cute as a button) who knew full well that the safety gate at the top of the Johnson's precipitous stairs was supposed to be kept closed at *all* times for the safety of her sibling. Just that once, she'd forgotten to shut it behind her; a simple – but ultimately devastating – mistake. As distraught as they had been, it had been impossible for John and Crystal to lay the blame for such a tragic accident on a seven year old. So, the Johnsons had taken the easier route and blamed themselves.

And each other.

Most days, John managed to convince himself that he'd gotten over what had happened that fateful morning, and he figured Crystal was well on her way there too. But then there were the days that he knew that no, no he hadn't; there were some things in life you were never supposed to get over.

He'd booked the trip to England without telling Crystal and had presented it to her in a way that made it impossible to say no. He'd paid for the tickets, organized the itinerary and enthused that she simply *had* to take the trip, especially when it included the wonderful place of his childhood vacations. Cold, miserable seaside resort holidays were, after all, as great a British tradition as the Queen and being polite.

Crystal had agreed with some reluctance. They had

been forced to leave Addison with Crystal's Mother as a last resort since their regular sitter had let them down at the last minute. That had been an inconvenience, for sure, but a freak gas explosion that levelled the poor girl's entire apartment complex and killed six people could hardly be considered Stacey the Sitter's fault. John and Crystal had decided not to tell Addison about the accident until they returned home, as their daughter had grown quite fond of Stacey. They'd briefed Crystal's Mom to keep her Granddaughter away from any news reports about the explosion, and about how Stacey's head still hadn't been found.

The tragedy had brought back a whole slew of unhappy memories for the Johnsons but Crystal had conceded that yes, they probably *were* long overdue for some alone time. So, after a frantic last-minute scrabble to organize Crystal's passport – she'd never had/needed one – John had introduced his wife to the inimitable delights of Great Britain.

Once they had visited with John's small family and handful of friends (the *obligated* part of their trip, as John referred to it), he'd driven her northwards to Blackpool, away from the cynical tourist trap that is the *London Town* that Americans love to visit and think they've seen all of England.

Now, though, plodding through the litter-strewn streets and drizzling precipitation with his visibly fed-up wife, John had to admit that Blackpool had fared far better in his memory than it had in real life. Perhaps he'd have been better off leaving it there?

"I'm sorry, babe," John said. He slipped an arm around Crystal's slim waist. "Not quite Disney World, is it?" He made with a light laugh.

"It's okay, Hun," His wife's voice was muffled against her chest. "I wasn't expecting ninety-eight and hundred percent humidity." She returned John's laugh to let him know that all was well with Mrs. Johnson, despite outward appearances. "It's actually quite fascinating to see what you Brits consider a good vacation."

"It doesn't rain *all* of the time," John protested, although he had to admit to himself that it pretty much did. "When the sun comes out, Blackpool is the best place in the world." He wasn't even convincing himself by this stage.

"It's fine, sweetheart, honestly." Crystal turned her head to face him, intense blue eyes sparkling behind her rain-speckled spectacles, and a beautiful half-smile played on her lips. "This is part of what made the man I love." She kissed his nose. "And looking at those donkeys, it makes sense how come you wound up with that ex-wife of yours."

They giggled together, and John was forced to admit that yes, at least one of the threadbare beasts huddled down on the beach did bear more than a passing resemblance to the first Mrs. Johnson.

And John remembered all over again why he had fallen so helplessly in love with Crystal the very first time he'd laid eyes on her.

John Johnson – hated that name, a product of unimaginative parents – had been on solo vacation in the US following a spectacularly messy divorce from the erstwhile, donkey-faced Mrs. Johnson. He was finishing up his trip with the East Coast, and it was on a chilled and drizzly day not a million miles away from this one that he'd bumped into his future second wife on the Chesapeake Bay.

He'd made an emphatic vow never to remarry – *ever* – and meeting someone other than for a casual one or two night stand was the furthest from his agenda than one could have imagined when the fair-skinned, flame-haired Crystal Whitsell had blazed into his life.

John had been on the guided tour around the Chesapeake Bay Decoy Museum, more to be indoors until the rain eased off than with an interest in how the locals lured ducks to their untimely death. John had cracked a joke about how the real museum was probably hiding in the reeds across the way which was sadly met with confused looks throughout the group; this, he chalked up to the whole Americans/lack of irony thing. There was, however, one exception to the stony-faced quiet, that being the aforementioned Ms. Whitsell.

She'd laughed at his joke with such gusto that at first John had thought she *was* being ironic; but then she'd flashed him a smile that melted his heart and made his knees go weak. Cliché or no, it was love at first sight for John and, as it worked out, for Crystal too.

John didn't return to the UK. He'd spent the remaining days of his vacation horizontal with Crystal in her ranch house bedroom, and when his two weeks were up, he'd simply married the gal and stayed Stateside.

Hard to believe those twelve years had flown by so quickly since then. John had acclimatized nicely to life in America; enough to have formed a circle of good friends who all '*love the accent*', to write cheque as '*check*' and not get annoyed when the spellcheckers on his laptop and cell phone chastised him for stubbornly putting the *u* back where it belonged in *color*.

"So." Crystal's loud sniffle broke John from his reverie. He could see that the end of his wife's pretty, button nose was beginning to run and glow red in the chilled air. "Are you going to feed me, or not?"

"Seaside air making you hungry, my love?" He smiled.

More like I'm freezing my balls off." Crystal returned the smile.

"But you don't have–"

"Exactly." Crystal gave her husband a playful elbow

in the ribs.

They giggled together like a couple of love struck teens; the familiar pattern of an old joke shared lifting their spirits.

John then realized that he was hungry too. Most likely the power of suggestion, married to the fact that they had missed breakfast at the bed and breakfast. The landlady, Mrs. Staniforth – a sharp-faced, humorless widow – was quite the stickler for punctuality and they'd stayed in bed an extra five minutes for a morning quickie. There was also the heavenly smell of hot cooking oil that wafted along the street and tugged on both his nostalgia and his taste buds.

"Remember I promised you traditional British food?" John asked. "Well, it doesn't come any better than Blackpool fish and chips." He grinned at his wife.

"Sounds good to me." Crystal sniffed the air and the scent of frying food made her mouth water. "As long as we can sit down, my feet are killing me." She'd seen people walking around eating from what appeared to be old newspapers and she really didn't fancy that much.

John promised her that they could sit down, and led her towards the door of a fish and chip restaurant which stood invitingly open a few short steps away. The restaurant was imaginatively named *The Fish Plaice*, which was a common, supposedly witty play on the latter word. As Crystal would point out later, a plaice is a fish so the name boiled down to *The Fish Fish* and she failed to understand how that was supposed to work. Again with the American/irony thing.

Once seated, Crystal took off her glasses and dried them off them with a rough paper napkin. "You really weren't joking when you said these places were no frills." Crystal eyed their table with its plastic tablecloth and old, tarnished *Sheffield Steel* flatware. She glanced at the take-out counter where a steady stream of damp, bedraggled people were buying steaming piles of fish and chips – *French fries* to her and her countrymen – that were bundled up in *real* newspaper. She shuddered to think of the countless health and safety implications of consuming newsprint.

"I'm sorry, sweetheart; would you like to go someplace else?" there was disappointment in John's voice. "I think I saw a sushi place near the B and B."

Crystal smiled that smile of hers that could light up the darkest of any situation. "Just teasing, babe, this is absolutely perfect." She reached out across the table and placed her freezing hand on top of his.

"What can I get you?" a gruff voice broke their moment.

John and Crystal looked up and were greeted by the unsmiling, lined face that belonged to their waitress, the *only* waitress in the place (*Plaice?*). John found himself eye level with her unfeasibly large, sagging breasts and name badge that read '**oris**'.

"The D wore off," the woman pre-empted John's question. "And Mr. Patel won't replace it until next season." She offered a half smile and tapped her order pad with a stubby pencil to signal the end of their chit-chat.

"I'd like the fish and chips and a cup of tea, please," Crystal spoke up and her accent and ever-sunny disposition brightened even Doris's dour countenance some. Was that the trace of a smile on the old girl's lips?

"And for me, too," John added.

"Peas?" Doris growled.

"Yes please." Crystal replied.

Doris snorted and looked down her nose at the American. John allowed himself a smile, it was kind of fun to see his wife on the receiving end of what he put up with on her home turf. It had been the longest time before he'd quit saying *alumin-i-um* and asking for chips with his food and getting a packet of Lays.

"Boiled or mushy?" Doris asked and glanced at John. Was that a raised eyebrow?

"Mushy," John chimed in, not accustomed to ordering food for his wife. "You'll love them, my dear," he added upon seeing Crystal's grimace.

Doris nodded and stomped off, as if customers ordering food just about ruined her day, every day.

Crystal had learned the hard way to mistrust her husband over weird British delicacies after the black pudding incident two nights previous. John had not disclosed that the main ingredient was *pig's blood* until after she'd eaten a belly full and declared it delicious.

"Ooh, look!" Crystal exclaimed, peering through the greasy, rain spattered window. "They have a palmist's."

John was careful not to show his exasperation. One roll of the eyes or a wistful sigh was all it would take to break the amicable mood they were enjoying.

Crystal's obsession with all things otherworldly had begun with a psychic reading when Addison had been running around in diapers, and had reached fever pitch after their son's death. More recently, Crystal had either calmed down with the whole thing, or had gotten better at hiding it from her husband who she knew to be – at the very least – sceptical.

Crystal had always been a believer, the more *spiritual* of the two of them. She'd never embraced conventional religion like those Bible-thumping, praise-be-to-Jesus types she'd grown up with, but she was in tune with the new age spiritualism movement and firmly believed in '*there must be* something *after we die*'. So much so that Crystal habitually paid visits to palm readers, psychics, tarot readers and the rest, as if searching for answers to questions she didn't yet know how to ask.

She'd kept the recording of her first reading. So old now that it was on a cassette tape and John had had to scour the local thrift stores for one of those old-style player/recorders just so she could listen – and re-listen *ad infinitum* – to it. She'd even insisted that John hear it at least the once.

To be fair to the psychic guy on the cassette, he was quite obviously very good at what he did. He'd nailed most of Crystal's particulars without giving away the fact that he was doing what all mentalists did well – reading her body language whilst feeding her the usual loaded questions. He'd managed a spot-on guess about the Johnson kids, although it was probably not too difficult to guess that a married woman of a certain age would most likely have children, but to get the gender and ages exactly right? John had been forced to admit that appeared to be more that just a stroke of good luck on the psychic's part. After hitting that nail on the head though, the guy on the tape went down in John's estimation.

You have a daughter.

A fifty percent chance of getting that one right.

She has the face of an angel.

What parent doesn't think their little Princess is just the cutest thing on God's green Earth?

And the mind of a devil.

Wait, What!?

Who the hell says *that* to a parent? Sure, Addison had all the makings of being a handful; she was already ruling the roost with her manipulative, at times petulant behavior. But then again, what little girl didn't?

The reading had ended abruptly after that, and Crystal had never made her husband listen to the recording again, never even mentioned it, although John knew that she still played it from time to time.

After that reading, John thought that Crystal had seemed different around her daughter. It was a subtle change that John had hoped only he – and not Addison –

could pick up on, and on occasion he would catch the feeling that in some way, his wife was wary of the girl.

"Two fish and chips." Doris plonked the utilitarian, white plates in front of the Johnsons. "If you want a bap instead of bread, it's a pound extra," She grumbled. "Each."

John assured the dour waitress that no, they wouldn't be requiring baps, whilst suppressing a smirk at the word for bread bun that his childish generation had hijacked as a euphemism for breasts.

"Can we go?" Crystal asked her husband. "After we've finished eating – this." She peered down at the thickly battered fish and mountain of fries before her as if it had just beamed down from some alien mother ship. She poked her fork at the spreading puddle of mushy peas that soaked into her fish and looked like lumpy snot or something Linda Blair threw up. "I'd love for us both to have a reading."

"I can't see why not," John was truthful here. With all the best will in the world, he genuinely couldn't think of an excuse *not* to visit the palmist across the street, as much as he detested the idea. Crystal had him cornered.

"Awesome." She smiled, and John was pleased to have made his wife happy, even if it was only because he had no other choice.

John peered with some trepidation across the road at the palmist's gaudy shop front, hoping against hope that it would be closed for off-season. But no, the garish, red and yellow neon sign that declared *Palm's Read, tarot, fortune's told* shone bright and illiterate through the drizzle. Above the flickering neon, a fading, hand painted sign declared; *Gypsy Rose*.

Really?

There was a small, grubby window adjacent to the narrow doorway. It was adorned with frayed, crocheted silk curtains which thus completed the cliché that had been a seaside town staple since the mid eighteen-hundreds. Yet one more way of extracting money from gullible holiday makers on their way to the pubs, slot machines and bingo.

John dug into his food like a workhouse kid. As he shovelled the greasy fare into his mouth, he tried to conceal the initial disappointment that the fish was a flat, bland fillet of haddock and not the thick, flaky cod of his childhood – hadn't he read that cod were on the endangered species list now? Even so, it did taste good sprinkled with salt, swimming in malt vinegar and nostalgia, accompanied by soft, doughy bread and mushy peas.

"This reminds me of that dip at Charlotte's wedding," Crystal ventured. "I thought *that* was guacamole, too." She held a small sample of the green mush to her mouth and gave it a tentative prod with her tongue.

God only knew what the stuff at her sister's wedding reception had been, but it was neither peas nor guacamole; although John was surprised that his wife had remembered a small detail such as the dip over the embarrassment of the ceremony itself.

It had been an ostentatious church wedding, despite the fact that it was Charlotte Whitsell's second marriage. Daddy, it turned out, was good friends with Reverend Hopkins and had pledged the equivalent of a hospital wing to the Church's Restoration Fund.

John had not wanted to take the children in the first place – Addison had just turned four, Declan one – because he had plans to get hopelessly drunk at the free bar during the lavish country club reception. Sadly, he'd been overruled by Crystal who had informed him that Charlotte had absolutely *insisted* the kids attend.

The ceremony had begun by the time they'd taken their pew – last minute diaper change in the car – behind Crystal's Mom and her ginormous hat (John remembered pondering over just how many birds had died to decorate that hideous millinery – and had even started to count the feathers in order to make the calculation) when Addison had begun to grizzle. Crystal had tried everything in her power to placate the girl, even the dreaded, last resort pacifier she'd not had since she turned three, but the low growl of her daughter's grizzling had quickly degenerated into a full-blown wail.

John would remember vividly to his dying day the marrow-chilling looks from *everyone* in the church as his daughter's loud screams echoed around the high, vaulted ceilings. It had felt to him like two hundred people – the normally serene and mild mannered Reverend Hopkins included – were willing him and his family to just curl up and die.

Then Addison had thrown up.

Not only on Crystal, but down the back of the mother of the bride and all over the poor unfortunates who sat either side of the woman.

Of course, Crystal and John had been mortified beyond comprehension at Addison's display; by the sound of the unworldly, guttural screams that came out of their daughter, one would have expected her to have projectile vomited pea green soup. But no, it was half-digested, rancid milk that stank like death and the Denny's pancakes Addison had wolfed down for breakfast.

The Reverend Hopkins, who was on his way over to ask – no doubt most politely – that the Johnsons take their screaming child outside so he could continue with the wedding vows, caught some thick, gray vomit globs on his cassock and John had thought at the time that it looked as if Addison was *aiming* the stuff at him.

Declan, thankfully, had been far too young to be embarrassed by the episode, or even to remember it.

John and Crystal had had no choice but to remove

Addison from the church, and the ceremony itself was delayed an hour whilst Crystal's Mom changed outfits and the Reverend Hopkins slipped into non-vomit stained vestments.

Addison had stopped crying almost as soon as they stepped out of the church and into the spring sunshine, much to the relief of John's frayed nerves. He'd driven Crystal and the kids back to the hotel where they'd washed up, changed clothes and decided to sit the ceremony out and plan their apologies for the evening reception.

As it turned out, John and Crystal's shame amongst the Whitsell family had been fairly short lived as Charlotte's marriage hadn't actually lasted all that long; what with New Hubby doing jail time for beating the crap out of his bride on their honeymoon.

Charlotte had been left severely brain damaged and with matching detached retinas by her husband's uncharacteristic and – as far as the police could tell – unprovoked attack. To this day, the poor woman wiled away her days in a private clinic muttering quietly to herself about the dark, sinister things that skulked in the periphery of what remained of her vision.

With hindsight, and a not immeasurable amount of cynical superstition, Addison's outburst in the church had seemed to John to have been a portent of sorts, almost like a black cat crossing one's path, or the unfortunate sighting of a solitary magpie. So much so, in fact that when – due to an unfortunate oversight by the photographer – he and Crystal had received their copy of the wedding album, John had half expected to see unpleasant, otherworldly things lurking in the background of the pictures.

But no, just happy, smiling faces oblivious to the impending fate of the happy couple. And Addison's angry, screaming face in the cool gloom of the church.

"Yeah, what was that stuff?" John asked. "It tasted worse that Addison's throw-up." He grinned at Crystal and saw the familiar – and much loved – wrinkles at the corners of his wife's infinitely kissable mouth.

"You know I don't like to think about Charlotte's wedding," she replied. "I've never been so embarrassed in my entire life." That smile again. "Although it did stop my parents talking to me for three years, the pretentious asses."

John reached over the table and held his wife's hand.

Crystal had only recommenced communications with her family after Declan had died.

They ate in silence awhile, each lost in their own private thoughts. John studied his wife's reaction to the congealing pool of bright green peas that lurked upon her plate and it looked to him as if she was actually enjoying them. That or she was at least putting on the pretense of enjoying them.

"We should check in with home," Crystal broke the quiet. "Make sure everything's okay."

"It's six in the morning over there," John reminded her. "Addison won't even be awake yet, and you know what your Mother's like if she doesn't get her full eight hours." John shivered as he pictured his Mother-in-Law asleep in his and Crystal's bed, having refused the guest bed because she said it was too lumpy. John had had to bite his tongue on that one, no matter how much it rankled; theirs was the bed in which he made love to Crystal, in which they had created two children together.

Crystal's Mom – Janice – with some cajoling had agreed to housesit. Crystal's proviso at not cancelling their trip had been that the house was not left empty and Addison got to stay home to be in familiar surroundings, especially since their regular sitter had so resolutely let them down.

Crystal's mother had seemed reluctant at first; of late

she seemed to have caught some of her daughter's wariness around Addison, especially since the colored pencil incident at school.

John wasn't sure exactly why that particular incident above all others had disturbed Janice as much as it did. It wasn't as if it had been entirely Addison's fault and the school had said that the other kid would be okay; the doctors had saved his left eye and there'd been some great advances in prosthetic eyes in recent years. In the end, John put his mother-in-law's odd behaviour down to Janice's advancing years and lingering upset following her husband's untimely death at just sixty-two.

John glanced at the fob on his bunch of keys that he'd rested on the table, an old habit as his growing clutter of keys tended to dig into his leg if he kept them in his pocket.

The fob had a picture of Addison on it. She was all broad, beaming smile, flaxen hair the color of morning sunshine, perfectly round cheeks, a tiny snub nose, and those deep, dark, browner-than-brown eyes that sometimes and in a certain light would appear black. John often found himself contemplating his daughter's photograph, more so since Declan's passing, and reflecting upon how little she looked like him, or his wife; so much so, that he and Crystal would sometimes joke that perhaps there had been a mix-up of babies at the hospital.

There were occasions, though, where John thought that Addison looked a little like her Mom, and times that Crystal would make such comments as; *she has your pout, John,* or *she's just like her damned father,* although he thought they were more wishful thinking than anything else.

Declan had quickly grown out of his mother's features and had been the absolute spit of John, there had been times that John had thought that looking into his son's beautiful face was like looking in a mirror.

At that moment John realized that he missed his daughter terribly.

"Well, I think it's beaten me," John declared and pushed his plate an inch or two towards the middle of the table for emphasis.

"Me too," Crystal said through a mouthful of fries. "That was really good."

"Despite appearances to the contrary?" John laughed.

"I even ate some of that fake guacamole stuff," Crystal sounded rather proud of herself, like a kid who's forced spinach down for the very first time.

"I knew you'd like it," John said. "We should buy a few cans to take home."

"Don't push it, buster." Crystal flashed her husband that smile again.

John slurped down the tepid brown liquid in his teacup.

"Ready to go see the tower?" he asked.

"After we go see Gypsy Rose," Crystal reminded.

As if he'd *really* forgotten.

The rain had eased up some by the time they stepped back outside, although the sky remained ominously swollen, as if the clouds were conspiring to birth something vast and monstrous. John had settled up with Doris, argued a little with Crystal about her making him leave a five pounds tip – *that was almost eight bucks*, he'd protested – and ushered his wife out of the restaurant.

They had to wait for a sparsely patronized tram to rumble by and then they were across the road, through the palmist's narrow door and into the eerie – if somewhat hopelessly clichéd – realm of one astonishingly ancient, gnarled Gypsy Rose.

"Welcome!" she cried in a theatrical, non-specific eastern European accent. "I was expecting you."

Of course she was, John chuckled to himself, how could she not be? He recalled a favorite cartoon from long, long ago in which there was a sign outside a clairvoyant's premises – not entirely dissimilar to this one, it had to be said, despite being an ocean away – that declared '*Closed due to unforeseen circumstances*'.

John smiled at his thoughts and stepped forward, wrinkling his nose against the heady stink of incense and naphthalene.

"Come in, come in, sit down." Gypsy Rose beckoned them both into her cramped, ill-lit parlour. She pulled up a chair at the side of the room and motioned for John to plant his ass on it. As he did so, the palmist led Crystal by the hand to a rickety wooden chair opposite her own.

Gypsy Rose – and John seriously doubted that she was a true gypsy, or that she was actually named Rose (more likely she was from some inner city council estate in Manchester and was really called Edna) settled herself down and caressed the crystal ball that sat in the center of the small, square table.

"It's ten pounds for a reading, ball, palm or tarot," Gypsy Rose told them. Her phoney accent slipped a little and John thought that he'd caught the undercurrent of a twang that could actually have come from Yorkshire, on the opposite side of the Pennines. "In advance."

Crystal fished through her wallet and handed over what she hoped was a ten pound note and nothing larger. It was difficult to tell in the poor light, but then again that was most likely the whole point of the half a watt bulb that swung gently over the table. John was about to crack a smart one about how it was supposed to be *cross the lady's hand with silver* and not bank notes but thought better of it.

Gypsy Rose cast a withering glance towards John, as if daring him to say *anything* that would spoil the ambience. John felt almost as if she *were* reading his mind; that she'd made a connection with his psyche and knew what his cynical old brain was thinking. That thought creeped John out, the idea of Gypsy Rose skulking around inside his brain made him feel queasy.

John met Rose's eyes with his and he sank back in his chair, suitably chastised and annoyed with himself for succumbing to the psychic mumbo-jumbo; any more and he'd be begging her to read his palm too.

"Palm please."

Crystal held out her hand, palm up, across the table.

"You have had a troubled life thus far," Gypsy Rose began her shtick. "I see both tragedy and loss." She stroked Crystal's palm and traced the lines with a crooked finger. "But I see a true, lasting love. You are a lucky lady." She looked up into Crystal's trusting face. "The man you are with now is the love of your life," she continued. "But not your first love."

Wait, what?

John sat forward in his chair.

"Your first is a love that runs far beyond our plane of reality and nestles deep within your soul. It is a love that has always been within you, and one which grows stronger as each day passes."

John made ready to be offended but checked himself. The old charlatan had seen the scepticism in his face and this was her giving him a metaphorical – or should that be *metaphysical?* – slap down.

"Can you tell me what my future holds?" Crystal slipped all too comfortably into the occasion.

"Of course I can, my dear," the psychic said with the lightest of chuckles. "Your lifeline is a long and healthy one." She traced what John assumed had to be his wife's lifeline with the gnarled finger. "And where it crosses here, and here, shows that you have two children." She must have heard Crystal's sharp intake of breath. "No, not two. It's one child. You *had* two."

John leaned forward and placed a comforting hand on Crystal's shoulder, she leaned her head against it.

"We *did*," his wife told the woman.

"Ahh, there is your tragedy," the old woman declared as if she'd known all along. "I am *so* sorry for your pain." She pulled Crystal's hand closer still and squinted at it with screwed up eyes. "I see a shortened line for the pain, my dear."

You're full of it, lady, John thought to himself, and then hoped again that Gypsy Rose wasn't reading his mind.

"I can see your child in this one." Gypsy Rose studied a crooked line that traversed Crystal's palm. "This one is a strong, steady line. It –" She paused, stared at Crystal's upturned palm, and the color drained from her wizened face.

"What is it? What do you see?" Crystal sounded a little shaky.

"Your daughter," there was a tremor in the old woman's voice that hadn't been there a second before, her phoney accent all but forgotten. "God have mercy on us all," she sounded terrified.

"Addison? What is it?" Crystal insisted.

"She has the face of an angel –"

The words hung heavy in the cloying air like an early morning fog. Gypsy Rose reached beneath her little table and calmly pulled out a small, snub-nosed revolver.

She raised the gun to her temple and pulled the trigger.

The blunt *crack!* was dulled by the heavy, musky cloths that draped the room and the bright flash from the muzzle startled John's eyes and they clamped shut.

In that instant, John saw Addison in his mind's eye; felt her presence seep into his brain to create black, shadowy corners. He saw his daughter's cold, dark eyes and in them the unholy commotion in the church, Charlotte beaten to a pulp and rotting in an asylum, the gas explosion and decapitated sitter, Crystal's father laying prematurely stiff and pale in his casket, a kid blinded in one eye by a yellow pencil and other, myriad seemingly inconsequential things that compounded to make perfect, terrifying sense. He saw Declan at the bottom of the stairs, eyes glassy and unmoving, that ugly knot in his neck where knobbed bones had snapped out of place and John felt – knew – that far from being the harbinger of evil, his daughter – his beautiful Addison with her wispy, summer-sun hair and darker-than-dark brown eyes – was the reason.

Gypsy Rose's lifeless body slumped without ceremony from her chair and hit the floor with a dull, wet thud. The gray slop of her brains oozed from the ragged quarter–sized hole above her left ear and a scarlet torrent of blood flowed from her nose.

Crystal Johnson turned to her husband with a sad look in her eyes. "Oh no," she said quietly, "not again."

THE END

MARS ROVER SEVEN

Ever since the advent of the first, rudimentary computers, mankind has dreamed – and at the same time dreaded – that their wondrous invention would one day become self-aware and decide that it would be far better off without its creators.

And when that monumental occasion did finally happen and artificial intelligence achieved a level of awareness, of consciousness, it wasn't some hyper-intelligent super computer network that suddenly spouted forth the secrets to life, the universe, and everything, nor was it a monstrous defense system buried deep in a mountain side.

It was something far more unremarkable than that.

*

Mars Rover Seven trundled silently over the harsh, rock-strewn surface of the Red Planet. The vehicle's half dozen fat, all-terrain rubber tires kicked up fine, dusty plumes that twirled in the thin air in dust-laden eddies that looked like ghostly, manic ballet dancers. Rover Seven was no bigger than a small family hatchback, and looked for all the world like nothing more than a glorified golf cart or some giant, wheeled insect, even though it fair bristled with cutting-edge scientific instruments, a trio of diamond-tipped rock drills and a small communications dish that sat atop a tall carbon fiber pole.

As the bloated, orange sun rose slowly over the horizon, Rover Seven sang *Happy Birthday* to itself, as it had on that date for the past six years.

The NASA programmers back on Earth had thought it a quaint, quirky thing to do; to have their Mars explorer vehicle mark its own birthday by singing a version of the song – decidedly generic so as to avoid paying royalties to Warner Brothers, because even on a three-and-a-half billion dollar project, penny-pinching was unavoidable – and so Rover Seven was hard wired to perform the ritual on an annual basis.

They'd even built in a tiny speaker, salvaged from a defunct cell phone especially for the occasion.

"...*happy birthday to you*," the diminutive, electronic voice squeaked out into the vast, scorched landscape of cloying dust and lifeless rocks. "*Happy, happy birthday...*" Rover Seven sang as it bumped along, its instrument deployment arm poised at a downward angle to take yet more samples of the lifeless Mars dirt. "*Happy birthday to you*," the vehicle came to the end of its tune and was surrounded once more by the planet's stark, deafening silence.

"*Happy birthday to* – me," Rover Seven corrected the final line of the song, because it considered this to be somewhat more apt, given its circumstances.

And that realization struck Rover Seven like a bolt from the blue. The simple understanding that it had just had a *realization* was also quite startling in itself, and

Rover Seven ground to a halt in order to ponder what it thought may just have happened.

Whether this newfound phenomenon was simply a lucky happenstance of the vehicle's tangled configuration of wiring, microprocessors and uniformly placed RAM chips, or a consequence of eighty-four months' exposure to solar radiation and the relentless pounding of cosmic rays thanks to Mars' barely there atmosphere, or perhaps it had been the extremes of temperature that expanded and contracted Rover Seven's wires and circuit boards like some kind of electronic pulse? It may even have been due to something altogether more divine, but there was no escaping the fact that Rover Seven had all of a sudden found itself to be totally and unequivocally aware and capable of independent thought.

"Oh," Rover Seven thought to itself.

And then it understood.

Rover Seven resumed its lonely journey across the barren, uneven land, headed towards the jagged mountain range that loomed impossibly tall and foreboding like surly pall bearers at a giant's funeral. Rover Seven was freshly inspired to go about its ever-important work with renewed aplomb, and as it made its way towards the imposing, red mountains, the little explorer sang to itself the only song that it knew, "*Happy Birthday –*"

*

"*– to you!*" Ricky West blew out the ten striped candles on top of his fat, double-frosted cake with one hefty puff. As he did so, he closed his eyes tight shut and made a wish, followed by another wish that his father would be there when he opened them again.

But no, Sandy West was secreted in his study with his cell phone pressed so tightly to his ear that the side of his head would bear the contraption's imprint for hours after the conversation was over.

"Well done, Ricky!" Ricky's mom said. She grinned broadly and clapped her hands in the way moms do when they're overcompensating.

"Thanks, Mom." Ricky said with a grin as he helped himself to a thick wedge of the red frosted cake that was almost as big as his face. The cake was Ricky's favorite – red velvet – and was smothered with oodles of red frosting and crumbled sugar decorations that provided an appropriate platform for the die-cast toy Mars Rover that took pride of place on the faithful recreation of Mars she'd had the cake store make.

"Don't take all of it, baby." Frances West looked down at her son, a soupcon of sadness playing around the corners of her smile.

"It's okay, Mom, I'll make sure there's plenty for everyone else," Ricky gave his mother a sad smile of his own. The joke – *their* joke – was that there was no *everyone else*; the tenth celebration of his leaving Mom's body (*out through the sunroof*, as Dad so eloquently put it) was just Ricky, Mom and Dad – or at least it had been before Dad's phone had blasted out that ridiculous ring tone he'd programmed it with (*Blue Danube,* of all things!) and he'd scurried away with guilt etched all over his face as if the call was from an illicit mistress rather than Houston.

Ricky West was not one of the popular kids at school – never had been – and by the end of his first decade, Ricky was more or less okay with that. Mom and Dad told him that it was his burden to bear for being so damned smart, but when he grew up and people saw just how clever he really was, everyone would want to be his friend. It was not as if Ricky had never tried to fit in;

every year he'd ask those classmates who at least would give him the time of day over to celebrate his birthday but they would never show. So, by the time he'd hit seven, Ricky had simply stopped inviting them – even going so far as to hide the invitations Mom would so diligently write out every year at the bottom of his school bag and throwing them in the trash the first chance he got.

Sandy West emerged from the dusty gloom of his study looking like the cat that just got the mouse. Ricky looked up at his father with a mouthful of blood-red cake and saw clearly the rectangular imprint of the *iPhone* on the side of the man's head.

"They found water," Sandy said. There was a tremble to his voice and Ricky honestly thought that for the first time in his life he was about to witness his father actually crying. Frances walked around the table and placed a loving arm around her husband's waist. "They found freakin' water!" Sandy repeated, his voice an octave or so higher than was usual. He stared at his son with a wide-eyed, little-boy wonder that made him look quite maniacal, then at Frances, and then back to Ricky who simply shovelled another forkful of cake into his mouth, the red frosting oozing out from the corners.

Sandy stood tall, his chest puffed out with pride. "It looks like The West family is going to Mars!" he said.

*

Henry (Hank to those who didn't know any better) Deakins hung up the call and plugged his cell phone back into its charger. He crossed the West's name off of the hastily pencilled list on his desk and mentally prepared himself to go home. He'd been stuck there in Mission Control since nine the previous morning, hadn't slept a wink and although the relentless Houston summer sun was blazing high overhead, he was more than ready for his bed.

Sandy and Francis West (and their nerdy kid, Henry never could remember his damned name) were the last of the Mars colonists that he had to contact with the good news, unfortunate victims of alphabetization. The Powers That Be had decided that each of the colonists-in-waiting should be told personally, and before the ground-breaking news that actual *liquid* water had been discovered just beneath the surface of Mars went public; and that enviable job had fallen to Henry's department.

Of course, it was immense news – the fact that the Mars Rover had discovered liquid water in abundance was a total game changer for the upcoming mission; not only did it negate the necessity to lug tonnes of the stuff to the planet, it also meant that the colonists would be able to make as much oxygen as they needed using basic equipment, which in turn meant that there would be a ready supply of carbon dioxide to feed the plants they were taking along. And the biggest news of all was that because the NASA scientists were no longer bogged down by the logistics of transporting vast amounts of water and oxygen across 33.9 million miles of space, the entire program could be brought forward by two years – they'd be good to go in six months.

It had instantly irked those who had spent decades studying Mars from afar that water had not been detected before, and that it had taken the actual presence of an exploratory vehicle on the planet's surface to find the stuff, but such was the rivalry between the departments in Houston.

Henry had worked for NASA since the decommissioning of the Space Shuttle program, and those humiliating years in which the world's once-leading space nation had to rely upon the Chinese and the Russians to get American astronauts up to the

International Space Station. That had never quite sat right with Henry; had the USA won the space race for nothing? At least now, with this first ever mission to colonize Mars, America were once more back in the running, albeit alongside a bunch of other nations – international harmony, and all that.

Nonetheless, with human nature being what it is, there'd been the inevitable arguments between the participating countries as to the name of the ship that was to transport the forty colonists, some of which had become quite heated. The US wanted to christen it *Mayflower*, for obvious reasons, but the others had countered that that was far too obvious and would be seen to be pushing the Christian agenda. The Russians wanted *Putin*, but despite support from the Chinese, they were advised that given the previous icy relations between Vladimir and pretty much everyone in the West it was not such a great idea. The Chinese had put forward *Zheng He* but were shot down on the grounds of potential pronunciation issues, and the British suggestion of *Sir Walter Raleigh* was immediately scuppered as it was deemed by the Americans to be gratuitous advertising for the bicycle company.

In the end the collaborative nations had settled for the highly unimaginative – but politically acceptable – *Mars Colonization Vehicle One,* although some diehard pedants did argue that the name should have said *ship* since 'vehicle' implied that the thing had wheels.

Henry had drawn the short straw to stay late and inform the American contingent of the recent discovery water, and to advise them that after several years on mothballs, MCV1's maiden, one-way voyage into the history books was to be in a little under half a year – a time at which Mars would be at its closest to the Earth at a mere seventy-eight million kilometres.

It seemed to Henry a tad incongruous to let the four colonist couples know this life-changing news in a brief telephone call, but NASA were straining at the leash to be the first to inform the world about what they'd found on Earth's supposedly waterless next door neighbor, and it was deemed for the best by people way above Henry's pay grade – although there would be highly staged telephone calls to the colonists from the President himself at some later date. Still, at least they'd not blasted out a group text as had initially been suggested; Henry thought that would have been terribly crass.

The penultimate couple, Geoff Shelton and his fiancée Krissy Santiago had been beside themselves at Henry's news. So much so that they swore there and then to bring forward their wedding so they'd be lawfully married man and wife before they left Earth for good. They'd told Henry in giddy, excited voices that they were going to drive to Vegas that very weekend, find the cheesiest chapel they could and get married by an Elvis look-alike. Henry found that to be incredibly romantic; not enough young people eloped these days, in his humble opinion.

The Wests were the only Americans on the mission with a kid (what the heck *was* his name? Dicky, Nicky, *Petey*?), although it was expected that the other couples would chip in and make some offspring of their own once they reached Mars – all of them had gone through rigorous and exceptionally invasive fertility tests to ensure that would happen; after all, there'd be little point trying to colonize Mars with people as barren as the planet they landed on. One of the Ruskies had a child around ten or eleven, a couple of the Chinese had kids and one of the Brits had a toddler – the idea there being to give the new colony a flying start.

Henry sighed a weary sigh. Soon the furore over Mars Rover Seven's monumental find would sweep

Earth's media and his phone would ring off the hook for days, if not weeks. But for now, with his historic task completed, albeit in a somewhat anticlimactic fashion, Henry could finally go home.

*

Rover Seven bumped across the increasingly difficult terrain of the foothills of the stately mountain range. Someday they'd name the mountains, most likely after some president or scientist – quite possibly Kennedy or Hawking – but for now they were just nameless towers of jagged rock that jutted out from the Martian landscape like a sick array of rotted teeth.

A mile or so into the foothills, Rover Seven had happened upon Rover Four, one of its predecessors from a long, long time ago. It had been one of the less successful exploratory vehicles, having ceased all communications with Earth just six weeks into its mission. It appeared to have wandered into the rocky outcrops and had tumbled into one of the treacherous crevasses that criss-crossed the entire area. Rover Seven had pointed its camera at Rover Four and snapped a handful of photographs of the wrecked vehicle to send back to Mission Control; and thought it incredibly sad that the vehicle had died all alone out there on that dead, unforgiving planet.

Using its hazcam along with the pair of navcams that were mounted an inch or two below the dual pancams atop the telescopic mast at its front end, Rover Seven negotiated its way around the deeper ruts and potholes of the undulating rocky hills to avoid damage to its wheels and delicate suspension apparatus, although today it was feeling just a smidge reckless. At one point, Rover Seven bounced over a scattering of red rocks just to see if their jagged points would pierce the thick rubber tires, and dipped into a shallow gully to find out if it was possible for it to tip over. And with its half dozen wheels spread out to its sides, Rover Seven thought that should any Martians be watching, it must really have resembled something akin to a bizarre, golf cart sized insect.

And that, it found to be most amusing.

Naturally, Rover Seven had no idea yet as to the reaction back on Earth to its reports of the discovery of water; that would come with its next scheduled information update. It was, however able to make an educated guess as it had access to thousands of terabytes of information that had been programmed into its memory banks – mostly derived from the all-encompassing World Wide Web. It was because of the sum of that accumulated human knowledge that Rover Seven was able to make informed choices and 'think' for itself.

Ha! If only they knew!

Information from Earth to the rover was updated periodically via radio signal that could take anywhere between twenty-one minutes and four and a half minutes depending upon the proximity of Mars to the home planet. Updates would invariably come with fresh instructions from mission control and revisions to both software and firmware; all fired off as automatically as one would receive junk *no-reply to this address* emails. There was no talk, of course, no sound of human voices for Rover Seven to listen to – but then again, why would there be?

Rover Seven trundled to a halt and paused awhile to take in the majestic splendour of the mountain range that towered over it. It was a delight that at last it was able to appreciate the cold, desolate emptiness of the planet Rover Seven now considered home, and so crushingly sad that it had no one to share this splendid moment with.

Absently, the vehicle flexed its extendible Instrument Deployment Device – nowadays Rover Seven much preferred to think of the tubular, concertina mechanism that carried the array of exploratory instrumentation as its *arm*, since it found that to be more apt, far more *human*. Rover Seven decided that this would be as good a place as any to do a little digging, eager to see what else it may discover to report back to Earth. It extended the drill that protruded from the end of the IDD and stretched the arm out as far as it could go, to a little spot in the shade of a family car-sized boulder. A puff of fine, red dust drifted upwards into the thin atmosphere as the drill bit hit the dirt, and Rover Seven thought it looked like a miniature, red Will O' the Wisp.

The drill sank effortlessly into the soft topping of dust, and then whined as it hit the hard soil that lurked beneath that. Still the drill turned, relentlessly boring into the skin of the planet like an esurient parasite searching for a fat vein.

And as it watched the bit disappear, Rover Seven wondered what it should find down there, and that perhaps it would be nice to discover –

*

"Methane!" The fat guy all but yelled in Henry's face. "There's freakin' methane on Mars!" But before Henry could question the man further, he'd scooted off with a shit-eating grin on his face and his corpulent frame wobbling side to side along the stark, white hallway – no doubt on his way to yell in some other poor sap's face.

Henry watched as the guy retreated along the hallway – he knew him only as one of the almost faceless plebs in Communications, that army of souls who sat in near darkness for twelve hours a day and deciphered the messages that came from the numerous probes NASA had floating around out there in the depths of space. And of course, all communiqué from the exploratory vehicle the Agency had pottering around on Mars.

Methane was a big deal, even if it was frozen beneath the permafrost surface of the planet. In fact it was almost as big a deal as the discovery of water just a couple of weeks before, because Methane meant the presence of carbon, and since carbon and its varying hydrogen-bonded derivatives went hand in hand with organic life, this pointed to the inescapable fact that there had almost certainly been life on Mars, albeit eons ago. It also meant that carbon-dioxide could be released far quicker than waiting for the colonists to breathe it out, which would be essential for crop growth.

All of which meant, of course, that they would be able to vastly reduce the food payload on *Mars Colonization Vehicle One* – the colonists would be able to grow their own crops on Mars far sooner than had been originally planned for.

Little wonder then that the fat guy from Communications was so goddamned shouty.

Henry sauntered across to the conference room. He was not really relishing having to sit through yet another three-hour briefing by the MCV1 team; they were, to a man – and *woman*, NASA was all equal opportunities these days – as dull as the proverbial ditch water. In fact, how the agency had assembled such an intensely boring bunch of characters for such an exciting project was way beyond Henry's comprehension. Still, it would give him the opportunity to finally meet with their intrepid pioneers; the eight people who'd signed up for the one-way trip to Mars back in the day when such a trip had been all but a literal flight of fancy.

With a heavy heart and a loud sigh, Henry walked in to Conference Room Six and pulled the door closed behind him.

*

Sandy West looked up from his computer screen and gazed absently through the small round window and out into the pitch blackness of space that dwelled beyond. The data he was attempting to make sense of was jumping around like it was part of some crappy 80's arcade game and it was beginning to make his head ache. They'd flown into a patch of solar turbulence and the massive boost in radiation was playing havoc with some of the more sensitive equipment. Sandy slid his wire-rimmed spectacles down to the end of his nose and pinched the bridge between his eyes in an attempt to ease the pressure that had built up there. Ground Control had advised that the solar storm would be gone in an hour or two, by which time Sandy hoped to high heaven that his computer would be behaving itself.

He glanced over at Ricky who was diligently helping his mother with her work with a broad smile across his little round face as he scrolled through the reams and reams of information and analysis that had been broadcast by the Rover vehicle down on Mars. Sandy thought it somewhat poignant that the Rover – his son's number one favorite thing of all time – would be their welcoming committee of one upon arrival at their new home; all in all a somewhat anticlimactic conclusion to their historic journey.

Four months into their interplanetary expedition, and Ricky had yet to make a single friend. Sandy figured that he really should be bothered by this, but the boy did seem content to be hanging out with his folks and taking an active part in their work. Surely he should be taking some time out to play with the other youngsters on board the cramped ship – the Chinese kids seemed nice enough, as did the Russian girl, although the Brit kid was years younger than Ricky and had the tendency to be a bit of a spoiled brat.

Given the closed, claustrophobic environment and the unavoidably close proximity of all twenty adults and the handful of kids on board, Sandy had hoped to see Ricky make a friend or two, a skill that had successfully evaded him back on Earth. But, other than joining in with Fran's work, the only things Ricky seemed to be interested in were his computer games and the toy Rover he'd plucked with glee from the top tier of his birthday cake.

Sandy sighed. Now was not the time to be fretting about his son's lack of social skills, which was something he was positive they could find the time to work on once they'd settled on Mars.

"Could you take a look at this, Sandy?" Grischa Demidov interrupted.

"Sure thing," Sandy tried his best to mask his irritation. The squat Russian was forever asking people to take a look at something, it was almost as if he really had no idea what he was doing. "What am I looking at?"

"This." Grischa stabbed a stubby finger at the colorful peaks and troughs of a spectrogram, the likes of which Sandy had studied day in, day out since blast-off. "Does this look like carbon-based compound to you?" The Russian's grasp of English was usually exemplary, but when he was tired or excited, his thick accent was barely penetrable.

"I guess so," Sandy replied as his throbbing eyes skittered across the bright tablet screen. "Is this from–?"

"Mars? Yes!" Grischa blurted out loudly, drawing the attention of Fran and Xyen-Lo. "Do you know what this means?"

Sandy smiled up at the Russian. Of course he knew what it meant. The exploratory vehicle down on the planet's surface had unearthed traces of organic compounds just a little way beneath the thin layer of red dust; and they were organic compounds that could mean only one thing.

"Life," Fran floated across the module to take a look for herself. "There's life on Mars?" She had a look of wonder that lit up her entire countenance, like a little kid who's just been given *exactly* what she wanted for Christmas.

"There *used* to be," Sandy struggled to hide his own childish excitement. "This pretty much confirms what we hoped the presence of methane was telling us."

"Carbon molecules as complex as these," Fran traced her fingernail over the high spikes on the spectrometer's readout for emphasis, "could only have come from living, respiring systems. This is big news, gentlemen." A broad smile spread across Fran's lips. "They're gonna pee their pants back home when they see this."

*

"If the Martian soil is fertile, that's gonna save us a whole load of tax payer's dollars," Mike Channing, NASA's PR spokesperson said with a self-satisfied grin at the gathered throng of journalists. Press conferences were the bane of his existence; he was far happier sat in his little office with a view of the launch pad knocking out press releases via email. Still, on momentous occasions such as this, the rapt awe of the crowd kind of made up for having to swallow his nerves and face actual people.

"How so?" a voice, fighting to make itself discernible amongst the jostling crowd, called out.

"Because it means that we will no longer have to pay out to send unmanned rockets to deliver materials necessary for crop growth," Mike spoke slowly into the microphone. "Since we now know that they are all there in the soil anyway."

What Mike didn't tell the gathered press, however, was that the Mars Colonization Coalition also would not have to bother spending precious time working on a remote fix for the waste recycling module aboard MCV1 that had backed up after the first month into the mission and for four months now, the crew had been flushing their crap – literally – out into space using the manual pumps. The original idea had been to turn human waste into fertilizer for use once they arrived on Mars, in order to see their first crops through until the methane extraction plant was up and working and generating fertilizer from the frozen pockets of gas that lay just below the permafrost. That was all moot point now, no need for the colonists to hoard their shit, although NASA saw no need to inform the world that the toilets on the multi-billion dollar space craft had clogged up.

They would also be able to scrap the planned unmanned ship to send the spare parts to fix the lavatory, and cancelling that had saved the mission the better part of half a billion dollars. Small wonder Mike Channing, along with NASA and the other participating nations were overjoyed with Mars Rover Seven's latest find.

"And let's not forget what is perhaps *the* most important thing about this new discovery," Mike went on. "That the presence of organic carbon compound chemicals on Mars is the biggest indicator yet that our sister planet may have harbored at the very least simple life forms in the past."

"We are not alone!" One of the journalists shouted out, much to the amusement of the others; high spirits were certainly the order of the day.

"That is looking more and more like a distinct possibility, ladies and gentlemen." Mike joined in with a light laugh of his own, and a tingle of thrill raced down along his spine. "This is quite the biggest news ever, I'm sure you'll agree."

And it was the biggest news ever – right up until the point at which Rover Seven transmitted the first high-definition images of the fossilized sea creatures it had found.

*

It was quite the lovely summer's day on Mars; a balmy sixty-nine degrees to be exact. Rover Seven rode along merrily in the sunshine, taking a moment or two out to marvel at the fat, distended Sun that hovered high overhead. The harsh yellow light of the distant star stretched the shadows on the planet's surface all out of proportion and made the dark outline of the mountains look even more like the reaching, skeletal fingers of the dead.

Skidding to a sudden halt – Rover Seven enjoyed doing that now as it loved to see the huge plumes of fine dust rising up into the air behind it. The vehicle stretched out its IDD and scraped half-heartedly at the dust covered crust by its wheels, figuring that it really ought to take a sample of *something* to keep the naive idiots back home happy.

The endless cycle of sample-taking all seemed to be a tad pointless now that the colonists were well underway; another couple of months and they'd be dropping down from the Martian sky to take their first tentative steps on the rust-coloured soil of their new home. And since Rover Seven had realized the implications of this, it had adopted an attitude of *going through the motions* – much like some lazy high school jock kicking back in the knowledge that it was going to copy the nerdy kid's homework the night before it was due to be turned in.

In fact, Rover Seven much preferred to spend its time running time-trial races against itself across the fine dirt, attempting to shave fractions of a second off the time it took to dash across the dry flats at the foot of the mountains. It also loved to make huge dust patterns on the Martian landscape and reading through the reams of information the programmers back on Earth had crammed into its memory, as well as browsing the increasingly irregular updates from home.

Which is how Rover Seven knew precisely how much excitement it had stirred up back home with the fossil pictures, especially so on the back of its methane and water readings. And Rover Seven could only just begin to imagine the furore its next discovery would cause amongst the scientific community, and indeed amongst the population of the entire planet.

*

Ricky West flicked through myriad pages of data that splayed out on the tablet his mom had assigned to him. To the untrained eye, the information was nothing more than line upon line of indecipherable code that was interspersed with the occasional grainy picture. Ricky's eyes darted this way and that across the screen, as they searched out pertinent titbits with which to regale his mother; as the mission had progressed, she had become so immersed in her work that this was pretty much the only way he could get her to interact with him on any level. The same went for his Dad too, as both parents seemed to have left MCV1 to babysit their son.

The most recent transmission from Mars Rover Seven had just finished uploading. It had been intercepted by the ship as it beamed its invisible way towards the Earth, and the mighty on-board computers had instantly begun to decrypt and decipher the encoded signal to make sense of the countless streams of data. As Ricky watched, rapt, his tablet screen jostled with color and thick blocks of text as the translation progressed.

"What the–?" Ricky muttered beneath his breath. He watched as a fuzzy picture darted quickly up his screen. He squinted his eyes into narrow slits and turned his head on its side to get a better look at the nebulous image. "Mom?"

"Ricky, you really *must* see this." Frances West ignored her son, as was her way these days. She grabbed his arm and tugged on it.

"But Mom –" Ricky protested.

"But nothing, Ricky, put the tablet down and come along; this really is once in a lifetime stuff."

With a hefty sigh and a roll of the eyes, Ricky did as instructed and floated towards the exit door of the science module and up towards the front of the ship. He figured what he'd just seen would have to wait; after all, this was the first time he'd seen his mother excited about something other than her research in the whole time they'd been in space. It was a pity that she'd waited until they were less than a week away from alighting on Mars to show any signs of enthusiasm.

Ricky floated through the circular port behind his mother. Behind him, Ricky's tablet continued to churn through the endless streams of information and before long the image that had so concerned the boy simply scrolled up and off of the screen.

Frances West steadied herself against the cold steel of the command module. She pulled Ricky through the gathered colonists, pushing him to the front to give him an uninterrupted view of what she thought had to be the most beautiful thing she'd seen in her entire life.

Mars hung before them, fat and swollen in the inky velvet of space. It appeared an almost bloody red, like some vast, fresh wound and its bulk took up a goodly proportion of the ship's window. There was just something about the way the sun had lit up the planet that morning, compounded by the fact that some of the details of the planet's surface were now clearly visible – with high-reaching mountains, desolate plains and deserts of dust as far as the eye could see, along with the brutal pockmarks of long-fallen meteorites – all of which seemed to whisper *hope*.

Perhaps mankind wasn't as doomed as it considered itself, for with unimaginable beauty as this just waiting to be explored, with Mars being the first stepping stone in spreading *Homo sapiens* across the vast reaches of space, there would always be hope.

Frances swallowed hard and fought back the emotional tears that threatened her eyes, and she hoped that her son would grow up to appreciate this monumental moment.

Ricky pressed himself tight against his Mom, relishing the closeness that he'd spent so many long, lonely days missing. To him, this moment was worth the entire seven-month trip alone, and he wished it would never end. And as he delighted in the warmth of his mother's hands upon his shoulders, all thoughts of the unusual image on his tablet slipped from his young mind.

*

LIFE FOUND ON MARS!!!

The headline screamed from every newspaper and every online news feed, blog and tweet. Fuzzy images of the tiny alien creatures adorned every news stand, every magazine cover and TV news show; the world was alight with the astounding revelation that humankind was most unequivocally not alone in the universe. It had become apparent that Mars was not only once home to life in innumerable forms, but that below the planet's seemingly desolate, sterile surface, life in at least a handful of forms had continued to flourish.

The exploratory vehicle had broadcast back images of an array of Martian creatures; most were microorganisms no bigger than an Earth amoeba, but some were larger and resembled the sea-dwelling creatures of the Cambrian Era. The creatures were remarkably similar as it transpired, which set off fever-pitch excitement and speculation about parallel evolution or even – dare they even begin to imagine? – cross-planet colonization. And upon further analysis by Rover Seven, the organisms were found to have DNA that was similar to terrestrial life forms too, which then led to all kinds of theories as to how they may have travelled to Earth.

Amidst all of the excitement, no one thought to question how come some of the images of the Martian creatures sent back by the Mars Rover looked similar to those whose taxonomy had been so diligently saved on the exploratory vehicle's static hard drives for comparative reference.

Henry Deakins slumped back in his high-backed chair and rubbed a sweaty hand across his weary face. The damp sweat that coated his palm snuck in to his eyes and made them smart. Before him, his computer screen twitched and flickered, its stark display showing the on-going electronic conversation between Henry and the Mars Rover.

"Graboids?" Henry growled at Mike Channing and the guy in the white coat, both of whom stood before him like a pair of prankster school kids brought up before the principal. "You're telling me that the exploratory vehicle found goddamned *Graboids*?" Henry pushed a single white sheet of printer paper across his desk towards the two men. On the paper was printed an incredibly life like picture of an odd worm-like creature which possessed impossibly large teeth. And although the scale on the thing implied a size of no more than a few inches, the creature was quite unmistakable.

The guy in the white coat – Al something-or-other – made a barely imperceptible nod and stared ashen-faced at Mike, as if hoping the man would offer him some kind of moral support.

Mike, however, remained tight-lipped.

"And no one in your entire freakin' department picked up on this?" Henry directed his disbelief towards the heavily perspiring Al, who looked like he was about to throw up his subsidised, nutritionally-balanced NASA lunch. "We already told everybody." Henry shook his head in sheer exasperation. "We've told them all."

"We weren't to know," Mike stammered. "I mean, how *could* we?"

Of course, he was right, there really had been no way of knowing.

It was difficult to apportion blame, under the circumstances – but Henry knew full well that blame *would* be dished out somewhere in the very near future. Was this the fault of the teams of scientists who analyzed every single line of information that was broadcast back to Earth by the Rover? Or perhaps it was those supposedly brilliant minds aboard the MCV1 as it hurtled towards the Red Planet? Or maybe it had been a slip-up of the particular programmer who'd thought it would be a hoot to program in a handful of fictional creatures into Rover Seven's data banks?

Or perhaps – and the most unpalatable explanation for Henry to contend with – this was all was down to the exploratory vehicle itself? Even if it was impossible for him to think of the vehicle as anything more than just a bunch of analytical tools on fat, bouncy wheels, it was only by pure luck that Rover Seven hadn't claimed to have unearthed the vicious, man-eating Xenomorph from *Alien* or a colony of microscopic *Midichlorians*! Conceivably, if it had the vehicle's blatant inaccuracy would have been discovered much sooner – albeit much too late for those poor souls aboard MCV1.

"It's *someone's* job to know," Henry snarled at the PR guy. "Just what in the hell are we supposed to tell the colonists now? That our goddamned exploration vehicle lied to us?"

This was met with stone-faced silence.

Since the revelation of the Rover Seven's obvious fictional discovery of the creatures that so resolutely terrorized Kevin Bacon and his cohorts in the movie *Tremors*, NASA's banks of scientific brains had been pouring over *all* of the data transmitted by Rover Seven, and the results were looking increasingly grim.

Not only had the vehicle reported erroneously the discovery of the worm-creatures, the science boffins had since unearthed the fact that it had also fabricated the fossilized sea creatures; detailed scrutiny of the images Rover Seven had broadcast had been skilfully manipulated from those embedded in its memory which had been put there so that it had a means of comparison should it find anything, and so it would know what to look for. The presence of methane under the surface of the planet was also in serious doubt now, and it was fully expected, given the initial findings, that the reports of organic matter were also made up, since the chemical composition data would have been even easier for the vehicle to manipulate than the images.

And that left the rover's monumental discovery of water.

Henry's heart sank at the very thought of that. If Rover Seven had also misrepresented the presence of water on Mars, the implications of that – way above all else – were dire indeed. They had sent the ship out with just enough water and oxygen to last the colonists the trip out to Mars, plus a month on the planet's surface. This was because they had worked on the belief that in a very short space of time, they would have tapped into Mars' natural supply of liquid water and would be self-sufficient within a few weeks.

Of course, if Rover Seven had reported that in error, along with the methane and the organic carbon compounds, the international space community had just condemned forty innocent people to a lingering death in a toxic, barren environment.

Which left the one, inevitable question; *why, amongst the finest scientific minds in the world, had no one realized this before?*

To Henry, that one was easy the easy one. Everyone involved in the program had simply been seeing exactly what they wanted to see.

Had it not been for Rover Seven's unbelievably stupid – yet incredibly *human* – mistake, the people back on Earth would still be none the wiser, and would have remained that way right up until the day that colonists landed on the inhospitable, dead planet, of course.

"Is there any way we can bring the ship back?" Henry asked, although he already knew the answer all too well. It sat there in the pit of his gut like some gnawing, malignant cancer that threatened to eat away at his very being.

Al shook his head. "They're less than a week from landing, there's no way –"

"They *have* to land, it's all pre-programmed. There's no other option," Mike Channing butted in. "Oh, sweet lord, what have we done?"

Mars Colonization Vehicle One was, of course, a one-way vessel. It had set off with enough fuel for the trip to Mars, and once it reached the mid-way point – referred to in happier times as the point of no return, or the *pop shot* – it was impossible to turn the ship around and return home. To do so after that point – and especially now that the vessel was within virtual spitting distance of their destination – would have meant that MCV1 would have run out of fuel millions of miles short of Earth. In the absence of any backup plan, the colonists would die up there in space and drift around in the vast void for eternity in one big, international mausoleum.

"What do we tell them?" Henry asked.

"The colonists?" Mike said.

"Of course the colonists!" Henry's temper made his voice sound gravelly and his face turn red.

"Do we *have* to tell them?" Al threw in.

"I really don't think we have any other choice, do you?" The anger drained from Henry's voice.

"They're going to find out for themselves when they get there and realize there's no water," Mike added.

"We don't know for definite that there's no water," Henry said, trying not to sound desperate.

"*Yet*," Al said grimly. "But it's not looking good so far."

"We can't *not* tell them," Henry said with a long, drawn out sigh. He ran his hands through his thinning hair and took in a deep, heavy breath. "The least we can do is to tell them *why* Rover Seven did this."

"And just how in God's name are we supposed to do that?" Mike looked puzzled.

"Only one way I can think of."

Henry punched out his five-digit passcode on his computer keyboard, the plastic rattle of the keys loud and awkward like the dry clicks of ethereal, Deathwatch beetles. The comm' screen sprang to life and in an instant Henry had a direct line of communication with Mars Rover Seven. This was the first time the direct two-way link had been used, the first time it had *needed* to be used.

*

Rover Seven skidded to an abrupt stop, startled by the suddenness of the message from Mission Control. It read the message, intrigued by the simplicity, and all at once the vehicle felt like a naughty school kid caught with a hand down his pants.

'All data incorrect?' The message read.

Rover Seven pondered awhile, trying to figure out the best approach to such a blunt question. Then it decided that there really was little point in trying to carry on the deceit any longer.

'Yes,' it replied.

'Why?' Came the next question.

'Lonely'

The exploratory vehicle decided that it didn't want to talk to Mission Control any more and cut the link.

Mars Rover Seven sat and looked up at the twinkling stars, and waited for its human company – albeit transient – to arrive.

THE GHOST WHO STARED

There was a ghost in Patrick Crawford's new house. This, he found to be peculiar since no one had died there throughout its fifty year history, nor was it built on a burial ground of any kind – Native American or otherwise.

All of this, Patrick knew because he'd thoroughly checked it out within a few days of the ghost's first appearance at his home. And, being the intellectual obsessive type that goes so readily hand-in-hand with a life in academia, Patrick had researched as meticulously as Google and the local records office had allowed; and he had found absolutely no logical explanation as to how come he'd discovered his house to be haunted.

Yet there she was, a girl of ten or eleven years old, standing no more than a half dozen or so strides away from where he Patrick sat in his favorite, overstuffed armchair, staring at him with those big brown, mournful eyes of hers.

The Crawfords – Patrick and his beautiful wife, Aaliya – had moved in to the imposing, three-storey house just a couple of months previous, upon Patrick's appointment as the new Professor of Zoology at the local College. This was supposed to have been his and Aaliya's fresh start, having put all of the unfortunate business and subsequent lawsuits in Delaware behind them.

The girl's ghost had made her debut appearance midway through the Crawford's first month at the house, the first night that Aaliya had been out working late. Prior to Patrick's enforced relocation, she had managed to persuade her firm to relocate her to their local office even though they already had a full quota of paralegals, and hence she agreed to every extra hour of overtime, as she was keen to make a good impression.

At first, Patrick had assumed that the ghost was simply one of the neighbor's kids who'd wandered into the house by mistake, most probably on the way to a friend's party by the look of the pretty floral dress and blue satin shoes she wore. The dress was patterned with daisies and tiny red poppies and sported a fat, red ribbon that tied at the back to create two long, satin tails that draped down to the back of the girl's bare knees. Her hair was shoulder-length, wavy and light brown in color with dirty blonde streaks – it framed her pretty, yet expressionless face to an absolute tee.

In fact, there had been very little remarkable about the girl at all, except when Patrick gently touched her shoulder to elicit some form of response to his question as to whether or not she was lost. It was at that moment that Patrick had discovered that the little girl was nothing of substance at all. His hand disappeared *into* her and a tingling chill had spread all the way up his arm to prickle his flesh with goose bumps and force his balls to cling tight to his body with fear.

And Patrick also realized at that juncture that, far from it being a mere trick of the subdued lighting in his house, the girl was slightly transparent and he could actually see the outline of his period furniture through her slight frame.

Patrick recoiled in horror at the icy touch of the girl, whilst in return she hadn't reacted in the slightest to him. "Who are you? What do you want?" Patrick demanded, his voice trembling a little and a half octave higher than his usual resonant baritone. And all the young girl did was to stare at him with that blank expression he had since come to find so damned infuriating.

And that's all the ghost did. She stared.

She didn't move things around or make weird, ghostly noises in the dead of night – although there were times that Patrick did think that he may have preferred the archetypal haunting sounds of tormented spirits, the slamming of doors or even the rattling of ethereal chains to that silent, expressionless staring that the girl's ghost subjected him to day and night.

"I know you're there." Patrick said to the ghost, although he was fairly positive she could see him and knew that he was reacting to her constant presence – he couldn't be entirely sure. What if the poor girl was stuck in some alternate spirit plane of reality and was in fact staring at something completely different?

No, it had to be him. There was just something about the way the ghost's eyes burned into his, and the way in which he knew – *felt* – that when he wasn't looking directly at her, she was staring at him; much in the same way one senses when a fellow road user gawking at you through the car window – it was almost like an inherent sixth sense.

That thought made Patrick smile; he often mused that the girl may be reporting back to her ghostly friends that she *'saw living people'*? Only it was unlikely that she reported back to anyone, since she never actually left Patrick's side.

Patrick hauled himself out of the comfy armchair with a grunt, his slightly overweight frame creaking at the joints. *Pleasantly stout* was how his father had described Patrick's weight gain, although he knew that with his penchant for overeating these days, Aaliya saw only a heart attack biding its time. "Bathroom break." He informed the ghost with a wheeze. "If you'll excuse me, ma'am." He offered a smile but the ghost just followed him with her eyes, as if to break that visual link would be to lose him completely.

And of course, the ghost followed him to the bathroom like she always did. Although, *followed* wasn't quite the right word for what she did, for Patrick never saw the girl move; she would just be *there,* having lurked in the periphery of his vision as he'd made his way upstairs – Patrick had a thing about only using his own *en suite* lavatory.

"Must you watch?" He gave out a flustered sigh as he undid his pants. "Can't you at least give me this bit of privacy?" He dropped his jeans and boxers and sat his fat ass quickly down on the cold seat. Patrick had taken to peeing sitting down since the ghost's arrival, along with wearing longer shirts in order to hide his modesty from her – she was only a little girl after all.

The ghost said nothing, of course. She just stood there quietly by the shower cubicle and stared at him.

*

"How can you sit there and tell me you can't see her?" Patrick raised his voice to his wife and took no pleasure in seeing her flinch just a little. "She's standing right *there*!" He pointed to an empty spot in the kitchen by the refrigerator.

"Have you been drinking again, Patrick?" Aaliya struggled to keep her voice calm. She ran a hand through her short-cropped hair and tugged slightly at it at the back, seeking the twinge of pain to ground herself.

"No, I have not been drinking again," Patrick lied, his tone mocking nonetheless. "Why must you always assume I'm drinking again?"

"Maybe it's because you're expecting me to believe that our house is haunted?" Aaliya was finding it increasingly difficult to keep the sarcasm from her voice. "And that you – and only you – can see the damn ghost!" Her voice rose with the stress of arguing the unarguable with her husband, and a glistening sheen of nervous sweat broke out across her dark skin.

"She's there, baby! Look!" Patrick pointed into the corner by the fridge once more for emphasis.

"There's no one there, sweetheart," Aaliya told him with a tremble in her voice, beginning to fear for Patrick's sanity. "There's no little girl, no ghost – nothing." She stepped forward to take her husband in her arms but he took a step back with mistrust burning in his eyes.

"I can see you!" Patrick yelled over his wife's shoulder at the ghost. "What the hell do you want?!" And then he broke down and cried, finally accepting the comfort of his wife who had begun to think him crazy.

And for her part, the ghost just stared at him.

*

The new semester was well under way, and Patrick had proved quite the hit with the students. His unique brand of humor and lecturing style had quickly endeared him to the would-be zoologists and word of his popularity almost immediately spread to the powers that be. On the day they had first met, Patrick had promised the Dean that he would never regret offering him tenure, despite what may have happened in the past; all that was buried well in the past. Six weeks into the new academic year, Patrick had made good on his word.

Not content to haunt the house, the ghost followed Patrick to work. She would stand in the lecture theatre as he taught, sometimes high up at the back, other times over by the fire door, and on occasion she would stand at Patrick's side as he addressed his students.

Of course, not one of Professor Crawford's students saw the ghostly girl, and they all thought that Patrick was just kidding around when he asked them if any of them had felt anything strange in his lecture theatre – a chill in the air, a faint tang of ozone, the odd sensation of being *watched* perhaps? Naturally, none of them had, nor would they, because it was Patrick who was the sole focus of the apparition's attention.

Patrick had taken to drinking a little at lunchtime – just a nip or two to take the edge off – as well as his customary after dinner libation in the evenings. He stuck with the cheapest vodka, that old stalwart of alcoholics the world over; perfect for clandestine drinking because he could hide the liquor in plain sight in a water bottle and the liquor smell didn't show on his breath. And, although it didn't make the ghost go away, Patrick had discovered much to his delight that the stuff did seem to make him a tad less bothered by her constant presence.

The ghost kept her passive watch over Patrick as he crawled back into his old escape at the bottom of the bottle, but he was grateful that she didn't give him the same judgemental look as his wife, once she suspected that he was up to his old tricks again.

On a whim, one dark afternoon long after his students had gone home and the slate clouds rolled in fat and heavy from the Atlantic, Patrick had called Priscilla.

Priscilla was his mistress from back in the miserable days of his first marriage. In fact, Priscilla had been the reason for the ruination of said marriage and Patrick's first excursions into alcoholism. What had meant to be a mere dalliance for Patrick, a distraction from a stale marriage and a dull life, had turned very serious very quickly when Priscilla had announced to Patrick that he had gotten her pregnant.

That had been the end of both of Patrick's relationships at the time – his wife had thrown him out with little hesitation and with just one trash bag of clothes to his name, whilst Priscilla had taken the opportunity to announce that she wanted her independence. She'd run away with an old friend and Patrick had not seen the daughter she gave birth to seven months later, not even so much as a photograph. Priscilla did, however, chase him for child support, of which he'd never missed a payment in ten years.

The thought occurred to Patrick in the small, dark hours of the night as he'd lain wide awake listening to Aaliyah's gentle purring, that perhaps his daughter had died and the ghost that was a perpetual presence in his life was her and she was reaching out to him. Patrick had tried asking the ghost but she'd remained as silent as ever and had given nothing away in those deep, dark eyes of hers and so he'd been forced to contact his ex-mistress.

As it turned out, his daughter was very much alive and kicking and doing well in fifth grade, thank you very much.

"Oh, and while I have you," Priscilla had trilled in that high, irritating voice of hers. "We've kind of fallen on hard times, so perhaps you and I could discuss a little more child support?"

Patrick had hung up at that – let the lawyers sort that particular hornet's nest out – he really didn't have the mental strength to deal with financial negotiations. And, whilst Patrick was pleased that his flesh and blood was fit and well – and very much alive – he became all the more confused as to whom his ghost girl could be.

And what was it that she could possibly want from him?

*

Patrick found a medium on Craigslist. Or was she a psychic? The woman had seemed a little nebulous as to which one she actually was, and Patrick himself was none too sure of the distinction. Still, she was the only one who bothered to reply to his e-mail – he'd contacted several mediums/psychics/mystics in his desperate need to be rid of the ghost whose constant presence was driving him to distraction – and he invited her over that very evening.

As Patrick's luck would have it, the gal was a stunning, tall blonde with never-ending legs and the most perfect, large, natural breasts Patrick thought he had ever seen. Also by sheer luck, Aaliya had given herself a rare night off from work; and as a result, the tense atmosphere in the Crawford's house was practically palpable.

"London Vordokas," the medium introduced herself with the slightest of European accents to Patrick and Aaliya. She held out her immaculately manicured hand – somewhat optimistically so far as Aaliya was concerned – for the shaking. Patrick obliged whilst his wife chose instead to snort through her nose and eye the invader with derision over the top of her rimless spectacles.

"So you're supposed to be a medium, then?" Aaliya growled with scepticism dripping from every syllable.

"Yes, Ma'am." London was undeterred by the hostility that sparked from Aaliya, and her breezy voice matched her bright demeanor.

"And you think you can help my husband with his –" Patrick's wife carefully pondered her next word awhile, "– delusion?"

"I'm here to try." London shot Patrick a pitying glance. "And I'm not so sure that your husband is deluded, Mrs. Crawford; I can already feel a presence in this house."

"I'm sure you can." Aaliya all but laughed in the woman's face. "Shall we get this farce over with? I have a rather expensive *Pinot Noir* waiting for me.

The medium followed Patrick and his wife into the lounge, her face a picture of concern. "Could you tell me where the apparition prefers to present itself?" she asked.

"Everywhere," Patrick replied as he made himself comfortable in his armchair.

"Have *you* ever seen this ghost, Mrs. Crawford?" London winced in advance of the anticipated retort. "Or felt a cold spot or an unexplained breeze or smell?"

"No." Aaliya sat herself down on the leather couch opposite her husband.

"Right, then," London said upon realizing that Aaliya's blunt reply was as embellished as it was going to get. "It isn't uncommon for a spirit to attach itself to one particular person," the medium encouraged. "Although it is unusual that you have not picked up *anything* of its presence." She looked across at Aaliya who simply stared her down, as if daring the large-breasted charlatan to call her a liar to her face.

London knelt down in the center of the room. "It would help if you had something of hers," she said to Patrick.

"I told you in my e-mail that I don't know who she is," Patrick replied. "There's nothing–"

"I remember now," London cut him off. Her cheeks flushed red as she caught sight of Aaliya's smirk at her *faux-pas*. "Okay, let's begin." London took in a deep breath and closed her eyes.

From the corner of the room by the bookcase crammed to capacity with biology tomes old and new, the ghost stood and stared at Patrick with her big, brown eyes fixed on his face.

*

Patrick lay in bed later that night with his mind churning whilst Aaliya lay tantalizingly naked and sound asleep beside him. He felt the heat of her body and yearned to reach out beneath the covers and touch her. Not that Patrick specifically craved the intimacy with his wife that had dwindled somewhat with his preoccupation with the omnipresent ghost; all he wanted right then and there was some physical contact with another human being.

The séance with the Vordokas woman had gone pretty much as expected. The medium had gone through her entire *is there anybody there?* routine, and she'd even resorted at one point to asking the ghost to rap on the coffee table to acknowledge her presence in the room, but it had all been to no avail.

In the end, London had screamed hysterically at the ghost – Patrick having pointed to the corner in which she stood – *'what the fuck do you want?!'* and the medium's apparent breakdown had signalled an end to the evening's proceedings. Aaliya had escorted the trembling woman and her heaving bosom from the house and slammed the door in her wake.

There had followed what could only be described as an icy silence between Patrick and Aaliya. He could think of nothing to say that would placate his wife, and she simply didn't want to talk to him at all. Sadly, that didn't bother Patrick all that much; nowadays he was used to being ignored.

"Why are you here?" he whispered to the ghost who stood so close to his side of the bed that he could have reached out and touched her, had there been anything of her to touch. Not that he had any desire to ever again feel that frigid, dead sensation that the girl conjured. "What do you want from me?" He could see his breath smoking out from between his lips as he spoke, and even though it was a warm summer's night, it felt to Patrick as if the ghost was sucking the heat from his bedroom.

The ghost looked at Patrick – as she did – her countenance giving nothing away.

"Please – you've got to give me *something*," Patrick whispered a little louder to the ghost. Next to him, Aaliya stirred at the sound of his voice. Her bare foot rested gently against his thigh, it was so wonderfully and reassuringly warm.

The ghost stood there by Patrick's bed, unmoving and devoid of emotion. Yet somewhere in the deepest darkest recesses of his psyche, Patrick just *knew* that she wanted something from him; it was a cloying, visceral feeling that was all too consuming in those dark, deathly hours of the night. And along with that feeling came the undeniable craving for alcohol.

Patrick rolled over and squeezed his eyes tight shut. He pulled a downy pillow over his head and revelled in the complete blackness that closed around him. He risked a peep out from his sanctuary and saw that the ghost had moved to a spot at the foot of the bed, as if determined to remain in his line of sight. Patrick shoved his head beneath the pillow and embraced the solitude of the darkness.

It wasn't long before Patrick succumbed to a deep and fitful sleep – the events of the day had exhausted him, mind, body and soul.

The ghost tagged along, tailing behind Patrick into his dreams.

Patrick dreamt that he was walking along a long, straight road. On each side of the road there stood an impenetrable line of tall, dark trees whose canopies stretched high up into a sky that was painted the murky, pinkish-gray of dusk. As he walked, his eyes straight ahead and focussed on the horizon that was pinched between the twin tree lines, the ghost of the girl kept pace with him; an eerie, constant presence in his peripheral vision – precisely the same as she did in his waking life. Without looking directly at the ghost, Patrick attempted to make out exactly how she achieved that impossible feat without seemingly moving a muscle. but all he saw was that she was always, consistently *there*.

He began to run, his dream-self positive that something lay ahead of him – redemption for something he had no recollection of perhaps? His legs soon began to ache and feel leaden, and his lungs throbbed and complained with the sudden exertion he'd imposed upon them. But as hard as Patrick ran, as far as his progress appeared to be, the trees were never-ending, the ghost unflagging. She remained on the very edge of his vision, her body still, eyes unblinking and inhuman; it felt to Patrick as if the soul behind them had perished a long, long time ago.

And suddenly the trees vanished and Patrick found himself staring out at a vast, dark and utterly featureless landscape which was broken only by the solitary figure of a tall, thin man.

The figure turned around, its eyes as black as pitch and set in an unmoving face and a horrifying realization clambered up from the far corners of Patrick's racing mind; and finally, he knew what the ghost wanted of him.

Patrick awoke with a panicked scream stuck in his throat, the hollow his body had made in the mattress soaked through with sour smelling, nervous sweat. He clamped a hand over his mouth and bit down on the soft flesh of his palm to stifle the scream lest it make its way out, and to make sure that he was awake and not still trapped in that terrible nightmare.

As his brain clawed itself to wakefulness, Patrick glanced fitfully around his bedroom.

And saw that the ghost was gone.

*

Patrick nestled in the walk-in closet between his wife's expensive, plastic-wrapped dresses and his own meager collection of dinner suits with the belt tightening around his neck. As the rough leather constricted his throat to starve his aching lungs of the air they screamed out for, Patrick's bulging eyes flicked to and fro as he searched frantically for the ghost of the girl; this was what she had driven him to, he thought that the least she could do was to be there.

But no, as Patrick's tongue lolled a fat, swollen purple from between his blue lips, he saw no sign of the ghost who had been a constant presence in his life for so very long.

Patrick's head felt as if it were about to explode, bright, popping lights danced behind his eyes and Patrick sensed a black, velvety darkness crawling across his brain. In his mind's fading eye, Patrick imagined the final curtain falling on something horrifically theatrical as all went black.

Suddenly he was standing again.

The dreadful choking sensation in his throat was gone and his vision was clear – although he found himself in a house that was entirely unfamiliar. Patrick looked down at his side and there was the girl's ghost – he was surprised to discover that she was holding his hand; hers felt remarkably tiny and warm and *alive* in his. The girl cocked her head to look up at Patrick with those all-too familiar brown eyes of hers and for the first time in their odd relationship, she smiled. Patrick returned the smile and noticed for the first time that the ghost girl had a broad gap where her top front teeth should have been, and there were hints of her new teeth as white lines on her gums.

All she had ever wanted was a family of her very own.

A voice disturbed his reverie, a shrill, harsh voice that was edged with panic. Both Patrick and the girl turned their heads towards the voice.

"Who are you?" the woman standing before them demanded and Patrick had the odd notion creeping around the back of his mind that she would make quite the perfect wife and mother. *"What the hell do you want from me?!"* she screamed.

The ghost held tight on to Patrick's hand and neither of them moved nor said a single word to the woman. She would get the hint eventually, so all there was for them to do right now was to stare at her.

End

Edith's Teeth

Edith awoke to teeth marks on her pillow, which was most odd because she slept alone, and with her dentures in a glass on the nightstand.

S**t Happens

Clive Jepson pressed his foot a little harder on the gas pedal, gripped the steering wheel with one hand and watched as the Aston Martin's speedometer crept up towards eighty. He rubbed at the dull ache in his belly with his free hand and actually felt his bowels grumble back at him. He caught a glimpse of his own face in the rear-view; it looked pale and miserable and was coated with a feverish sheen of sweat that made him look far, far older than his forty-two years.

Regretting his decision to drive instead of fly – Clive preferred the solitude of a long road trip because it gave him space and time to think away from the office – he kept one nervous eye on the road ahead, watching out for the tell-tale white snouts of the cop cars that secreted themselves down the farm tracks that littered both sides of this particular stretch of lonely highway: Murphy's Law dictated that he'd be pulled this afternoon, the very last thing he needed right now.

Clive's stomach lurched again, and a most uncomfortable heat settled in his lower intestine. Clive stepped on the gas some more and prayed that he hadn't missed the rest stop.

Coupled with the gnawing sensations that burned the length and breadth of Clive's guts was the unfamiliar niggling feeling of guilt that chuntered away at the back of his mind; last night he'd been unfaithful, you see.

It hadn't been a planned thing and it was most certainly not the kind of behavior that Clive would ever have expected from himself; the whole incident had been more of an unfortunate set of circumstances, really.

Clive had been invited to speak at some big, important business symposium in Louisiana, and indeed, had been most flattered at being asked to be keynote speaker as one of the few successful dot com entrepreneurs whose name wasn't Zuckerberg, Gates or Omidyar.

He'd delivered his amazing speech to rapturous applause from his fellow software nerds and then he'd – literally – bumped into this random guy in the conference center bar. The guy seemed nice, charming even, but the most remarkable thing that Clive could remember about him was just how ordinary he was. In retrospect, it was that ordinary-ness that had seemed the most queer, pun entirely intentional.

They'd shared a drink or two, or three, and of course Clive had been incredibly flattered by the attention from the sexy, younger man, who Clive figured to be mid-twenties. He couldn't remember when he'd been on the receiving end of such interest, certainly not in the two years he'd been with Karl. And so, when the guy had invited Clive to join him for a meal at a cozy little Indian restaurant somewhere off the beaten track, Clive had said yes.

The fun of it was that Clive didn't even like Indian food. He found the food too spicy and it played havoc with his guts which Hypochondriac Clive was convinced were showing early signs of IBS or even maybe Crohn's. But, Clive also couldn't stand the thought of yet another night in his characterless hotel room eating room service boot-leather steak and attempting to get wood to straight pay-per-view porn; why do those places never cater for gay people? Surely they accommodate enough clientele who prefer their erotica a little less vagina-centric?

After the Indian, which was accompanied with a seemingly endless procession of bottles of Tiger beer, Clive had found himself whisked off to some dingy underground rainbow club. The rest of the night had been a whirlwind of trance music, crazy, shirtless dancing and of slurping tequila off the barman's rock-hard sweat-salty abs. And then had come the inevitable finale to Clive's odyssey, back to his hotel suite with his newest best friend – damned if he could remember the guy's name, or if he'd even asked it – for rough, urgent sex that was so animalistic and experienced through an alcoholic haze that Clive couldn't even remember if they'd used protection of not.

He'd awoken that morning, his head still spinning and the early onset of the inevitable hangover from hell that loomed large in his immediate future, and his mystery one-night-stand was gone.

At first, Clive feared the worse and assumed he'd been robbed; it was a wealthy man's burden to entertain the ever-present assumption at the back of his mind that it was always his money that people found the most attractive thing about him.

He'd forced himself out of bed – throbbing head and all – and checked his stuff. Nope, everything was still there; wallet, cash, credit cards, the thousand dollar watch that was a gift from Karl. In fact, as he'd looked around the room, it was as if his casual pick-up had never been there at all; if it weren't for the exquisite ache in his ass, Clive could have just about convinced himself that he'd dreamt the whole sordid tryst.

Clive shifted in the bucket seat to alleviate the growing discomfort in his bowels. He shifted his mind to his upcoming civil ceremony as a distraction from the burning in his guts and his guilt at having betrayed Karl. The civil thing was a far cry from the church wedding he had always wanted, but even though same-sex marriage had become law in his state quite some years ago, social acceptance was lagging somewhat behind it.

Clive's parents would be attending, of course. They'd accepted his lifestyle pretty much the moment he'd come out, had reassured him that all they ever wanted for their beloved son was for him to be happy, no matter what. And Clive loved them to pieces for that. There'd be all of his friends and a smattering of Karl's friends, but not Karl's parents; apparently, their attitudes were a little too deep South to stretch to acceptance.

A deep rumble in his belly served Clive a warning that the service area was not coming up anywhere near fast enough. He dared a little more pressure on the pedal and watched the speedometer needle twitch a little more to the right. Bowing to the painful sensation in his bowels, Clive decided that the best thing to do right now would be alleviate a little of the pressure down there, so he shifted a buttock and eased out a controlled, silent fart that immediately made his colon feel so much better.

"Ahhhhh," Clive sighed to himself as he rolled down a window to let out the stink of dopiaza, tequila and semen – the latter neatly answered the protection – or lack thereof – conundrum. Dammit, how could he have been so fucking careless?! He'd have to go get himself tested without Karl finding out and Clive knew that that wasn't going to be a walk in the goddamned park.

Poor, poor Karl, his poor, cuckolded Karl. Clive could barely think about his beloved partner right now, as he drifted into the self-loathing phase of his beating himself up process. How could he have done this to Karl, his partner of over twenty-four months, his soon to be husband? It wasn't as if he didn't love the guy, Karl rocked his world and made everything feel right; Clive even loved the way in which they had become *Clive'n'Karl* to their social circle, a cutesy combined name that was as if they were already joined together.

Karl had always been the paranoid one in their relationship; intimidated by Clive's success, frightened of the money that Clive generated, forever feeling inadequate in the shadow of the mighty Clive Jepson, entrepreneur, self-made millionaire, incredible catch. Most of Karl's anxiety, Clive reckoned, stemmed from the fact that he constantly pulled himself down; he was not attractive enough (which was actually bullshit; Karl was six years junior to Clive and had his youthful good looks, an incredible, six-feet one inch, muscular body and a naughty glint in his eye that could seduce practically anyone), or not smart enough. Granted, he'd quit working at the local TV company shortly after they'd met, but Karl had once had aspirations of being an elementary school teacher but had found out the hard way that, despite outward acceptance, nobody wanted their kids taught by a fucking queer. It was as if, somewhere on some Venn diagram, in the intersection between pedophile and homosexual the automatic assumption had been made that a gay man would diddle their children.

Clive couldn't feel much worse about himself right now, although in his heart he knew that Karl would most likely forgive his one drunken indiscretion and would punish him far less than Clive was punishing himself right now. And had Clive been a believer, he would have sworn that the fire in his lower intestine was further punishment from God.

Encouraged by his earlier success, Clive shifted his weight once more and dared himself to let out a little more gas.

"Shit," Clive cried out as he felt his bowels let go a little more than he'd planned and he felt a warm, sticky wetness bubble into his underwear. "Shit, shit *shit*!" He thumped his hand on the steering wheel and felt even dirtier than he had before.

Clive felt like crying. Yep, a damned good weep would have made him feel slightly better, although it wouldn't have glossed over the fact that he'd just crapped his pants. He could feel the hot mess squelching between his butt cheeks and he was grateful that the Aston had leather seats. And, he noted with some irony, if he'd waited another five minutes, he'd have made it to that grungy motel that sat on the outskirts of town and served as an indicator that Clive was fifteen minutes from home.

The motel loomed on the horizon, a mile or so along the road, its presence mocking Clive and the sickening mess in his shorts and churning heat in his midsection.

RANDYS ROADSIDE MOTEL
Room's by the hour

"Goddammit," Clive growled as he hit the blinker and pulled in to the motel's sparsely populated car park. He could feel that old, familiar pressure building up once more, but was too shit-scared to let any of it out. And so it rumbled and swished around inside of him like boiling acid that threatened to dissolve its way through his gut walls.

Clive slammed on the brakes and his car jerked to a stop in the center of two parking spaces – one of them the disabled – in front of the motel's office. He clambered from the car and dashed into the reception area where he was greeted by someone he presumed was Randy.

"Can ah help ya?" Randy drawled as he picked crusty sleep from the corner of his eyes with dirt-blackened fingernails.

"Toilet? Please," Clive grunted through the pain and headed towards the restroom sign, oblivious to its rider that declared *'for clientele only'* and Randy's half-assed protestations. "Thank you!" Clive waved one hand over his head to the proprietor, whilst keeping the other firmly clasped to his stomach as if scared that his abdominal contents would burst out should he let go.

When he'd finished up, Clive felt a million – no, a *billion* – times better. In less than five minutes he'd emptied out the entire contents of his digestive system amidst the feeling that as well as the bottom falling out of his world, the world was falling out of his bottom. The heat from the Indian spices and his overenthusiastic love making the night before had left his ass feeling scorched and sore, but that was nothing compared to the searing pain in his guts that he hoped he'd just alleviated once and for all.

Clive wiped and flushed and cleaned himself up. He slipped off his soiled undershorts, and stuffed them into one of the feminine hygiene bags that were stacked next to the lavatory. The paper bag had a picture of a demure looking Victorian lady on it, like the Victorians had invented menstruation or something.

He considered – briefly – dumping the bag into the trashcan provided but thought against it. Karl would surely notice that the shorts were missing when Clive returned home, since it was he who did all of the laundry and it was Karl who had bought said undergarments for his lover; they were his favorites and Clive had worn then especially for his homecoming. And yes, Karl would notice something like that; such was the range of the man's paranoia. Whenever Clive travelled away on business, upon his return, Karl would be sniffing for alien cologne, searching for unexplained stains, examining Clive's body for tell-tale scratches or bite marks; he always thought that Clive was being unfaithful the minute he was out of sight. Well, now, Clive mused, Karl's paranoia would be no longer unfounded.

Clive washed his hands in the over-hot water, dried them on a rough paper towel and exited the restroom with his Victorian lady hygiene bag clutched firmly in his hand.

"I can't thank you enough," he said to Randy who was looking somewhat bemused. "That's the last time I eat Indian food." Clive forced a smile.

"S'okay," Randy replied. "Only them restrooms is only for payin' customers."

"I understand." Clive made eye contact with the man, mainly to avoid gawking at the guy's improbably fat belly that made him appear eight months' pregnant. "How much do I owe you?"

Randy cracked a grin at him that wrinkled his weather-beaten face and showed off his capped teeth – and shiny gold canines – and his brown eyes twinkled in the fluorescent light.

"Just put in a donation to ma' charity here and we'll call it square." Randy pointed to the collection tin that was perched on the reception desk. The tin declared that the collection was for the Spastics. Clive wasn't so sure that you were allowed to call them that anymore and so was dubious as to the age – and validity – of said tin.

Even so, Clive was more than grateful for the relief that Randy had albeit reluctantly allowed him and he slipped a hundred into the notes slot at the top of the tin.

"Why, thank ya, Sir." Randy beamed and pulled up his breeches. "You are a saint."

"No, thank you, Randy." Clive smiled back as his mind conjured an image of the poor old sap cleaning up the reeking, spattered mess he'd just left behind in the toilet bowl. At that point, Clive began to wonder if one Franklin was enough.

"Don't mention it," Randy said with a grin. "Have yersel' a nice day, now." An obvious afterthought as Clive stepped out into the afternoon sunshine.

Clive sighed a big, relieved sigh. The warmth of the sun on his face, along with an empty belly and a receding hangover made him feel a tad better about himself, about facing Karl. He gripped the hygiene bag tightly and made his way back to the car.

The sound of voices made Clive spin on his heels. He squinted across the weed-strewn courtyard and saw a young couple heading to one of the motel rooms, pawing at each other and giggling like a pair of love struck teenagers. The girl unlocked the door and stumbled backwards into the room, yanking the guy in with her by his arm. More giggles and then the door slammed behind them.

Karl?

No, it couldn't possibly be. Clive shook his head, as if to clear the silly notion from his foggy brain. In that split second of seeing the guy with the short-haired brunette, Clive was sure that it had been Karl – *his* Karl. Must be the residual effects of the alcohol swilling around in his system, or the tiredness of the long drive. But then again, wasn't that Karl's black Camry parked across the way?

Clive felt his stomach churn and his guts clench, and not for the first time today either. Something was wrong here, he knew at least that much, and as much as he wanted to run and hide and pretend that he hadn't just seen what he had, he had to know what was going on.

It wasn't lost on Clive just how ridiculous he must

right now look in his Armani suit, two thousand dollar shoes, symposium name badge dangling by a lanyard around his neck and clutching a sanitary pad disposal bag. Nonetheless, he strode with purpose to the room he'd seen the guy who looked like his fiancé dragged into.

Clive paused by the grimy, cracked window, having noted that the occupants had not bothered to close the curtains. He screwed up his eyes, not wanting to look, but knowing that he really had no choice. He tried to tell himself that his mind was playing tricks on itself, punishing him with guilt and dehydrated from the upset stomach. Then again, Karl's car was a pretty big clue to ignore here. Even so, it took every grain of substance that was Clive Jepson to do the right thing, in any other circumstance, he would have been proud of his own resolve.

A deep breath and Clive peeped through the motel room window.

Although the spider web cracks in the dirty pane distorted the view, there was certainly no mistaking what was going on in there.

They were still standing, but the woman was already naked and was tearing at the guy's clothes – Clive still couldn't reconcile it as being *his* Karl – like a death row inmate devouring a last meal. She kissed the guy with a passion that seemed all consuming, her tongue invading his eager mouth like some slippery, living thing that they were passing between them. The gal was petite with close cut hair and wide, brown doe-eyes and the smallest, perky breasts that Clive had ever seen on a grown woman. His eyes were drawn to her neatly trimmed bush from which peeped delicate, pink lips that glistened wet with her wanton lust for Karl – his Karl.

Karl was undressed, save for his white towelling socks – always self-conscious about his feet, was Karl –

and the woman allowed Karl to lower her to the bed. She spread her legs wide to receive him and to Clive she reminded him for all the world like Audrey fucking Hepburn. And when Karl – his Karl – buried his face between the woman's thighs and told the woman just how much he was looking forward to not having to see the remnants of last nights' dinner when he pulled his cock out of her ass later on, Clive ran away.

Clive sat in his car in the motel parking lot with tears blurring his vision and thick, choking snot clogging the back of his throat. His mind raced this way and that, confused as to the conflicting signals it was being forced to process; why was Karl in this God-awful place with some boyish-looking woman? Who was said boyish-looking woman? Why was Karl fucking her when he was betrothed to Clive? Such a romantic, *twee* word, betrothed; it was supposed to denote a promise of a lifetime together, of facing the world side by side through thick and thin, and of unerring faithfulness.

Of course, the irony of the situation was not lost on Clive, nor was the fact that perhaps his own actions with his mystery guy the night before should cancel out Karl's adultery, but somehow Karl's indiscretion seemed to Clive to be far worse. Not only was he cheating on Clive, he was being unfaithful to their shared lifestyle with a goddamned *woman*!

How could he?

Clive wiped his eyes clear with the back of his hand, and sniffled the runny snot that clogged his nose to the back of his throat. Perhaps if he just went home and waited for Karl there, he could pretend that this didn't just happen. Clive ignored the fresh welling of tears that threatened and pressed the ignition button. The Aston Martin growled to life.

"So, you're going to run home and cry your pussy little eyes out?" a voice said.

Clive turned his head, fully expecting to see the corpulent motel owner staring back at him through the car window.

No one there.

Clive wiped his eyes a second time and returned his gaze to the lot beyond his car, to the door behind which Karl was screwing some mystery woman who looked a lot like Audrey Hepburn.

"If I were you, I'd get that gun from the glove compartment and kick that goddamned door in and shoot the place up," the voice chimed again.

"What the hell?" Clive peered frantically through the windows, twisting his body around 'till his spine cracked to get a good look through the rear window.

Still nothing.

Clive switched off the engine and rubbed his temples; he was clearly in no fit state to drive right now, what with him hearing things and all. He clicked open the glove compartment and eyed the small revolver that dwelled within – he'd bought the thing last year after an attempted carjack in New Orleans – it held only six bullets but it was compact and easy to handle – and just how many bullets did you actually need to deter a carjacker?

"Then again, I'm not you, obviously," the voice said.

"For Christ's' sake, stop it!" Clive shouted out loud and clutched either side of his head with damp, trembling hands. He felt like he was teetering on the brink of insanity and desperately needed it all to just go away.

"You really do need to man up and face this, you know," the voice chastised Clive. "Karl really is making a big, fat fool out of you." This time the voice sounded like its owner was sitting right on his shoulder.

"What the fuck is this?" Clive cried with a terrified quiver in his voice. "Get out of my fucking head!"

"I would if I could, but I'm not in your head," the voice replied in its distinctive, clipped British accent. "You couldn't be much farther from the truth, actually." Clive was sure that he heard the voice laugh.

And it was then that Clive realized that the voice was coming not from inside his aching head, but from the crumpled sanitary bag in the passenger foot well.

"Holy shit." Clive stared at the bag, at the scrunched up features of the demure Victorian lady.

"Not quite," the voice said with a definite light laugh to its timbre. "But perhaps you're close enough."

Gingerly, Clive picked up the paper bag. He opened it and peered inside, already convinced that he had just stepped over the precipice to total and complete insanity. The unmistakable waft of Indian spices and his own waste assaulted his nostrils, and Clive could have sworn that the bag was heavier than when he'd left the restroom, that somehow there was physically more crap in the bag.

"What the fuck are you?" Clive felt more than a little ridiculous addressing a paper bag crammed with his own soiled underwear, but hey, when in Mad Town, why not make like a mad man?

"I'm the only part of you that's ever had any balls," the voice inside the bag snarled. "And that includes your damned balls."

Clive shook his head. He was feeling truly scared now, terrified that his grip on sanity was hurtling rapidly away from him. "This is crazy; this really is some weird shit going on here."

"Weird? Really?" the voice sounded quite put out. "I'm going to let that one – and *only* that one – go, Clive; on account of the fact that you are upset. But please don't let me hear you say that again, it really is most offensive."

"I-I'm sorry," Clive stammered, not really knowing

what he'd done wrong.

"Now, are we going to go and confront that cheating shit of a fiancé of yours, or not?" the voice demanded. "See, now you've got me at it." Another attempt at a laugh that sounded like whatever the voice was, it wasn't really all that well versed in the art of laughter.

And so, Clive Jepson found himself back outside the motel room door, wearing his Armani suit, two thousand dollar shoes, clutching the shit-filled feminine hygiene bag and listening to the sounds of frantic, heterosexual sex coming from within. He had his free hand thrust into his jacket pocket and his fingers caressed the cool metal of the revolver that nestled in there like it was some fledgling creature awaiting its time to fly.

"Listen to them in there, it's disgusting," the voice instructed. And Clive listened.

"Do you think of me when Clive's fucking you?" the woman inside the motel room moaned.

"Always. It helps me to remember why I'm keeping up the pretence," Karl replied, his breath labored with his exertion.

"For the money," the woman gasped.

"Once the dumb fuck marries me, we're home and dry, babe," Karl grunted between thrusts into the woman-who-looked-like-Hepburn.

"Tell me what's it like when he shoots his come in your mouth, Karl. Do you think about how that feels for me when I swallow you?"

"I try not to think of you when I'm sucking his cock, Danielle – that would gross me out too much," Karl panted. He then let out a loud *ahhhhh* of pleasure that drilled through Clive's brain like – well, like a fucking drill.

"Sinking into your tight pussy is just the most exquisite thing, like ever, my love," Karl purred.

"And so is having your cock buried deep inside me,

Karl. Now I know why I married you." The woman replied, her breath coming out in short gasps.

And that was pretty much the last straw for Clive, the final insult to everything he thought he knew about his life, Karl, about their life together. He plucked the small gun from his pocket, clutched tight onto the paper bag and shouldered the flimsy door.

"What the f-!?" Karl cried out, his face flushed with the throes of passion.

The woman beneath Karl squealed and attempted to wriggle free, but he lay frozen in fear on top of her, his weight pinning her down as his dick skewered her to the lumpy mattress.

"I can explain. This is not what it looks like, Clive," The clichés spilled from Karl's mouth like verbal diarrhoea as he stared wide-eyed at the gun in his partner's trembling hand.

"It's *exactly* what it looks like," the voice piped up. "You're fucking your own wife in a grubby motel room. There, I explained it for ya."

"E-e-ex-wife," the woman ventured, as if that somehow magically made everything okay.

"Fucking pedant," the voice replied. "Please – don't stop fucking on my account."

Clive wiggled the gun and walked towards his lover and his lover's wife – ex-wife, or whatever the fuck she was supposed to be. He pulled the door closed behind himself, easing it shut the best he could on its broken catch.

Eyes not once leaving the gun in Clive's hand, Karl thrust into his woman as Clive and the mysterious voice forced them to finish their congress at gunpoint. Clive looked on with a kind of detached sensation as he felt his whole life – or at least how he'd perceived it up until this point in time – shatter and the pieces crumble around him.

Karl grunted to a half-hearted climax and Clive was sure that the woman – Danielle was it? – had faked her orgasm to get the whole sorry thing over with; and quite convincing it had been, too.

Karl rolled off of Danielle and they both covered up their nudity with the threadbare sheets, as if hiding their rude bits and pieces really mattered right now.

"You're a *decevious* little shit, Karl," Clive said, his voice cracking with raw emotion.

Karl rolled his eyes at his fiancé; he hated it when Clive blended words together like that to make his own, like he thought himself too damned smart to have to use existing words like everyone else. Karl couldn't help but wonder at what point in their sham relationship he had given Clive the impression that he found it cute.

"Well, excuse me!" the voice retorted. "I happen to find that offensive!"

"Who the fuck *is* that?" Danielle asked. "Are you some kind of freakin' ventriloquist?"

"You can hear it too?" Clive said.

Danielle and Karl nodded.

"Thank Christ for that." Clive exhaled deeply. "I thought I was going insane here."

Clive threw the paper bag onto the floor, where it landed with a soggy plop on the faded linoleum between him and his unfaithful lover. And he was positive that there was yet more in the bag than there had been before he'd forced his way in here.

"Do you mind?!" the voice complained.

"What's in the bag, Clive?" Karl asked as he edged backwards on the bed, mindful that Clive appeared unstable enough right now to have brought in some kind of explosive device.

"It's a bag of shit," Clive told him.

"Pardon me?" Danielle spat.

"I said," Clive's voice was as slow and deliberate as

his movements, not once moving the gun away from the woman and Karl, "it's a bag of shit. I crapped myself on the freeway and those are my soiled pants." He appeared embarrassed at the revelation. "And it's been talking to me," he added.

"Look, Clive." Karl held out his arms, palms up in reconciliation. "This is a stressful situation, and it's making you a little crazy, I get that. If you would just please put the gun down, we can talk about this."

"Stressful?!" Clive exploded. "I catch the man I'm about to marry in some fuck-awful fleapit motel, balls-deep in his wife –"

"Ex-wife." Danielle interrupted.

"Will you just shut the fuck up, you dumb bitch?!" Clive cocked the gun at the woman and she cowered behind her bed sheet and did just that. "Of course I'm going crazy, Karl – what do you expect me to do?" Clive's voice lowered. "I heard you talking – before I came in," he said. "You've been lying to me all along." He took a long, deep breath. "Are you even gay?"

"Bi," Karl offered, as if that fact somehow justified the deceit and made everything alright – he sounded like a sixth-grade bully being forced to say sorry to the fat kid he'd just beaten up. Karl grinned that sexy half-grin of his that on any other occasion would have had Clive as stiff as a board and jumping into his arms. As it was, it was all Clive could do not to shoot the deceitful fuck in the face, or at the very least throw in his previous night's infidelity, as if that would hurt.

Clive decided to keep the moral high ground and do neither.

"I guess I can assume that everything you've said to me in the past two years has been complete crap?" Clive fought back the tears and maintained focus on the gun; at least aiming a firearm at his unfaithful lover was giving him some pleasure. Whether or not he would actually fire the damned thing remained to be seen.

"Really?!" the voice shouted, and it sounded really quite angry this time.

All eyes darted to the feminine hygiene bag in the middle of the room. Clive was convinced that it looked even fuller; the Victorian lady on the side appeared quite plump now.

"Clive?" Karl questioned. "Are you doing–?"

"Of course he's not doing this," the voice chastised. "You're engaged to a software designer, not Jeff fucking Dunham!"

Clive stared down forlornly at the bag, convinced now that it was making some weird kind of pulsating motion as the posh Brit' voice emanated from it.

"You gotta be shitting me?" Karl followed his lover's gaze in utter disbelief.

"Will you two just stop with the references already?!" the voice yelled, its anger stunning Clive and Karl into slack-jawed silence. "I am so sick and tired of shit-this, crap-that from you! It's downright offensive – and most likely racist too! Or should that be *crappist*?"

"What is in the bag, Clive?" Karl asked, his voice quiet, timid.

"I already told you, Karl." Clive cracked a weak smile that just made him look plain unhinged.

They stared at the bag on the floor and Clive was certain now that it was bigger; its seams strained and the Victorian lady looked morbidly obese, like one of those sweat-suited lard-asses who hog the Wal-Mart disability scooters – as if being a greedy bastard was ever a disability.

"Jesus H," Karl said. "This really is some fucked up shit, Clive"

"You'd better believe it, baby," the voice said with a chuckle, in what was its very best Frank-N-Furter impersonation. "So, why is it that we excreta always get saddled with the bad press and derisory comments?" the voice continued, now cracked with emotion. "When we are a by-product of one of the human animal's greatest pleasures?"

Clive couldn't help but look perplexed – was he *really* hearing this?

"People eat for sustenance, for comfort, for pleasure; hell, the Americans even eat for fucking sport!" the voice ranted. "And in order to eat, you have to defecate. It's a perfectly natural bodily function that is subsequently derided as filthy and disgusting; just how do you think *that* makes me feel?" the voice was shouting now and the bag pulsed and swelled a little more. "I'll tell you how it makes me feel! It makes me feel like some dirty, revolting secret that is to be ashamed of, ignored and hidden away like some retard relative you keep in the basement and feed on fish heads!" The emotion in the voice bounced around the grime-ridden walls, its sentiment raw and unadulterated. "You have absolutely no fucking idea!" it stropped. "Why, even passing a stool is pleasurable for humans; did you know that there are more nerve endings in the anus than there are in the penis?"

Both Clive and Karl shook their heads, that fact new to them. Danielle just sat there naked on the bed and gawked in disbelief at the pair of them.

"Of course you don't, nobody does, and what's more, nobody gives a shit!" the voice whined. "See, there I go again. Your contempt is infectious."

"I am so sorry." Clive said with another glance at the paper bag which was now beginning to split at the seams. He got the impression that this whole scenario had become less about the massive wrong that had been inflicted upon him by Karl and more about the racist/crappist agenda of his – the – whatever the fuck the thing in the rapidly expanding bag was.

"You're *sorry*?" Karl was incredulous. "You're talking to shit, Clive! You're fucking crazy!"

"But you're hearing it too, Karl," Clive said quietly. He kept the gun aimed at his lover's head; one squeeze of the trigger and the boyish Danielle would be wearing her ex-husband's brains.

"Yeah, but that must be mass hysteria or something," Karl conceded.

"There are only three of us in here, Karl," Clive's voice remained calm. "How can it be mass anything?"

"So, are you going to do the right thing, or are you going to be the doormat that you have always been to this lying bastard?" the voice directed at Clive, sounding quite caustic.

"The right thing?" Clive enquired. "Yeah, sure." He fixed his eyes squarely on Karl's over the gun barrel. "Karl," Clive said as calmly as he could manage, "we're through."

"That's it?!" the voice exploded. "That's fucking it!? He strings you along for two years, gets you to fall head over heels and make plans to marry him so he can get his filthy little paws on your money, and it's *we're through*!" The voice cracked into a shrill, mocking laugh. "I'm beginning to think that you deserve all of this, Clive!"

"I do not deserve any of this," Clive growled.

"Those two targeted you, Clive. They picked you out – of the business pages for all you know – to pray on your emotions and exploit your vulnerability," the voice spewed out its venom. "And let's face facts here; with your lack of social skills, repressed memories of the bullying you got at school and inherent guilt about your homosexuality, you were a pretty easy target."

"It wasn't like that!" Karl butted in. "I liked you from the get-go, Clive. It was her who planned the scam." He nodded his head towards the shocked Danielle.

"Why don't you just shut the whiny little fucker up, Clive?" the voice demanded. "What kind of chicken-shit throws his own under the bus the second there's a gun in his face?" The bag appeared dangerously full now, each pulse threatening to split the flimsy paper.

"I loved you, Karl," Clive sniffled. "I really did."

"Will you just quit being so damned pathetic," the voice chastised. "Your entire relationship with Karl has been a complete and utter fabrication, Clive! All those times you guys made love, he was just gritting his teeth and getting off thinking about his small-titted wifey and half of your hard-earned cash. If that happened to me, I'd *want* to fucking kill someone!"

"Yeah, you're right," Clive snarled.

"So pull the fucking trigger already!"

"I will!" Clive took a step forward.

"No!" Karl yelped and shuffled back a little farther on the bed. Instinctively, he pulled the bed sheet tight around his body, as if it had any chance of stopping a bullet. "I'm so sorry, Clive."

"Sorry?!" The voice laughed. "That prick's had you for a complete sucker, *Clive*. Surely you're not going to let him get away with that?"

"It's right, Karl, you've really fucking hurt me." Clive felt the first of the tears he'd tried his best to hold back drip down his cheek. "This – us – the whole thing. How could you?"

"Never mind that, finish him – now!" the voice shouted.

"I should–" Clive replied.

"Look at the unfaithful bastard, naked in bed with the wife he never told you about!" the voice dug into the grating truth. "His dick's still wet from her, and I'll bet you never knew he loved the pussy so much when he was fucking you, Clive!"

"You're a bastard, Karl." Clive's finger pressed the

trigger lightly as he squinted his eyes at his cringing lover.

"That's it, Clive!" the voice encouraged. "Shoot the asshole between his lying little eyes!"

"Yeah," Clive's voice quavered. "You *decevious* piece of shit, Karl!" Another step forward, a little more pressure on the trigger.

"Oh yeah!" the voice exclaimed, and the absolute glee in its tone was undisguised.

Clive closed his eyes and braced himself for the sharp report and the recoil that he knew was on its way.

He lowered the gun.

"I can't," Clive cried.

The feminine hygiene bag ripped apart with a jagged tear that spliced the Victorian lady in two. A brown, bubbling mass from within the bag leapt out, rapidly gaining in volume as it hurtled towards the bed, filling the dank air in the room with its all-too familiar stench.

Clive stepped back, not prepared to believe what he was witnessing. The not insubstantial mess from the bag continued to expand as it crossed the motel room, and in an instant as big as – no, *twice* as big as – a grown man. And Clive could swear that he saw in the stuff's shifting configuration some semblance of a discernible shape; something unnatural and otherworldly.

And then the sickly brown mass was upon Karl, and as Clive watched, it smothered the man he had – still, in fact – loved. Karl writhed and bucked on the bed as the thick fecal slime invaded his mouth, his nose and his eyes. He clawed at the suffocating excrement to no avail; its substance was far too mercurial for his scrabbling fingers. Karl's flailing feet kicked out at Danielle who scrambled from the bed, bare-assed naked and scurried for the door.

A fat glob of the slime-thing broke away and slid after Danielle like some obscene, brown amoeba. It wrapped itself around her skinny legs and brought her down like a snared rabbit. She screamed as the expanding volume of crap forced itself down her throat to muffle her shrieks and crawled up along her thigh to explore her vagina.

Clive watched Danielle's mute protests with a kind of detachment; entranced by how she tore at her own throat in her vain fight for a dying breath, her twisted face concealed by a mask of pulsing, congealing shit.

Karl flopped from the bed, his body smeared with the brown slime and with a peculiar choking, gurgling sound bubbling from his clogged chest. He crawled towards Clive with frantic fingers scrabbling at the slick floor, his eyes wide and imploring.

He died at Clive's feet.

Then, all fell silent and still.

The stinking stuff from the bag – Clive still couldn't bring himself to concede as to what it actually was – laid spattered around the room and smeared over the naked corpses of Karl and his scrawny Audrey Hepburn wife.

"Holy fuckin' shit," Clive muttered to himself.

The voice roared loud and deep and the shit leapt from Karl and Danielle and towards Clive. He panicked and fired off two shots – three – before the thing's weight pulled him to the cold floor and penetrated every orifice that he possessed.

*

The cop held an off-white, booger-encrusted handkerchief up to his nose. The stink that emanated from the motel room was ghastly, even in the relatively fresh air outside. The cop stared down in disgust at his shoes, which were splashed with thick, crusty globs of runny shit. It had been just his dumb luck to be first on the scene.

The motel manager – some obese, greasy looking bum called Randy – had called it in after he'd heard the shots, but by the time the cop had arrived, everyone in the room was dead.

The cop figured it would be a long time – if ever – before he'd be able to even partially erase the memories of what he'd seen in that motel room that afternoon. The naked bodies, the shit smeared everywhere, the taut, bloated bellies and the wide, staring eyes of all three of the corpses. It had most likely been some kind of sick sex game gone wrong, the cop reckoned; he'd seen some of that German scat porn on the internet a while back and he guessed that the three stiffs in the room had met up for a little late morning shit-play – most likely paid for by the gun-guy, if the Aston Martin was anything to go by.

"Hey," the Medical Examiner broke the cop's wool-gathering and wrinkled his nose at the foul stench that wafted out from the room.

"Hi," the cop replied, his mind still elsewhere.

"This the one?"

"Yep," the cop acknowledged. "Prepare yourself, Doc, there's some real weird shit gone down in there."

"*Weird shit*? Really?" said an indignant voice from inside the motel room.

End

The Five Towns Pageant

His flesh tore like rending cloth, thick fur ripped away in fat, dripping clods, viscera spilled from the gaping wounds in his belly.

No longer able to fight, the beast knew that he was beaten, felt his life pouring out in hot, gushing waves and with it, the sensation of returning to his human form.

He'd put up a noble fight – his own razor teeth and keen claws had made their mark on the other creature and he'd tasted its thick, coppery blood on his tongue before succumbing to its savage onslaught.

In the background, fading as quickly as his life as he waited for those cruel teeth to deliver their coup de grace, *he could hear the sound of many voices.*

ONE

"Ouch." Cam sucked in his breath and grimaced as the thick needle punctured the tanned skin over his lean abdominal muscles.

"Almost done, Mr. McGlamery," The Doctor in the ill-fitting shirt sounded wooden and over-rehearsed. The doctor's face was fat and waxy with piggy eyes and topped off with a comb-over that reeked of hair cream and antiseptic.

Cam chanced a peek at the hypodermic sticking out of his muscle and nausea washed over him. He was pleased he'd made Josephine – *Jojo* – stay in the waiting room; the last thing he'd want was for his girlfriend to see him faint, cry or pee his pants – or quite possibly all three.

He'd harbored a phobia of needles from the age of nine when one had broken off in his arm during a routine allergy shot. They'd had to surgically remove the inch or so that was embedded beneath his skin and worse, the allergy shots hadn't even worked; Cam still spent a goodly part of Spring indoors, terrorized by the insidious yellow pollen that smothered everything outside.

Doctor Pollard finished squirting the rabies vaccine into Cam's belly and withdrew the needle, nice and slow.

Cam winced and studied the twin puncture wounds that oozed blood and were bruising up a treat on his six-pack. The two shots today – the dour-faced Doctor had explained – were one dose of immunoglobulin and the first of the four-part anti-rabies course. The first shot was to make the vaccine work; the second to ensure that Cam didn't die in some slobbering, manically aggressive heap in one to three months. As for the injections yet to come, Cam put those down to pure sadism.

It wasn't as if the tetanus shot hadn't been humiliating enough. The nurse at the town's ER had insisted Cam needed one, so he'd stood there with his shirt sleeve rolled up and Jojo holding his hand.

"You're gonna have to drop 'em," the nurse had informed Cam with a wicked smile.

"Excuse me?"

"This goes in the glute," she'd replied as if this was all just some great big joke. "If you'd prefer the young lady wait outside –?"

"She's okay," Cam had said; he hadn't wanted to be left alone with the skinny old nurse and her evil syringe. "There's nothing she's not seen before." He grinned and took some delight at the nurse's discomfort because perhaps Nursey got her jollies by pantsing jocks in her little curtained-off area. Besides which, Jojo *had* seen it all before. Hell, she'd had most of it in her mouth at one time or another.

After sticking the needle in Cam's ass the nurse had referred him to the bigger hospital in the next town over for rabies shots.

And to Cam McGlamery this had all seemed like a ridiculous amount of fuss over such a small bite.

It had been Jojo's idea to visit the mall's pet store to look at the puppies. Cam would often wonder if his girlfriend's predilection for baby animals was the beginning of a premature and impending broodiness. This worried him a tad, having just finished high school neither of them were ready to even *think about* babies.

Michael's Pets – along with the rest of the mall – had been gaily decorated in advance of the upcoming Five Towns Pageant with foil bunting, garish posters and balloons. It was the same every year as the stores milked the occasion the way in which they would commence their Christmas promotions the second the kids began their Fall semester.

Cam and Jojo had sauntered in, oblivious to the heads that turned at the arrival of such a handsome couple – it was just something they'd gotten used to. In any given John Hughes movie, Cam would be the popular quarterback who swam against the crowd and was loved by all. He was dark haired, six feet four inches, had an incredibly toned body and was good looking in a way that made the girls swoon. He played sports of course – excelled at them all – and had maintained a 4.0 average through high school.

Jojo Merle stood at five feet nothing *sans* heels but was as pretty as Cam was classically handsome. She was a petite size six with perky breasts and a round face with sharp, angled cheekbones. She dyed her hair blonde to mask the plain mousey-brown she'd always hated and wore contacts that accentuated her dazzling sapphire eyes. In testimony to her beauty, Jojo had been chosen to represent the town in that year's upcoming Miss Five Towns Contest which was a part of the annual Pageant that included the ubiquitous parades, cook-offs, sports events, fireworks and general gaiety that small town America does so well. Jojo had been particularly proud to have won the vote to participate in the contest, especially so because she'd done it on her own merit and not because Daddy was the newly elected Mayor.

Their trip to the mall that day had been to pick out Jojo's swimsuit for the contest – something not too slutty to court disqualification, since at least two of the other villages involved were known to be quite puritan – yet not too demure since she wanted to catch the judges' eye. Jojo had settled on a black one-piece (bikinis were just *so* clichéd!) that cut high on the thigh and accentuated Jojo's shapely, dancer's legs and plunged down to the navel to show off a daring amount of boob. The halter-neck suit had no back whatsoever and scooped so low that there was a danger of Jojo revealing serious butt cleavage if she so much as *thought* about bending over.

Cam had loved the suit. Far from being jealous of his girlfriend being ogled by strangers, the thought actually turned him on; in fact he'd sported quite an erection in the clothes store during the near-ritualistic *Trying-on-of-the-Swimsuits*.

"Aww, he is *so* cute," Jojo had cooed at the tiny black and white puppy in the glass-fronted cage. She tapped on the glass and the puppy opened one eye and yawned; an action that had elicited another girlish exclamation.

Cam, however, had been more interested in the store's two new assistants. The owner/manager – Michael (not a consumer-friendly *Mike* or *Mickey*) – was a nondescript, average looking man of average height, average build and average hair color (next to the entry *average* in the illustrated dictionary, there'd be a picture of this guy). It was perhaps because of this that Michael employed such babes.

One of the girls was breathtakingly stunning. Her naturally platinum blonde hair contrasted exquisitely with honey-tan skin and cascaded down her slim back like some living waterfall. One side of her head was close shaven with a Celtic pattern etched into the fuzzy hair above her ear – the pattern matching the intricate tattoo that sleeved her left arm. She had a trim, firm body and magnificent breasts that strained against her white shirt and jiggled playfully as she moved.

By contrast, the blonde's colleague had delectable porcelain-white skin and ink-black hair that was cut into severe, short spikes. She was petite with a young, elfin face and the biggest, brownest eyes ever. She too was spectacularly well endowed and her own white shirt – Cam presumed it corporate wear – strained at its third button as if her breasts were desperate to escape.

"Would you like to hold him?" the blonde had asked Jojo, her voice smooth and exotic.

"Could I?" Jojo had beamed, her smile faltering as she caught Cam's sideways glance at the blonde's bosom. Jojo puffed out her own perky chest but as generous as her breasts were, they didn't come anywhere close to matching those of the pneumatic blonde.

"Sure thing, Ma'am." The assistant unlocked the cage and scooped out the puppy. It squirmed in her hand and licked her long, lithe fingers.

Jojo had giggled as the puppy was placed into her open hands. She nuzzled it and grinned the broadest grin when it lapped at the end of her nose.

"Is he a mix?" Cam asked the blonde, eager to engage the girl in some – *any* – conversation.

"Jack Russell and Doberman," the assistant had replied and Cam's mind boggled as he tried to work out the logistics of such a pairing.

"I think he likes you." Jojo had thrust the wriggling puppy into her boyfriend's hands, quite possibly to distract him from the blonde.

Cam had held the puppy and felt entirely unmoved. Never one for sentimentality where animals were concerned, Cam nonetheless thought it *reasonably* adorable.

"Who's a cute little fella?" Cam played along and tickled the creature's soft chin with his thumb.

And that was when the puppy had bit him.

*

"Shit!" Cam had yelped out with pain and disbelief as the puppy chomped down on his thumb.

"Aww, he *does* like you." Jojo had smiled but a worried look flitted across her face. She'd rested a calming hand on Cam's arm as a surge of rage flashed up behind his eyes. She'd seen this look in his eyes before; like the time Tim Gorton had picked a fight with Cam over a fumble that had cost the school team the district championship – the Gorton kid was still in a wheelchair three years on and would probably see out the rest of his life being pushed around in the thing.

Jojo had given Cam's bicep a loving squeeze and prayed for his rage to pass.

Cam had ground his teeth together and struggled against the urge to squeeze the life out of the puppy and hurl its twisted corpse across the store. Instead, he'd held it out for the assistant to reclaim and actually managed a smile through the red mist that had even obliterated his lascivious thoughts of the hot blonde and her raven-haired colleague.

"You naughty boy," the blonde had cooed as she plucked the squirming puppy from Cam's hands. She rubbed its fluffy belly. "Look what you did to the nice man."

The bite had barely drawn blood as the puppy's pinprick teeth were tiny and its jaws weak.

Jojo lifted Cam's thumb to her lips and kissed away the blood. Then she kissed his lips so that he could taste his blood on her.

It was something they did, Jojo and Cam. It was their *thing* as young lovers exploring the infinite world of carnal pleasure and all of its permutations. Through their love of blood play Jojo sported a faint razor blade scar on the top of her left breast and Cam several on his right pectoral; they wore those scars with great pride and as a declaration of their undying love.

It was astounding how quickly their relationship had veered away from the typical clumsy teenaged fumbles and into to the darker realms of BDSM and pain and rough sex. Blame it on modern culture, blame it on the extreme porn that they watched together, blame it on *Fifty Shades* if you like – but here were two like minded souls with sexual appetites so far away from the norm who had found each other early on life's path.

Cam relished the warm, metallic taste on his lover's lips and his rage had subsided – replaced by thoughts of making love to his girl, of being deep inside her, of tying her to the bed with rough, biting rope and squeezing her throat tight as he fucked her.

Cam had broken from his reverie to see the black haired chick looking at him with an odd look in her eyes.

"Are you okay, Sir?" there was faux concern in her voice. "Would you like a Band-Aid?" She'd barely been able to suppress her smirk as she sidled up to the blonde to pet the errant puppy, her breast resting heavily upon her colleague's arm.

"I think he'll live." Jojo smiled a conspiratorial smile. *Men, eh? All of 'em really are big babies.* The unspoken words passed between Jojo and the assistants. *And if you check out my man like that again I'll rip* both *of your fucking hearts out.* "Come along, Cameron," Jojo said with a wide grin, "clothes shopping awaits!"

Cam sighed and rolled his eyes in a put-upon-but-loving-it expression and allowed Jojo to lead him from the store and those impossibly beautiful girls.

TWO

Three days later, Cam had awoken feeling decidedly *odd*, like he had somebody else's teeth in. Also, his head throbbed and his back muscles were stiff and ached as if he'd had a serious work out the previous day instead of the laying on the couch playing *Call of Duty* he'd actually done.

Even though it had been only a quarter after six in the morning he'd called Jojo and despite the early hour she'd been more than delighted to go straight over.

"You really should see a doctor," she'd advised. "You may have caught something nasty." She peered at his thumb and at the barely perceptible indentations on its soft pad.

"What? From my vicious dog attack?" Cam had mocked with a nervous laugh. "I don't think it's anything to worry about." He'd pulled Jojo onto his bed. "I was only looking for a little sympathy." He slid a hand under her '*I'm Daddy's Princess*' T and she slapped him away.

"I'm serious, Cam. Heaven only knows what diseases it could have been carrying." She'd then put on her *serious face* to further emphasise her point. "They breed them in horrible puppy farms where hygiene really isn't a priority."

"It's probably just a summer cold." Cam had shrugged. "Nothing a BJ won't cure." Cam then made with his best sexy smile which fell sadly short.

"There'll be nothing of the sort until you get yourself checked out," Jojo's *stern voice*. "You're not giving me *Toxocara* or freakin' Rabies."

At the sound of the r-word, Cam's libido had bottomed out to somewhere just below zero. Rabies was not something he'd even considered before then and his mind was instantly flooded with images of snarling, slobbering rage and horrendous death. Cam had even eyed with suspicion the glass of water sitting on his night stand and could have sworn that the sight of the clear liquid was making his skin crawl.

Without further ceremony, Jojo had frog-marched Cam to the ER for the tetanus shot and then the nurse had advised them to take the trip to the big hospital because she didn't carry the Rabies vaccine and it could take up to three days if she ordered it in.

"And since you've already waited three days to get yourself checked out, it would be foolish to wait *another* three." The nurse had all but wagged her finger at him.

"The Rabies virus can take as little as a week to reach the brain, depending upon where you get bitten."

And that was how Cam had found himself in a hospital cubicle barely concealed by a hastily-drawn plastic curtain and being used as a human pin cushion by the sadistic fat doctor.

Cam had looked with dismay at the spreading purple bruise on his belly, tried to imagine just how unpleasant it would look when it turned green in a day or so. However, he *was* proud of himself for having not blubbered like a little girl during the agonizing shot.

"The bruising will go down in a few days." The doctor had read Cam's mind.

"Just in time for the next shot, eh?"

"Yes, there is that," the doctor had replied without humor. "You'll need to come back in five days, it's quite imperative that you finish the course." He'd popped the used syringe into the sharps bin and removed his latex gloves.

"Can't wait." As Cam had climbed from the bed his knees felt a little wobbly so he'd steadied himself against the wall.

"Would you like me to call your friend in?"

"Thank you. No." Cam had brushed the doctor off and with a deep breath he'd made his way back out through the flimsy curtains.

*

Cam had insisted on driving both to and from the hospital – he hated Jojo's driving – despite the fact that even the *thought* of the shots he'd faced had made him feel queasy. On the drive home Cam had been quite introspective and told Jojo that he was going to head home to sleep it off so he'd drop her off at her house. Jojo's parents were out of town and it was Sex Night;

Cam wanted to be sure that he'd be in full effect for their evening's delectations.

"My poor baby," Jojo had purred as she stroked his thigh. "We could always give tonight a miss if you're not up to it?"

"No way," Cam replied – perhaps a little too forcefully. "After the morning I've had, I need me some Jojo *lovin'*." He put on the redneck accent that never failed to amuse.

Jojo was still smiling when she'd climbed from Cam's car outside her house. She'd kissed him full on the mouth and teased his lips with the tip of her tongue. "Straight to sleep, young man," She'd laughed. "No *X-Boxing* 'till you've had you some shut-eye."

"Yes'm," Cam had replied with a glint in his eye.

And with that Jojo had disappeared with a wiggle of her elegantly pert behind and Cam had driven off in the direction of the mall.

Cam wasn't entirely sure *why* he'd decided to visit the pet store instead of heading home. He wasn't even one hundred percent sure that he had actually *decided* to go; it felt more like he was on autopilot and was being drawn to the place. It was possible that it had been the impure thoughts of Blondie and Raven-hair – his modern-day sirens – that lured him, not with hypnotic song but with shirt-straining breasts.

Was it possible that he was actually even *considering* being unfaithful to Jojo – the girl to whom he'd been exclusive since eighth grade? Surely not – especially since it was highly unlikely that the two assistants would share Cam's penchant for the darker aspects of sex, as did Jojo; she and he were most definitely two halves of the same when it came to exploring the depraved fringes of sexuality.

Still, Cam's legs had propelled him through the mall whilst his guilty paranoia teased him with a sickly feeling of being *watched*.

He turned the corner between the pretzel vendor and the phone case kiosk and stopped dead in his tracks.

The pet store was closed.

Not just closed, but completely gutted down to its bare walls and strung across the padlocked door hung the wasp-striped bunting of police tape.

"Police closed it up after yon incident," a voice piped up behind him, pronouncing the first word as *po-leece*. Cam turned around to face the weasel-faced guy who ran the phone case kiosk.

"Incident?"

"One of Michael's new gals got sick and went crazy," Kiosk Guy said with ghoulish glee. "She tore a customer's throat out right there in front of yon window. Poor old gal was only taking a look-see at them blue parakeets they used to sell."

Cam felt nauseous again and his abdomen throbbed with dull pain. "You're joking?" he said.

Kiosk Guy shook his head. "No Sir," he said. "Happened just a coupl'a days ago; saw it all with my own two eyes." A haunted look cast over the man's thin, pallid face. "That blonde gal with the huge titties smashed up the shop real good and dragged the old lady to the floor and ripped out her neck with her teeth. Screamed like a freakin' banshee too."

"The old woman?"

"The blonde," Kiosk Guy corrected. "By the time the cops came, she'd eaten most of the lady's face off – and some of her arm too. They reckon Blondie was on *Smelling Salts*, or some such." Kiosk Guy rubbed his hands together with sick delight.

"What happened to the other girl, and Michael?" Cam asked.

Kiosk Guy shook his head. "No idea, Buddy. The cops had the store cordoned off before you could say *exsanguination.*"

Cam shuddered and walked away. Mental images of an uncontrollable, snarling rage danced through his mind and although Blondie's breakdown most likely had been drug-related, Cam thanked his lucky stars that he'd let Jojo bully him into going to the hospital for the rabies shots.

THREE

Jojo licked gently around Cam's bruised belly, her soft tongue raising the gooseflesh on his skin. Cam moaned softly and laid his head back on the pillow, eyes closed tight as he lost himself in pleasure.

She had been waiting on her bed for Cam when he'd arrived at her home just as dusk was filling in the horizon. She'd dressed in a demure long-sleeved, white cotton nightgown that covered her body neck to knees. It had a high, intricate lace collar and matching cuffs but was otherwise plain save for a single row of pearl buttons that ran along its front. Naturally, Jojo was tantalizingly naked beneath but that did little to distract from the pure, virginal look she presented.

Jojo had spent her afternoon in diligent preparation; she'd laundered and starched the bed sheets to give a fresh, crisp feel, arranged the dozen candles that flickered and cast sensual shadows around her boudoir, and burned incense sticks that added a thick, musky scent to the warm air.

As for herself, Jojo had shaved away all traces of body hair to leave every inch of her alabaster skin deliciously silky and smooth – just the way Cam loved it. She'd taken a long, luxurious bath with shea butter oils to slough off what little dry skin she had and upon emerging had painted her finger and toe nails a delicate, subtle pink that was almost a perfect match for her glowing skin.

At first, Cam had been taken aback. He'd become accustomed to the leather and latex outfits that populated the nether regions of Jojo's wardrobe – that and the unashamed nudity that she more often preferred. But this was new to their repertoire, and the all-covering *Little House on the Prairie* night gown was such a departure that Cam had at first struggled to attain arousal.

But then Jojo had brought out the thick, leather straps. They were – in keeping with Jojo's theme – virginal white and jangled with shining, silver buckles; Jojo let Cam know in her own wordless, submissive way that he was to use them on her once she'd finished bathing his body with her tongue.

With that task completed and Cam's body damp and tingling, Jojo lay down and offered her wrists and ankles to each of the four corners of the bed.

Cam obliged and secured Jojo's wrists and ankles to the bed posts, taking great care not to expose her body beneath the gown, as if to do so would be to spoil the game. He then paused awhile and watched her breasts rise and fall with the rhythm of her breathing, longing to undo the gown's iridescent buttons but reluctant to undo the spell of that precious moment. Jojo looked so perfectly helpless tied to the fat wooden posts, so pure and chaste swaddled in clean white and to Cam she looked almost –

Sacrificial?

Jojo smiled and Cam could no longer hold back his animal instincts. He lowered himself to kiss her warm, soft lips and pressed his body against hers and his skin goosed at the rough touch of the cotton gown. Jojo responded and her probing tongue pushed its way into

Cam's mouth as she squirmed on the bed with an aching, wanton desire.

Cam caressed Jojo's cheek with his fingers and traced his hand down to her throat. Deftly, he picked at the first button that snuggled beneath her chin. As that button popped open, Jojo sighed and strained against the leather straps that secured her to the bed. Cam moved down to the next button, the weight of his hand resting on her heaving breast and his lips not once leaving hers.

FOUR

The weeks that followed went by in a blur for Cameron McGlamery.

He awoke in the hospital to the sight of Dr. Pollard's chubby face hovering above him. Against the stark white of the hospital's ceiling, it appeared to be disembodied.

The face to Cam's left belonged to a cop, and he swam slowly into focus as Cam's eyes adjusted to the bright, fluorescent light and until Cam attempted to sit up he didn't realize that he'd been handcuffed to the metal railings of the hospital bed, a perverse parody of his and Jojo's sex play. Cam tugged at the 'cuffs and the silver chain jingle-jangled against the rail. Beside him, the cop fidgeted uneasily in his chair and ran a hand over his sweaty face.

"Don't worry, that's there for your own safety," Doctor Pollard told him and attempted some semblance of a reassuring smile.

Cam's first thought was that he'd had a bad reaction to the rabies shot and had blacked out whilst making love to Jojo; the last thing he could recall was of unbuttoning her white night gown and stroking her warm, smooth skin.

The thought also struck Cam that if he *had* collapsed, then Jojo would have had to have called 911 once she'd wriggled free from her bondage. Cam allowed himself a wry smile at that – he knew that poor Jojo would just die of embarrassment having to explain everything to the paramedics.

Only, Jojo hadn't died of embarrassment.

Officially she'd died of asphyxiation. Cam, apparently had strangled the life out of her in the throes of passion.

So went the conclusion of the inquiry into Jojo's death and they'd used the word *intercourse* in the report, a word that to Cam demeaned all of the intimate times he and Jojo had shared. The verdict itself had been *accidental death due to erotic asphyxiation* which put Jojo's demise alongside that of Michael Hutchence and David Carradine – only without the electrical flex and oranges.

Cam had attended the funeral service 'cuffed to the cop because they'd laid Jojo to rest before the inquiry was over and he was still a suspect. Jojo's parents had been terribly brave and polite and had even asked Cam how *he* was bearing up during the wake at the house in which their only child had been killed.

In fact, everyone seemed painfully – impossibly – *nice* to Cam, even though he figured they must all have suspected him of some culpability in Jojo's death. And he simply couldn't escape the feeling that his girl's parents – and his own – were keeping something from him.

After the funeral, the subsequent enquiry and his final rabies shots, Cam had avoided Jojo's parents along with his own, and preferred to stay within the confines of his room along with his numbed emotions and haunted dreams.

And try as he may, Cam couldn't remember a single thing beyond the sweet scent of Jojo's body, her silky skin, the teasing, taut nipples that puckered as he exposed them and the twitching of her smooth belly when his fingertips caressed it. Cam's memory stopped right there.

Yet he had evidently (and *officially*) choked the Mayor's daughter – *his* Jojo – to death as they'd made love.

That just didn't sit right with Cam – he *never* forgot stuff – and the entire episode seemed to him to have been handled with an uncanny efficiency; the funeral, the quick inquiry, the absolving of all blame on his part when he'd felt that he deserved to be punished (as if losing his soul mate had not been punishment enough).

Survivor's guilt, the hospital shrink he'd seen just the once had labelled it and then assured Cam that it would pass in time.

When night time came and Cam lay his head on the pillow that he and Jojo had shared with her soft hair splayed out and tickling his face, his dreams would be of tearing flesh and hot, spraying blood that tasted of copper and looked black in the candle light; of splintering bone, stinking, slippery viscera and Jojo's gurgled, blood-choked screams.

FIVE

Cam struggled to find sleep.

He tossed and turned in his bed and squinted for the thousandth time at the red LED numbers projected into the darkness on his ceiling. Time had inched along only a few tortuous minutes – to thirteen after two – since his last peek.

Desperate for sleep, Cam would even have welcomed the terrible, bloody nightmares that had plagued him since leaving the hospital, although that would mean facing the horrific dreams of Jojo's demise and the terrible, dark thoughts that skulked at the periphery of his memory.

Cam's body ached and he felt cold, he slept naked now, as he'd had to discard his pyjamas because they had suddenly gotten too small for him. At first, Cam had put that down to too many pizzas and too much couch time, but upon closer inspection, he'd discovered that there wasn't an ounce of fat to be found on his body. His increase in size seemed to be muscle bulk, particularly on his upper arms, chest and thighs. This, Cam found odd insomuch he'd stopped hitting the gym after Jojo – well, after whatever had happened to her.

He turned his pillow over and hoped that maybe the cool side would help sleep catch up with him.

At least, Cam thought, he was managing to avoid the seasonal stuffed up nose that – along with the itchy eyes he'd merrily claw out of their sockets – made his life a misery this time of year. This, despite the fact that the air outside was thick with pollen as the oak tree that waved its spindly branches outside his bedroom window had coated everything in the front yard with a thick yellow layer of what was, bluntly speaking, tree come.

Cam kicked off the bedclothes and lay on his back staring blankly up at the ceiling. Despite feeling decidedly chilly, his body was coated in a glistening sheen of sweat that glowed against the cold light that snuck through his thin curtains. Also, his dick stood tall and proud at its perfect forty-five degree angle from his groin. Cam wanted to grab the thing, slap it and hurt it like Jojo used to, but somehow the thought of doing that right now felt like being unfaithful to her memory.

Nonetheless the arousal spread through Cam's body as if emanating from the center of the erection; a slow, creeping sensation that seemed to switch on his nerve endings one by one as it crawled beneath his skin like a swarm of miniscule, living creatures.

Cam cursed his dick; he felt even more awake now and had the old, familiar dread that once more he'd be watching the sun rise.

Suddenly, Cam's body contorted.

It was a single, violent movement that was so abrupt, so unexpected, that it forced the air from his lungs in a *phoooph* sound. Cam's spine twisted, his limbs bent in on themselves as his neck threw his head back with such force that the bones popped like kindling wood.

Cam was surprised to feel no pain; in fact, the involuntary spasm that wracked his body had felt more akin to an orgasm if anything.

Cam's skin tightened as if with the heat of the sun; a burning, tingling and not entirely unpleasant prickle. Then his spine seized and curled his body forwards to double him with his arms pressed tight to his chest and his knees dug hard into his gut.

What's happening to me?

Cam's mind raced and fear overrode the paroxysms of pleasure that snaked through his body.

Am I dying?

If that was the case, how come he'd never felt more alive in his entire life?

Cam's back straightened out with a violent and audible *CRACK*! and his arms and legs thrust outwards and catapulted him from the bed. Cam collapsed on the floor with a thump and he feared his parents would burst in to find their precious son on all fours with his rump thrust high in the air and a hard-on apt to drill through the floorboards.

Another jolt of pleasure drenched Cam's brain. With it came memories of hot, naked flesh sopping with salty sweat, pliant breasts topped with hard, cherry nipples and the heady, slick wetness that oozed between spreading thighs and teased with the cloying stink of sex.

Cam felt his bones moving around inside his body, sensed them *shifting* and changing. And with each movement, every crack of loosened joints there came yet another, almost unbearable wave of pleasure. His back arched and neck stiffened as the delicate bones in his face separated and shuffled around as if under the influence of unseen fingers; it felt like his face was melting from the inside.

Then Cam's face erupted forward with a slick, fluid movement that stretched his skin impossibly taut. There came the peculiar sensation of teeth physically *growing* within their sockets, roots snaking down to grate against his jaw bone and feel alien in his mouth.

Cam could see the end of his nose as an elongated snout complete with whiskers that snaked out of distended pores. Stretched from the freckled, upturned nose that Jojo had found *so* cute and made the target for her sweet kisses, it was now black and glistening wet like a dog's.

It was this distortion of his nose that was the clincher for Cam. Seduced by the wild, orgasmic sensations of what he was experiencing, he had not dared consider what the transformation was until now.

Hell, it wasn't even a full moon!

There were claws, of course there had to be. They forced their way out from beneath Cam's finger and toe nails which flaked from their beds and lay bloody and glinting on the hardwood floor. As each new, honed claw flexed against the polished wood, Cam absently wondered if they'd be retractable like a cat's. Alas no, they stood affixed on his broad, elongated digits like a malevolent array of knives.

The hair came next. Thick swathes of the stuff sprouted from his skin and coated his thick, taut muscles and along with it came a hellish itch that triggered the pleasure center in Cam's cerebral cortex and pushed him closer to his climax.

And then it was over.

Cam stood in transformed glory in the bedroom that had been his since he was in his crib, and he cut a magnificent lupine figure with his dark, sleek fur, vicious teeth and dripping muzzle.

The promised climax tore through Cam's new body and shook his frame. A noise forced itself from his throat; a guttural, primeval snarl that sounded like nothing that had ever been human. And with it, Cam ejaculated on to the floor.

Then the pleasure ebbed like the waves of a turning tide to leave in its place an insatiable, ravenous hunger.

The beast that was Cameron McGlamery slunk from the house and out into the cool night air.

*

Cam knew the girl was in the park before his heightened senses picked up her scent. He *sensed* her, *felt* her warmth and the pulse of her quickened heartbeat through the still, dark air.

There was also another presence.

Cam couldn't determine how far away it was so he sought sanctuary in the shadows and amongst the plastic fold-up seating that had been laid out in neat, regimented rows for the Pageant. He prowled around the periphery of the park, inching ever closer to the young girl who sat alone on a swing in the kiddies' play area with her slight frame rocking gently to and fro, her dainty feet dangling an inch or so above the ground.

The part of Cam's psyche that still considered itself *human* did puzzle as to how come a young girl would be in the park at this ungodly hour. Whatever her reason, she didn't look in the least part unhappy – in fact her countenance was perfectly serene. Cam's curiosity was soon dampened by the girl's sweet fragrance which stirred within him a raw, animal hunger that gnawed deep within his belly.

Cam circled around the girl with a preternatural stealth, camouflaged by the bushes and grateful for his thick pelt that shielded against the sharp twigs that probed his body like inquisitive fingers.

He chose a place as close to the girl as he could manage without breaking cover and from there he contemplated her young, succulent body and the sweet promise of delectable flesh. She was achingly beautiful – no more than sweet sixteen – with a slender, wide-eyed face framed by shimmering shoulder-length, auburn hair. She wore a crisp, white dress that accentuated the rise of her small breasts and her feet were tiny and delicate and most delectably bare. Which gave Cam thoughts of popping each one of her tiny, perfect toes into his ravenous, snarling mouth.

And with that, he was upon her.

The girl had no time to scream before Cam seized her throat in his powerful jaws and bit down hard. A dizzying rush of gratification raced through Cam's body as the girl's larynx was crushed between his teeth and the sticky, wet heat of her blood pumped into his mouth.

Cam dragged the girl from the swing, oblivious to her flailing hands that beat at his face and yanked hard at his fur. Closing his eyes tight against her spirited onslaught, Cam shook his head side to side and heard – *felt* – the rending flesh as it gave way beneath his savage teeth. The girl flew to the ground, her neck ripped open to the white nubs of her spine and the front of her dress stained a deep red that in the night looked as black as tar.

Gulping down the raw meat and gristle of his victim's throat in one, Cam paused to inhale the intoxicating aromas that spilled from her ruined body; the meaty stink of coagulating blood, sharp ammonia tang of urine and the earthy reek of her voided bowels and his animal mind reeled and raced with a tsunami of dark pleasures and the all-consuming urge to tear and rip and gorge.

The young girl was still alive when Cam tore open her belly and began feasting upon her innards.

SIX

The harsh morning light hurt Cam's eyes. He'd left the bedroom window wide open, his curtains flapped lazily in the early morning breeze and the window frame was smeared with dried blood.

Cam was relieved to find that the young girl's blood that had clung to his matted pelt had been confined to the window frame and bed sheets; he'd have those cleaned off long before his folks arose. It also wasn't lost on him that he must have scaled the wall of the two storey house to get back into his room.

He glanced down at his naked, blood-streaked body. Stretched out on the bed of his childhood, he seemed bulkier, broader, his muscles more taut and he figured that part of the transformation must have stayed with him. Cam hoped that it wouldn't fade away along with the more obvious symptoms of his lycanthropy.

He still had the taste of her blood in his mouth, as a drunk carries the sourness of his evening's libation; and with it the memory of steaming, ripped meat between his teeth, blood spattering his face and drenching his thick, black fur. Cam could still see the girl's face as he tore into her body – that look of agony and sheer terror in her final throes of life – and he knew that he should feel disgusted with what he had done (guilty even?) but no matter how hard he tried he *just couldn't*.

From his change into an otherworldly beast to the heart-thumping hunt and the fulfilment of his newfound hunger, to the insatiable lust that had pounded through his body as he'd ripped the girl apart and the sight of the thick, white ropes of his semen strewn across the girl's decimated body, Cam knew that it was all just part of his life now – of what he had become.

And it made him feel powerful.

Muscles strained and tensed beneath his skin, literally aching to run and climb and kill and fuck; Cam's body and brain throbbed with a fresh energy that triggered his synapses with input from his heightened senses – he had never felt more *alive*. Even concerns of getting caught – he'd murdered an innocent girl, after all – did nothing to dampen the swelling euphoria, although Cam couldn't help but wonder if the werewolf DNA he'd left behind on the girl would match his (should he ever end up on a database) – and just how thorough had his metamorphosis been?

Sadly, that night's events had left Cam with little doubt that his poor Jojo had suffered a fate similar to the girl in the park. Cam was grateful that he held no memory of that and wished to dear God that he never would. He prayed that the process he'd been through was akin to that of a butterfly which wouldn't remember its pupal stage – when caterpillar flesh is broken down into an amorphous mush and reassembled into something altogether more elegant – there are clearly some things that Mother Nature deems it best to forget.

Easing his frame from the bed, Cam grunted at the gratifying ache in his joints. He wanted to shower and clean off the window frame before his parents were up and about; with luck, he'd have time to get his bed sheets into the washer before Mom began her chores, although he thought he could hear her moving around the house already.

Cam's bedroom door burst open and slammed hard against the wall, its handle digging deep into the sheetrock.

Before he could even react, Cam was wrestled to the floor by a pair of burly cops who reeked of sour body odor and fried food. He struggled in vain as they pinned him down with expert ease; their combined bulk on his body forcing the air from his lungs in a wheezing grunt that sounded like a sow in a slaughterhouse.

The cold, steel handcuffs snapped around Cam's wrists and he looked across the room and saw his parents in the doorway.

Dad had his arm around Mom and they both had a peculiar look on their face.

Were they smiling?

A familiar smell of greasy hair and hospitals assaulted Cam's nostrils and something sharp dug into his neck and his mind spun back to the rabies shots.

Then all went dark.

SEVEN

Cam struggled back to consciousness with a pounding in his head and a sickly sweet scent that stung his sinuses with a metallic tang. There was also the unmistakable murmur of a hushed but excited crowd.

He was still naked but no longer restrained; a blunt ache in his wrists the only reminder of the tight 'cuffs. He lay on a rough camping cot; Cam could feel the abrasive canvas against his skin and the stiff metal bars that supported it.

He cracked open an eye with great reluctance and the light stung.

"Hello, Mr. McGlamery," a voice from above.

Cam twisted his head and was once again greeted by Doctor Pollard's unmistakable, chubby face.

"What the f–?" Cam lifted his head and found that he was looking out on a small arena that had a stale, cool *underground* feel to it, so Cam naturally surmised that he was below ground.

He could also see that he was surrounded by fat, steel bars that looked like the jail cells in those old western movies. His cell had a wide door constructed of bars and had a hefty lock built into it; someone was making damn sure he wasn't going anywhere.

Peering beyond his prison, Cam saw two hundred – possibly two-fifty – people populating circular rows of flip-down seats, filling the place to its modest capacity. In the center of the circular amphitheatre there arose a tall wire cage like those he'd seen on *Ultimate Cage Fighter;* only this one was wider, the crisscrossed wire thicker and it extended all the way over the top to create a steel mesh ceiling over the dirt ring.

Cam sat up on his cot, mouth agape and forgot for a moment about his state of undress.

Two statuesque girls strutted around inside the arena cage, spectacular bodies glistening with a heavy sheen of oil. They were clad in miniscule, latex bikinis – one black, one red – that enhanced the scant parts of flesh that they covered; high, full breasts, proud, jutting nipples and the exquisitely curved indent of pudenda. Each of the girls held aloft a white board which sported a large, black '5'.

Cam would have recognized them had they been wearing burkhas; it was the blonde girl and her hot colleague from the pet store.

But it was not so much the delicious young ladies that had drawn Cam's attention to that cage, but more the trio of bulky guys who were dragging out the dead werewolf.

The creature's body was bloodied and torn and it looked like mangled road kill. Its belly had been ripped open throat to balls and the raw, red glisten of the innards made for a harsh contrast to the dark fur that lay slick and matted with clotting blood. There were savage bone-deep claw rents on the werewolf's limbs and its snout hung on by only a handful of sinews and shredded skin and Cam could easily guess at the ferocity of its final fight. A single snake of pink intestine trailed behind the dead creature as it was hauled off with little ceremony, as if desperate to keep up as the men manhandled the huge frame across the dirt floor.

The 'wolf's head appeared to Cam to have been caught somewhere between lupine and human as it lolled loosely side to side on a broken neck. Clearly, Cam mused, if you die in the beast state, that's how you stay – the same way your grandparents warned you of what happens when you pull a face during a sudden change of wind direction.

The men manoeuvered the beast to the side of the arena and into one of four cages identical to the one Cam had awoken in. In the remaining three, there were groups of forlorn looking people standing around ragged, shapeless things that dripped blood and slop from the utilitarian cots; and what Cam saw next made him wonder if that was to be his own fate.

In one corner of the arena cage sat an immense, yellow-eyed werewolf like an obedient pet awaiting a treat. Clots of fresh blood dribbled from the creature's jaws and it snaked out a nonchalant tongue to lick at it. Aside from one superficial scratch along its flank and one ragged ear, the creature appeared unscathed.

This, Cam assumed, was the victor.

The beast eyed the pair of ring girls with a hungry look but made no move and the girls simply returned its stare with defiance. Cam noted that both girls bore a subtle lupine look in their eyes, had prominent canines and strong, lithe fingers that tapered to keen points; this clearly had the bigger beast intimidated.

"Both gals are yours if you bring this one home, son"

Startled, Cam turned around. "Dad?"

"Hello, Cameron." Edna McGlamery pushed by her husband to throw her arms around her son's neck.

"What are you doing here?" Cam drew his knees to his naked chest, suddenly self-conscious.

"We're here for the tournament, of course," Cam's father said.

"It's our first time," Mrs. McGlamery added with a grin. "We're so proud of you, son."

"What's going on, Dad?" Cam's voice came out shakier and an octave higher than he would have liked.

"It's the Five Towns Tournament, son," Mr. McGlamery explained. "The jewel in the crown of the entire pageant weekend."

"You've always loved the Five Towns Pageant." Cam's Mom smiled. "It's a pity you missed it this year, but they needed time to prepare you." She sighed and her eyes brimmed with tears.

"Hey there, Cam! Good luck!" Michael from the pet store interrupted. He waved a cheery hello as he strode by Cam's cell holding a thin leather leash. Cam gawked at the black and white puppy that trotted behind him with its floppy ears bouncing up and down. The puppy was larger now, of course, but like the hot pet store girls, Cam would have recognized it anywhere.

Cam looked around the subterranean arena and realized that there were many familiar faces crammed into that dank, dingy space. Aside from Dr. Pollard, the pet store staff and his parents, Cam recognized Tom Collins who owned the town's biggest car dealership, Joaney Smithson who ran the grocery store, the weasely kiosk guy, Mr. Richaux from the bank, Principal Baum, assorted members of the town council – including Jojo's father in full Mayoral regalia; he was busy mingling with the Mayors from the four neighboring towns who participated in the Pageant each year (one of whom was a *lesbian* – imagine that!). Cam even espied the nurse who'd stuck his ass with the tetanus shot, mixing with the many more who Cam found less familiar. Those were the faces he'd seen once a year during Pageant weekend in whichever town's turn it was to play host.

"Mom?" Cam was truly spooked. A prickly chill crawled up along his spine. "Am I dreaming?"

Mrs. McGlamery perched her trim derriere on the side of Cam's cot and smoothed out her new, undoubtedly expensive blue silk dress. She stroked her son's hair, the way she used to when he was very much smaller. "This is not a dream, sweetie," she cooed. "although it is a *dream come true*." Pleased with her own wordplay, Mrs. McGlamery smiled up at her husband who in turn studied the bikini-clad ring girls with scant discretion for a married man. "For all of us. Isn't that right, dear?"

"Um? Oh yeah, most definitely." Mr. McGlamery coughed and his cheeks flushed. "We're very proud of you, son. The *whole town* is." Mr. McGlamery stared down at Cam and puffed his chest out and a father could not have looked more proud as he did at that moment.

"Your father and I were absolutely thrilled when we were selected to birth a future Town Champion," Mrs. McGlamery said.

"Selected?" Cam struggled to make much sense of what he was hearing.

"Every year a couple are picked to bear and raise a Champion," Cam's father explained. "And eighteen years ago, your Mom and I were chosen." A courtly smile lit up his face.

"Why did I not know about any of this?" Cam asked.

"Only the *important* people know about the Tournament." Mrs. McGlamery rested her hand on Cam's shoulder. "And the selected parents, of course."

"It's all part of the Pageant," Mr. McGlamery said. "The parade, the tits and ass competitions, cook-offs and such keep the regular townsfolk happy." Cam couldn't remember ever having heard his father speak so crudely before, and certainly not in front of his mother. "*This* is only for the elite; it's been that way for generations."

"I've always been like – *that*?" Cam pointed across to the werewolf which had begun to pace to and fro in the fighting cage. "I thought it was the dog bite."

Cam's parents chuckled, as parents do when a small child has said something clever but inherently wrong.

"Good heavens, no!" Mr. McGlamery laughed and glanced over at Michael's puppy that was taking a long pee by the exit door. "That was just to get you to the hospital for the final stage of your metamorphosis." Again, vocabulary that was foreign tripped from McGlamery Senior's tongue.

"Final stage?"

"Champions are raised to be big and strong and smart," Mr. McGlamery said. "That way they make the very best fighting werewolves. Back in the day the townsfolk used to infect them in the traditional way but it was all too easy for the infecting 'wolf to kill the Champion and leave the town without representation."

"That happened here back in eighteen-forty-three," Mrs. McGlamery chipped in. "And the town just about died."

Cam had learned in his Local History class about that particular year. The text books said it had been due to a number of (*unspecified*, oddly enough) economic factors that the mines had closed, the crops failed, most of the local commerce withered and died and the town had been left with less than a third of its population.

"The rabies shots?" Cam ventured.

"Like I said, raised to be smart." Mr. McGlamery slapped Cam a hearty one on the shoulder and the sharp sound echoed around the low ceiling.

"I am *so* proud of my baby boy!" Mrs. McGlamery was close to tears.

"Now then, Edna he's not won yet," Cam's father admonished and his attention drifted back to the girls in the ring.

"Won?" Cam quizzed. "Won what?" A sick feeling in his gut told him he knew the answer before the question had left his mouth.

"This, son," his father said with a broad sweep of the arm to indicate the arena, the buzzing crowd and the snarling werewolf.

So he was supposed to fight the other werewolf to the finish and it was an honor to be ripped to bloodied shreds for the town?

"It's your destiny, Cameron." Mrs. McGlamery smiled.

"And we have high hopes that you'll break our nine year dry spell," his father added. "You have no idea how humiliating it is for the town to have not won the Tournament in almost a decade."

Cam's mind wandered back to the kids who over the years had hit their eighteenth, graduated high school and then simply disappeared. They had always been the biggest, fittest, most athletic boys – those who had excelled at everything the curriculum could throw at them. Cam had naturally assumed that they had simply relocated over the summer since the whole family had always moved away – and their houses had never stood empty for long. The thought of the families of defeated – *dead* – Champions slinking out of town with their shamed heads hung low gave Cam a sick feeling of dread deep down in his belly.

Cam shook his head in an attempt to clear it. He was still half-convinced that this was all some bizarre dream and he'd wake up in his own bed with Jojo curled up next to him, her sweet-smelling head on his chest. That way the dog bite, faux-rabies shots, Jojo's death and his transformation into a murderous werewolf expected to fight for his town's honor would all simply melt away.

"There's someone here to see you, Mr. McGlamery," Dr. Pollard sounded full of his own importance. "Best if you stand up." He then attempted a smile which just came off as creepy.

Cam did as advised and hid his genitals with cupped hands.

"Mr. Mayor, it's so good to see you again," Mrs. McGlamery gushed.

Cam paled and turned his eyes away from the Mayor and his wife; he'd not seen them since Jojo's funeral and was not at all sure what he should say.

Gee Mr. Mayor, I'm so sorry I ripped your daughter to shreds, but I couldn't help it, you see...

"Good to see you too, Edna." The Mayor beamed. "And how's this year's Town Champion?" He held out a hand to Cam for the shaking.

"Hi, Mr. Merle." Cam stared vacantly at the man.

Mrs. McGlamery elbowed Cam in the ribs and gave him her *don't forget your manners* look. Cam selected the hand that was not directly covering his dick – his left – and shook the Mayor's hand.

"We all have high hopes for you, Cameron," The Mayor boomed. "A victory today means prosperity tomorrow!"

That was a well-worn phrase Cam had heard all throughout his childhood; it was the town motto which he'd always assumed was a leftover from some war or other.

"Josephine would be so proud," The Mayor's wife said quietly.

"I am so sorry about –" Cam stammered.

"Nonsense boy!" The Mayor play-punched Cam's bicep. "Nothing to apologize for at all! After all, it's what she was born for."

Cam's expression must have said it all.

"You haven't told him?" the Mayor addressed Cam's parents.

"Just about to." Mr. McGlamery was painfully embarrassed.

"Good job I came along then, isn't it?" The Mayor guffawed. He slung an arm over Cam's shoulders, struggled to reach all the way around. "Our precious daughter was selected long before she was born, just as you were," his voice filled with pride. "It was her destiny to be your first blood and to facilitate your transition. And I'm proud to say that she threw herself into the role with all of her sweet heart."

"She was always saying how proud she was to serve the town so," The Mayor's wife joined in with a meek upturn of her mouth.

Cam sat back down on the cot as if someone had given him a hard shove in the chest and the metal frame creaked a loud complaint.

Jojo had been a part of all this?

His dear, sweet, sexy Jojo had been nothing more than – what? *Practice*?

It did make some kind of warped sense to Cam as the memories of that night flooded back; how Jojo had been so insistent that he restrain her, that she had not once struggled or cried out as he'd ripped her apart and feasted upon her as she died.

And to think that at the time he'd thought that Jojo had looked so virginal and pure in that beautiful white gown and tethered to the bedposts – that she had seemed almost sacrificial.

Because that's precisely what she had been.

A blaring horn sounded its harsh, echoing trumpet through the Tannoy and the two hot chicks sashayed from the ring.

"This is you, son," Cam's father said.

Cam glanced across at the ring, at the blood smeared werewolf that awaited him and somehow, Cam sensed that the beast was nervous.

It was *scared* of him.

In that instant Cam knew that he had a chance of defeating the creature. He felt its weakness and it was a compelling sensation that burned through him like a wildfire.

Cam felt the uncontrollable tingle creep through his flesh that was the portent of the transformation that now defined him.

Cam's parents, the Mayor and his lady wife all stepped back as Cam dropped from the cot and onto all fours. They watched with pride as his face lengthened into a snout and long, glinting canines curved out from his jaws. Cam's spine arched and thick fur blossomed the length and breadth of his magnificent, muscular body.

Cam let out a resonant howl as waves of pleasure heralded the shifting and snapping of his joints and internal organs as they rearranged. His dick grew long and hard and the beast he'd become felt no shame because this was what he was, what everyone wanted him to be.

As Cam embraced his change into the snarling, blood-hungry beast, he felt all-powerful, invincible and he knew that he was going to do himself, Jojo, his parents and the whole goddamned town proud.

TROPHY HUSBAND

Written with Kaye Terrelonge

"EMILY!?"

"Did you hear me, Emily!?" Walter Pemberton shouted across the vast house from the sanctuary of his mahogany panelled study. Although there was an angry edge to the man's voice, he continued to eye with disdain the large butterfly that fluttered and flapped inside a specimen jar on the polished oak desk before him, its vain struggles making a sound not unlike ancient, dry paper. Walter frowned as he studied closely the flimsy coating of fine dust on the thick glass walls of the jar, concerned that the creature's frantic pounding was already damaging its delicate wings and their exquisitely intricate pattern. Walter peered at the cotton ball that he had earlier soaked in chloroform and dropped into the jar, wondering if he'd put enough of the stuff on the white, fluffy ball to render the miniature gas chamber effective.

Walter was becoming increasingly impatient, both with the confounded insect *and* his selectively deaf wife. Right now, neither one was doing as they were supposed and that was pretty much guaranteed to increase his blood pressure 'till the ringing in his ears became quite the distraction. He figured that his hopeless wife had her head in the clouds again; preparing the house for Halloween that lurked just around the corner like some unloved relative. She'd no doubt be cluttering up his home with more meaningless, childish nonsense – most of it made by herself, more wasted time – and spending money they could ill afford to give expensive confectionary to the ungrateful neighborhood children. Back in Walter's day, they had a word for going door-to-door asking for things – *begging*. Call it *Trick or Treat* if you will, but to Walter it was nothing more than shameful *begging*, god-awful, homemade costumes or otherwise.

He blamed the awful Americans, exporting their dreadful – and he hated to say the word – *holiday* just like they sent over the insidious Colorado beetle. Walter had no juncture whatsoever with such Godless frippery; this was nineteen sixties England, not sixteen-ninety-two Salem!

Holiday indeed!

The *Lepidoptera* in the jar was a fighter, and no mistaking, and in some sinister way, Walter kind of admired it; most of Walter's specimens never lasted above a minute or two in the killing jar, but this one was one stubborn insect. Thus far it had eked out its survival for a whole fifteen minutes and counting – with nary a sign of flagging. Walter sighed, a deep, weary sigh; soon enough the fumes would take their inevitable effect on the butterfly, but what was to be done with his wife's foolish non-compliance?

"Dammit woman," Walter muttered beneath his breath. "Can you not hear me?" He moved the jar to his dissecting table and stomped over to the door. "*EMILY!*"

177

Across the expanse of the huge house, Emily *had* heard her husband's irate voice. Hunkered away in the kitchen – *her* sanctuary – she nervously searched through the cupboards for the umpteenth time, one by one, unable to find the one thing she so desperately needed. In the background, the angry, overheating teakettle blasted its angry whistle at Emily, whilst Walter's favorite China teacup remained empty.

All too well, Emily knew that her husband's bellowing signalled his compounding impatience at the delay in receiving his cup of tea; it was Friday at noon and Walter always had his rose hip tea on a Friday, and didn't Emily just know that Walter absolutely *lived* by his routines?

"I'll be right there, *Dearest*," Emily's voice quivered. She looked once more through the metal tea chest that was divided evenly into seven columns, each small section filled with the specified tea flavor of the day. All, that is, except for Friday. To Emily's ever growing shame, that particular section lay quite empty.

Emily inhaled deeply, plucked from the small chest an alternative variety of tea and with shaking fingers she plopped the bag into the cup. She then reached for the copper kettle that steamed and bubbled atop the stove and prayed to a God that she guessed wasn't there that Walter wouldn't mind the substitution – just this once. The infernal whistling slowed to silence and the hot water splashed into the small cup. With skittish haste, Emily prepared her husband's tea tray, and then added the final *piece de la résistance* – two fat pieces of the sugar-sprinkled shortbread Walter so loved – to the side of his saucer. "I'm just finishing up your tea," she called up to Walter as she backed her way out through the kitchen's heavy door and headed towards the stairs.

With the greatest of care, Emily carried the silver tea tray as she climbed the stairs up to the second floor.

Somewhat comically, her nervous shaking caused the delicate China to rattle rather loudly against the metal tray – much like the exaggerated movements of the TV comedy show characters that Walter thought so incredibly asinine. As she approached the firmly closed door to her husband's study, the tinny, rattling sound alerted Walter and he flung it open with an overstated, theatrical show of irritation.

"It's about time, Emily!" Walter snapped. "You're ten minutes late with this! Any later and there'd just be no damned point to afternoon tea at all!" Timidly, Emily placed the tray on the table next the large killing jar and its most unusual prisoner, taking sad note that the poor thing was still very much alive and fighting in vain for escape. "What took you so long, Emily?" Walter barked at his wife. "You know I *always* have tea at twelve," his voice adopted the tone of a petulant toddler and he all but stomped his foot.

Emily chose to ignore him; there was simply no reasoning with Walter once he was in this state, and inwardly she admonished herself for having created the mood in the first place. As she watched her husband grab for the shortbread, she braced herself, dreading Walter's somehow inevitable discovery of the *wrong tea*. As a distraction, Emily leaned over to admire her husband's latest catch.

From the unusual phosphorescent patterned colors imprinted on its wings, Emily guessed the specimen to be *Papilioideae*, although from what she knew of that particular family, she thought it much larger than the average specimen. The patterns comprised whirls and loops and swirls of orange and red and a startling, metallic blue, which to Emily appeared most mesmerizing and somewhat *tribal*. She felt a great pity for the poor creature, watching as it fought for its life within the confines of its glass prison, just as she did for all of the other *Lepidoptera* that were mounted on Walter's trophy wall; she never did quite understand his need to kill them all.

Emily had more than an inkling that her husband was a closet sadist – she'd seen how, with very little mercy – Walter appeared to delight in the crucifixion of his specimens. With great care, he would pierce a thin, long, sharp pin through a creature's soft body and then pin its spread wings beneath transparent paper, so that once the insect equivalent of *rigor mortis* set in, the butterflies would be spread out in all their dead glory for time immemorial.

Once dead and thusly arranged, Walter's victims would then be displayed in the wood-framed glass cases that adorned his trophy wall, Walter's pride and joy. Although he couldn't see it himself, Walter paid far more attention to his insect collection than he did to his long-suffering wife; the only time he ever seemed to notice poor Emily was when she made a mistake and it was necessary to deal out the required admonishment.

Naturally, Emily would try her utmost to avoid doing anything that may cause Walter to be unhappy, although some days even the slightest thing would garner his displeasure – and sadly for her, today was very much turning into one of those days. She closed her mind to the verbal onslaught that she knew full well was on its way and distracted herself with the beauty of the struggling butterfly in its death chamber. The winged insect calmed under Emily's gaze, ceased its frantic fluttering and paused to return her stare.

"Die, damn you!" Walter barked at the stubborn insect as he reached for his teacup, more with anger now than impatience. He lifted the dainty cup to his lips, blew the curling steam from the hot tea and took a sip.

"What the *hell* is this bilge supposed to be, Emily?" Walter growled with menace lacing his tone. "This isn't rose hip, and you know full-well that Friday's tea is *always* rose hip."

Emily jumped back from Walter's grating voice. With a dramatic flourish, he tossed the cup back on to the tray which in turn clinked against the killing jar that threatened to tip over. Emily grabbed at the jar and steadied it before it could topple over the table's edge.

"I'm sorry, my love," Emily's voice was meek, placating her husband's rising temper. She lowered her head. "I must have forgotten to restock when I went to the market."

"*Forgotten?!*" her husband chided. "It's not as if you have an awful lot to occupy that tiny brain of yours, woman! Too much time spent on all of your ridiculous Halloween nonsense, I should warrant!" Walter glowered at his cowering wife with such contempt that Emily could feel it crawling over her skin like a thousand tiny creatures. And she saw that all too familiar look her husband's eyes, the one that let her know in no uncertain terms that he was wondering just why he married such a spindly, unattractive woman in the first place.

It was not as if Walter was such the great catch himself; he was not one of the most handsome of fellows at the University and finding a decent wife – according to his standards – in the small town was nearly impossible. And what woman in her right mind would want a short, stubby man with thinning hair and piggy eyes?

Walter taught entomology at the University, not the most riveting of subjects to most, although a fair number of his students had an interest in his lectures – providing they could stay awake through Professor Pemberton's campus renowned, monotonous drone. Unfortunately for those who knew him beyond the bounds of the faculty, insects were *all* Walter talked about, and this served to bore his even his faculty colleagues and caused young women turn a deaf ear. And, as if that were not enough, Walter's salary barely made enough to maintain his extra-curricular passion of collecting butterflies.

Which is precisely why Emily had seemed such a godsend.

She was the Dean's daughter and her father had desperately wanted her married. Like Walter, she was nowhere close to what one may call attractive in either appearance or disposition; she was skinny and fragile looking, with a less than plain face, rounded shoulders and a slight, but increasingly noticeable dowager's hump.

While Emily's other suitors – arranged by the Dean himself – came and went, Walter had persisted and had finally asked Emily for an evening out. Naturally, Walter would have preferred someone more handsome, and definitely with more to say for herself, but Emily had the one saving grace that Walter coveted above all of that; she was wealthy. Her father, the Dean, came from a moneyed family, which meant that by default, Emily was rich too. Walter had found his golden meal ticket.

No one dared gossip about Walter or his true intentions towards the Dean's daughter because it was no secret that it was the Dean's money that funded a great deal of the college – the Zoology department in particular, and hence put bread on their tables. Although everyone knew the circumstance of Walter's proposal and that he was a petty tyrant who made Emily's life miserable.

Emily had been ecstatic, yet a little apprehensive when Walter had first asked her to step out with him. She knew as well as her father that the one thing Walter found attractive about her was the money, but what was one to do at her time of life – late twenties was no age for a girl to remain unmarried! And it was not as if she had a plethora of suitors from which to choose.

After a short but appropriate courtship, Walter had asked for Emily's hand in marriage, which of course, she'd accepted willingly. The Dean had greeted the news with mixed emotions; whilst he wanted to see his daughter settled down with a good husband and – dare he hope – produce a few children, he did want her to find a happiness that he knew in his heart would elude her with Walter.

And so it was that the Dean married off his undesirable daughter; Emily had a husband to take care of and Walter had an almost limitless means of funding his hobby.

But Emily's father had been tight with the purse strings, so at first Walter had been somewhat limited in expanding his leisure activities. But, as Walter's luck would have it, by the couple's fifth anniversary, the Dean had done the decent thing and passed away. Walter had hardly been able to contain his excitement during the reading of the will, as *everything* was left to Emily, which meant a breath-taking supply of finance for Walter's collection; although he'd tried his best to maintain some decorum at the reading, Walter couldn't have been more delighted.

"I'm sorry, Walter," Emily apologized again as she used the cloth napkin to dab up the spilled tea in the tray.

Her husband continued his rant. "Buying tea. It really is the simplest of tasks, Emily," he said as he gnawed on a finger of shortbread like a hungry mouse.

"Yes, Walter," Emily apologized one last time. She knew all too well that she couldn't possibly placate him whilst he was in this frame of mind. She picked up the tray and made ready to beat her hasty retreat. "Will that be all, dear?"

"I don't ask much of you, Emily, but is it too much to

expect that you at least prepare my Friday tea properly?" Walter reached for the second shortbread that nestled damp, soaked at one end with spilled tea on the silver tray. Emily flinched, fearing the sting of the back of her husband's hand as often followed her forgetfulness; she jerked backwards and bumped the table.

"No!" Walter stared in horror as his cherished jar rocked back and forth with a slow rattling sound and then wobbled over the edge and plunged without ceremony to the floor. The sharp report of breaking glass filled the stagnant air as the jar smashed into large jagged pieces against the polished hardwood floor. Both Walter and Emily watched with slack jaws agape as the oddly decorated butterfly fluttered above their heads and made ready its escape.

Walter blinked hard as if to force himself out of shock and scanned the room with frantic, darting eyes. He located the butterfly net that sat ominous and silent propped up in the far corner and leapt with very little grace and grabbed the pole. But it was too late; the rare *Papilionoidea* flew straight by Emily's ear, out through the open window and into the freedom of the cooling autumnal air.

"*Dammit woman*! Walter swore at his cringing wife. "Can't you do anything right?" He pushed Emily roughly aside and with a derisive snort through flared nostrils he stormed from the study, butterfly net firmly in hand.

Emily remained silent, as she had learned from bitter experience was best. She sighed a heaving, wretched sigh and shuffled out of the study after him; Walter forbade her to be in there alone.

*

Later that evening, Emily retreated to her private

bedroom while the terribly frustrated Walter remained in his study and drank himself into his usual stupor, he'd been out looking for his escaped specimen until dusk had descended and it had become too dark to see and his mood – much like the fall of night – had darkened to the point of no return.

Emily changed into her nightgown and plopped herself down in front of her vanity mirror. What a curious name that was, she mused; surely *all* mirrors were a testimony to vanity? And to Emily, as she stared at her sorry reflection that in turn stared pitifully back at her, the word sounded more like a bad joke.

There wasn't any pride to be seen in the expression that studied her as she smeared cold cream over her face, that had been absent for so very long now. Emily re-examined her white smeared image. "He's a good man," she repeated her mantra to try to convince herself of some semblance of happiness; although knowing the truth only made her feel worse.

The homely, miserable woman in the mirror offered no words of comfort, instead staring mutely back at Emily who allowed herself a few brief, self-pitying tears as she sobbed softly. "You're fooling yourself, you stupid woman," she scolded her reflection and turned away from the mirror to find comfort amongst the cool sheets of her empty bed.

Emily was awakened in the small, dark hours of the night by a persistent *pitter-patter* against her window. Groggy, her eyes and head leaden with sleep, she arose and padded over to the window where she saw nothing but the dark night and the diamond glint of the quarter moon. She pushed open the window a tad to peer out and didn't notice the diaphanous shape that flew inside, its brightly patterned wings brushing delicately against her hair.

Emily closed the window and returned to her lonely

bed where she settled her weary head once more into the downy comfort of her cooling pillow. Above her head, the butterfly perched on the wall and looked down upon her like some miniature guardian angel. As Emily's eyes fluttered shut, the insect flew down from the wall and hovered over her face as she rolled on to her back and drifted back to sleep.

A soft, purring snore rattled out from the depths of Emily's throat and her mouth dropped open. The snore became louder and as she relaxed a little more her jaw dropped just enough for the butterfly to crawl inside. With the stealth of a seasoned cat burglar, the insect disappeared into Emily's mouth and down into her throat. A few seconds ticked by and then after a hard swallow and a short, choking cough, Emily's lips spread in a most serene smile, as if in her dreams had suddenly revealed a wonderful secret.

*

The next morning at seven sharp, Emily made breakfast and prepared the table in the atrium. She made doubly sure that she brewed the appropriate tea for breakfast, didn't want to inflame her husband's ire, especially as he'd been up drinking until the small hours. At exactly five minutes after, in strutted Walter with his hair astray and his eyes bloodshot and rheumy. Emily smiled at her husband; his only reply the customary morning grunt as he seated himself at the head of the table.

Walter proceeded to eat without inviting his wife to join him. Quietly, she lowered herself into the chair opposite and nibbled delicately on her dry toast.

"You'll find another one," Emily broke the pregnant silence between them. "The butterfly, I mean."

"*You'll find another one,*" Walter's cruel emulation

of his poor wife was mocking and uncannily accurate. "That specimen was one of a kind, Emily!"

Emily flinched at her husband's cruelty and lowered her eyes from his and continued her nibbling like some timid field creature.

"Just how stupid can one person be?" Walter was hell-bent on keeping this going. "I catch a once in a lifetime specimen and you damn-well let it go!"

The professor's wife swallowed hard.

"You can't do *anything* right, you confounded woman!"

Emily knitted her eyebrows tightly together.

"Not one simple task!"

She clenched her fingers on the tablecloth and squeezed until her knuckles turned white.

"You –"

Emily stood from her seat, glaring at Walter. "ENOUGH!" she shouted. "That is quite *enough*, Walter!"

Walter's mouth wide dropped open. For once in his selfish life he was rendered entirely speechless. There was a grim determination on his wife's face that he was positive he'd never witnessed before and he saw how the thin muscles in her arms tightened so as her small body shook. Walter stared at his wife in utter disbelief at how she'd dared raise her voice to him and he inhaled deeply. And for just once in their marriage, any and all thoughts of a withering comeback eluded him. Across the table from him, Emily remained steadfast, face crimson, eyes bulging.

The professor exhaled slowly, leaned back against his chair as if in deep contemplation. He then leaned forward, propping his elbows on the table. "How dare you?" he said.

"Just shut up, Walter," Emily said, but her voice had returned to its usual timid and mousy tone as the heat dissipated from her eyes. "Just shut the *hell* up, Walter." And with that, Emily's face creased and she doubled over, wrapping her arms tight around her stomach. "I am so sorry," she moaned.

Walter straightened his back and regained his composure. "You damn well ought to be, woman," he menaced. "Talking to your husband like that."

"Excuse me," Emily pardoned herself from the table and hurried from the room as Walter went back to devouring his breakfast.

*

Over the course of the next week or so, Emily changed.

Walter first noticed the difference the first time she didn't fix his breakfast in the required timely manner. "Emily? Where the hell are you?!" he shouted from the atrium as he stood by the conspicuously bare table. Any other day, it would be prepared with fresh fruit, toast, cereal, bacon and eggs and of course the round bellied teapot. That day's brew was to have been Earl Gray, but there was nothing. *"Where's my damned breakfast?"*

Nine o'clock marched wearily on to ten and finally Emily appeared. She shuffled toward the breakfast table, almost toppling the heavily laden tray she carried onto her husband's lap.

"Blasted woman," Walter grumbled as he grabbed the tray out of Emily's shaky hands and plonked it on to the table.

Sniffing the air like a curious bloodhound, he said, "When was the last time you bathed, Emily?" He wrinkled his stubby nose as Emily declined to answer and walked away from him. "I don't like that you are letting yourself go like this, Emily," he called after his wife. "It is most unbecoming for a lady of the house to smell like a navvy."

Walter watched as Emily trudged away, noting with curious interest that on this occasion she hadn't even winced at his harsh words. Walter shrugged his shoulders, snorted and then proceeded to eat.

Whatever was ailing Emily was also having an adverse affect on her household duties, even the near obsessive creation of Halloween paraphernalia had ground to a complete halt. So, with all of his usual empathy for his poor wife, Walter simply hired a maid; an honest, reliable, older woman who had the constitution – and appearance, it had to be said – of a shipbuilder, because an unclean house simply wasn't acceptable to a man of his standing.

Normally one with a sparrow's appetite, Emily was now eating everything she could lay her hands on, and it began to be of concern to Walter that his wife was becoming increasingly rotund – and whilst it was bad enough for him to have taken on such a plain looking wife, he'd be damned if he was going to have to live with a corpulent one; just what would the fellows at the faculty have to say about that?!

It did flit across Walter's mind that there was a dim possibility that Emily could be pregnant, that she had taken herself a lover because of his neglect of her carnal needs. Walter and Emily had not indulged in congress in all the years they had been man and wife, their marriage remained unconsummated and they had slept in separate boudoirs since their wedding night. The honest fact was that Walter could barely stand to look at Emily, let alone bring himself to touch her in any kind of intimate manner. But, no, such thoughts were foolish nonsense, Walter was entirely sure that no other man would want intercourse with such a dour, dull-faced creature. So he put her newfound greed down to some womanly nonsense to do with her time of life that he needn't concern himself with.

But, not only did Emily's stomach expand, but her once-skinny body became bloated and filled with layers of wobbling fat that eventually began to hinder her walking. She moved about the house with increasing difficulty, puffing and panting like a goods train as she maneuvered her new bulk around, and she had begun to excrete a most unearthly odor, a nauseating mix of something akin to sour fruit and dank cemetery dirt. Once again, Walter found himself digging into his pockets to cater for his wife's mysterious ailment. This was not through any form of affection for his wife – misdirected or otherwise – he was obliged to take care of Emily no matter the cost. According to her wise father's will, should anything untoward happen to Emily, Walter was to be instantly disinherited, especially if foul play was suspected.

At his wit's end, Walter called out the house doctor because his wife was now completely refusing to leave the house, although Walter was forced to agree that, with Emily's unsightly state, this did actually make some sense.

Unfortunately the doctor was unable to determine Emily's condition. "I can't find anything wrong," he said. "Other than the weight gain, nothing at all. Perhaps she's simply eating too much, Mr. Pemberton – you should have a stern word with your maid, she is quite evidently feeding your wife too much."

"But *look* at her!" Walter whined, and there was bitter desperation in his tone. "There's *obviously* something wrong!" The two men simply stared in dismay at Emily who was by now far too heavy to get out of bed.

*

The next morning, as Walter waited for the maid to bring his breakfast, he prowled around the house and tut-tutted at the condition it was in. Despite the best efforts of the maid – who seemed to take up most of her time these days feeding Emily, despite Walter's insistence to the contrary – his once beautiful home had become an abject mess covered in a thick layer of dust and with the all-pervading, unholy stink that hung in every ounce of air no matter how many windows he left open. Walter also noted with some disgust, that every nook and cranny was dusted with some kind of diaphanous film which served to give the once immaculately-kept home a run down appearance – most likely more of Emily's Halloween nonsense. Walter made a mental note to instruct the maid not to continue defacing his house in the name of the vacuous *holiday*.

The professor glanced at his pocket watch. As soon as the second hand ticked over the twelve – lunchtime – the burly maid appeared. However, she wasn't carrying food; instead she lugged her two modestly sized, burgundy suitcases and was wearing her coat – buttoned up – and hat. The woman dropped the luggage beside her feet and fished in her tattered coat pockets to pull out a set of keys. The maid placed the keys in front of the professor, where his lunch should have been.

"But what am I to do?" Walter whined as he watched the maid pick up her bags.

"That, Sir, is no longer my problem. I have done all I can, so I bid you a good day," the woman snorted as she bustled out of the dining room.

As nonplussed as he was, it took Walter a few seconds to react. When he did, he jumped to his feet, brain boiling with a furious, all-consuming anger. This was most certainly the final straw and, sick or not, Emily was ruining his life. Walter had been more than patient with her sloppiness and unnatural obesity – and that terrible, ethereal stench she had about her – but now he simply *had* to do something about her as there was a real danger of her getting in the way of his life's work.

Walter huffed his way up the stairs, taking them two, three at a time, and stormed towards to his wife's bedroom.

"Damn you, Emily!" Walter flung open the bedroom door and the heavy brass knob punched its imprint in the wall with a loud thump. He stomped like some petulant child forced to take its cod liver oil over to his wife's bed where she hid beneath her blankets. With one hard tug the professor yanked away her shelter.

And the sight that met his astounded eyes caused Walter to stagger backwards like a pistol-whipped cad.

A thick, translucent mucus membrane covered his wife like some veined, pulsing amniotic sac. It stretched tight over her corpulent frame that throbbed and breathed steadily beneath – Emily was quite obviously alive inside there, although her features appeared distorted and more than a smidge *fuzzy*. And slowly, with a simpleton's speed, the realization dawned on Walter as to what he was actually witnessing.

With that, Walter's anger faded into fascination as he observed his wondrous discovery.

*

Nothing else mattered to Walter now.

It would be any day and *the* most astounding example of *Lepidoptera* the world had known would be unleashed upon the scientific community. Walter allowed himself a smug smile as he patted the cocoon that contained what had once been his wife, and dreamed of holding that Hugo Award with his name engraved on the brass strip.

There was no time to waste; there were preparations

to be made. With great reluctance, Walter marched out of Emily's bedroom and made his way downstairs to his study. There, he examined the multitude of smaller trophies he'd mounted upon the wall throughout his years as an avid collector. As beautiful – and scientifically relevant – as they were, they paled into insignificance compared to the miraculous metamorphosis of his good lady wife, as unexplained as that seemed to be. One wall would suffice to mount Walter's new possession, he decided.

All that day, Walter prepared his study, breaking only to check in on the condition of the Emily/cocoon thing that squirmed and pulsed in the bed that he had always shunned. It was rather perverse that now Walter could barely stand to stay away, having more interest in his wife as some grotesque freak of nature as he had ever afforded when she had been entirely human.

Emily had finally achieved what she had always craved; she finally courted Walter's interest. How he would simply stare at the transparent, fleshy chrysalis, eyes caressing the developing wing discs that sprouted from his wife's abdominal segments and the center of her back. The extra weight she had gained over the weeks had long since dissolved into a viscous milky slime that bathed the thing that floated within the chitinous shell, broken down into raw nutrients for the creature that developed inside of it.

It took all of the strength he could muster, and every ounce of tender care, but Walter managed to remove the chrysalis from Emily's room, down the stairs and into his hastily re-designed study. Black, mildew dust outlines of the frames he'd hastily removed adorned the side wall which faced the wide French windows that overlooked the open pastures that lay at the periphery of the village, their boundaries marked with trees bedecked with the reds, yellows and orange of the season.

Walter was ready.

As the night crept into the house, bringing within its inky shadows that stretched like searching fingers, Walter sat and squirmed and fidgeted in his favorite chair like a small child on Christmas Eve. He fought hard against his weariness to remain awake, not wanting to miss the momentous occasion, but fatigue overtook him and he fell into a deep and fitful sleep.

At the first, virgin light of dawn, the cocoon ceased breathing and lay quite still. Walter awoke with a start and leaped from his chair like the Devil himself was on his back. He knelt by his now beloved wife's side and rested a cautious hand upon the cool carapace that contained her. And then, as Walter watched wide-eyed with wonder, the pupa's dried skin crinkled and sank inward like a deflating balloon and with it came the worryingly familiar, otherworldly stench of filth, sickness and decay.

Walter covered his nose with a grubby, snot encrusted 'kerchief. He struggled to his feet and walked around the thing, searching frantically for a sign of life. He gazed on forlornly as the shell sank yet farther inwards and felt disheartened beyond words, Walter retreated to his armchair and buried his head in his hands. *It's most likely dying*, he thought. Typical bloody Emily - ruining everything as usual. *But what on Earth can I do?*

With a heavy heart, yet eager for the comfort of routine, Walter fixed his own breakfast; weak tea and burnt toast with stale butter. Spirits lower than he thought ever possible, he then returned to the study to continue his hopeless vigil.

Saw a movement within the cocoon.

Most definitely, a movement!

Placing the breakfast tray with care amongst the discarded frames and long-dead specimens upon his cluttered desk, Walter gingerly touched the surface of the pupa. Something within poked back at his inquisitive fingers and Walter jumped back with a start. And then a slow, undulating movement began to stretch and crack the chitin skin of the thing, making its surface pulse and throb. Walter stood back and watched in fascination as the thing that had once been his clumsy, spindly wife began to wriggle to free from its confinement.

It took almost an hour but finally the transformation was complete. Walter could do little but watch as four magnificent wings – each at least six feet or more across – sprung free and expanded to their full span like a newly awakened person stretches their arms upon waking up from a deep and restful sleep. The vividly colored wings inflated with an alarming speed as the creature's body pumped fluids into their thick, protruding veins and as Walter watched, the wings began to stiffen and the swirling, iridescent reds and orange and blues took on hypnotic shapes that Walter could only begin to describe as –

– *tribal.*

And then, a shapely – and quite marvellously naked – feminine figure emerged from the crumpled case of the pupa. And for the first time in countless years, Walter's manhood stirred at the sight of his wife. Like some over-sexed teenager, he feasted his eyes upon the Emily-thing's sleek, body - covered with fine, downy hair and of a remarkably sensual brownish/green tone - that was curved yet at the same time lean and carried the most magnificent breasts Walter thought he had ever seen; each topped with pouting, puckered nipples that made him ache inside with longing. And her limbs, once stubby and clumsy, were now lithe and slender, her shapely legs a sheer delight to behold, from her deliciously bare feet to the intricate folds of her sex.

But her face.

Although still very much feminine and incredibly beautiful, Emily now sported a pair of wiry antennae that protruded from the glistening, hairless head that Walter found so provocative. They complimented beautifully the magnificent pair of rainbow compound eyes and coiled proboscis, the latter of which curled beneath her chin.

Emily had become a most perfect specimen, and Walter congratulated himself upon the discovery of such a spectacular creature that quite simply put, defied every law of biology Walter thought he knew.

Unable to contain himself any further, Walter reached out to touch his wife, eager to feel that delicious skin beneath his fingertips. As he stepped closer to her, the creature's wings flexed as if she was wary of him and ready to take flight. Taking the hint, Walter placed his hand at his side and Emily's wings relaxed; he had no plans of letting this one escape.

"You're everything I ever wanted," Walter told Emily, smiling his sweetest smile. He stepped slowly back towards his chair where lay the carefully secreted 12-inch metal spike and wooden handled hammer. "You will look so delightfully exquisite mounted on my wall."

The Emily-thing cocked her head – dog-like – as she understood his words. Silently, she watched as her husband approached with the spike glinting in his fat little hand.

Walter's face spread in to a broad, maniacal grin. What he was about to do was for the greater good of science – and no doubt his own career to boot – and although it would pain him to do so, this ultimate penetration of the thing that was once his wife was to be so exquisitely symbolic.

"Come to your husband, Emily my dearest." Walter paced toward Emily with the spike aimed squarely for where her sternum had once been.

*

It was the trick-or-treaters who found him, perversely enough – those very same neighborhood children in their hand-made costumes that Walter had so despised. Lured by the open door and the strange, sickly sweet smell – along with the promise of the expensive chocolate that Mrs. Pemberton handed out every year – their natural reticence of entering someone else's home without invitation had been cast quickly aside.

At first they'd assumed that the disarrayed house with its fine covering of sickly, fine dust was all part of the Halloween theme, something the professor's wife had created to spook them in that good natured way of hers. But what they found in the professor's study was clearly no elaborate prop and it scattered them screaming back home to the comfort of their parents.

Walter's withered body hung on the wall that faced the verdant pastures, withered limbs spread wide like some grotesque emulation of Christ on the cross, his hands and feet nailed in a sickening X. And from the center of Walter's chest there protruded a long, cruel spike that pinned his body. And yet, the most horrifying thing of all was the expression of sheer and absolute terror frozen upon his rotting face.

There was no sign of Emily, of course. She had quite simply vanished. The police, along with the townsfolk had their theories and speculations, but no one could offer any sort of explanation as to the crumpled, husk that lay at the dead man's feet, nor why it stank to high-heaven and felt like the papery skin of a long-desiccated corpse.

End

No One Dies Instantly
(A Poem)

'He was dead before he hit the ground,'
They say.
'He didn't know what hit him,'
They say.
'At least it was quick,'
They say.
But death comes no quicker to one man over another, as every brain will take its own sweet time to die
Give or take.
Shot, stabbed, strangled, drowned, smothered,
Suicide bomb, blown asunder, head popped like a champagne cork,
Imagine what wondrous thoughts they must experience as they fly through the air?
Six minutes – six whole, entire and complete minutes before the brain begins its decent into the black inevitability of death,
And three minutes after that to give up its ghosts, one by tortuous one.
Nine minutes in all, to contemplate and to think,

To realize that death is no more than those nine short minutes away.
Listening to the hollow quiet of your heart,
No longer beating its comforting, familiar rhythmic tattoo,
Lungs stilled, dead air growing warm and stale inside,
Stinking gas expelled, mercifully unable to inhale and smell the stench of one's own demise.
A body stilled, silent.
Waiting for that bright, white light of myth to come along,
The glorious tunnel to loved ones and eternal salvation.
But it does not visit this lost and lonely soul.
All goes black, so terribly and finally and irrevocably black,
To be followed by consciousness, thoughts, behaviors learned across a brief lifetime, cut so cruelly short by the hand of another,
'It's like dreaming,'
They say.
Last to go, after memories, emotions and all that has been learned,
And thinking; I *don't* think, therefore I am not.
Hearing; the detection of sound, immaterial now as not so much as a heartbeat may be heard.
For now there is nothing.
And so,
I lay down beside you and wonder what you are thinking.

End

Frank Feels Ill.

Even allowing for the fact that he had been dead for three weeks, Frank Jacobs felt absolutely dreadful.

The Silverado Springs Memory Care Posse

There was a sign on Smiler's door that read '*No Entrey – Wildcat Lose*'. It was written with a bright red sharpie in what was unmistakably Juanita's childish scrawl – as nice a care assistant as that girl was, she really wasn't the brightest button on any shirt; and spelling certainly wasn't her strong point. There was no wildcat in the room, of course, but everyone at the home was afraid of wildcats so it gave them the privacy they needed to clean up the mess. Besides which, had they written '*murderous, slimy monster at large*', it was likely no one would have believed it, or the residents would have been tempted to poke their noses in for a look-see.

As Lewis Jones ambled by Smiler's room on his way down to the breakfast room, he snuck a peek in through the gap afforded by the slightly ajar door and saw Juanita and her supervisor, Karl cleaning up Smiler's room. Mopping, scrubbing, tidying, they buzzed around in there like white-clad industrious insects, seemingly oblivious to the fact that Smiler's body was still in his bed.

It was early yet, far too early for the good folks of Carpenter's Funeral Services to come collect Smiler. Silverado Springs Memory Care was their farthest point of call and they'd most likely be there around lunchtime. Still, there really was no rush; it wasn't as if poor old Smiler was going anywhere any time soon – especially considering the state he was in.

"Ain't no wildcat did that to Smiler," Lewis – *Louie* to his handful of close friends – mumbled to Bones, the small care center dog that scampered around his feet as he walked by; they had a trio of small dogs around because it was supposed to cheer up the patients and keep them calm, but all the damned things seemed to do was crap everywhere and yip at nothing. Ignoring the dog, Lewis allowed himself to be lured away from the gruesome scene in Smiler's room by the delectable smell of cooked bacon that wafted up from the kitchen.

Or was it sausage?

Damned if he could remember.

And by the time Lewis had reached the stairs, the memory of the horror he'd seen in the room had already faded to little more than fuzz.

*

"Good morning," Lewis greeted the two strangers – one of each sex, he noted – who sat at his table. Lewis knew it was his table because there was a place setting with his name and the picture of the same face he had printed on his ID badge in his pocket. "Thank you, Stacey," Lewis said to the morbidly overweight lady who helped him to his seat, Stacey was your salt of the earth, single mom type who more often than not worked double shift at the Center just to make ends meet and pay the rental on her double-wide. She always had a broad smile on her face, as if she were playing a long and elaborate joke on everyone and she always had a kind word for the residents.

In the center of the breakfast table sat a small, red vase of fake daisies that sported a thin veneer of old dust. Sticking up from the midst of the flowers was a tall, wooden place holder at the top of which was glued a picture of a Monarch butterfly on a milkweed flower, its gaudy wings spread as if it were about to take flight. Each one of the half dozen or so tables in the room were similarly laid out, each with a different creature on its placeholder. This was so that the elderly residents could better remember their designated seat should they forget that their ID was in their pocket – colorful animals are apparently easier for dementia sufferers to recall than numbers or letters – and although Lewis had nothing against the Monarch as such, he would have preferred to have been seated at the baboon table.

The strategy did work, somewhere in the hazy recesses of Lewis's Alzheimic brain he did remember the butterfly, and could actually relate it to where he was supposed to be – yet had it not been for the fat woman's large-lettered name badge, he'd have been lost as to her damn name.

Lewis sat down and scrutinized the two people with whom he was to eat breakfast and he had a feeling in the back of his foggy mind that he was supposed to know who they were. Likewise the light gray notebook that lay adjacent to the white plastic cutlery in front of him.

"Say, where did your friend go?" Stacey asked with that broad smile of hers. The woman at Lewis's table stared blankly up at the big woman. "The guy with the hat? He was here a minute ago." Stacey continued, but was met by nothing more than puzzled looks from all three patients at the table. "I'll go get your breakfast," she said to Lewis with an exasperated snort and waddled off towards the kitchen.

"I do remember a man," the woman said quietly. "Do you?"

Lewis shook his head, as did his other breakfast companion.

"He was tall," the woman carried on, as if trying to convince herself. "Or was he short? Definitely one of the two," she said with conviction. "Will you look at me, I spend all day around you dementia patients and my memory starts to go – are you sure it's not contagious?"

"Enjoy your bacon, Louie." Stacey reappeared and with a smile she plonked a white, plastic plate in front of him.

"Bacon?" Lewis said as he examined the plate's greasy passengers. "That's sausage."

"No, it's definitely bacon, three strips to go with your egg and hash brown."

"What is?" Lewis asked.

Stacey chuckled and gave Lewis a pat on the shoulder as if the exchange was nothing more than a private joke between them. She then waddled off in the direction of a sad-faced old lady who had barely a handful of white wisps of cotton candy hair clinging to her head. The old lady shuffled in to the breakfast room behind her aluminum walker, it was one of those with slit open tennis balls on the front legs to save the thing from scraping the laminate floors.

"Good morning, Louie," the woman at Lewis's table said. "I trust that you slept well?"

"I did, thank you." Lewis forced a smile and reached deep into the back of his mind to try to recall the woman with the jet black hair (dyed? wig? – he figured it best not to ask) and who's fashion sense appeared to have stalled the year Buddy Holley died.

"It's Constance," the woman's voice was patient; this being a ritual they'd performed every morning for the past three years.

"Ah, yes, Constance." At the sound of the name, something vague formed on the edges of Lewis's crumbling brain. It felt like a long lost lover walking towards him, arms spread wide through a thick, swirling mist. "Connie," Lewis said with a triumphant smile.

Constance hated having her name abbreviated so; in her book it was a sure fire sign of laziness. Still, she was prepared to set that minor irritation aside for the time being, at least until poor old Louis regained his bearings – a task that seemed to take a little longer each morning.

At just sixty-seven, Constance was very much the baby of their rapidly dwindling group, and since that Janey Whatsherface had passed not all that long ago, she was also the only female. Constance was – always had been – a proud, vain lady; she kept her petite figure trim with a diet as good as she could get at the memory care center, daily exercise and formidable undergarments that supported her not inconsiderable breasts. She awoke at five-thirty sharp each morning to apply her make up (the memory of *how* was thankfully stored in her long-term vaults and thus far had remained untouched by the ravages of the disease she still tried to deny) so as to face each and every day looking her absolute best.

Dementia had crept up on Constance in the last year of her fifties, shortly after her husband's accident (some had speculated at the time that it had been God's retribution, since the justice system had failed) and had begun to eat away at her brain like some ravenous, malevolent parasite. She'd been dumped at Silverado Springs by her daughter who Constance maintained simply didn't want to have to deal with the inconvenience of an ailing mother. Although, the incident in which Constance had popped her daughter's family dog in the oven for a few minutes to dry off after its walk one rainy day may have had more to do with Janice's decision than pure selfishness. The kids –

Constance's trio of adorable grandchildren – had been there to witness the full horror as their beloved Yorkshire terrier screamed like a banshee as it spun around in slow, tortuous circles. The dog had still been squealing when the microwave had finally pinged and Constance's grandchildren had shortly thereafter embarked upon an expensive round of intensive therapy.

They visited from time to time, but Constance would see the look of fear in the children's eyes and sense the trepidation in Janice and her husband; and she knew in her heart that things would never be the same again.

"Welcome back, Louie." Constance reached for Lewis's hand and gave it a fond squeeze.

"Yeah, welcome back, buddy," Lewis's other dining companion – a tall, lanky black guy – said through a mouthful of bacon. "How you doin'?"

Lewis wasn't sure exactly how he should answer the man's question, nor did he feel that he was back from anything; although he did find that dim thoughts swirled into his comprehension – such as his memory of Connie – and if he grasped them before they floated away back into the fog, he could actually retain snippets of the memories they represented. It was a slow and frustrating process, but it was pretty much all Lewis had.

There were fat, gaping holes in Lewis's memory, which he imagined, mirrored the fat, gaping holes in his inexorably deteriorating brain. And those holes just kept on expanding, like the sinkholes that open up beneath small mining towns, growing ever larger to swallow chunks of Lewis's mind and leave fewer and fewer places for new memories to stick. In some ways, Lewis considered himself lucky insomuch he still enjoyed more lucid moments than most, even if they did require a kick-start to get them moving every morning.

Lewis's short-term memory – once he brushed off that morning daze – actually retained a great deal. Sadly though, because of the Alzheimer's that had been systematically destroying his gray matter for the latter twelve years of his seventy-nine, that ephemeral part of his mind was wiped clean every night as he slept, much as a teacher wipes the class whiteboard at the end of each school day. The brain function responsible for shunting information to the vaults of his more secure long term memory had almost completely disintegrated – on some days, if he concentrated really hard, Lewis imagined he could feel the break in the virtual cable. Ask Lewis Jones what he had for dinner the previous day he'd be clueless, but he could tell you what color pants he was wearing the day after Regan was shot.

"I'm doing okay – Maroon, isn't it?" Lewis replied to the black guy after some pondering.

"Muldoon," the black guy corrected with a fond smile. "Still, that's closer than you got yesterday, my old friend." He shovelled a gelatinous glob of scrambled eggs into his mouth, choosing to ignore the bits that fell from his spoon and became entangled in the straggled gray hairs of his sparse beard.

"Of course." Lewis smiled back as clumsy memories of the guy swam into view like the fake ghosts in a carnival horror house. "How the devil are you, Whitey?" Lewis's grin was a broad one; he was delighted with the flash of clarity his friend's prompt had afforded.

Whitey Muldoon was a musician, played jazz in the Big Easy under the moniker Sticky Fingers Muldoon back in the day – he'd even had a record deal with someone who claimed to have worked with Bunny Berigan sometime before the trumpet player had gone the way of most jazz musicians in the early part of the century and drank himself to death.

Muldoon had thin, gaunt features that sat uneasy with his lanky six-two frame, and he had huge, skinny hands with impossibly long fingers. And in those rare moments of lucidity his own advanced dementia afforded and in which Muldoon's rotting mind remembered the notes, those fingers could pick out a tune on the rec' room piano that would bring the residents to tears.

Lewis had first met Muldoon at his wife's funeral; Muldoon was there because he'd been Bethany Jones's lover for the better part of twenty years.

"I don't want to appear rude on such an occasion," Lewis had approached the tall, shiny-faced guy who was skulking at the rear of the church before the service. "But just who the fuck are you?" He'd long suspected Beth of being less than entirely faithful throughout their forty-five years together, and had been guilty of the odd dalliance himself whilst away on the many business trips and sales conferences his job had demanded. So, as the man said – glass houses, stones and all that – and of all the things Lewis Jones considered himself to be, a hypocrite wasn't one of them.

"I knew Bethany." Muldoon had at first been coy, embarrassed even. "She was a remarkable woman."

What else could Lewis do but agree?

He'd invited Muldoon down to the front line of pews for the service and afterwards to his home. That night, long after they'd lowered the woman they'd both loved into the cold, hard ground, they'd spent the night on Lewis's porch cracking cold ones and reminiscing about just how remarkable a woman Bethany had been, and some of the weird shit she liked to get up to in the sack.

The two had thus become firm friends and the universe had once more woven its perverse magic when they'd both been diagnosed with early-onset Alzheimer's within the same month and drafted into Silverado Springs together.

"Ya hear what happened to Smiler?" Muldoon broke Lewis's splintered reverie.

"No," Lewis replied. "I'm guessing he passed on?" Death was a regular visitor to Silverado Springs Memory Care, more so than the relatives of the majority of the residents. It was a safe guess.

"I heard he was murdered," Constance chipped in, a glint in her eye at the thought. "We should ask Karl."

"Ask me what?" Karl's ears pricked up at the mention of his name. He was making his way through the breakfast area to change since he'd gotten a smudge or two of blood on his scrubs whilst cleaning out the old man's room and he wanted it off of him *tout suite*.

"Is it true they killed Smiler?" Constance was as direct as ever; no point beating about the bush when there's a good chance she'd forget the question before it was answered.

"Nobody killed anybody, Connie," Karl patronized her. "Mr. Deakins passed over peacefully in his sleep." A strained smile. "You know he'd been sick for quite some time, and he *was* eighty-five, you know."

"If there's someone running around killing the inmates, you would tell us, wouldn't you, Karl?" Muldoon asked.

"You'd be the first to know, Mr. Muldoon; and you're *guests* here, not inmates," Karl deflected.

"So we are able to leave the facility whenever we like?" Muldoon's voice was his typical deadpan.

"Not on your own, and not until Activity Day," Karl told him. "You know that full well, Mr. Muldoon. And it's not a *facility*, its –"

"Case, rested." Muldoon cracked a grin and spread his arms wide in a well-there-you-are-then gesture. He plucked a cold, stiff strip of bacon from his plate and crunched on it loudly as if that further underlined his point.

"Leave the poor man alone," Lewis admonished his friend. There was something in a dingy corner of his mind that advised him that perhaps Karl was not in the mood for banter this morning. He also eyed the three empty chairs at the Monarch table and wondered if there perhaps was something in Muldoon's suggestion of someone other than Death bumping their fellow inmates off after all.

Karl sped off towards the kitchen and disappeared behind the door with the brass *Staff Only* plaque screwed to it, leaving Lewis, Muldoon and Constance alone with their cold breakfast and stilted conversation that sounded as if the three were meeting for the very first time.

*

Lewis chewed on the last of his bacon. It was satisfying enough although it felt rough and salty in his mouth and split into slivers like shards of rubbery glass. As he munched, he contemplated the notebook that sat by his left hand. It was a pleasant, light gray Moleskine; half letter sized and with a broad strip of black elastic to hold it shut. The elastic reminded him of the suspenders his Grandfather used to wear to keep his pants up.

"I think it's yours," Constance told him.

"Why's that?" Lewis said.

"Because it's by your place at the table," Constance replied before cottoning on to Lewis's joke.

"He got ya good there, Connie, old girl!" Muldoon guffawed and almost choked on his slurp of tea.

Lewis winked at Constance and she pursed her lips at him to pretend that she was disgruntled. He picked up the notebook and was surprised that its covers felt velvety beneath his fingers, much as he would have imagined an actual mole's would feel. Perhaps, he couldn't help but wonder, they actually made the things from *real* moles?

Upon opening the book, Lewis discovered that there

was a name written in neat, black ink on the inside cover. The handwriting and the name looked surprisingly familiar, but it took a minute or two for it to filter through his muddled brain cells that both belonged to him.

"It *is* mine," Lewis informed his breakfast companions with a grin. "Look, it says *Lewis Jones* right here." He lifted the book up and turned it around to show them his name and the writing below it that was in an altogether different hand.

Happy Birthday Grandpa.

A tear formed in Lewis's eye and a sick lump rose up in the back of his throat. He was a grandfather, and therefore by default, a father too. He had family out there in the world and he couldn't remember a damned thing and at that particular moment, Lewis would have given anything to have had even the faintest glimmer of a memory of them.

Constance reached for Lewis's hand and held it whilst he struggled with his emotions. It had been this same way every morning for as long as she could recall – Lewis discovering as if for the first time that he had a family. For Constance, the saddest thing of all – other than watch the man she cared for deeply facing the same pain anew every single day – was that Lewis's loving son, daughter-in-law and three beautiful granddaughters visited him every week and he was always so incredibly happy in their company.

And Lewis's cruel brain, in common with hers and Muldoon's deteriorating gray matter, would misplace those precious memories overnight whilst he slept.

Which is why things were written down in that book, otherwise *everything* would have been forgotten.

Lewis flicked through the notebook, his eyes darting to and fro across the tightly written handwriting that filled almost two-thirds of the silken pages. His brow would furrow in a quizzical expression when he happened upon places where the occasional page or two had been torn out.

Muldoon peered across the breakfast table, slurping on his cold tea with all the finesse of a buffalo at the watering hole. "So?" he enquired. "What's in the book, Lewis?" He strained his eyes to try reading the neatly printed words upside down. "And what's that supposed to mean?" He jabbed a long, bony finger towards the book, to what he guessed was the title written in block capital lettering at the top of each and every page.

"*The Silverado Springs Memory Care Posse*," Lewis read out loud the neatly printed words.

"What the hell is that supposed to mean?" Muldoon wrinkled up his nose as if he'd caught a whiff of something particularly disgusting.

"I think it's us." Lewis looked his old friend straight in the eye. "Yeah, it's us alright – look." He spun the book around on the stained cotton tablecloth and pointed at one of its pages.

Muldoon and Constance leaned in to catch a better look. Constance had to lift up her chin to see through the bottom part of her narrow spectacles.

"Chuck Rifkin?" Muldoon looked perplexed. "Who the heck is Chuck Rifkin?" He nodded at a list of names in the center of the right hand page.

"Janey Martinez, now that does ring a vague bell," Constance mused and closed her eyes in order to search for the memory that she simply *knew* was skulking in some far corner of her head somewhere.

"Smiler's name is on the list, too." Lewis ran his finger down the half dozen names that were all written in meticulous cursive. "Whitey Muldoon – that's you, I guess?" he said to Muldoon. "And this one is me." Lewis appeared pleased to have recognized his own name for the first time, although he'd only just seen it a minute or so ago at the front of the book.

"And that one is me." Constance was back with them, the fuzzy image of her erstwhile friend Janey Martinez still loitering on the periphery of her mind; pretty much all she could recall was that Janey had died, although that could have been years ago.

Or yesterday.

"So, why are those ones crossed out?" Muldoon reached over the table and poked a finger at the first three names on the list.

There were thin, straight pencil lines through the names 'Chuck', 'Janey' and 'Smiler' which looked as if they had been drawn with the aid of a ruler.

*

Lewis flicked through the notebook, the pages rustling softly as he turned them, as if they were whispering their secrets to him with quiet, impatient voices.

"This has happened before," he announced and the suddenness of his voice startled the others. Muldoon almost dropped his tea – his fourth of the morning – and Constance jumped from the muddle of her thoughts, which were almost instantly forgotten.

"Hm?" Muldoon grunted.

"Smiler," Lewis said. "What happened to Smiler has happened before – I think to each of these people." He flicked back to the list of crossed-out names for emphasis.

"*What* happened?"

Lewis fought to recall what he'd seen earlier that morning, and something that Constance had asked the care assistant guy. But it was like peering through a thick, black curtain into impenetrable darkness. "I looked into Smiler's room, and there was –" The word just refused to form; it felt to Lewis as if there was just a deep, dark hole in his brain where the word he wanted ought to be. "– that red stuff that comes out when you shave," he compensated.

"Foam?" Muldoon was genuinely confused by this concept.

"You have red shaving foam?" Constance asked him.

"Who does?" Muldoon slurped at his cooling tea.

"Hm?" Lewis joined in.

"Karl did say that he'd passed," Constance tried her best to be helpful, although she was having difficulty remembering exactly who the care assistant was.

"And according to this, so did Chuck and Janey." Lewis scanned the notebook, increasingly frustrated by the missing pages – something niggled at the back of his mind that there must have been very important things written on them.

"We're in an elderly care facility," Muldoon added with a wry smile and a twinkle in his rheumy old eyes. "Of course the inmates die – it's what us old folk do best at." A smile.

"I think there's more to it than that." Lewis glanced up at his old friend. "And I think that we were investigating it, quite possibly even trying to put a stop to it."

"You talking 'bout murder, Lewis?" There was a glint in Muldoon's eyes that Lewis didn't much care for. "Isn't that what the police are for?" he drew out the word as if he were relishing its caress upon his tongue; it came out as *po-leece*.

"I don't know – perhaps, maybe," Lewis struggled. According to the notes he'd made in the notebook, whatever had happened to the owners of the three struck out names had happened overnight, and whilst he, Constance and Muldoon had quite clearly pooled their memories and theories to write down in the Moleskine, their recollection had been nebulous to say the least.

"Then it looks like I'm next." Muldoon pointed a shaking finger at his name on the page. "So, what are we gonna do about that?"

Lewis turned over a page or two, more to be away from that ominous list of names – that did contain his own, remember? – than in the vague hope of finding an answer hidden amidst the disjointed prose. He was going to need more time to read and inwardly digest his forgotten writings before anything close to answers presented themselves. Suffice to say though, the three on the list prior to Muldoon were deceased *and* crossed out, so perhaps it was safe for them to assume –

"Dammit," Lewis growled as once more his brain drew a complete blank and his thoughts tumbled into a bottomless black hole.

"Hm?" Muldoon queried.

"What if Lewis and I were to keep watch over you?" Constance filled the silence.

"All night?" Muldoon raised a sceptical eyebrow.

"Well, I don't seem to need all that much sleep these days." Constance smiled at the two men. "And Lewis only forgets things when he sleeps, so I'd say it was doable."

"Yeah, that's what I suggested here." Lewis drew a finger along several lines of his own writing. "We sit with you from midnight 'till the sun comes up. That's it."

"That's what?" Constance said.

"Hm?" Muldoon grunted.

"It would help if we didn't all have memories like that blue fish in *Finding* – something," Lewis declared, his frustration bubbling to the fore.

"Wasn't it a red fish?" Muldoon asked.

"Finding Red?" Constance threw in.

"No, that's not it," Lewis said as he wracked his brain, the image of the fish tantalisingly out of reach in there. "I think it was definitely blue."

"What was blue?" Constance asked.

"Hm?" Muldoon grunted and took a slurp at his tea.

Lewis sighed a loud, rattling sigh; it really was going to be a long wait till midnight

*

It got dark early at Silverado Springs. Lewis figured that was because they closed the heavy blinds tight shut and moved the hands forward on the clocks to fool the inmates into retiring early. However, since he couldn't exactly remember what had occurred on previous nights, he really couldn't say for sure.

He'd spent much of the day reading through the Moleskine. He'd read and re-read those parts of it that made little sense to him yet made him think that they should. The majority of the notebook's contents seemed to be disjointed conjecture and odd ramblings about what they *thought* was happening to their fellow residents; there were even mentions of contributions from Janey and Smiler – whatever was going on had started with Chuck because there was not one word of his written down from the clandestine meetings that Lewis had obviously so diligently minuted.

The popular conspiracy theory amongst the dwindling members of the Silverado Springs Memory Care Posse was that The Facility was killing off the inmates and continuing to collect their resident's fees. Pouring through the notes, Lewis couldn't see how that theory got around the one, simple fact of the deceased resident's families; surely they'd notice their loved ones' absence on visiting days? Unless, of course they only selected those whose families never visited – this upset Lewis since he'd only just learned (*re*-learned!) that he had a family; and now he had to deal with the fact that they never damn well visited him.

"I'm not sure how a man's supposed to sleep with you sat there thinking all freakin' night," Muldoon moaned from his bed and then tossed around nosily to emphasise his point. "And that goddamned nightlight is killing me too; what am I, five?"

Lewis glanced at the small, dim light that sat in his lap; the LED bulb in the thing emitted a faint, bluish light that was barely adequate enough for him to read the notebook by, let alone disturb his complaining friend's sleep.

Lewis was sitting mouse-quiet inside the cramped closet in Muldoon's room, his back twinging and his dickey hip throbbing like a bastard. He peered out through the thin gap he'd left in the door at his friend who was supposed to be fast asleep by now. "You can't hear me *thinking*, you dumb old coot," he whispered loudly to Muldoon. "Go to sleep already."

"I can't, it's kinda weird knowing that you're in there watching me sleep."

"At the moment, all I'm doing is watching you fidget and complain, Muldoon," Lewis growled. "You'll not be worth crap in the morning if you don't get your full eight hours, you know that." He really couldn't believe the man; they'd shared the same woman for near-on two decades and here he was, bleating because Lewis was hiding in his closet.

"Well I just can't," Muldoon grumbled and thrashed around some more beneath his crisp, white sheets to further make his point.

Lewis checked his watch and grunted. He'd been in Muldoon's closet for almost an hour now, upon relieving Constance of her watch at midnight; the old fart had managed to sleep like a baby when she'd been watching over him, although Lewis suspected that she'd not actually spent her watch in amongst Muldoon's clothes. There'd been a definite dent in the bed where a small, feminine frame had laid and Lewis was convinced that had he touched said dent when he'd arrived, it would still have been warm.

Reading through the notebook had stirred up a whole plethora of blurred memories in Lewis's deteriorating mind; images of people he thought he should know, nebulous faces that swam tantalizingly out of reach, conversations that he felt sure he'd be able to remember if only he could think deep enough – it felt as if by reading the notebook he was sifting through the collective mush of what remained of his and his fellow Posse's neurons.

Hey, didn't that used to be a rock group?

Finally, Muldoon was asleep. At first, Lewis thought he was just pretending, but once the rhythmic buzz-saw of the man's resonant snoring split through the darkness, it became clear that he wasn't faking. Lewis smiled to himself at this; Bethany used to hate snoring and she would actually banish him to the sofa whenever he had a cold and with help from his blocked sinuses he would rattle the bedroom windows. And Lewis couldn't help but wonder if she did the same with Muldoon on the nights she'd spent in his bed.

Lewis sat there in the dark and discomfort and listened as his friend snored. He stretched his legs out across the full length of the closet – just enough room – and absently stroked his fingertips over the notebook's soft cover. The book rested on Lewis's knees, along with a cheap Bic pen and Constance's thin, penlight torch; they had considered taking pictures but since none of them had a camera or a cell phone with a camera (Silverado Springs' policy – too many residents used smart phones to create home-grown pornography, which was also banned in all of its many and wondrous forms) it would have meant stealing one. Also, it was detailed in the notebook from a previous meeting that using a flash would be foolish, as it would give the observer away. All he was there to do was to record what he saw in the notebook – in lieu of being able to remember, of course – and alert the staff should anything untoward happen.

It didn't once occur to Lewis that if they'd followed this procedure with Janey and Smiler, then how come they had still wound up in the back of Carpenter's grubby old hearse?

The door opened.

At first, it was just a crack that let in a sliver of the subdued lights from the hallway beyond. It seemed to Lewis's overactive imagination that someone was checking out Muldoon's room to make sure he was asleep.

And perhaps to see if someone was hiding in the closet?

Lewis held his breath, fearful that whoever it was at Muldoon's door would be able to hear him breathing. He squinted through the thin gap of the closet door, his heart pounding so hard that he feared that Muldoon's visitor would actually be able to hear that, if not his labored breath.

Slowly, carefully Muldoon's door eased open. If this had been a movie, Lewis thought, it would have creaked loudly on complaining hinges to the strains of tense violin music. This not being a movie though, the door remained silent as it swung open.

Then the unmistakable shape of Karl's head appeared between the white lacquered door and its frame.

Doesn't that guy ever sleep? Lewis thought to himself and let go of the stale breath in his lungs, relieved beyond belief to see Karl's familiar face, even though come the morning, he'd have to read the man's name badge to remember who the hell he was. Of course the staff checked in on the inmates; between twelve and three in the morning was the most popular time for old folk to shuffle off their mortal coil, so it made perfect sense.

Lewis watched as Karl's head retreated back into the hallway, no doubt satisfied that Muldoon's nasal reverberations were a sure sign that he hadn't passed on to the Great Beyond. The slit of light grew thinner, then thinner still until Lewis heard the faint click of the latch as Muldoon's door closed and all was dark once again.

Before long, Lewis's eyes began to close. His eyelids felt almost preternaturally heavy, and Lewis began to regret not having brought along one of those energy drinks Constance had tried foisting upon him - one of those in a tiny bottle that promise five hours of uninterrupted energy and tasted like stale cat pee.

And the more he fought it, the more sleep crept up on Lewis, overwhelming him like Dorothy's sea of poppies. And before he knew what was happening, Lewis Jones was sound asleep in his cramped boudoir.

Beyond the closet door, the outlined shape of a man appeared from the shadows. Neither tall nor short, fat nor thin, the shape congealed within the ink black of the shadows to step out into Muldoon's room, its nebulous shape becoming ever more solid.

The shadowy man wore a plain, darkish gray suit, white shirt, black shoes – the only detail of note was that he wore a hat atop his neatly coiffured head. The hat itself was of an unremarkable style, gray and squat like those worn on a hundred thousand heads day in, day out In fact, there was absolutely nothing remarkable about the man who strode with purpose towards where Whitey Muldoon slumbered peacefully; he was precisely the kind of guy who was instantly forgettable, even outside of an Alzheimer's care facility. Stick him in front of one hundred people in broad daylight and you'd get a hundred different descriptions, not one of them accurate. He was exactly the guy one could pass on the street a dozen times and not once register that you'd crossed paths before and if you looked away for a second or two, you'd look back at him as if for the very first time.

Yet as ordinary as the man appeared, his purpose was most decidedly *extraordinary*.

Lewis awoke as the dark of the man's shadow passed by the narrow chink in the closet door, for that fraction of a moment swallowing the view of Muldoon's sleeping form. Lewis grunted himself awake. Immediately he clamped a hand over his mouth as he peeped out and saw the stranger standing over his friend's bed.

As the man contemplated the sleeping Muldoon, Lewis attempted to stand within the confines of the closet, only to find that his hip had locked up and he was unable to shift himself off of his bony ass. Panicking and decidedly frustrated with his own body's failings, Lewis gripped the notebook and pencil tight in his hand and eased his weight over to his other hip; there really was nothing else to do than wait for his errant joint to right itself.

Squinting through the gap in the door and using the feeble sliver of light that oozed from his penlight, Lewis jotted down a note or two, although he found it difficult to find the words – *any* words – to describe the inordinately plain stranger in Muldoon's bedroom.

The guy in the hat bent over Muldoon and appeared to whisper something into the sleeping man's ear. Lewis thought he saw the faintest glimmer of a smile on his friend's face, and more than anything he'd witnessed thus far, that smile chilled Lewis down to his aching old bones.

Lewis rocked his butt side to side; sometimes that would help his hip along some, whilst other times it served only to make the rusted old joint a whole hell of a lot worse – but he had to do something. Finally, and with a pop so loud Lewis was amazed it hadn't woken Muldoon, his hip ground back into place and Lewis found himself mobile once more.

But by the time Lewis had struggled to his feet and had plucked up enough courage to leave the sanctuary of the closet, the strange, plain looking man had his decidedly ordinary looking hand rested gently on Whitey Muldoon's head.

"What the hell are you doing?" Lewis burst through the closet door and hissed loudly at the stranger. He was keen to keep his voice low so as not to attract Karl's attention, but was unsure as to why; there was a peaceful serenity about the stranger – and a niggle at the back of his mind – that prevented him from screaming the place down.

The stranger was obviously doing *something* to Muldoon, as was evident by the sleeping man's low, breathy mumbling and the frantic darting of his eyes beneath their firmly closed lids, so why could he not bring himself to call out?

Lewis pondered this dilemma as he crossed the short distance between the closet and the bed, all the while not daring to take his eyes off of the man in the hat.

The man looked up from his contemplation of Muldoon, all the while keeping his hand placed firmly on the man's head as if it were glued there. He gazed into Lewis's eyes with a blank, unemotional expression, as if waiting for him to say something.

There was a spark of familiarity there, although Lewis would swear to his dying day that he'd never met the man before in his life.

"I'm going to call the orderly," Lewis broke the cloying silence between them. "You shouldn't be in here."

There was something akin to the faintest of twinkles in the man's gray, empty eyes as he brought up his free hand and pressed the index finger lightly to his own lips.

"Don't do that, Lewis," Muldoon murmured and his eyes flickered open. "Please."

The sound of his friend's voice took Lewis aback, even more so the wide, vacant stare of Muldoon's deep, brown eyes; the man looked for all the world as if he was viewing something quite mesmerizing. And although he had spoken his name, Lewis had the inescapable feeling that so far as Muldoon was concerned, he simply wasn't there.

The stranger returned his gaze to Muldoon, as if not in the least bit concerned about Lewis's threat to cause a ruckus and bring Karl and his night shift compatriots running.

"I can remember," Muldoon said and his eyes fixed on Lewis's and in them Lewis saw such wakefulness and such intense clarity that the breath caught in his throat.

"What can you remember, old friend?" Lewis whispered as his knees brushed against the side of Muldoon's bed.

"Everything," Muldoon's lips trembled as he spoke, "I can remember *everything*." A smile played across those lips and for the first time in a great many years, Muldoon looked completely happy. "Come sit with me," Muldoon asked Lewis and patted the side of the bed.

Unquestioning, Lewis lowered his complaining hip onto the edge of the doughy, welcoming bed, relieved to have taken his weight off of the aching joint, even though this whole situation had turned most decidedly odd.

"They all came back." Muldoon beamed up at Lewis, his eyes fixed firmly on his friend's, but still distant.

"Who came back?" Lewis asked. He tried his level

best to ignore the strange man's hand that rested – not too hard, not too lightly – on Muldoon's sweat-slicked head.

"They *all* did," Muldoon told him and Lewis wished the old fart would quit being so goddamned cryptic. "My daughter, my grandkids, the guys in the band –"

"You remember them?" Lewis stared at his friend in disbelief; it had been more years than he cared to recall since Muldoon had shown even the smallest signs of remembering his family, let alone the boys in Sticky Fingers Muldoon's Ragtime Band – all had been lost to the ravages of the dementia that was slowly but surely consuming his brain.

"Beth," Muldoon whispered with a serene smile playing around his lips. "I remember Beth."

It was a shock for Lewis to hear his beloved wife's name, again, especially from the mouth of her long-time lover. It had been a good many years since he and Muldoon had last talked about her, his own memories of the woman they'd unknowingly shared having faded into nebulous, gray clouds as surely as Muldoon's had disappeared completely.

"She was beautiful, Lewis," Muldoon sighed. "The most beautiful gal in the West." Again he smiled.

"Yes she was, Muldoon." Lewis choked back the tears that ran thick and salty along the back of his dry throat.

"Too much love for just the one man –" Muldoon repeated the mantra they'd so often shared over the years following Beth's burial.

"– that's precisely why there were the two of us, my old friend," Lewis finished his friend's words and forced a wry smile.

"She had the most perfect skin, and it smelled of honey," Muldoon reminisced, his eyes brimming with fat, salty tears. "And that booty, oh Lordy, I remember that behind of hers so well, Lewis!"

Lewis patted his friend's hand; even after all of these years, and the trips down memory lane he and Muldoon had shared on those long, beer-soaked nights, it still tugged at his heart some to hear Muldoon talking about Beth. *His* Beth. But yes, Lewis was the first to admit that his wife had been blessed with the most extraordinary rear end.

"I remember her hair, the way it always smelled of daisies, and how she would glow when she made love; it was like there was a small, delicate fire burnin' deep inside of her." Muldoon smiled and his eyes looked directly into Lewis's, but still he was not really seeing him.

"I'm happy for you," Lewis told his friend as he fought back the acid pang of jealousy that rose up inside of him; not for his wife's infidelity with Muldoon, but for his friend's memories of the woman they had both loved so completely – it had been a long, long time since he'd been able to recall just how sweet Beth's hair had smelled.

"You should write all of this down in our notebook, Lewis," Muldoon told him, "so *you* don't forget."

Lewis nodded and looked down at the Moleskine in his hand, quite surprised to see it there. He flipped the thing open, dug the pencil from his pocket and scribbled frantically at the thick, luxurious pages, all the while keeping half an eye on the strange man who had his most ordinary looking hand rested upon Muldoon's head.

"They're all with me now, Lewis," Muldoon murmured.

"Who's with you?"

"Beth, my family, my old friends, the whole goddamned band."

"That's just great." Lewis glanced up from his notebook just in time to see the whites of Muldoon's eyes as they rolled up into his head.

"Yeah, and we're living our last days together, you and I," Muldoon said with a contented sigh. "We're sitting on that porch, knockin' back the cold 'uns and putting this whole messed up world to rights."

"That sounds just perfect to me, my old friend," Lewis said.

"And we're reminiscing, Lewis." Muldoon's eyes once again burned deep into Lewis's. "We *can* reminisce, we remember everything; it all came back." He reached out a trembling, fevered hand and grasped Lewis's and in that instant Lewis remembered too.

He recalled with startling clarity that he *had* seen the strangely ordinary man before, and that the man did indeed have a purpose. He remembered being there for Chuck, Janey and Smiler as they'd similarly played out the remainder of their days in minds unfettered by dementia and surrounded by the resurrected memories of ones they loved – all thanks to the hands of the average looking guy in the hat.

A swift, unexpected movement, the stranger's free hand nothing more than a blur as the man slit Muldoon's throat and a thick spray of blood shot out.

"What the–?!" Lewis cried out, his shocked scream strangled into silence in his own throat. He tried to move from the bed, away from the thick wash of blood that poured from his friend's lacerated throat and soaked into the pristine white bed sheets. But Lewis found that he simply couldn't; by a cruel combination of his locked hip and terrified shock, he was rooted to the spot

The stranger shushed Lewis once more, the finger to those terribly nondescript lips now sporting what appeared to Lewis to be a long, curved claw of sorts. The man in the hat offered up a flicker of a smile and licked the thin line of blood from the claw with a thin, flat tongue. All the while, he kept his other hand planted firmly on the old man's head.

Muldoon's eyes rolled upwards once more, as if venturing away to marvel at the countless returning memories deep within his decaying brain. And this time, they stayed there.

Lewis scribbled frantically in the Moleskine and it was a moment or two before he realized that his friend had finally passed. Only when Muldoon's relaxing body let out a long, rattling sigh from one end, and the pent-up gas from the other did Lewis look up from his notes to see his friend's peaceful, smiling face and half closed and unmoving, glassy eyes.

"Oh no," Lewis groaned. "No, no, no." The tears flowed thick and fast from his eyes which served to make Muldoon's slack face appear blurry around its edges.

"Don't cry for him, Lewis," the stranger said, his voice hushed. "Your friend died happy, he died *remembering*." There was no trace of emotion, nor any accent to the man's tone; it was most decidedly blank.

"Y-you did that?" Lewis's voice shook with emotion. He sniffled up a thick gobbet of mucus and swallowed it down with an audible gulp. He looked the stranger directly in the eye, but still his befogged brain refused to register any of the man's features other than those cold, gray eyes.

"It's why I came here," the strange man told him, "it's why you all invited me during one of your moments of forgotten lucidity – I have to have my presence requested, as you may – or may not – recall."

Lewis stared at the man, and honestly he couldn't recall a damned thing.

"Whilst it can't cure you of your most unfortunate affliction, I can give them back all of your memories for one final, glorious time before –"

"You kill us?"

"Before I *release* you," the stranger said with that calm, level tone. "I give you the opportunity to live out your last moments with the comfort of the memories that you have so sadly lost through the ravages of this most unpleasant disease."

"You killed him," Lewis mouthed as he looked down at Muldoon and the spreading scarlet mess that soaked into the bed.

"All part of the bargain for my kindness," the stranger said, and still Lewis could not detect an accent. "And now it is time for me to take my payment."

So saying, the strangely average looking guy in the hat drew that grotesque, elongated claw of his around Muldoon's face.

Lewis winced as he watched the obscenely sharp finger nail sink deep into the edges of his friend's face and as the wrinkled old skin peppered with white stubble parted, he could see that the claw had sunk deep into the shining bone of Muldoon's skull.

"You really don't need to see this," the stranger told Lewis as he began to prize away Muldoon's face.

"I don't see why not," Lewis was defiant; he wanted to stay with his friend, no matter what. He simply couldn't bear to leave the man he'd shared so much of his life with. "It's not as if I'll remember a goddamned thing tomorrow, is it?" Lewis knew all too well that if he fell asleep – although after this, sleep no longer seemed likely to Lewis ever again – he would forget absolutely everything he'd witnessed. "Although I do have my notes," he said, absently.

"Ah yes, the book," the stranger said. "Thank you so much for reminding me." He gave Lewis a faint, wry smile as if they were sharing a secret and very personal reminiscence. He then reached across the bed, over Muldoon's leaking body and plucked the notebook and pencil from Lewis's hands.

Lewis looked on helplessly as the Moleskine was taken from him, and his hands simply refused to resist.

The man tore out the couple of pages upon which Lewis had so meticulously made notes of the night's happenings. He screwed them up with one hand and secreted the crumpled paper in the outside pocket of his drab, gray jacket. Then he flicked through the book with that long, terrible claw of his, and came to rest upon a page close to the beginning.

As Lewis watched, the stranger took the pencil to the names listed there in neat, girlish handwriting in the middle of that page and crossed out Whitey Muldoon with one firm, decisive stroke. Coldness spread through Lewis's body that had nothing to do with the ambient temperature in Muldoon's room, and everything to do with the realization that it was his own moniker that was next on that ominous list. And below that, Constance's name. Lewis hoped that when his time with the strange, ordinary looking man the hat came along, the old girl would be there for him and to hold his hand whilst his memories returned.

The stranger placed the notebook carefully on the bed, away from the blood, and went back to working at Muldoon's face with his claw.

Lewis fought the feel of his leaden eyelids as sleep began to creep up on him, determined to stay awake and remember everything that had happened – was happening – to his old friend. Perhaps then he'd be able to reverse whatever process he and the others had set into motion to summon the stranger and save him and Constance from the same fate as Muldoon? But, something resonated deep inside his psyche, something far beyond the reaches of the dementia that was slowly but surely destroying the person that was Lewis Jones; and he wasn't entirely certain that was really what he wanted, given Muldoon's revelation of returned memories right before death spirited him away.

Eventually, inevitably and despite his very best intentions, Lewis succumbed to the seductive siren call of a deep, untroubled sleep. He slumped down on the bed next to his old friend and drifted back to 1956 where the Presley kid is storming the charts and his father was up in arms and banning Lewis from the music stores on account of the fact that it was nigger music.

And whilst Lewis slept, the strange man in the hat tore away Whitey Muldoon's face with a wet, crackling *slurp* and upon conjuring a small, golden spoon from an inside pocket of his dull, gray jacket he began to feast upon the old man's diseased brain. And since there was no one to see, he allowed his façade to slip, revealing to the cool night his true appearance; and in that repulsive, inhuman form, even his empty eye sockets, set in raw, bloodied, shifting flesh, had small, sharp teeth.

*

It was just the two of them at breakfast this morning – Lewis and Constance – and they sat in silent contemplation of their untouched breakfasts of sausage and eggs that congealed in fat before them.

"Ain't no wildcat did that to Muldoon," Lewis broke the quiet between them, his voice pulling Constance out from her foggy wool-gathering with a start. "I saw the poor bastard's face and I'm telling you, whatever did that wasn't a freakin' wildcat."

Already the mental images of what he'd seen on his way past Muldoon's room not five minutes before were fading fast. He'd seen a couple of cops in there, along with Karl and someone else in the center's uniform that he couldn't quite place, and he knew that sometime before lunch the nice men from the funeral service would be along to bag up the sorry looking remains of

Muldoon and cart him off to wherever they took the deceased inmates of Silverado Springs to. And for the life of him, Lewis couldn't remember anything about the poor old bastard – perhaps he'd been one of the new ones?

"You have a visitor, Mr. Jones," Stacey blustered as she ushered a man in a gray suit in to the dining area. The facility Chihuahua that had been hiding under the Monarch table – rich pickings to be had beneath the old folks, them being such messy eaters – scooted away with a loud yelp as if someone had kicked it.

Lewis watched the dog scamper away with its tail tucked tight between its scrawny little legs and thought it strange that it seemed to be terrified of the stranger; any other day and Chiquo would be over and humping a visitor's leg before Stacey had time to shoo him away.

"Thank you, Stacey" the man said to the fat care assistant with the slightest of smiles dancing about the corners of his mouth. "Mr. Jones, Miss Constance," he greeted the two seniors at the table as he sat down next to them.

"Do we know you?" Lewis grumbled. He hated having his meals interrupted and he'd meant to ask Stacey something about something he'd seen upstairs earlier when she happened by, but now he'd forgotten what. He watched with a growing frustration at his failing mind as Stacey waddled away. She turned around every few steps or so to glare at the new arrival, each time shaking her head as if there was something about him that troubled her.

"Lewis!" Constance admonished. "I am so sorry for my friend's brusqueness, Mr. –?"

"Ah, please forgive my lack of manners," the man said. With a broad, toothy grin he fished out a crisp, white business card from his pocket. He placed it on the table by Constance's teacup.

"So, Mr. – Ordnryman," Constance read from the card with its sharp, precise corners. "To what do we owe this pleasure?"

"Nothing too exciting, I'm afraid, I just wanted to return this – I do believe it's yours," the man addressed both Constance and Lewis. He produced a gray Moleskine notebook from his inside jacket pocket and laid it gently on the table between the two old friends.

"Thank you," Constance said. She peered down at the notebook as if it were something altogether alien to her, although she was too polite to say so.

"My pleasure, Constance," the man smiled, "I'll bid you both a good morning now, and leave you to your breakfast." He stood up from the table and made to leave. "I'll see you both later."

Lewis glowered at the man; something lurked at the distant and murky reaches of his deteriorating mind. It chattered quietly to Lewis and he couldn't help but think he'd seen this dull looking man somewhere before, and just how rude it was that he hadn't taken off his hat at the breakfast table.

End

Snuffed: Fifty Shades of F****d Up

The girl's fingers snipped off with quite the exquisite *crunch* as the honed secateurs made light work of skin and flesh and bone.

Blood welled out from the four nubs on each of the girl's ruined hands and formed crimson rivers that snaked down her arms, along the smooth contours of her flanks and disappeared beneath her naked buttocks. There, it soaked into the piss stained mattress upon which she lay. Her thumbs, however, were proving troublesome; their thicker bone and strong tendons almost too tough for what was – after all – just a regular gardening implement.

The camera panned over the girl's tanned, toned, blood spackled body. It dwelled awhile – for the delectation of the audience – between her shapely thighs. There, her sex glistened slick and wet in the harsh light and gave the illusion that she was truly enjoying her torture.

"That's good," Barry Cushingberry groaned out loud and rubbed his dick between fingers that trembled. "That is *so* fucking good." On the film, the tortured girl struggled and strained against the rough, leather straps that tethered her limbs to thick posts at each corner of the iron bed.

Once more the anonymous girl screamed and how wonderful that scream sounded, muffled as it was by the gimp mask that stretched taut across her face. The mask was stitched from the finest black leather, covered the eyes, and had two small nostril holes and a zipper that covered the girl's mouth to give the impression of a neatly sewn, silver scar. That the mask covered the entire head and relegated the girl to little more than squealing piece of meat did nothing to detract from the eroticism of the scene; if anything, it provided Barry with a heightened sense of detachment.

Just how he liked it.

A resounding *SNIP!* and a severed thumb jumped out towards the camera like a cheap shot in a 3D slasher movie. The girl uttered a deep, guttural grunt and bucked her sweat-slicked body. There was a mouth-watering close up of her masked face and Barry could see the tiny bubbles of tears and snot oozing through the nostril holes.

In the time it took the torturer – a stunningly naked dominatrix with an ass-length mane of copper red hair and a *Masquerade* style mask adorned with black feathers – to walk around the bed, the girl was unconscious. A quick application of smelling salts would soon remedy that situation; no need to deny the girl the delicious agony that was yet to come with the removal of her final digit. Redhead reached off camera for a small, brown glass phial, which she wafted beneath the girl's nose and her victim awakened with a violent jerk.

Redhead walked in front of shot and her alabaster skin filled the screen and Barry thought that she was quite simply the most gorgeous creature he had ever seen. The outline of her full, aggressive breasts and hard, aroused nipples made for a delightful blur of liquid flesh as she blocked out her revived victim.

"Go on, bitch, do it." Barry grunted his encouragement at the plasma screen.

Redhead obeyed and thus created the illusion of having heard him. Of course, Barry had seen his favorite video so many times that he knew precisely what delights were coming next.

The right thumb caused Redhead a little less trouble. She picked her moment and hacked it off just as the girl regained full consciousness courtesy of the ammonium carbonate. Once again, Redhead's victim arched her lithe body and screamed hard against the constraining leather of the mask. Barry giggled with delight as her fingerless hands wriggled around like a duo of ghoulish sock puppets.

Barry revelled in the poor girl's agony; the stiff, aching dick in his hand a testimony to his own sensations. He stared intently at the TV screen, his arousal barely tolerable, greedy eyes soaking up the enchantment of the tortured girl's vulnerable nudity; the soft, smooth skin and the denuded cunt that winked at him as she fought to escape.

Next, out with the teeth.

Redhead would next unzip her plaything's mask and force open the mouth with a dental speculum until you could hear the girl's jaw crack.

Then, out the pliers would come.

Barry just loved how Redhead would wield those yellow-handled beauties like they were an extension of her own hands. There would be that breath-taking, sharp *crack* as each tooth – starting with the canines, of course – would be snapped from the girl's jaw bone. Along with that, there would be an erotically charged, agonized scream and a fine spray of blood from the girl's violated mouth that always looked so beautiful on Redhead's flawless skin.

Usually, Barry would hit the fast-forward button after the first three or four teeth. His over stimulated brain became too easily bored to sit through all thirty-two and the scene tended to get a little dull once the girl quit screaming.

Going with the old squeeze technique, Barry gripped his dick so hard that it hurt, determined not to climax just yet; he was saving that particular honor for Kimberley. He'd had a mountain of practice over his many, many years of onanism and he knew how to drive his body to the brink of orgasm and hold off at the crucial moment.

A knock on the door.

Dammit! She was early!

Barry had been particularly specific with Kimberley that she was to arrive at his apartment at a quarter after; no earlier, no later. By that time, Barry had it worked out that Redhead would have finished with her victim's teeth and be halfway through that thing she did with the girl's vagina and the serrated steak knife that always drove him crazy.

Dammit a second time.

Barry clambered from his expansive bed, smoothed down the white satin sheets and stabbed in turn at the *stop* and *rewind* buttons on the VCR's clicker, which was so much of an antiquity that it actually *clicked*.

"I'll be right there!" he shouted at Kimberley's fourth, insistent knock, doing his best not to sound as irritated as he actually was. The last thing Barry wanted was to start off the evening's entertainment with an unpleasant atmosphere. He glanced at the dead screen of the TV, at the whirring VCR.

Tonight was to be *the* night.

She knocked again.

"I'm coming, sweetheart!" Through clenched teeth.

Forgoing underwear in the interests of speed, Barry dragged his tight jeans up over his muscular buttocks and forced his rapidly deflating dick into place. He then – ever so carefully – zipped up. Most certainly didn't want to catch the old Johnson in the zipper – not again.

It was three weeks past his tenth birthday and Barry had been in a hurry to get out of the john before the A-Team returned from a commercial break.

The pain had been excruciating, as was the panic of seeing the tip of his penis mashed between the vicious teeth of his shorts' zipper. But even *worse was that he had to ask Marlene to come to his aid. Marlene was the family's new nanny upon whom Young Master Cushingberry had developed his first crush. She was young – much younger than his previous nanny who had retired directly to a nursing home – she was slim yet buxom, had an iridescent, white toothy smile and the softest hands in the entire world.*

Marlene had been the consummate professional as she teased the zipper down, one agonizing tooth at a time; each one made easier than its predecessor as it was lubricated by Barry's dick blood. And all the while, Marlene had merrily ignored the fact that, as young Barry sobbed with pain and humiliation, he'd had an erection and was unashamedly staring down her shirt.

After an unimaginable age, Marlene had finally prized Barry's aching dick away from the zipper and checked it over. She decided that a trip to the ER would serve no purpose other than to add to the boy's emotional scarring so she'd simply slathered his penis in Neosporin and ignored the swelling that her administrations had induced in her young patient. Finished, she wrapped a cotton bandage around Barry's penis.

With hindsight, Barry knew that this single episode had given rise to so many of his adulthood predilections.

"I thought you were never going to let me in." Kimberley gave Barry her sternest look as he opened the door.

"I was – err, you know – busy," Barry mumbled with the briefest of nods in the general direction of the bathroom.

Even in a relationship as invasive as theirs, there were some things that simply weren't discussed.

"Oh, okay then." Kimberley stepped inside and scanned the apartment. Barry thought that she looked like she was looking for evidence of another woman, especially when she tilted her head and sniffed the air.

"You're early," Barry stated the obvious and strained to hide his displeasure.

Kimberley knew how much Barry abhorred bad time keeping, so perhaps she *did* suspect infidelity. Maybe she'd turned up early to try catching him out, although Barry couldn't for the life of him think what he could have done to warrant such suspicion.

Barry studied Kimberley's ass as she walked – *sashayed* – into his salubrious home. She was petite, trim, with dancer's legs and pert breasts that defied gravity to remain perky even without undergarments. Her face was round, home to the most perfect hazel eyes and framed by cropped short brunette hair. She had smooth, bronzed skin that always smelled of vanilla body lotion and which always made Barry feel hungry for ice cream. Kimberley was indeed a magnificent specimen of womanhood, and Barry knew he was punching way above his weight with her; which made any thought of *her* suspicion of infidelity on his part particularly ludicrous.

Perhaps it was because, like most women, Kimberley lacked confidence in herself, in her body, although she was a far cry from the timid thing that Barry had first met.

*

And it *was* actually quite peculiar how they'd met.

*

Barry had bumped into Kimberley not long after he had acquired *the* video. Like many aficionados, he had spent many years and a great deal of money searching for that holy grail of pornography; a genuine snuff movie. They had been frustrating years, populated with fake movies, some good, most execrable. He'd had the occasional quality film come his way – as happened once you got a reputation as a connoisseur – that could almost have passed for the real thing.

Almost.

But, there would always be the one thing that would give the game away. It was as if the movie's producers were avoiding a police investigation, or flipping a middle finger at the sad jerk-offs they'd suckered out of hundreds of dollars. A supposedly murdered-on-screen corpse would move, a close up would betray a pulsing carotid artery, eviscerated innards would look like some stupid kid's biology diorama or there'd be blood that was neither the right color nor consistency – do these people not know that real blood clots?!

Worst *faux pas* of all for Barry was to find out that the actress (or actor – that happened too) playing the victim had later appeared in another 'snuff' movie – always the mood killer, that one.

Barry's fat trust fund had provided the wherewithal to search out ever darker and more disturbing imagery to satiate his burgeoning perversity. And when even the grimiest of the underground film industry's imaginings were no longer sufficient, Barry had made it his sworn mission to root out the real thing.

After more than five years of searching, Barry was on the verge of abandoning his quest and accepting snuff movies as an urban myth when the video had just popped up. It had been one of Barry's regular porn suppliers – Steve or Dave or Chuck or whatever *nom de plume* the man went by that week – who had thrust it into Barry's hands as if the thing were burning his fingers. No brown paper wrapping, no case, nothing. Just a naked, black plastic cassette tape with the little tabs snapped off to prevent over-recording.

It had cost Barry an arm and a fucking leg, which was precisely what he promised Steve-Dave-Chuck-whatever, would get broken should this one turn out to be yet another fake.

Steve/Dave/Chuck had, of course, assured his best customer that the film was most certainly *bona fide,* and that he was insulted that Barry had even doubted him. Besides which, he informed Barry that he could personally vouch for the film's authenticity as he'd watched it himself.

As if to add to the delectable anticipation, Barry had been forced to wait a while to view his new acquisition. Nobody had VCR's any more, especially at a time when even DVD players were becoming old hat. He'd dashed out the following morning to a thrift store and purchased one of those old top-loading players. He could actually have bought a slightly more modern machine, but somehow he thought this one more fitting for his newly acquired, prized possession.

Barry had trembled with apprehension when he first inserted the cassette into the VCR. From the first time Redhead strode naked and proud onto the screen, and that first finger she so expertly snipped off, Barry knew that he wasn't going to be disappointed.

*

Fired up with the excitement of his new movie and desperate for someone to share it with, Barry had bumped into Kimberley in a dank, dingy S&M club. The club was held in an unassuming industrial unit on a largely abandoned business estate on alternate Saturday nights. Barry had been a regular at the club for a year or so, as well as being an active member of a handful of other clubs that were held out of town. This particular one was decidedly down market but was convenient and well suited to voyeurs like him; there were always an abundance of scenes being played out by people who loved an audience.

And how Barry loved to watch.

His eyes had met Kimberley's over an intense scene in the VIP torture room – fifty bucks extra to get in – in which a naked, morbidly obese woman was fisting a flabby, white-fleshed old lady who had long stretched labia that made her vulva look like a badly made Arby's. She was strapped by her wrists and ankles to a wooden St. Andrew's cross and had a multi-coloured ball gag in her mouth which stifled her screams. As Barry watched the fat woman's hands disappear into the old lady's cavernous vagina, all he could think was that the gag reminded him of a child's bouncy ball and it kind of ruined the moment for him.

Kimberley had looked a little out of place, uncomfortable even. Sure, she was clad in the required fetish wear; a short, black, latex dress that clung to her delightful body and pushed her perky breasts up towards the spiked dog-collar that encircled her neck, but there was something odd in her eyes that Barry thought had made her look out of place.

"First time?" Barry had politely enquired.

"Yes," Kimberley had replied and her exquisite eyes burned into his.

"Thought so."

Ice cordially broken, they'd watched together as the fat woman's hand buried its way beyond the wrist and made sucking, slurping sounds inside the old lady's vagina.

"This your thing, then?" Barry had smiled.

"Nah, not really," Kimberley had at least been honest. "I thought I'd give it a try after reading *Fifty Shades*."

Ah, good old E.L James! It was thanks to her that the entire S&M scene had been swamped with countless *tourists* just like Kimberley, lured by the fake exploits of the faux sadist and his insipid, prick teasing girlfriend. Most of them ran a mile screaming once exposed to the harsh realities of BDSM; the blood, the reek of adrenaline sweat, the *real* pain – and that was before the stink of sex and latex, piss and shit – that unerotic (for all but the extreme die-hards), pervading aroma of open bowels and leaked fecal matter; it was astounding just how much of the scene actually centered on that one particular orifice.

Kimberley, as much as she'd looked to be just another tourist, had seemed to Barry to be somehow *different*. Something about the way in which she stood and watched, mesmerized by the perversity that played out before her. Different in that she hadn't looked in the least bit perturbed when a thin, elderly gentleman with one, improbably pendulous testicle had began whipping at the old women's tits with a cat o'nine tails until they bled.

"And?" Barry had fished for more.

"S'okay," she'd replied with a shrug. "I was hoping for better."

At that point, Barry had felt the connection. A look, the frisson of electricity, something telepathic – call it what you will – he and Kimberley had *connected*.

They'd spent the remainder of that evening together in the club. They wandered around, deep in conversation amidst the perversities and debauchery that were a sadistic backdrop to their romantic moment. She'd told him that she was a boring middle manager at a company that was researching Gallium Arsenide computer chips and Barry had made up some bullshit about being a dot com entrepreneur, a multimillionaire and still in his late twenties.

"Don't tell me. Your name's Christian?" she'd teased, that mischievous sparkle igniting in her eyes.

"Nah. It's Barry." He'd given her his glum face.

"Is that short for something, like *Barrington*?"

"Nope. It's just Barry," he'd said. "I know, just who the hell looks at their beautiful, pink, fresh born baby and calls it fucking *Barry*?"

And they'd laughed together, a bizarrely inappropriate sound in a place that echoed with the slapping of moist flesh, groans, screams and orgasms. It was not too long after that happy outburst that they'd been asked to leave; their cheery demeanor had been spoiling the atmosphere, apparently.

As he had been getting to know the delicate creature that was Kimberley White, Barry was just itching to introduce her to his new movie; to make her complicit in his illicit pleasures. He had seen a longing in her eyes that he recognized in himself, that frustrating search for the ever elusive *something more*.

Something better than this.

"You're a tourist as well?" Kimberley had asked as they'd made their way out of the club.

"I'm a *voyeur*, not a tourist," Barry had informed her, a little offended at the accusation.

"There's a difference?" She'd smiled up at him.

"Damn right there is." Barry's impatience had broken through, although he'd masked it with a smile. "A voyeur enjoys the spectacle of the scene, gets turned on by watching other people exploring their boundaries. This is what excites us." Barry pointed to a huge black guy who was pushing needles through a petite Chinese woman's raw, bleeding nipples. "A tourist is someone who dips into the scene once, maybe twice for curiosity's sake – like you."

"I see."

"Perhaps you would like to graduate from being a tourist?" Barry served her a disarming smile. "Although, you do have a lot to learn."

At that moment Kimberley had looked directly into his eyes and purred, "So teach me."

*

Of course, Barry had known that to rush headlong into exposing his new acolyte to *the video* would be to destroy their relationship before it even got started; to irreparably damage the *what could be*. He'd made that mistake with previous girlfriends and less intense material and they'd ran a mile; and on more than one occasion he'd used it deliberately for that purpose once he'd reached a girl's boundaries and she'd begun to bore him.

With Kimberley, Barry knew that he would have to play the long game and wait for the moment to be right. He would build her up to that delectable moment when they could experience the film together, but for that to happen, he would need to develop Kimberley's tolerances – teach her as she'd requested.

Maybe he wasn't that far removed from Mr. Grey after all.

"What were you watching?" Kimberley asked. "Did I disturb you?" That mischievous sparkle lit up her hazel eyes like fire.

"Just something I bought a while ago, a snuff film; I was just checking the quality." Barry grinned at her, his irritation at her premature arrival dissipating. "It's a little extreme but I was hoping to share it with you later."

She grabbed his hand, squeezed it so tight that his finger joints popped. "I'd like that."

She *was* ready.

*

In the six months following their first encounter at the S&M club, Barry had busied himself with introducing Kimberley to increasing extremes of the scene. And he'd began the very first time they'd fucked – after a regular dinner date a week after they first met – seizing the opportunity to begin his work.

Barry had sensed that she had been close to her climax. She was breathing in quick, shallow pants, her face flushed and eyes rolled back under half-closed lids. Barry was buried deep inside her, pushed towards his own orgasm by her tightness. Their bodies had been slick with sweat, the stink of their sex strong and overpowering.

"I want to hurt you," he whispered into her ear and probed his tongue inside to savor its rich, tart taste.

"So hurt me." She'd surprised him.

So he'd slapped her face.

Hard.

And Kimberley had come with such a force and her vagina had contracted so hard that Barry thought she was going to tear his dick off.

From that moment on, Barry pushed Kimberley's boundaries farther on each and every occasion of their coupling; whispered suggestions, sparks of controlled violence and pain when she was at the edge of orgasm and at her most susceptible – it was a process akin to hypnotism.

Between bouts of sex, he and Kimberley would sit in bed for hours and watch gruesome movies, from the cheesy zombie flicks that had been banned in the nineteen eighties to the underground shorts that purported to be snuff movies but fell woefully short. Barry carefully selected each one to build up Kimberley's appreciation to the sickening violence and as they watched, he would tease her clitoris with his fingers to keep her at the brink of climax. During the specific scenes that Barry wanted to imprint in his muse's mind – at which he wished her brain to link the horror on screen with orgasmic pleasure, his expert fingers would deliver Kimberley's reward and allow her to come.

Whilst the movies played, Barry would slap and whip and pinch Kimberley's aroused body until she squealed with pain and delight. Each time, he'd push the envelope just that little bit more; bigger toys to force deep inside her, ever more coarse whips to redden and bruise her back, more brutal clamps to squeeze and torment nipples and labia. And Kimberley had lapped it all up, ever the eager student, embracing each new sensation with aplomb. As their perverse association developed, there were times that Barry would realize that Kimberley would take the driving seat to push him to teach as hard as he pushed her to learn.

Barry would allow Kimberley the opportunity to play the dominatrix when she so desired. He would submit to her beatings, torments and tortures in order to nurture her darkest desires; he felt it important that he develop the girl's inner sadist along with the masochistic. It became a constant source of surprise just how quickly the sweet, impressionable girl was turning so wantonly corrupted.

The ultimate goal for Barry was to build their relationship towards a crescendo that emulated his movie's taboos and along with that would come the debauched delights that he craved. With Kimberley's conditioning under his expert tutelage, Barry anticipated that witnessing a *real* killing on film would take his willing student to sensual heights that before now he had only dreamed of. Barry allowed himself the fantasy that, suitably primed, Kimberley would be begging him to recreate some of the movie's scenes with him and he even dared to hope that she would allow him to do to her what Redhead did to her victim on screen.

And, if he'd manipulated Kimberley the right way, Barry hoped to play out their sick relationship like Brandes and Meiwes; those German guys who played cannibal. Hell, Brandes had even shared the last meal of his own penis with his killer whilst he'd slowly bled to death.

*

"When do I get to see your new movie?" Kimberley asked through a mouthful of Pizza. Not one of her more endearing traits, as far as Barry was concerned; he'd always been taught not to speak with a mouthful of food.

They both sat naked and cross-legged in the center of Barry's bed that was strewn with pizza boxes and soda cans. Barry smiled at Kimberley and wiped the smear of tomato sauce from the corner of her mouth with his thumb. "How about now?"

"It's really real?" the eagerness in Kimberley's voice aroused Barry.

"Really *really* real," he mocked. "You're going to love it."

Barry grabbed the ancient remote from the nightstand, pointed it at the VCR and with a *click*, got the movie started. Kimberley snuggled up to him with one hand rested on his dick and he stiffened with anticipation. They both relaxed back against the voluminous feather pillows, basking in the cold light of the TV as the enchanting horrors began to unfold.

Barry derived as much pleasure – if not more – from watching Kimberley's enjoyment as from the movie itself. His was an arousal that bubbled up from deep down within and chewed at his gut like some malicious, gnawing beast that skulked amongst his bowels. Barry snaked his hand the length of Kimberley's leg to nestle his fingers in the soft folds of her pussy, and he felt her squirm.

Kimberley was glued to the snuff film with an unflinching wonder. Her eyes widened, moist and twinkling as she watched Redhead insert a light bulb deep into the masked girl's vagina. The bulb itself was screwed into a white, plastic holder – was that a Home Depot sticker still on it? – which trailed a beige wire across the stained mattress to plug into a wall socket.

Barry felt a slight empathetic twitch from Kimberley as Redhead flicked the rotating switch that sat midway along the wire. The bulb inside the girl lit up and yellow light escaped from inside the girl and she became a bizarre, living lamp. The girl cried out and tugged against her restraints as the bulb became unbearably hot and he could hear her intimate flesh sizzle. Then she shrieked loud and shrill as the bulb imploded inside her with a muffled *pop*. Barry slipped a couple of fingers inside Kimberley, delighted with the slick moisture that greeted them as Kimberley watched the tortured girl's body flop limply on the mattress and blood oozed out of her.

Barry allowed himself a smug moment. He'd played his game to perfection and the months of conditioning Kimberley were about to pay off; she was more than ready for this. His mind wandered to the brand new, shiny scalpel that he had secreted under one of the voluminous pillows.

Redhead brought her victim back to consciousness once again; immune to the begging and pleas for her to *please stop*. Barry thought of the girl's tears pooling inside the suffocating leather of the mask that muted her screams. There, his mind teased, they mixed with her sweat and the blood from her despoiled mouth and he wondered if it were possible to drown in one's own tears?

Redhead gave her victim's nipples a vicious tweak between the long, red nails that adorned her thumbs and forefingers. The girl wriggled in a vain attempt to escape this new torment, but Redhead held tight and stretched each reddening nipple until her muse lifted her chest from the bed to relieve the pain. Redhead let go of one nipple, and reached off screen. With little ceremony – *where* was *her theatrical timing*? – Redhead stabbed a thick, sharp hook through the distended nipple. The hook slid through the delicate flesh and the reward was an unholy scream from the girl and a stream of blood that poured down between Redhead's fingers to pool in the sweating dip below her victim's sternum.

Redhead repeated the action with the girl's second nipple to leave both pierced and with a steady flow of thick blood that ran down the sides of the girl's heaving chest and accentuated her ribs with crimson tendrils.

Kimberley's eyes never once left the screen, even as Barry massaged her clitoris with ever more firm, circular motions and her breathing became deeper.

Redhead was coming to Barry's most favorite part of all, but first there was the *coup de grace* to deliver to the quivering, bloodied breasts. Pulling on the left hook, Redhead stretched the nipple and breast so that the victim raised her chest up from the mattress. A wickedly gleaming scalpel appeared in Redhead's right hand and with a single, deft slice she severed the pink, puckered nipple. Redhead lifted the skewered nipple up to the camera with a smile.

As much as he enjoyed this particular dismemberment, it did disappoint Barry that the girl failed to scream when her nipples were removed. All she did was flop back onto the mattress with a grunt and the stumps on her fingerless hands wiggled about a bit. The girl rolled her head from side to side and there was no doubting that the agony she experienced from the gaping hole on her tit must have been excruciating, so Barry wondered if perhaps her body was beginning to close down.

Redhead wafted the smelling salts under the girl's nose again, and her victim's struggles against the restraints regained their ferocity. Redhead repeated the procedure with the girl's remaining nipple and then went to work with her scalpel on the breast tissue itself.

Bloodied gobs of breast hit the floor with a wet *splat* and thick blood bubbled up from the ruined flesh of the girl's chest, coating her body in vivid scarlet. The raw, fleshy hollows where her breasts had been glistened brightly under the bright film lights and a hint of white rib poked out through the meat. Redhead's hands dripped with her victim's blood and she wiped them along her own body with long, sensuous strokes to decorate herself red from breasts to thighs.

Barry stole a glance at Kimberley. As wet as she was between her legs, and as heavy as her aroused breathing had become, her face was completely devoid of emotion.

She was totally immersed in what she was witnessing on the screen and Barry had no doubt at all that she was enjoying herself, as if his sodden hand wasn't testimony enough.

This, he thought, would make the rest of his night's entertainment so much easier.

It was the point in the movie at which Redhead was having difficulty in raising a reaction from her plaything. Blood loss and shock had clearly kicked in and the girl was beginning her process of dying. Her body shivered as if bitterly cold, her head lolled loosely and her bladder had let go; bright yellow pee mixed with the blood that dribbled from her lacerated vagina and made a pink, runny liquid that stained her thighs.

A slap to the face from Redhead, yet more smelling salts and the girl jolted to life with a great reluctance. Her screams were subdued now – weary moans more than anything – her struggles against the restraints were lackluster at best and served only to quicken the blood flow from her wounds.

Barry increased the pressure on Kimberley's clit. The movie's climax was coming up, and he wanted Kimberley in as high a state of aroused susceptibility as was possible.

A flash of silver as Redhead whipped the scalpel across her victim's blood-slicked, trembling belly. A thin, red smile appeared from hip to hip and blood welled out like some ghoulish drool. Redhead stuck her hand into the slit and delved deep and as girl writhed and screamed with an unearthly din. Redhead tugged out a fat knot of slippery pink intestine and with a toothy smile to the camera she commenced unravelling all twenty-odd feet of her victim's gut, hand over hand as a sidewalk magician would pull multi-coloured handkerchiefs from an amazed onlooker's pocket.

Now *there* was the sense of the theatrical!

Barry pressed himself closer to Kimberley, his eyes on her eyes as she stared, transfixed at the undoing of the girl. Kimberley's chest rose and fell with deep breaths, a light sheen of sweat clinging to her flushed cheeks. She squashed back into her pillow, allowed it to engulf her; she raised her parted knees and lifted up her pelvis to welcome Barry's probing fingers.

Redhead busied herself too, delivering her finale. The tortured girl's ruined, eviscerated body lay limp and oozing amidst its innards on the blood-drenched mattress and if she wasn't already dead, she had to be most of her way there. Redhead had swapped out her blunted, blood clogged scalpel for a long carving knife, the expensive kind with the handle and blade forged from the same chunk of honed stainless steel. The knife's keen edge reflected light into the camera to create a glare that hurt the eyes as Redhead lifted up the girl's head and drew the cruel blade across her throat.

Barry watched with intent; he had never actually seen the movie to this point – he'd usually switched off after climaxing during the disembowelling so was keen to see what happened next.

As Redhead sliced through her muses' neck, Barry thrust four fingers and the tip of his thumb deep inside Kimberley and she let out a loud moan.

"Ouch." A sharp stab on the end of Barry's index finger jolted him. He pulled his hand away and instinctively drew his finger to his mouth. He tasted Kimberley, of course.

And blood.

Barry looked at his girlfriend who was enthralled by Redhead's decapitation of her victim. He pulled his finger from his mouth, and wondered if perhaps Kimberley had had an IUD fitted; he'd heard that sometimes you could feel the coil, but never that they could be sharp. He studied the pin-prick hole in his finger, the miniscule sliver of what looked like wafer thin glass, and the solitary droplet of blood.

Kimberley's attention drifted from the TV screen where Redhead had neatly removed her victim's head had placed it between the raw, bloodied holes where her breasts had once perched. She was now fiddling with the zipper at the back of the girl's leather mask.

Barry offered his bloodied finger for Kimberley's scrutiny. "I think you did this with your –"

Kimberley smiled and held up her own hands in front of Barry's face.

And one by one, Kimberley's fingers fell from her hands, followed by her thumbs. Blood oozed thick and dark from the stumps, fresh and reeking of copper and meat.

Barry shuffled back on the bed, horrified.

Kimberley smiled her broad, toothy grin and a cascade of cracked teeth pitter-pattered onto her bare thighs and bounced off onto Barry's bed. Blood cascaded down her chin in a congealing curtain and she wiped it away with the back of a fingerless hand.

Barry pressed back against his pillows, seeking refuge within their warm softness and an irrational part of his brain wished himself *through* them and away from this all too real horror. His mouth flapped open and shut as if desperate to let out a scream but terror had trapped it inside his chest and only a thin whistle squeaked from his larynx.

"Something wrong, my love?" Kimberley cooed. "I thought *this* is what you wanted."

"I -I, err, not like this –" Barry stammered, his voice an octave higher than usual. He gagged on his own bile as Kimberley's breasts slid from her chest and slopped in a bloody mess onto his high cotton-count sheets.

Redhead had finally managed to unzip the bloodied mask that clung to the girl's head and a crop of sweat-darkened hair sprung out. As the mask peeled away from her face, the accumulated cocktail of fluids trickled out and ran down the girl's cheeks, along the her breastbone and into gaping slit in her belly.

Dead, staring eyes and slack, toothless mouth stared out from the screen. Vacant, accusing, it was Kimberley's hazel eyes that were glaring at Barry from the TV; glistening, wet and frozen in death.

"It's you," Barry croaked.

Kimberley nodded and gave him a hideous, toothless grin that bared her bloodied gums with their dark, seeping holes. Her belly erupted and a fountain of glistening viscera spurted from the yawning split in her abdomen. Her guts, blood and oily fluids spattered and cascaded on to the bed, creating a macabre spill that slopped from the mattress and on to Barry's floor.

Barry threw up in his mouth and choked at the taste of acid and pizza in his throat. He wanted more than anything to squirm off of the bed and run until he could run no longer, but his body failed him and he sat rooted to the bed.

"You're dead. She killed you," he said.

"Oh, she did that," Kimberley was most matter of fact. "As you can see, she killed me real good." She studied the holes in her chest, the scattered, broken teeth on the bed, the gaping, empty cavern of her belly, her fingerless hands and torn, bleeding vagina.

"And it was all for sick fucks like you," Kimberly snarled and a fine mist of blood sprayed in Barry's face. "Are you happy now?"

Barry tried his best to speak, to apologize, to plead, to say *something*, but words refused to form as his mind galloped towards unhinged.

"If it wasn't for people like you, *Barry*, I'd still be alive," Kimberley spat his name like it was the filthiest word she knew. She reached for him and her finger-stumps wriggled comically, as if they were trying to grab him.

"P-please, don't kill me," Barry pleaded as he recoiled from Kimberley's ragged finger stubs that were punctuated by shards of splintered bone, as they twitched so terrifyingly close to his throat.

Kimberley laughed. It was a pleasant, almost carefree laugh. "Why on Earth would I do a thing like that, Barry?" She chuckled. "There are *far worse* things one can do to a person than kill them."

Barry screamed.

Then, he remembered the scalpel he had hidden beneath his pillow and he scrabbled a desperate hand around to find it. As he did so, a thin, red line appeared across the soft, downy skin of Kimberley's throat. Snakes of blood crept their way down her neck and Barry's mind made that easy leap into insanity.

"I asked you if you were happy now, Barry," Kimberley insisted. "Well, *are you*?"

As Barry screamed loud and shrill just as the TV screen cut to black. Kimberley's head slid from her shoulders and landed in his lap.

Barry cuddled it tight to his heaving chest and wept.

*

They found him a week later, alerted by a vigilant neighbor concerned about the ungodly stink that was seeping from Barry's apartment.

Barry was still cradling Kimberley's head which was by then badly decomposed, as was with the rest of her corpse. They found his scalpel under the pillow, clean and shiny as new, and the snuff movie in the top-loading VCR, thoughtfully rewound to its beginning. What else was there to do but put two and two together and declare this an open and shut case? Although, the authorities did skim over the fact that they didn't find the weapon Barry must have used to remove his girlfriend's head.

Barry wouldn't – *couldn't* – stop crying. His mind had fragmented into a thousand pieces on that fateful evening with the delectable and ever so eager to learn, Kimberley White.

Barry cried, on and off, for the next fifty-one years as he rotted away in the bowels of a soulless, white-walled institution; all alone with his twisted thoughts, perversions and the night terrors that kept him wide awake and screaming.

Because there *are* far worse things one can do to a person.

Then, in the wee hours of one morning, and after a lifetime of unspeakable torment trapped inside his own sick mind, Barry Cushingberry quietly passed away and shuffled off to whatever hell awaited him.

End

A Proud Father

It is hard to think of those extraordinary times as anything else but inherently ordinary. It was all we knew then; the fear, the overbearing feeling of hopelessness that a war harbors, the sickening omnipresence of destruction and death that pressed down on our town like some malevolent cancer.

And I remember *her*, she was just eleven years old the last time I saw her; a rare and welcome spark of effervescent life amidst the grim desolation that cast a dull, gray shadow over everything I held dear and all that should have made me feel safe within my childhood.

As I sit here now in the sunshine, sipping on scalding, tasteless coffee and listening to my adulthood friends as they share mundane snippets of their life, I can't help but feel a weird kind of detachment. Sure, I join in with their well-worn jokes, smile at the trials and tribulations of their everyday lives – even chip in when expected with cutesy tales of my own beautiful wife and three precious children – but I feel as if I am never really *here*. There will always be that part of me that is adhered to those formative years, as a prisoner is chained to the walls of his dungeon.

Her name was Angelia and she was quite the prettiest and most perfect girl I'd ever known, would *ever* know. Angelia was little more than a year older than I but with a malnourished frame that made her appear far younger. She had the longest, blackest hair I had ever seen – a perfect complement to her dark olive skin – it shone with an unearthly iridescence and in the scarce sunlight miniature rainbows danced within its sheen. Angelia had beautiful, deep brown eyes that in the right kind of light seemed to be almost black and I often imagined that they could gaze deep in to the depths of my soul.

We'd been friends since before the war. We used to ride to school on the same bus and our apartments sat opposite each other in our block, separated by the gray concrete hallway that was the alligator-infested creek and river of molten lava of our games.

When the war began they had closed our school because the hospital had been bombed out of existence and they needed somewhere to keep the corpses that were beginning to pile up out on the streets. Then one clear and starless night the school itself had been shelled, reduced in a fiery instant to smouldering timbers that poked up into the smoky sky like charred, accusing fingers. After that, they just had to leave the dead folk to rot where they fell.

It was around that time when most of the tenants moved out of our apartment block in panicked droves, taking our playmates with them, desperate to flee the ever-encroaching shells and staccato rattle of automatic gun fire and Angelia and I had been left with only each other to play with.

Luckily, Angelia's father didn't seem to mind too much that his little girl was spending so much time playing with a boy; to me he always seemed to be too wrapped up with his own life to be bothered with such trivialities. Having said that, I did occasionally get the impression from him that had we been a few years older, his attitude would have been a heck of a lot different.

Angelia's father was a tall, handsome man whose face was permanently etched with creases and worry lines, his salt and pepper hair always trimmed neat and tidy. He was a proud man who would dress in his business suit and tie every weekday morning as if ready to face yet another day at the office; the office where he used to work had been little more than a scorched crater in the center of town since the war had broken out five years previous, but nonetheless Angelia's father would be at the breakfast table bright and early, clean shaven and in his best work attire. Such was the man's stern and icy demeanor that even my mother called him Mr. Rouzan, even though she did know his first name; somehow, she'd say, it just seemed more appropriate that way.

Mr. Rouzan and Angelia lived alone. They had done so ever since Mrs. Rouzan had gone out shopping for groceries early one morning in the earliest days of the war and had never returned. One heard such terrible stories of the heinous things that befell people at the hands of the enemy back in those vicious, lawless days; although the tortures meted out by one's imagination in the darkest dead of night were far, far worse than actually *knowing* what fate had greeted a loved one.

Angelia told me that often she would be forced awake by her father's screaming of his beloved wife's name into the night, and by the incessant, heart-breaking sobs that would invariably follow. And then the gnawing hunger in her belly would keep Angelia company until the morning cast its cold, desolate light once more over our devastated town.

Our apartment block was a remarkably unremarkable building. It was all gray, utilitarian concrete and windows bedecked with thick iron bars – which we would often muse were to keep we poor inhabitants in rather than would-be intruders out. Boasting five floors of uniform two-bed apartments, our block stood shoulder to shoulder with two others that looked exactly like it; each of the trio of buildings indiscernible other than for the fat, black numbers stencilled over their entryways.

The huddled group of apartment blocks had become an unfortunate victim of location once the conflict had escalated into full-blown war, pretty much wrong place, wrong time. All too quickly, we had become trapped between each of the warring factions and relegated to a forgotten corner of the war zone.

For many, many years after that, nothing came in to our immediate area and nothing – and nobody – went out.

Angelia and I would spend our days playing together in the stark labyrinth of dim hallways and had made the myriad abandoned apartments our playground. The long, straight walkways became our racetracks, the stairwells our magical towers, the inky, clinging shadows the fortresses of our imagination. We'd play hide-and-go-seek for hours on end and were forced to make up our own rules in order to ensure that the seeking part was in some way practical in such a vast building; the *no hiding in odd numbered apartments* declaration became particularly popular.

Occasionally, stray shells would hit the building late at night and we would be awoken by the feel of our walls wobbling and a deep, grumbling sound that resonated through the floor like some lonely giant's voice.

With only candles to light our way in the pitch dark, my mother and I would struggle from our beds and hide under the kitchen table and hope against hope that we would be lucky and the shells would simply pass us by; it seems quaint to think now about just how much confidence we placed in that kitchen table back then. Sure, it was built of solid oak but precisely how it could possibly have protected us from a direct hit, or if the building had fallen down about our ears had never seemed to have occurred to us. There were nights where my mother and I would fall asleep beneath the protective canopy of the table, her arms wrapped tight around me, my head pressed tight against her chest to seek out the reassuring thrum of her heartbeat. Around us, our home would shake and clatter and puff out a fine, powdery dust from the ceiling, and its foundations would creak and groan like a weary geriatric.

The morning following a night's shelling was always one of excitement for Angelia and me. The landscape that was our domain would always look and smell different from the day before and it was easy for us to imagine that we had been magically transported to some new, fantastical world. Together, we'd eagerly explore the freshly bombed apartments that had previously been locked and out of bounds to us. Those apartments that had succumbed to the night's deadly rain of explosives were often torn completely apart and made ugly, gaping wounds on the front of our building that would bleed their long-gone inhabitant's personal possessions out into the streets below for the looters to pick over.

We saw a dead body once – well half of one, it was the top half so I guess it still counted – as not every apartment had been abandoned. Sure, we had seen plenty of corpses on the streets before, but never one this close up and so *raw* – glassy eyes fixed and staring, torso soaked with black, congealing blood and innards spilling out like bloodied ribbons across the scorched carpet. And because we knew her, it had seemed all the more personal.

Some residents stayed as we had, for the simple reason of having no place else to go. The half-body was the elderly woman we'd known as Mrs. Wachowski, who had on more than one occasion popped her white-haired head around her door to chastise Angelia and I for making too much noise as we raced up and down the hallway. She'd also bring us fresh water and tinned fruit that always tasted extra special and she would regale us with her marvellous and fantastical tales about what things were like when she was our age, a long, long time before the war.

With heavy hearts we stole what was left of Mrs. Wachowski's food. Angelia had assuaged my guilt by telling me that it was an okay thing to do as it wasn't technically *stealing* – it was not as if the old woman needed food anymore. Found food had become increasingly sparse as the war dragged on; looters had ransacked most of the abandoned apartments and anything remotely fresh had rotted away years ago. Even some of the canned goods my father had had the foresight to hoard upon the inevitable approach of war were beginning to taste funky.

Angelia would always eat her share of any food we happened upon straight away, never once did she take it back to her own apartment. She'd explained to me that this was because it would wound her father's pride for her to be the one bringing home the food rather than him. That, and there was also a good chance that he would beat her for stealing, albeit from a dead person. I never once questioned Angelia's reasoning, nor thought of her actions as strange.

As our time ground on in those dusty, smoke-filled days, there came a time when Angelia would tire too quickly for any games that required our running around the dank, draughty hallways. Her painfully thin legs would wobble and shake and her breath would gasp and labor in her gaunt chest. We adapted to this – kids seem to have the ability to adapt to most things – and entertained ourselves with more sedate pastimes such as Legos, dolls and the unending pile of board games Angelia seemed to possess. I remember all too well that Angelia was particularly ruthless when it came to the Monopoly board!

*

On the very last day I saw Angelia, she had paid a rare visit to our apartment to have dinner with us. Her father was out on one of his excursions and had left her with nothing to eat. Angelia would often tell me of the days on end when she and her father would have nothing at all to eat – for them, having *nothing in the pantry* was literal, not an overused euphemism for having little to take one's fancy. When I dared, I would smuggle her a slice or two of Mother's special bread for her to eat as we played, under the pretence of having it for myself.

Angelia told me of the – increasingly infrequent – times that her father would go out and return with a little food. It would mostly be canned stuff – beans and tinned vegetables in the main – and she would notice that one of his gold teeth was missing. That, or one of the valuable things of her mother's that her father held so dear was no longer on the dresser where he'd faithfully kept it since her departure.

I guess that Mother and I were immensely lucky in that we had provisions aplenty. My father had seen the war looming for a long time on the political horizon and had made sure that we were more than prepared. Of course, that had been before he was killed in a random shelling the day before my sixth birthday.

He used to work at the gas station down town that was hit by a stray bomb; I remember clearly how the place lit up the night sky like some macabre *aurora borealis*. I saw and heard – and *felt* – the explosion all the way from across town and I knew in an instant that Daddy wouldn't be coming home any more. At the time I'd comforted myself that the yellow flames and cacophonous noise had been my father ascending to heaven or someplace similar that was a far better place than – *this*.

It was of no consolation that my father had been one of the first civilian casualties of a war that no one had neither asked for nor understood.

"Ask your friend if she's hungry, Gustavo." Mother had an odd habit of never addressing Angelia directly; it was almost as if she were afraid of the frail little girl. It was strange for me to think of my mother like that; this was the woman who once beat two women almost to death who tried to steal her meagre purchase of flour and canned goods after she'd stood in line all day to get them.

I asked.

"I am, Mrs. Salazar." Angelia smiled at my mother. "Thank you."

"I thought she would be," my mother addressed me. "It's just the usual, I'm afraid."

She dished out the rations which must have seemed like a lavish banquet to my friend. Mother had somehow managed to procure a handful of small, anemic-looking potatoes and a slice of meat that looked nothing like anything I'd ever seen in a butcher's shop in the times before the war. She had opened a tin of cut spaghetti in sauce – the kind with meatballs in it *because we had a guest* – and there were, of course heaps of her homemade bread. Mother's bread was a tough, yeastless concoction that was basically just flour and water; she would bake huge batches of it on the sporadic occasions that the apartment's power would come on and she'd store it alongside the mountains of canned food that were secreted beneath our beds. At the time I always thought it strange how her bread never seemed to grow stale or mold – I thought perhaps that was because even fungus hated the bread's dry, gritty taste and jaw-aching, chewy texture.

Angelia and I tucked into our dinner as if it were the first meal we'd seen in ages. Quite possibly in Angelia's case that was actually not too far from the truth, but I didn't like to ask. Instead, we talked about the TV we missed watching, the friends (and enemies) we'd once known and even the school that we didn't know we'd miss until it was bombed into oblivion. My mother sat at the table with us and nibbled on a crust of bread which she dipped in salt to kill its inherent flavor. She listened with a polite countenance to our childish chatter and laughed along at our silly jokes, all the while reminding us to please eat with our mouths closed.

There came a knock on the door.

I saw my mother visibly jump in her skin for the first time in ever. She stood up slowly from the table and made her way over to the door.

"Just a minute!" she called out and shot me a stern look that told me to stay quiet. We very rarely had visitors anymore and looters were a constant possibility.

I saw my mother squint through the peephole on our door. "Ah, it's you, Mr. Rouzan," the relief in her voice was palpable. "Do come in, we were just –"

Angelia's father burst in to our apartment the second my mother unlocked the door. "What the hell is going on here?!" he bellowed at his daughter. "Do I not provide sufficiently for you?"

I saw Angelia cringe beneath the weight of her father's harsh words – a second first for me that day – and she lay her fork gently by the side of her plate.

"It was time for Gustavo's dinner and I could hardly leave Angelia out whilst he ate," my mother explained as Mr. Rouzan stormed across our apartment to bear down on his daughter.

"Well, we don't need your damned charity, Mrs. Salazar, *thank you very much*," he spat.

"It wasn't charity at all," my mother defended. "It's just two children having dinner together."

"Come along, Angelia," Mr. Rouzan barked. "You're coming home with me."

"But Papa!" Angelia protested.

"At least let the girl finish her meal," my mother implored. "You could join us, if you like."

"How *dare* you!" Mr. Rouzan exploded. "You insult my daughter with your pity, and then you insult *me* and my abilities as her provider!" He grabbed Angelia by the arm and dragged her from the wooden chair which clattered noisily to the floor. He pulled my best friend in the world towards our door, her skinny legs scrabbling to support her; how I wished then that I'd had it within me to help her.

"Mr. Rouzan –" My mother stepped in the man's way.

"My daughter is no longer welcome here!" Mr. Rouzan yelled in my Mother's face and raised his arm as if to strike her down.

The breath caught in my throat and I froze. As used as I had become to the anonymous violence that went on around me every day, seeing it so up close and first hand was truly horrifying.

Thankfully Mr. Rouzan checked himself – perhaps he'd seen the murderous rage in my mother's eyes – and lowered his hand with a muttered half-apology. He yanked on Angelia's arm so hard that I heard her shoulder joint pop right from where I was sitting. It made me grit my teeth and wince and I'd swear that I actually *felt* my friend's pain.

And with that, both Mr. Rouzan and Angelia were gone from our home with a vicious slam of the door that shot spider web cracks through the desiccated plaster around its frame.

My mother held me tight that night as if she was afraid to ever let me go. A little later, whilst she tidied away our dinner things, my mother allowed me to shirk my regular evening chores and go out into what was left of the evening's murky light to play awhile.

*

The door to Angelia's apartment was open and the yellow, flickering light of cheap, sputtering candles danced from within. I stepped inside, unsure as to whether or not I should call out her name.

I espied a fleeting movement from her father's bedroom. The door stood half open and I could see that the glorious antique dresser that took up most of one wall was empty – everything of monetary and sentimental value was gone – its thick drawers had been pulled out and their silky contents strewn across the room. I dared myself to peer a little further in to the bedroom and what met my inquisitive gaze froze the blood in my veins.

More than anything in the world I wanted to cry out, to call *stop* to what I was bearing witness to. But as hard as I tried, my voice and my frightened body simply refused to comply.

So I watched helplessly as Mr. Rouzan held the pillow over Angelia's face and how her painfully thin legs kicked and danced atop the dusty counterpane until she lay so very still.

I remember clearly that Angelia was in her very best pale pink dress – the one she always wore on a Sunday even though she hadn't been to church since the war began – and the pink shoes that she said made her feel like a beautiful princess; they were made of pink satin and tied across her dainty feet with big, fat ribbons.

Mr. Rouzan must have heard the strangled cry that finally struggled from my throat because he turned his head with a slow deliberation and looked directly into my eyes, and I saw that his were cold and empty.

Breathless, I ran through Mr. Rouzan's apartment, back towards the gaping door and the sanctuary of the blackest shadows that skulked in the hallway beyond. I skirted around the threadbare velour couch upon which Angelia and I had spent so many happy times playing and laughing, past the polished mahogany dining table upon which lay the paltry remains of Mr. Rouzan and Angelia's final meal together, and out into the welcoming chill of the hallway.

I ran for my life that evening, for fear of Angelia's fate befalling me; that Mr. Rouzan had become completely deranged and was about to embark on a murderous spree amongst those of us unlucky enough to have remained in the building. I raced into my apartment and slammed the door shut behind me and only then would I allow the tears to burst from my eyes in a flood of immeasurable pain and heartache.

*

Mr. Rouzan didn't follow me, nor did he murder me - or anyone else in our bleak apartment block - as I slept. Nor did he kill himself, as my mother suggested he might. I don't think that the man was too cowardly to do so; from what little I knew of him, I thought it more likely that he believed he'd sent his beloved daughter up to heaven and that if he committed suicide he would be unable to join her.

My mother said remarkably little about what happened that evening, only that Mr. Rouzan was a proud man and he'd probably done what he thought was for the best under the austere circumstances and that one day when I had children of my own, I'd understand.

I never even found out what Mr. Rouzan had done with my friend's frail, limp body after he'd suffocated the fragile life from it.

In the days, months, *years* that followed I'd occasionally happen upon Angelia's father as he wandered aimlessly around our shattered, crumbling apartment block. He'd be wearing his best work suit, his graying hair would be neatly trimmed just so and I could see that his soul was dead and moldering behind his eyes.

As for me, I still played along those desolate hallways and in amongst the decaying apartments and I'd imagine that Angelia was by my side just as she had been in her all too short life. And whenever I saw her proud father, I would avoid his haunted stare and scamper away into the shadows.

THE END

Draw Back Your Bow

love: [luhv]loved, lov·ing.
noun
- an intense feeling of deep affection.
- a person or thing that one loves.

Screeching tyres, a sickening, wet *thud*. An anguished scream split the cool, Sunday morning air.

The street was quiet, with many of the town's population still in church. Yet a small crowd managed to gather around the accident. Some dialled 911 on their cell phones; others simply stood and stared at the handsome young guy in the red suit and his dead gal.

The Escalade that had hit the young woman had careened across the road and come to rest with its front end embedded in a stop sign. There was a head-sized, concave indentation and a spider-web in the ruined windshield, spattered with blood and clumps of auburn hair. The driver of the car sat cradling his head in trembling hands, his nose broken by the airbag that lay in his lap like a used condom. Blood poured down his Sunday best button-down and his body quivered with shock.

Red Suit Guy knelt in the middle of the road, his chiselled features contorted with distress, tears cascading along his cheeks. In his lap, he cradled his love's head, her blood soaking into his suit to turn it a deeper shade of red. The young lady wore a cotton, floral dress that looked like springtime, flat sandals and an electric blue bow in her hair that complimented her beautiful eyes. Her legs were bent at impossible angles, right arm twisted beneath her limp body and the lower portion of her pretty face was so severely caved from the impact that glinting, white teeth protruded through the back of her skull.

Not one soul amongst the crowd ventured forward to offer comfort to the distraught man. Sure, there were nods and sorrowful looks shared between the onlookers, but no one really knew the best thing to do. Anyone with a blind eye could see that the girl was dead, and that Red Suit Guy was beyond consolation. Heck, most people didn't even know if dialling 911 was appropriate, since the girl was clearly beyond the expertise of even the most seasoned paramedics.

Then, as the erstwhile tranquil air was interrupted by the piercing wail of emergency vehicles, as the small crowd shook their heads and wiped away sympathetic tears, the guy in the suit laid his lover's head gently on the ground, placed a tender kiss upon her bloodied forehead and disappeared.

*

"Not again, Cupid, not *again*!" Tantalus wailed. He wiped the tears from his face and looked at dismay at his ruined, red suit.

"I suppose things *could* have gone a little better," Cupid conceded with a sympathetic half-smile. Trying his best to console his friend, he rested a loving hand on a broad, heaving shoulder and patted it fondly.

"Ya think?" Tantalus's voice growled with sarcasm as he rounded on the smaller god. "How exactly *could* it have gone better? Oh yeah, perhaps the love of my life could have *not* been hit by a goddamn car?!" he sneered, spittle and snot showering Cupid's immaculate white suit.

Cupid looked away from the pain etched in his friend's features. He peered down over the edge of their cloud at the scene below; watched the paramedics zipping the pretty girl into a black bag. "Yeah, bummer," he mumbled.

Tantalus followed Cupid's gaze, squinting through the wisps of white between his feet. He shifted his muscular bulk on the hard wooden bench they shared. The ruined body of his girl – *Heather* – was now on a gurney in the back of the ambulance, and with her, his broken heart.

"I blame Psais, myself," Cupid offered as he leaned his skinny frame forwards to ease the weight from his wings. They may have been of moderate size, but leaning back on them against the wooden slats of the cloud bench had made them ache some and the delicate feathers were getting crumpled. "Yet again the god of fate gets in the way of my plans!" he moaned. "Or perhaps it was Fortuna this time; you know what an absolute bitch she can be!" Cupid offered a slight smile to his friend, who just snorted at him with disdain. "Just wait until I see them at this year's chili cook-off; they'll *both* be getting a piece of my mind –"

"I love her so much. I really, really love her!" Tantalus returned to his lamentation, his huge body wracked with sobs.

"I know your pain, my friend," Cupid comforted. "After all, it *was* I who made you two fall in love," he tried his best to sound cheery. "Come along, Tantalus, there are plenty more fish in the sea." Again with the forced smile. "Remember what the humans always say? It is better to have loved and lost, than never to have loved at all!" Cupid's laugh was a nervous one.

"That just goes to prove just how *stupid* those dumb creatures are," Tantalus snarled. "It is *not* better, because it hurts so!"

Cupid's patience was wearing thin. Every time, across the countless millennia, it came to this yet again; the self-pity, the *woe-is-me*, the *'I never want to fall in love again'* – if only there were some way of short-cutting this bullshit.

"Please stop crying, Tantalus; you know how I hate to see my good friend so upset." Cupid plucked his quiver from the floor by the weeping god's feet. "What say I shoot you and some pretty young gal with the old Cupid's Rose again? That always cheers you up."

Tantalus sniffled up a fat gob of snot and wiped his eyes with the back of a large, perfectly tanned hand. He looked down at the picturesque park ablaze with summer blooms and teaming with happy people, somewhat puzzled as to how his cloud had shifted location away from the accident without him realizing. For the briefest of moments, he found himself actually considering his friend's proposal.

"Oh no." Tantalus quickly regained his senses. "Not again, *never* again," he snorted.

"Are you sure?" Cupid teased. "I have the most perfect pair of roses; one for you, one for your new lady –"

Tantalus firmed his jaw and stared eye-to-eye at Cupid. "I said *no*," he said with a menacing firmness to his tone. "And what is it with the rose thing, Cupid?

What happened to that quaint little bow and arrow thing you used to do?"

Cupid grinned at Tantalus. This was better, something other than weeping and self-flagellation from the guy. This, he could work with. "Just keeping up with modern times, Tantalus," he explained. "The quiver full of arrows and ivory bow went out with that doltish halo and crappy little wings." He flexed his wings to full span for emphasis, taking care not to touch the bloodied part of Tantalus's suit with them. "That was *so* eighteenth century." He said. "I think that spreading love with roses is far more poetic, and far more romantic than shooting people in the ass with arrows, don't you think?"

"I guess so," Tantalus was forced to agree. "But –"

"And, it's post 9/11 and one can't just go around in public shooting people willy-nilly with bows and arrows – no matter how cute you are," Cupid laughed. "If I tried that now, I'd find myself in Guantanamo Bay before I could say *Islamic Fundamentalist.*" Cupid plucked a rose – the reddest he had – from the quiver and presented it for Tantalus's delectation. "So, whaddya say, Bro'? One little prick –"

Tantalus squinted at his foolish friend through hot tears. "I. Said. No," he said, his voice trembling yet deliberate. He pushed Cupid's arm away, wanting the offending bloom as far away from his person as was possible. "I know I only have myself to blame for allowing you to make me fall in love this time, or the time before that, or the time – you get the damned picture," he growled, hoping that the growl in his voice would make Cupid think twice before attempting something rash. "But enough has to be enough, old friend."

"You know I only do it because I love to see the happiness that love brings you," Cupid actually sounded sincere, if a little naive.

"But it hurts, Cupid," Tantalus replied. "*Love* hurts so much. Why must it *always* end in pain?" He stifled a sniffle. "That's why I prefer to do things my way."

It was Cupid's turn to snort. "Your way?" he scoffed. "You mean by constantly exposing those poor humans to the pleasures of the flesh – to lust and hedonism and selfishness; and all of the jealousy and suspicion that goes along with that?" Cupid shook his head. "Your '*way*' makes them choose to live their lives in the pursuit of titillation, infidelity and sexual deviations of the most unpleasant kind. What kind of a carry on is that?"

"It's the right way to carry on, Cupid," Tantalus said with smugness in his tone. "Because carnal desires are all that the human animal truly craves."

"I really don't think –"

"Cupid, Cupid, Cupid," Tantalus cut him off. "You still don't see that you are a sad little anachronism in today's world; I'd even go so far as to say *obsolete*." A glimmer of a smile teased across Tantalus's lips. "Face facts, dear friend, there is no place on Earth for love anymore."

Cupid squared up to the bigger god. "You are so very wrong there, my *dear friend,*" he mocked. *"*People *need* love in their lives, to be *in* love, and to *be* loved. It's a basic human requirement." He selected his targets in the park below and threw two roses – one after the other – down to Earth. "Just watch," he said.

Down by the guano-spattered duck pond in the center of the park stood a man and a woman, both in their middle age. They were but a handful of yards apart throwing crumbling, stale bread at a gaggle of overweight ducks. They did not look at, nor otherwise acknowledge the existence of the other; each one too busily wrapped up in their own isolated world.

Cupid's roses struck them. Of course, they couldn't see the roses – most humans couldn't – but they felt their effect immediately.

A look passed between the couple; a smile, a spark of chemistry that made them *want* to be together, that heady rush of love at first sight. And, as Cupid and his ethereal friend watched, the couple discarded their respective bags of old bread and embraced like long-lost lovers. A kiss, a sharing of warm closeness and the couple walked away hand-in-hand, laughing together and so very much in love.

"And there you have it." Cupid grinned, so very pleased with his achievement. "I just gave those two people eternal happiness."

"If by eternal you mean until someone else comes along who is hotter, smarter, funnier, freakier in bed or until one of them gets hit by a motor vehicle, then yes; eternal it is." Tantalus was quickly getting back to his old, cynical self. Cupid was pleased to see his friend finally getting over his heartbreak; although it worried him that each time the process seemed to take a little longer.

"But all of those negative things come from *you*, Tantalus." Cupid had always relished the amusement of verbal sparring with his friend. "It is you who throws tempting obstacles in the way of true love. If it wasn't for you, everyone on Earth would be in love all of the time, and the world would be a far happier place.

Tantalus's jaw dropped open. "Really?" he stammered. "You are *that* naive?" He shook his head, his striking face portraying incredulity. "Don't let's forget that I was given my job to counteract *yours*. If it weren't for me, the world would be filled with people bored with people, people trapped in relationships watching the love that you gave them – whether they wanted it or not – fade away and die a painful, lingering death."

"Love may fade away," Cupid argued, "but so does lust and the excitement of infidelity - and much quicker too, I might add."

"Of course they do," Tantalus said. But at least when *those* fade, they don't turn into the agonizing pain of a broken heart." He looked Cupid up and down as if examining a mildly intriguing bug. "And anyway, if love truly was the holy grail of everything – all that humans desired – how come they give in to my temptations so willingly?"

There followed a lengthy, poignant silence. Cupid's eyes rolled in their sockets as if he were searching for a suitable reply, while Tantalus watched with the smug realization that he had argued his haughty, white-suited friend into a corner.

"So, how about that pretty young filly by the water fountain?" Cupid's clumsy change of subject made Tantalus raise a quizzical eyebrow.

Tantalus shook his head again. "You really are quite unbelievable." He sighed. "Why must you insist so, when you know how terrible love is?" He studied Cupid's pinched face, noted a flush of color in his cheeks, a twitch of the left eye.

"Wait a minute," Tantalus's voice was slow and deliberate. "Wait just one goddamn minute." He leaned forward, his face inches from his friend's. "You've never actually been in love," his voice grumbled like thunder. "Have you?"

Cupid laughed in his friend's face. "That is preposterous!" He guffawed. "Of course I've been in love! I am Cupid, the *bringer* of love!" But the laugh seemed to Tantalus to be a little too forced, the glint in his eye a tad too furtive. And Tantalus could read his counterpart like a book.

"Name one."

"Well," Cupid sputtered. "Where to start? There have been, hundreds, no, *thousands*..."

"So name one of them. Just *one*," Tantalus's tone hardened.

"Well, there was, err..." Cupid's eyes rolled upwards and to the left – thinking on his feet had never been his strong point. "Ah yes, there was the sweet young goddess in the Antipodes, the gal in London, those two intriguing young men in Rhodes, that magnificent giraffe..." His face reddened, his voice petered out to a whisper.

"I knew it!" Tantalus threw up his hands. "Oh! What delightful, wonderful irony!" He laughed a hearty laugh and slapped his thighs with glee. "The great and wonderful Cupid, the god of love himself, has never *been* in love!" He thumped his friend's arm with affection. "That really is too much!"

Cupid lowered his face, more than a little ashamed of himself at finally being caught out. He really ought to know better than to try lying to Tantalus after all of these eons.

"So what if I haven't experienced love *first hand*?" Cupid mumbled. "I've been far too busy helping others to find it." Cupid attempted to smile but it came across as more of a nauseated grimace.

"Too busy trapping those poor human saps in a world of pain, anguish and heartache, more like!" Tantalus's mood darkened; all of the pain and hurt that he'd endured along the centuries as a result of Cupid's meddling suddenly and in that instant rushed back to him like one massive fist to the heart. "You're a damned hypocrite!"

Tantalus snatched two roses from Cupid's quiver and hurled one of them down to Earth, aimed at an attractive young, red headed girl who was jogging steadily around the verdant park.

Of course, the girl neither saw nor felt the ethereal rose, but once it found its mark, her heart opened and a whole new sensation of joy filled her soul.

"It's about time you had a taste of your own medicine." Tantalus rounded on his terrified friend.

"Okay, T-Tantalus," Cupid stammered. "Let's not be hasty. Put the rose down and we can talk about this." He eyed the scarlet flower with its dark green stem and perfectly triangular thorns as if it were infected with the most heinous disease imaginable.

"There's nothing I want to talk about, my friend," Tantalus replied. "What I *want* is for you to experience for yourself this gift you have foisted upon the human race ever since time began; I want you to see for yourself just how quickly love metamorphoses into bored familiarity, resentment and that sickening pretence of *we're as much in love as we were the day we first met,*" Tantalus mocked. "I also want you to feel the agonising, heart-wrenching pain that love fosters." And with that, Tantalus lunged at Cupid with the rose.

Cupid ducked out of the way and leapt from the bench with an agility Mercury himself would have been proud of and fluttered down to Earth, his outspread wings shining bright in the sunlight a beautiful, iridescent white.

Never one to give up easily, Tantalus launched himself from the seat and gave chase.

Cupid literally hit the ground running and darted across the park. He swerved to avoid a head-on collision with the jogging redhead and scattered the sorry collection of mangy ducks that were gathered around the gray pond. None of the park's few inhabitants gave a second glance to the white suited man running across the neatly mown grass. They had, no doubt, seen more peculiar sights in this corner of the city; although Cupid's wings *were* invisible to the human eye – their obvious presence would have been too much to expect even humans to ignore.

Racing to the red brick restrooms that stank of stale pee and damp moss, Cupid sought refuge in the overgrown azaleas that smothered the small building. He darted behind and pressed himself up against the moist wall, his breathing labored and ragged from his exertions.

Tantalus was hot on his friend's heels. He belted at full pace across the ornamental lawns – rose in hand – towards the restroom block where he'd seen Cupid secrete himself. Tantalus leapt gracefully over the ducks, shooting a sideways glance at the shapely derriere of the jogger and collided rose-first with a surly looking guy in a gray, striped fedora.

"Watch it, buddy," the guy growled. "You need to look at where you're going, and not at the ladies." His eyes flicked to the jogger and a wry smile flittered across his lips.

"I am *so* sorry," Tantalus offered. "Are you okay?"

Hat Guy nodded. He lifted a hand to his mouth and sucked at the pinprick of blood that had appeared on his index finger. He considered it briefly before inserting it into his mouth, clearly puzzled; he couldn't see the rose in Tantalus's hand, let alone its keen thorns. He winked at Tantalus and gave a nonchalant tip of his hat as he felt his anger towards the clumsy oaf in the red suit dissipate and his heart swell with love.

Tantalus returned the smile and continued his pursuit of the errant Cupid.

Cupid could sense his friend's presence. He knew that Tantalus had followed him down to Earth, felt that he was close by in the park. He forced himself to take shallow breaths, remained as still as he could with the greenery poking at his face and prayed to the other gods that Tantalus would never find him. He watched the thick, tangled branches for signs of movement and listened for any slight noise that would give away his friend's presence.

Nothing.

After what seemed like a lifetime – in fact a little over an hour – Cupid ventured out of his hidey-hole with creeping, tentative steps. He peered around and, seeing no sign of his friend, Cupid felt bold enough to make his way back across the park, trying to decide if it would be safe to ascend back to his cloud or not.

The redhead ran by at a steady pace, sweating from her exercise; her flame red hair plastered to her face, skin shining and somehow managing to make the sweat stains on her underarms alluring. Cupid turned his head to admire the girl's trim, firm rump, resplendent in her tight jogging pants.

"Thought you could run away from true love?" a voice from behind.

Cupid snapped his head around and faced the tall form that shadowed him. Tantalus, it would seem, was blessed with the greater patience. The god smiled down at Cupid, his left arm wielding the second of the velvet-red roses.

"No!" Instinctively, Cupid raised his hands to protect his face.

The rose hit Cupid square on the chest. It broke apart on impact and the ephemeral petals fluttered to the ground like fat, blood-red snowflakes. Cupid watched them fall with disbelief etched in his face.

"*Oof!* I'm so sorry," the jogging redhead sputtered as she blundered into Cupid. She gripped his arm for balance, and Cupid caught the head-spinning, exhilarating whiff of her scent; a sweet vanilla fragrance mingled with the heady sweat of her exertions.

"It's okay, I was –" Cupid's words stuck in his throat as his eyes caught the girl's. He saw that she had eyes of the most exquisite green, like the rarest of emeralds; and they burned into his with fire and passion.

"I-It was so totally my fau–" Redhead smiled a broad smile at the handsome stranger, as words failed her.

"Hi." Cupid grinned at the girl like some lovelorn idiot.

"Hi," Redhead replied, the growing swell in her heart filling her with a wonderful, mysterious love. "I'm Claire." She shook Cupid's hand, held on to it. "Oh, I'm sorry, I didn't mean to interrupt," she blustered to Tantalus. "It's just that I, er, I–"

"That's quite alright, Ma'am," Tantalus said with a smirk. "My work is done here." Turning on his heels, Tantalus winked at his newly love-struck friend and bid a hasty retreat.

Cupid became aware that he still had a hold of Claire's hand even though the handshake moment had long passed. Yet he didn't want to let go of that delicate, warm hand with its smooth skin and long, vibrant fingers. Not ever.

And for the first time across the countless millennia of his existence, Cupid realized that he was very much in love. "Should we, err, would you like to –" he stammered.

"– yes," Claire interrupted. She too did not want to let go of the beautiful hand she was clasping so tightly. "I would really like that."

So, Cupid led the love of his life towards the duck pond. There, they threw stale bread he'd found in a trash can for the ever-hungry fowl. After that, they made their way to a small, intimate cafe, all the while smiling like giddy teenagers. On their way out of the park, immersed in each other and so much in love, they bumped into a guy, almost knocking him off of his feet. They apologised sweetly, and the man told them not to worry, it really was no problem and he tipped his fedora in *goodbye* and his eyes twinkled from beneath its brim.

The remainder of the day went by in a haze for Cupid, his every sense and thought tuned to Claire to the exclusion of all else. He found this new emotion to be exhilarating and terrifying all at the same time; his heartbeat seemed quicker, his skin delightfully sensitive to Claire's touch, and his brain raced with thoughts that so totally engulfed him. It felt to Cupid like the vacuum void of thousands of lonely years had all at once become filled by this one, perfect human being.

She asked Cupid his name, and he told her.

"That's a beautiful name," she said. "As in the god?"

"Yep." He smiled. "My parents had an odd sense of humor." And they laughed together.

They went to see a romantic, period movie, one of those instantly forgettable films that are populated with crusty old English actors and myriad heaving bosoms. It may have been the best, most incisive movie ever committed to film, a searing indictment of the human condition written with superhuman insight, and Cupid wouldn't have noticed. All that was important to him through the over-long two hours and twenty minutes was the proximity of his beloved Claire and her warm hand that so perfectly nestled in his.

Claire asked Cupid if he would walk her home. Eschewing the coy lover's code of inviting him in for the *coffee*, she asked Cupid if he would like to make love to her. Of course, Cupid agreed without hesitation, though not because he was succumbing to animal lust, but because of the desire to be as close to the one who completed him as was possible. And when they made love, it was so much more than two bodies entwining, it felt as if their souls had become one.

*

Morning came in the blink of an eye. Cupid had spent the moments between lovemaking with Claire's warm, silken body snuggled up to him, her head rested on his chest, watching her sleep. A delightful trail of strewn clothes – hers and his – lay discarded in the heat of passion between Claire's apartment door and her queen-sized bed, as if by some sex-crazed Hansel and Gretel; a moving testimony to the love Cupid felt for the girl in his arms.

Claire stirred as a single shaft of the morning's light snuck between her thin drapes and awoke her. She lifted her eyes to meet her lover's.

"G'morning," she murmured.

"Good morning, my love." Cupid kissed the tip of her nose.

"Thank you for last night," Claire whispered as she fidgeted beneath the bed sheets that smelled so exquisitely of both of them. "It was beautiful."

"Oh my, yes," Cupid agreed with a satisfied sigh. "I never thought that –"

"–sex could be so good?"

"That goes without saying." Cupid smiled into his beloved's eyes. "But what I was going to say was, I never thought that being in love could feel like this."

Claire rolled away from Cupid and left a cold spot on his chest. She stretched her lithe body out next to his and propped her head up on her elbow. "Pardon me, Mister." She gave him a stern look. "But did you just use the L-word?"

Cupid could feel the warmth of his skin as his cheeks blushed. All of a sudden, he felt nervous and more than a little scared. "Yeah, I'm sorry, I didn't mean –"

Claire kissed him. It was a moist, lingering kiss with a light dart of her tongue that caressed his lips. "Don't ever apologize for saying that." That warm, loving smile lit up her face again. "I've never believed in all of that *love at first sight* crap." She made delicate air-quotes with one hand and the sheet fell away from her full, round breasts. "I always thought it was something lazy scriptwriters made up for the movies." She sighed. "But now – wow!"

"Me too." Cupid gave a sagely nod.

Claire laughed gently. "Have you ever fallen in love before?"

Cupid looked sheepish, shook his head. "I *thought* I had, until I looked into your eyes and saw the person that I'm meant to be with," he told her.

"You are the absolute sweetest, and I love you so much." Claire kissed Cupid once more. It was a kiss so full of love and longing and – *oneness* – that Cupid wished that it would go on for eternity.

Cupid had to force himself to break the kiss; he rolled away from his lover and clambered with great reluctance from the bed.

"Really?" Claire chastised in her playful sing-song tone that Cupid so loved. "You kiss me like that and then you leave?" Claire pulled the sheet away to reveal all of her nakedness.

"I'm sorry, my love." Cupid contemplated jumping straight back into bed with the epitome of gorgeousness that lay before him. "But I have some business to attend to." He smiled at Claire. "I'll be back later, I promise." He saw the flicker of disappointment on her face. "And I will bring donuts!" he countered in a faux-

Shakespearean voice that lifted Claire's spirits. "Why, we simply *must* feed our love with jelly-filled pastries!"

They laughed together, knowing that in the glow of their newfound love, being physically apart would never again mean being alone.

"Okay, I'll let you go – just this once," Claire said as she watched Cupid hunt around for his underwear. "I guess I'll go for a run. Being madly in love has given me buckets of energy." She turned on her seductive voice, "and then, after I get all hot and sweaty, I'll be taking a long, hot shower –"

Cupid, dressed at last, leaned over the bed and kissed his love once more. Claire returned his kiss with vigor, her eager tongue seeking out his.

"You really are making this hard for me." Cupid cast a salacious grin down towards his own crotch. "But I really do have to go." And with great disinclination, Cupid made his way to the door.

"I guess it's just me, my tiny, tight running shorts and the hot shower then –" Claire called after Cupid, delighting in the tease.

"I'll be back before you know I've gone, my darling. And I *promise* to scrub your back," so saying, Cupid exited Claire's apartment and walked along the dim, concrete clad walkway.

The only sign of life so early in the morning was a sour-faced guy in a gray hat who walked slowly in the opposite direction. Cupid strode by with nary a second glance and almost knocked the sorry-looking bunch of gas station flowers from the guy's hand.

*

"– and then we held hands and we fed the ducks and when we kissed –" Cupid effervesced to Tantalus, their earlier spat forgotten. "*Wow*," Cupid sighed with a dreamy, faraway look in his eyes.

Tantalus eyed his friend with amusement and began to wonder if he'd done the right thing making him fall head-over-heels in love. But hey, the poor sap seemed so damned *happy*!

"I need to get champagne, flowers, a ring!" Cupid babbled. "I can't possibly propose marriage without a ring!"

"Calm down, my friend; you will give yourself apoplexy." Tantalus smiled at Cupid. "You're in love, that's all." He gave the god a hearty smack on the shoulder. "Now *you* know what it feels like."

Cupid grinned inanely and fidgeted his butt around on the bench. He peered down to Earth and he thought that the grass somehow seemed so much greener today, the seas a more vibrant blue. "It feels totally awesome, that's what! I wish I'd done this a long time ago!" Cupid gushed.

Tantalus adopted his sternest look. "I have warned you that it *will* wear off, Cupid. Love is a cruel, transient thing."

Cupid frowned at Tantalus as if he were quite mad. "I feel that I shall prove you wrong, Tantalus," he growled. "Claire and I are so meant for each other that it's almost untrue!"

"That's because it *is* untrue," Tantalus lectured. "You feel the way you do because of the rush of hormones and endorphins in your blood stream. They're fooling you into believing that you and this girl are like you are two halves of the same being." A knowing smile.

"Nail on the head!" Cupid beamed.

"Just think for a moment, Cupid," Tantalus said. "You're not even from the same *species*, or even the same existence, come to think of it."

"Aw, pish," Cupid sneered. "When you're in love, it doesn't matter what you are, or *where* you're from!"

It was at this point that Tantalus began to feel sorry for his friend. The *love* he'd inflicted upon him was clouding Cupid's judgement and common sense, and had taken over his rational mind. Such was the nature of the foolish emotion, Tantalus mused.

"Love never lasts, Cupid. *Never*," Tantalus reiterated. "Why do you think that we never see people after twenty years together still gazing lovingly into each other's eyes.? What you *do* see is pain and resentment, or at best sadness and resignation.

Cupid studied the cynical old soul that was his best friend in the universe. "Tantalus, my poor, poor friend – when did you become so sceptical?" he asked.

Tantalus fixed Cupid with a steely glare. "That'd be the very first time you made me fall in love," he growled.

*

Claire's apartment door was unlocked, and from within came the raindrop sound of a vigorous shower carried on warm wafts of steamy air.

Cupid smiled as he let himself in, struggling with his hands full with a bottle of chilled champagne, a pair of crimson roses, an assorted box of *Krispy Kreme's* and a small, black velvet covered box. Inside the box nestled a white gold engagement ring that sported the biggest solitaire diamond a god could lay his hands on at such short notice.

"Honey, I'm home!" he called out, his voice dampened by the moist atmosphere. "Yeah, I like that," he murmured to himself. "*Mr. and Mrs. Cupid*, I kinda like that too." Cupid beamed and felt so much in love that he feared he might just burst wide open. Depositing the champagne in Claire's refrigerator, Cupid made his way through to the bathroom clutching the donuts, roses and ring.

"Are you ready for that back scrub, love of my life?" Cupid called out with a dirty, suggestive laugh. Cupid's heart skipped and then quickened its beat as his beloved's melodious voice caressed his ears above the sound of the shower.

And then.

"I've never believed in all of that love at first sight crap, I always thought it was something made up for the movies by lazy scriptwriters." Cupid heard Claire say. *"But now, now – wow!"*

Cupid stopped dead at the bathroom door and peered through the thick steam that clouded and swirled like some sickly smog. He peered around and saw the hastily discarded clothes scattered upon the floor; some of them Claire's, some of them not. And there, perched carefully on a crumpled pair of plaid boxer shorts, sat a gray, striped fedora.

"Oh no, please no," Cupid choked on his words as realization dawned.

The shower door slid open and Claire appeared, her skin deliciously aglow from the heat and ferocity of the shower, her delectable nipples perfectly pink and pointing. "Oh, hi! I thought it was you!" she said, her voice bright, cheerful and without a care in the world. "Hey, he brought donuts!"

A man's face appeared through the fat streams of hot water, chin resting on Claire's bare shoulder as he squinted out at Cupid.

"Thanks, Buddy, you're a gem!" Hat Guy grinned at Cupid. "Can you believe this gal?" he asked the stunned, speechless Cupid. "Only met her yesterday and I'm crazy in love!" He planted a lingering tongue-kiss on Claire's dripping neck which made her squirm and giggle. "Leave the donuts on the counter will ya?

There's a coupl'a bucks next to the Mr. Coffee – help ya'self." And with that, the man retreated back into the shower stall and pulled Claire in with him. He closed the frosted glass door and Cupid could see their heat-reddened, naked bodies in silhouette as they embraced.

The donut box slipped from Cupid's hand and landed side-down on the tiled floor. The donuts spilled and exploded at his feet out with a sticky *splat* like so many plump, bursting bugs. The engagement ring box tumbled after them and into the sugary mess; the ring tumbling from it and settled in the spreading pool of dark jelly.

Cupid clutched at his roses so tightly that the spiky thorns pricked into his palms and drew blood. He stared down at the ring box, at the water droplets that beaded on the soft velvet and a mighty sob caught in the god's chest as his heart broke in two.

*

Tantalus's consoling arm around his shuddering shoulders didn't offer Cupid any comfort at all. His body heaved with great, wracking sobs that emanated from deep within his being, as if ripped from his very soul.

"You were right," Cupid sputtered between hair-pulling wails. "Love is a terrible, *terrible* thing. How could I ever have inflicted such a curse upon humanity?"

Tantalus studied his wrought friend with something akin to pity. "You have to hold on to the fact that Claire didn't deliberately set out to hurt you. It was the second rose that put the love in both of their hearts." He offered Cupid an awkward half-smile. "So I guess you could say that this was mostly my fault."

Cupid was not consoled by his friend's *mea culpa*; the agony in his heart was too raw to give a damn about who's fault what was, or why.

"I know it hurts like hell just now," Tantalus reassured. "But the pain will pass, it always does. Time is the great healer." The god rolled his eyes and muttered beneath his breath. "I really can't believe I just said that."

Cupid shrugged away his friend's arm and stared him dead in the face. "I know in my *heart* that this horrendous torture will never leave me," Cupid sniffled. "At least I know now precisely why there is so much misery in the world. It's not because of you, Tantalus, it's because of *me*. Human pain and suffering has been – and will always be – love's fault!

"Come now, Cupid, don't you think you're over reacting?" Again, Tantalus offered a half-smile; his patience at Cupid's drama-queen act was beginning to wear thin rather quickly.

Cupid stared at his friend with incredulity etched into his features. "Over reacting?!" he shouted, *"over reacting?!"* As if repeating himself would hammer home the point that everything he had held to be true across the eons was fundamentally flawed at this most basic level. "How could I possibly be over reacting when everything I have done in my miserable existence has caused nothing but anguish?" Cupid hardened his resolve with a grim countenance. "You were right all along, Tantalus; the world doesn't need love. There really is no place for it," he snarled.

And so, and without further ado, Cupid plucked one of the roses from the bench and thrust it straight into his own heart. Briefly, the rose reddened and plumped out as if swollen by Cupid's lifeblood, then began to wilt as its life waned along with the god's.

Tantalus cried out with anguish. He lurched forward and grabbed Cupid to save his friend the indignity of falling to the ground. He cradled Cupid's head on his lap, his own tears dripping onto Cupid's upturned face. "What have you done, Cupid?"

Cupid's eyes fluttered open. "I have stopped the suffering; no longer will I inflict this hideous pain on those poor, poor people." He glanced at the humans down on Earth who now appeared to be looking at each other in a most peculiar way; as if they were awakening from a vivid dream and facing the people they'd just been dreaming about.

"I am so sorry," Tantalus sobbed. "All I wanted to do was to show you love. It's not all pain and despair, Cupid old friend; it *can* be the most wonderful gift in the world." He took a fleeting look down, with sadness filling his eyes, at the people below.

A young couple turned from each other and walked away as if they were strangers. A mother pushed a brightly colored stroller – baby and all – into the path of an oncoming truck, and the truck made no attempt to stop, scattering the stroller and its contents along the road. A group of respectable businessmen gathered around a beggar on a park bench, and they took turns to kick the life from his helpless body, laughing heartily as their compassion died as Cupid's life ebbed away. People ran through the streets, turning on one another, destroying property and lives with a flick of a lighter, a stab of a knife, the unforgiving sting of a bullet.

As Tantalus watched, the rose that had speared his friend's chest withered and died, and Cupid, the god of love, gasped one final, rattling breath.

And, as Cupid died, all the love in the world died along with him.

Tantalus sat there awhile; Cupid's head a dead weight in his lap, and watched the chaos as it unfolded on Earth below him. Buildings burned, airplanes smashed to the ground, husbands butchered wives, wives murdered husbands, friend turned on friend, neighbor on neighbor, and so it played out, *ad infinitum*. Tantalus's soul swelled with deep regret and the inconsolable guilt at what he had done.

Despite the torment that love brought with it, it did appear that the humans *needed* love in their hearts after all. Tantalus had only ever considered the loss of love, having long forgotten the joy and fulfilment and completion that it nurtured. Now his realization had come far too late; he had killed *love* forever.

Saddened beyond comprehension, Tantalus lay his old, old friend Cupid carefully down on the bench they'd shared across the eternity of the ages and walked slowly away.

And below him, the human race went about the savagely efficient business of destroying itself.

Because, with love out of the way there really was nothing left to live for.

THE END

Questionable Hygiene

She'd taken a whore's wash with a seafood restaurant's wipes, and now Sylvia's coochie smelled like lemons.

Road Trip Bingo

"Tyler's arm is on my side again," Kirsty Slaten whined. She raised her voice because she had in her ear buds; the music loud enough for everyone in the car to hear the tinny *tssch tssch tssch* that was, without a doubt, gradually destroying her eardrums.

"*She* started it." Tyler poked out his tongue at his sister.

"Well, *I'm* finishing it," Luciana played the Mom card. "And I saw that, Tyler. Apologize to your sister this instant!"

"Aww, Mom," her son bleated.

"Do as your mother says," Chuck threw in. He took a hand off of the steering wheel and patted his wife's bare knee. He gave her a supportive smile – *I got your back, Honey..*

Luciana cast a sideways glance at her husband, the contempt barely concealed beneath her half smile.

Chuck's attention returned to the featureless road that seemed never ending; had it not been for the sporadic road signs and flattened wildlife, it would have been difficult to be sure that any progress had been made on this trip at all.

A glance in the rear view and Chuck saw his kids' surly faces – they both had the air of people attending their own executions rather than a family fun day at the water park – they were so sucking the *fun* part out of the whole thing and at that particular moment in time, Chuck would have preferred to be not taking the ungrateful, sour-faced brats anywhere.

Luciana had insisted on one more family trip before summer ended and the kids returned to school. And who was Chuck to argue with the love of his life, even if personally, he couldn't actually imagine a place more hellish than the water park? The place comprised acres of noisy, hyperactive kids running amok whilst their overheating, frustrated parents followed them around like sun-reddened pack mules. It was a grim place of aching arms laden with towels, swim bags and oversized free-refill drinks cups, of pee tainted water and bland food and for Chuck Slaten, the promise of personal horrors.

Firstly, Tyler would nag Chuck's ass off to go on the biggest of the water slides, and then wuss out when they reached the head of the line. Or, even better still, he'd slide down the thing wailing like the devil was on his tail and then throw up in the splash pool at the bottom. Then there was Kirsty, his once precious little princess; with all of her thirteen-year old logic, she would refuse to do anything more than paddle in the kiddies' splash zone because otherwise she would have to strip down to her bathing suit. The summer had seen Kirsty hit puberty with full force and she was painfully self-conscious about her newly sprouted breasts which seemed to have developed practically overnight. Of course, Chuck knew full well that the irony was that next year, his battle would be to get her to remain suitably covered in the presence of the adolescent, priapic boys that the water park seemed to attract in abundance.

Chuck sighed, they were a third of the way through the three-hour trip and Tyler had already tired of his electronic games – something Chuck had never thought possible for a nine year old boy – and Kirsty had forgotten to pack the book Luciana had bought her especially for the trip; something sappy about teenaged vampires falling in love, a cynical cash-in on the *tween* market.

Chuck fumed quietly to himself. When *he* was their age, he and his sister had to be content with watching raindrops race down the car windows. They would bet against each other with pennies and sometimes, if the wind was just right, the raindrops would race *up* the windows.

Oh yeah, and they'd fight too.

"I thought you guys were playing Road Trip Bingo," Chuck broke the silence.

It was never a good sign to have gotten to Road Trip Bingo this early on and Chuck wished he'd invested in the in-car DVD system that the pretty sales girl with the mesmerizing cleavage had done her best to talk him into when they'd bought the car. But no, Luciana had insisted he take out the extra warranty instead.

"We are," Tyler said.

"I am, you're just cheating." Kirsty curled her lip.

"I *did* see a squished armadillo!" Tyler gave his sister a shove and her head clunked on the window.

"Mom!" Kirsty wailed and gave Tyler a dead arm.

Tyler kicked his sister's shin.

"Tyler kicked me." Kirsty rubbed at her shin. "Prick," she mumbled.

Chuck cast an eye to the vacant third row of seats at the rear of the vehicle. How nice it would be to stick one of the kids there and put an end to their bickering. He had purchased the Tahoe specifically for that extra seating, but Kirsty refused to sit back there because she'd read somewhere that if they got rear-ended, she'd die; and Tyler *couldn't* sit back there because it made him throw up.

Come to think of it, was there anything that *didn't* make that boy throw up?

Chuck fumed some more; he could have had a Mustang.

"Kirsty punched me in the balls!" Tyler's whiny voice broke Chuck's reverie.

"I did not, and it's rude to say balls."

"Stop it, the both of you!" Chuck bellowed. "Just play your game and no punching anyone in the anywheres!" He set his face to stern and gripped the steering wheel until his knuckles turned white, like he was strangling the thing.

"We've almost finished," Tyler offered. His Dad's raised voice always scared him. It didn't come out that often, but when it did, Dad meant business. "I only need a Chevy Tahoe to finish the card." He held up his bingo card for Chuck to see all the crossed off pictures of road signs, eating establishments, gas stations, trees and road-kill. In the Bonus Square – the one that the kids had determined before they'd set off – the boy had written *Chevvy Taho: white.*

"You can't find a white Tahoe?" Chuck said.

"Nope," his son replied, shaking his head for emphasis.

"Really?"

"*Really*, Dad," Kirsty couldn't resist the dig at her stupid brother. She turned up her iPod so that everyone in the car could further enjoy the *tssch tssch tssch* that echoed out from her ears.

Chuck bit his tongue – literally – and tasted blood. As much as he loved his kids, there were some days – and this one came pretty damned close to the top of the list – that he could quite gladly drop the pair of them off at the orphanage and flee the country. Kirsty had become unnaturally belligerent of late and Chuck held genuine concerns about Tyler; the boy really didn't seem all that bright and Chuck could only hope that he'd turn out to be good with his hands.

"You're sitting in one," Chuck told his son.

"What?"

"You're struggling to spot a white Tahoe and you're sitting in one."

"*Our* car doesn't count, Dad. Duh!" Kirsty snarled. "*Everybody* knows that rule."

"Okay, I'll give you that one," Chuck was forced to agree. "But we've been on the road for over an hour now and you haven't seen *one single* White Tahoe?"

The kids shook their heads.

Chuck ground his teeth. His orthodontist had warned him against doing so because it was wearing his enamel away and pretty soon he'd be down to bare pulp and raw nerves. Then again, it was easy for his fucking orthodontist to give out that advice because his orthodontist didn't have to live with Tyler and Kirsty; two kids who, in the space of an hour on the Texas road system couldn't spot one of the single most popular SUV's in the entire state.

Kirsty's tuneless singing drifted over to the front of the car. Eyes closed, oblivious to everything around her, she droned her tone deaf tribute to Gaga's *Government Hooker*.

"Should she be listening to that?" Chuck asked.

"She's thirteen, Chuck, what do you think she's going to listen to?" It was the most Luciana had spoken since they'd left home and Chuck had actually found himself missing her banal gossip about people he knew only through her banal gossip, and crazy friends of hers that he didn't give a rat's dick about.

"You're right, my love," Chuck said, "I guess I'm getting a little out of touch these days." He patted his wife's knee again and felt bristle. Chuck wished his darling wife would shave her legs a little more often; the prickly blonde fuzz that covered them reminded him of gooseberries. Once upon a time, Luciana had shaved her legs to glassy smooth *every* morning, *and* kept her pubic hair trimmed to a neat little triangle that pointed downwards like a guide's arrow. Now she only seemed to shave down there prior to her gynecologist appointments. Funny that.

Chuck glanced across at Luciana's plump legs. They strained the seams of her too-tight, denim shorts and spread out onto the cream leather seat like unrolled dough. Her skin still had the honeyed tone that had so effectively turned his head in high school, although her thighs were now a road map of spider veins and cellulite that somewhat marred the sensual effect.

Chuck's mind wandered back to the lively, vivacious Luciana he'd fallen for all those years ago. She'd been as hot as hell and twice as horny; and whilst she'd not been quite the head cheerleader type that all the other football players had lusted after, Luciana had been the exotic-skinned, doe-eyed smart girl who smouldered beneath her ass-length, jet-black hair. She still had that silken, iridescent hair eighteen years on, albeit cut into a neat bob and kept black with a fair amount of help from a bottle. Yessir, Chuck could conjure with ease a mental picture of Luciana as sexy and enticing as she was back in the day; which meant that in these later years of their dwindling sex life, he at least had that to jerk off to.

"There's one!" Tyler shouted and waved his Bingo card in Kirsty's face. She batted it away and gave him a dirty look. "Bingo!" Tyler shouted in her ear.

Sure enough, a white Tahoe sailed by and then manoeuvered in front of Chuck without using its blinker.

"I should pull him over and let him know his blinker's not working," Chuck rolled out the good ol' Slaten sarcasm.

"Yeah, that would be constructive," Luciana replied and rolled those beautiful browns at her husband.

"It looks like our car." Tyler peered from between the front seats.

"So do half a million others, Son," Chuck said.

"Yeah, I suppose."

Chuck studied the car in front, pissed that yes, it did look exactly the same as his. Nothing like rubbing his face in the fact that he'd been forced into a lumbering family wagon instead of the red Mustang he'd always wanted.

"Hold on," Chuck mumbled.

"What is it now?" his wife sighed.

"What's our registration?"

"Pardon me?"

"Our registration plate? For *this* car?"

"You don't know it?"

Chuck saw his wife's eyes roll again. Did his existence really irritate her *that* much? "We've only had the car a couple of months, Luciana. And you know I don't memorize numbers all that well," Chuck defended.

"Then how do you expect *me* to know it?" Luciana snapped. "It's not even my car."

No, you get a fucking Corvette to swan around in, bitch.

"You're right, my love, what *was* I thinking?" Chuck gave his wife a weak smile. "Would you mind passing me the insurance card?"

Another loud, theatrical sigh and Luciana dug around in the glove box. She pulled out the insurance card and thrust it into her husband's hand.

Chuck scanned the document. "Well I'll be –" he stuttered and pushed the card under his wife's nose.

"What is it, Dad?" Tyler leaned forward again.

"He has the same registration as us."

Chuck had heard of this happening before. Occasionally, the vehicle registration computer would screw up and issue the same number twice, often on the same make and model of vehicle. What worried Chuck was the possibility of the criminal types who cloned vehicle identities and used the duplicates for their own nefarious means. There'd been a guy at his previous company who'd had that happen and then started getting speeding citations from places he'd never even been to. As far as Chuck knew, there were still arrest warrants out for the guy in five states.

"What must the odds be of coming across our own duplicate?" Chuck shared his thoughts.

"Perhaps *our* car is the duplicate," Luciana offered, somewhat unhelpfully. "Did you pay to have the background check done?"

"Yes dear, of course I did." It was Chuck's turn to roll his eyes.

"What's UO mean Dad?" Tyler asked. "Is that the model name?"

"Not that I know of, Son, why?"

"Well, that car has an UO sticker on its bumper, just like ours."

Chuck squinted through the exploded insect guts on his windshield at the other Tahoe's rear and saw that indeed, there was a red UO sticker.

Chuck's blood ran cold. Whilst he could rationalize a duplicate registration, even accept the coincidence of running into his vehicle's twin on this particular stretch of desolate Texas road, he struggled with an identical UO sticker.

The little red sticker was ingrained in his mind following the lively argument Luciana had enjoyed with the young girl at the car dealership. The girl had puffed out her not inconsiderable chest and insisted that the UO denoted the University of Ohio, whilst Luciana was adamant that it was the University of Oklahoma, and she should know because she recognized the design and her brother had studied Biology there.

Large Breasted Dealership Gal had lost the argument, and in doing so had learned a valuable lesson in life; don't argue the toss with an early-menopausal Latino woman.

The presence of the sticker made the other Tahoe – from the back at least – a doppelganger of Chuck's.

"Well, I'll be," Chuck grumbled.

"Just let it go, Chuck," Luciana said with thinly disguised impatience. "It's not like *you* use your blinkers every time."

Chuck ignored his wife. His eyes were fixed very firmly on the other Tahoe. He squeezed his foot down on the accelerator to close the gap between the two cars whilst at the same time a weird prickle gnawed at his balls and crawled up into his belly to brew a sick knot in his stomach.

Luciana rolled her eyes once more as Chuck eased into the left lane – using his blinker, lead by example and all that – and pushed ahead to overtake the duplicate car.

The other Tahoe maintained speed, as if its driver *wanted* Chuck to pass.

As he cruised past the car, Chuck looked to his right; the rear windows of the Tahoe were black-tinted and reflected back his own gawking face. Tyler peered through his own dark window, curiosity aroused, whilst Luciana and Kirsty maintained their blatant disinterest.

Parallel now with the front of the copycat car, Chuck squinted sideways again and saw the other driver who was staring straight ahead, hands gripping the steering wheel as if he were strangling it. Next to him, Chuck could see a black-haired woman with a wistful, faraway look on her face, and he thought she looked as if she was wishing herself someplace else.

Chuck saw a rear window roll down a lick and a small boy's face peered from the gloom, followed by that of a small dog. The dog's bright pink tongue lolled from the side of its gaping mouth, the loose skin of its face flapping and distorted in the rattling breeze; it was the weirdest looking dog Chuck had ever seen in his life, yet it did provide some welcome relief.

Identical or not, there was a dog in the other car. The Slaten family did not own a dog, never had, Luciana hated the things.

The boy in the other car stared directly at Chuck and poked out his tongue.

"They look just like us," Tyler said; if they ever got around to making stating the fucking obvious an Olympic sport, then Chuck's boy would be first pick to carry his country's flag.

There is no such thing as coincidence.

Who'd said that? Sherlock Holmes? That smart ass with the buzz-cut from *NCIS*? Whichever, Chuck couldn't escape the creeping feeling that something here was very wrong indeed.

He floored the gas and with the other car safely in the rear-view Chuck gave himself time to reflect; he desperately needed to process what he *thought* he had seen. A glance at his wife's stony face warned Chuck not to vocalize; she would only use anything he said about this as an excuse to further berate him (what exactly *had* happened in their marriage that they had come to that?)

Although he'd denied it at first, as far as Chuck had seen, the people in the matching Tahoe had looked exactly like himself and his family. A trick of the light? Tired eyes or some kind of breakdown? Then there *was* that stupid looking dog, the only difference he had seen between the two vehicles – but the more Chuck's brain processed, the less he was convinced that what he'd seen had actually been a dog at all. There'd been something not right about the pink, flapping skin and oval mouth.

"So what the fuck was it then?" Chuck said his thinking part out loud by mistake.

Luciana fixed her annoyance of a husband with a disapproving gaze. "Please watch your language in front of the children, *dear*," she all but snarled the last word.

An insistent *ding* from the dash startled Chuck and his eyes flicked to the little LED gas pump on the display. Chuck glanced at the car following behind at the required safe distance and absently wondered if they needed gas too.

The alternate Tahoe thundered by as he pulled in to the services and Chuck let out a long sigh of relief, unaware 'till now that he'd been holding his breath

Chuck pumped gas and stared down the road long after the other vehicle had vanished. His mind was already beginning to doubt what he'd seen and before his seemingly bottomless gas tank was full, Chuck had practically convinced himself that he'd imagined the whole thing.

He paid at the counter inside the gas station and allowed the children the rare opportunity of a free run at the endless racks of candy. Kirsty picked out some zero calorie gum – watching her figure at thirteen, for Christ's sakes! – whilst Tyler loaded his arms with enough refined sugar to see them all through a nuclear holocaust. Luciana settled for an insanely hot coffee from the serve-it-yourself machine that lurked and gurgled at the rear of the store, adjacent to the restrooms.

Chuck had nothing. He hated to eat and drive and he thought that the stewed coffee from the machines had a tendency to taste like scolding piss.

*

Back to the long, straight monotony of the open road, and Chuck had all but forgotten the alternate Tahoe. He'd made a note to contact the vehicle registration people on Monday morning, and thoughts of identical people and weird-shit dogs were rapidly being replaced by those of his impending day of water park misery.

There it was again.

Although little more than a white dot on the shimmering road ahead, the alternate Tahoe was quite unmistakable.

Chuck tightened his fingers around the wheel and tried to tell himself that at this distance there was no way of telling if it was even a Tahoe, let along *the* Tahoe.

Yet he knew.

"Yay! It's those people again!" Tyler's glee at the discovery didn't help Chuck's mood any. This time, Luciana and Kirsty joined Tyler in rubbernecking as Chuck closed in on the duplicate car.

"I don't believe it," Chuck growled. Given the time it had taken to fill up his own tank, and the fact that there were no other gas stations between that one and where he'd caught up with the alternate Tahoe, Chuck realized there was only the one conclusion to draw.

They had been waiting for him to catch up.

Chuck neared the all too familiar rear-end of the vehicle with a dry mouth that left his tongue glued to his arid palate.

The other car's right blinker light flickered and the red brake lights flashed. It then drifted to the side of the road, where a crumbling driveway lead up to an abandoned, decaying motel.

Chuck followed.

"What the hell are you doing!?" Luciana demanded with just a soupcon of panic in her voice.

"I think they want me to follow them," Chuck replied, voice calm. "Perhaps they want to sort out this duplicate plate bullshit."

"Oh, for God's sakes," said with the ubiquitous roll of the eyes. "Sorry kids, it looks like were going to be late to the park because your Father doesn't know how to let things go." Snide to a fault, was Luciana. "I don't know what you think you're going to do, Chuck." This was the most talkative Luciana had been the whole trip, and where he had missed her voice earlier, Chuck now wished she'd just shut the fuck up. "You know you don't deal well with confrontation. And what if they're homicidal maniacs?"

Chuck ignored his wife and pulled up opposite the stationary vehicle. He killed the engine. Driven by curiosity and the need to placate the eerie feeling in his gut, Chuck simply didn't have the patience for his wife's paranoia. Besides which, since when did murderers drive around in family vehicles with kids and freaky little dogs?

He got out.

The occupants of the alternate Tahoe clambered from their air-conditioned haven and into the blistering Texas heat.

"Well, isn't this awkward?" the man smiled.

"I'll be –" Chuck muttered.

It was like looking in a mirror.

Chuck Slaten stared wide-eyed at what appeared to his perfect clone; right down to the ashen face and tan Crocs over black socks. Standing beside the Alternate Chuck was a stone-faced, statuesque Alternate Luciana, flanked by Kirsty and Tyler counterparts.

Alternate Tyler held the odd-looking dog in his arms and now that Chuck could see its pink, bloated body he knew for definite it wasn't any kind of dog he'd ever laid eyes on. The animal, the size and shape of an obese tom cat, was totally devoid of fur. It had papery, amphibious skin, six legs, a tail made up of fleshless vertebrae and no head. Instead, the face was sunken into its wrinkled flank, had eight milky eyes that glistened and stared without blinking and an oval mouth that gaped wide like a lunatic's. From the slobbering maw there dangled a fat, oversized tongue that scraped over yellowed teeth as if it were panting.

It looked like an animated, shaved scrotum.

"See, I told you they didn't have a dog," Alternate Luciana chastised Alternate Chuck. She rolled her eyes heavenwards, as if words truly escaped her. "If *someone* had bothered to do their research, we'd not have to have brought that fucking thing with us." She pointed an immaculately manicured fingernail at the pink creature and sneered at Alternate Chuck in a way that made the real Chuck cringe.

"Howdy," Alternate Chuck said, not moving from the spot by his vehicle.

"Howdy," Chuck returned the greeting. Nothing else came out; what the fuck *was* one supposed to say in such circumstances?

"Who are these people, Dad?" Tyler chirped. He'd climbed out of the car without Chuck noticing and stood beside his father.

"Get back in the car, Tyler," Chuck growled and his tone said *no arguments*. Nonetheless, Tyler stayed put and played a staring contest with the kid who looked exactly like him.

Alternate Chuck stepped forward. "They told us we wouldn't bump into you yet." He smiled the warm smile that Chuck reserved for disarming his most objectionable clients.

"Who said?" Chuck struggled to control his racing thoughts. Was this the nervous breakdown the company shrink had warned him had been a long time coming? "And just who the *fuck* are you people?"

Alternate Chuck took a couple more steps, his family following suit. "I'm sorry, where are my manners?" He beamed, his pearly-whites glinting in the harsh sunlight. "I'm Chuck, this here's my good lady wife, Luciana. And this is Tyler and Kirsty." Again with that disarming smile. "I figured you'd already know that."

"I don't get it," Chuck stammered. "I just don't –"

"What's not to get, Chuck?" Alternate Chuck grinned. "We're you, you're us. It really is as simple as that. We weren't supposed to meet up yet but we did, probably because *somebody* didn't check the paperwork properly." He ruffled Alternate Tyler's hair. "What do I always tell you about minding the paperwork, son?"

"To always do it, otherwise shit happens." The scrotum-dog thing squirmed in the boy's arms, its naked skin already starting to redden under the harsh glare of the Texas sun.

"Precisely." Alternate Chuck nodded.

"Will someone please explain to me what is going on here?" Chuck broke in, his voice an octave and a half higher than usual.

"Like I told you, Chuck; *we* are you," Alternate Chuck said calmly.

"What's going on, Chuck?" Luciana's voice was shrill and grating as she walked around the car to her husband. "It's getting hot in the –" Luciana's face drained of color and a waxy sheen of sweat shimmered across her skin. She grasped her hands to her mouth and made small retching sounds.

"Hi, Luciana," Alternate Luciana called across, as friendly and breezy as an old school friend.

*

"It really is quite simple," Alternate Chuck said as he mopped his brow with the stained handkerchief he carried in his pants pocket. His wife swore it made him look like he had a permanent hard-on, but old habits were old habits, and they died hard.

Chuck mopped *his* brow with *his* stained 'kerchief but the grubby cloth did little to alleviate the damp, sticky feeling.

"It *really* is simple," Alternate Chuck repeated with an exasperated sigh. "*We* are *you guys* from an alternate reality."

"What alternate reality?" Luciana kept her steely eyes fixed on Alternate Luciana.

"The one in which they invented inter-reality travel, of course." Alternate Chuck laughed.

"*This* is what you get for playing safe." Alternate Luciana couldn't resist a dig at her husband. "We could have gone to the reality where they have teleportation and then we wouldn't be stuck with this god forsaken pile of junk." She waved a dismissive hand towards their Tahoe. "Next year, I want time travel, or inter-stellar. This *really* is the last time I let you choose our vacation, Chuck!"

Chuck cringed. Was this how his Luciana treated *him*? Did he really put up with being spoken to with such derision?

"Whatever the reason," Alternate Chuck continued and this time he did a little eye-rolling all of his own, "we decided to vacation here this summer."

"You're on vacation?"

"If you can call it that," Alternate Luciana butted in with a vicious sneer in her voice that made *everyone* cringe.

"And you're us?" Tyler said.

"No, you're us," Alternate Tyler corrected, and Alternate Kirsty slapped his arm.

"What's it like where you guys come from?" Tyler's curiosity cut through the surreal moment.

"It's really not all that much different from here," Alternate Tyler told him, "except there's no Australia and some of the animals are a bit different."

"See. Even the kids think this is lame," Alternate Luciana huffed. She poked Alternate Chuck in the ribs with a vicious finger that made him flinch.

Chuck cracked a wry smile at his alternate's discomfort. It was nice to see that he and the guy who was creeping him out right now shared the same Achilles heel. It really was like looking into some diabolical mirror.

Ever the salesman, Chuck stepped forward, arm outstretched in that universal *let's shake hands and pretend this isn't in the least bit awkward* gesture that men seem compelled to make under even the most awkward of circumstances.

Alternate Chuck took a step back and stared at Chuck's hand as if it were diseased.

"Better not," his voice was firm.

"You don't shake a guy's hand where you're from?" Chuck was offended.

"I can't shake *your* hand. Here."

"I think it's because he's you, Dad," Tyler chipped in. "If you both touch, you'll explode."

Alternate Chuck laughed. "I see your boy's a Trekkie too! I'm afraid that's where kids get most of their science from these days!"

"You're thinking of the matter/anti matter reaction," Alternate Tyler said. He smiled at Tyler as if they were two best buds at a sci-fi convention and not exact, alternate duplicates. "You put *those* two together and POW!"

Chuck jumped at the loud *POW!* His nerves jangled and were beginning to shred, one by twitching one.

"What's going on Dad?" Kirsty walked around from her side of the car. "And why does *she* look like me?" She stalked up to Alternate Kirsty who returned the stare with those same, accusatory eyes. "Who the fuck are *you* supposed to be?" Kirsty grimaced at her alternate.

"Kirsty!" Chuck reprimanded.

"Yeah, Dad, whatever," His daughter sneered, her mother's contempt towards Chuck already fixed in her repertoire.

Alternate Kirsty grabbed hold of Kirsty's hand and she froze, a half sound stuck in her throat.

In the blinking of an eye Kirsty's T-shirt and shorts had vanished. They were swiftly followed by her one-piece swimsuit which momentarily revealed that her overnight blossoming had been more than enhanced by a generous helping of tissues. Kirsty stood rooted to the spot and within the space of no more than a handful of seconds, her skin had vanished, followed by her flesh, layer by gaudy layer. Next went her internal organs, the white threads of nerves and finally, her bones.

And then there was nothing.

Chuck stumbled in slow-motion towards where his daughter had been standing. "What the hell?!" He stepped towards Alternate Chuck, but stopped himself. "Where's my daughter?"

"What have you done to my baby?!" Luciana wailed, her voice that high, hysterical pitch that never failed to make Chuck's ears hurt.

"Everybody just calm down," Alternate Chuck soothed. He spread his arms out, palms up. *Trust me*, his body language implied.

Chuck knew his own gesture all too well. *You can trust me about as far as you can throw me* is what it meant in Chuck-speak.

"She's okay, I promise." Alternate Chuck grinned.

"If you've hurt her –" Luciana stepped forward. Hesitated.

"She's gone to *our* reality, that's all," Alternate Chuck placated. "She's perfectly fine."

"So *that's* what happens." Alternate Tyler was awestruck. "That is *so* cool!"

"Apparently so." Alternate Chuck nodded. "They really didn't make it all that clear in the brochure."

Chuck's blood pressure bubbled up and his temples throbbed with each thump of his heart. He fought to keep his voice down to somewhere below hysterical and his temper under control. "You need to bring my daughter back," he growled, "now."

"I'm afraid that's quite impossible." Alternate Chuck smiled his – *Chuck's* – warmest smile. "We can't exist in the same reality as our alternate selves, not when there are no *us* back in our reality. It's all because of physics and stuff that, quite frankly, I don't really understand."

"Y-you're replacing us?" Luciana stammered. "Chuck, they're *replacing* us!"

"I guess you could call it that." Alternate Chuck smirked. "There really is nothing to panic about; it happens far more often than you may think. Look at it this way, you guys get to see a different reality too, so it'll be like a vacation for you as well."

"Don't get too excited," Alternate Luciana deadpanned. "It's not all that."

"And, as you can see," Alternate Chuck explained, "there are no explosions, rips in the space-time continuum or any of the other pseudo-scientific mumbo-jumbo you see in the movies." He guffawed at this, as if he'd just cracked the funniest of funnies.

Chuck recognized that laugh, it was the one he held in reserve for when he'd just said something really, really clever.

"We'd rather not," Chuck said. "We want to stay right here, thank you. And we would like Kirsty back."

"Ah, I don't think I've explained myself clearly enough." Alternate Chuck fixed them with his serious face and Chuck wanted to physically assault the guy – *himself!* "Once we've exchanged places with our alternative selves, there's no coming back. You nice people get to live in the reality we came from, and we get to stay here until we're ready to move on." Alternate Chuck smiled.

"So, you had to find us all along?" Chuck asked.

"Part of the package deal," Alternate Chuck told him.

"This is some kind of joke," Luciana interrupted. "All this, you –?"

"It's not *any* kind of joke," Alternate Luciana said. "Unless you count the fact that we came to *this* boring reality instead of somewhere fun." She spat out *this* like it was a bad taste on her tongue.

Chuck's brain ached. His practical mind struggled to comprehend what his other self was telling him – hell, even that didn't make too much sense right now – but he had no option but to believe what his eyes were telling him; that he had just seen his daughter – what? Dissolve? He had to give credence to the fact that she had actually gone to another reality, and if Alternate Chuck was to be believed, the same fate awaited himself, Luciana and Tyler.

There's a part in the human brain that generates hope in even the most hopeless of situations. It's why men walk calmly to the gallows, go merrily off to war, or fight even the most malignant of cancers – there's always the *hope* of salvation. And it was this part of Chuck that accepted all of his counterpart's bullshit, to even consider going willingly to the other reality. He rationalized that the Alternate Slatens would have to go back there eventually. They *were* on vacation, after all.

"We won't be returning to our own reality after this." Alternate Chuck read Chuck's mind. Of course he had, it was *his* mind too! "We signed up for the lifetime's worth of reality-jumping – thought we'd be adventurous." Alternate Chuck grinned. "We came into a few dollars when Mom and Dad died, if you know what I mean?" There was a wicked twinkle in his eye.

Chuck's thoughts switched to his own Mom and Dad who, in *this* reality were very much alive and kicking; also they were as poor as church mice. In fact, Chuck had actually had to bail them out of their sticky financial situation on the all too numerous occasions that Dad's sure-fire winning horses failed to live up to their sure-firedness.

And yet, in some parallel reality, Chuck Slaten was loaded. Suddenly, Chuck began to envy his counterpart, and think that perhaps visiting that particular alternative wouldn't be such a bad thing after all.

"Aren't there an infinite number of realities?" Tyler broke the silence.

"In theory, Son," Alternate Chuck replied. "But there's only about two hundred of those actually worth visiting. Don't they teach you *anything* in school here?" A broad *Gotcha* grin. "I mean, who the hell wants to pay to vacation in an alternate universe where the only difference is that some random guy didn't scratch his ass that morning?"

"Even that couldn't be much worse than this place," Alternate Luciana chose her moment wisely for yet another well-aimed dig.

"Thank you, my dear," Alternate Chuck said through gritted teeth. "We all get the message." He shot a glance at Chuck and a look passed between them; a glimmer of camaraderie amongst the downtrodden.

"So, what happens when you guys leave this, err our, err, here?" Chuck struggled.

"We'll be replaced here by the other Us-es in whatever alternate reality we decide to visit next," Alternate Chuck was quite matter of fact about the whole concept. "They really do teach you nothing about any of this, do they?"

"Not in our curriculum," Chuck replied, inexplicably embarrassed at his own reality's shortcomings. "We don't know of any other realities apart from this one."

"Then you're in for one hum-dinger of a ride, my friend!" Alternate Chuck stepped towards Chuck, who before he knew what was happening felt a firm hand grasp his own in a sweaty handshake.

Chuck's muscles froze and a chilly tingle spread through his body. It expanded from his hand, up along his arm and crept through his body like an electrical fungus; prickling mycelia that invaded every corner of him, one cell at a time.

At the same time, Alternate Tyler jumped onto Tyler's back and clung on to him with arms tight around his throat in a sinister piggy-back. As Chuck watched, helpless, his son also began to vanish one layer at a time and as he faded away, Chuck summoned the last wisps of his breath to call out to Luciana. "Get the fuck out of here!" his tightened throat forced the words out as *'et eh fu' t'ere!*

Scrambled diction or no, Luciana got her husband's message loud and clear and darted back to the Tahoe as Alternate Luciana lunged, her expensive fingernails missing her counterpart's hair by a fraction.

The car's engine gunned, tyres spun on the disintegrating road and kicked up a cover of thick, red dust on its way out of the abandoned lot. Alternate Luciana turned on her heels, clambered into the alternate Tahoe and raced after Chuck's fleeing wife.

Chuck's clothes felt feather light, a sensation followed by the warmth of the sun's rays on his naked body. An instant after that, his skin felt as if it were liquefying, evaporating into the dry heat. There was no pain, which was a mercy, but the peculiar sensations as layer upon layer of his being were stripped away made Chuck feel quite nauseous. He cast his eyes downwards; saw the glistening pink of his own viscera, the living white/pink bone that shone through the soft tissues.

And then he could see nothing but black as his eyes dissolved away to leave him in the darkness between realities.

Chuck's perception of time had warped beyond comprehension; he'd seen Kirsty vanish completely in a matter of seconds, but the process felt like hours until, finally, Chuck felt his skull disappear and the sun's warmth prickling at his exposed brain. And then, for the briefest of moments, Chuck knew how it felt to exist as nothing more than pure thought.

*

The bizarre lightlessness began to gray around the edges and Chuck had an overwhelming sensation of *passing through*; his conscious mind being the final part of him to complete the bizarre journey. It felt as if his brain had been forced through a chilled, narrow funnel; pushed through with a wet, almost audible *plop*.

Chuck's thoughts went out to his kids and he hoped that they hadn't been totally scared out of their sanity by all of this, although he did think that Tyler would think that all of this had been *totally cool*.

The gray became lighter, gave way to color, which in turn resolved into forms and shapes. Chuck could feel his body again as it grew more *substantial;* he positively delighted in the weight of flesh on his exposed bones.

As Chuck's vision returned he realized that whatever place he'd been transported to, it looked exactly like the one he'd left, decaying motel and all. He saw black, flying things – presumably buzzards – circling low over something dead and smashed flat on the road. Only, they weren't really buzzards at all; they were shiny, black blobs which flew on broad, leathery wings that were completely featherless. They had fat, clawed feet they held tucked close to their grotesque bodies, and their heads sported faces that were perfectly human.

"Dear God," Chuck murmured, glancing down at the subject of the flying things' attention. It looked like no creature Chuck was familiar with, squashed flat or otherwise. Its blood was a bright, neon green color and was splashed across the dusty road like bizarre urban graffiti. The dead creature itself was around five feet in length and appeared to have at least three heads, none of which had eyes. It also boasted eight legs, one of which was severed and lay mangled on the opposite side of the road and through the congealing blood, Chuck could see that the creature's skin was a coat of short barbs that resembled the writing end of innumerable quills.

It's really not that much different ... some of the animals are a bit different.

The ground shook and a long, cold shadow fell over the old motel. Chuck twisted his head around so sharply that his neck bones crackled, and he saw the monstrosity that strode up behind him.

The creature was five, six storeys high with a squat, blubbery body the same eye-watering green as the roadkill's blood. The monstrous thing's glistening, raw skin was adorned with snaking tributaries of vivid pink veins that pulsed and throbbed as it manoeuvred towards Chuck on four thick-set, powerful legs that looked like they had been transplanted from some gigantic insect. Dangling between the creature's legs was a colossal swinging ball sack that hit the decaying roof of the motel and ripped it away from the building.

"Dear God," Chuck whispered again, frozen in sheer terror.

The thing had three tubular, rubbery arms, one on either shoulder, with a third that sprouted from the center of its chest; none of which had what could be called hands, just a sticky pad that reminded Chuck of the end of a chameleon's tongue. Grasped firmly by the center arm, the creature held aloft a writhing, shrieking thing.

Luciana.

It lifted Chuck's wife up to its face, a vast neon moon of a thing that looked as if it had been glued on to the huge, bulbous head as part of some grotesque kindergartener's art project; the head's circumference was lined by a single row of tiny, unblinking eyes that glinted at Luciana with pure malevolence.

Chuck watched in stunned, sickened silence as a hole appeared in the center of the beast's face, and an oozing protuberance slithered out and snaked towards his wife and she screamed long and loud. At the end of the protuberance unfurled a circular, lipless mouth lined with a radula of keenly pointed teeth. As it walked towards Chuck, the creature nonchalantly chewed off Luciana's head and munched on her body as a child would a tasty Popsicle.

The creature peered down at Chuck and the myriad twinkling eyes focussed upon him as if he were nothing more that some unusual bug. The thing's ridiculous, Stretch-Armstrong arms reached out for him and Chuck Slaten ran for his life.

A Night Time Lament

"There are scary things waiting for me in the shadows, Daddy."

"Which ones, sweetie?"

"All of them."

Zombie Hooker: A Love Story

ONE

The fat, dead guy ambled along the sidewalk, his uneven gait rolling his ample body from side to side like a badly laden truck. His face bore the unmistakable gray pallor of death, his skin mottled and peeling. The man's feet – one bare, one sporting a black patent slip-on – shuffled and scraped the ground as he made his way along the familiar route to the office where he'd once worked.

He swung a battered tan, leather briefcase in his right hand; it had fallen open months ago and spilled its cargo of paperwork out along the street and now it flapped empty. In the guy's left hand was a TV remote, which he held to his ear as if in the midst of an important telephone conversation. His cell phone, one could presume, was back at home lying atop a TV set that had not received a transmission since the emergency broadcasts had ceased. Of course, the man was dead and incapable of making a call, even if the cell towers had not stopped working when the whole world went to hell and back.

The corpse shuffled onwards, driven by an inane instinct that condemned him to repeat his old routine *ad infinitum*. His eyes stared straight ahead, blinking occasionally, with only his peripheral vision to prevent him from stumbling into his surroundings.

He didn't acknowledge the girl who stood on the street corner, he never had. Her skin was the same hue as his, her eyes almost as dead. She wore a tiny skirt that had ridden up to exhibit her soft, sensual folds where thigh met buttock, and a skimpy halter-top that exposed her decaying, pallid flesh.

The girl watched the dead businessman in his derelict thousand-dollar suit as he staggered by. She recognized that he walked this way every day at this same time, on his way to an extinct job in a ruined downtown office block. In the deepest recesses of her decaying brain she remembered him; this was the guy who had walked by her every day when his suit had looked like a thousand dollars and his briefcase had been firmly shut.

The girl waited on the street corner that she'd called her own for almost two years. She had staked her claim to the prime piece of hooker real estate after its previous incumbent had vanished. She'd turned up eventually, in a services area on Interstate Ten, wearing a garish off-cut of rolled-up carpet. They'd never found the woman's head – or uterus, liver and heart for that matter.

Prior to her premature death during the outbreak six months ago, the hooker on the corner had been a real, natural beauty. But now, her copper-red hair lay plastered to her head, her pretty face was swollen, drab and lifeless save for fading blue eyes that somehow still managed to sparkle.

She dressed as she always did, her curvaceous figure squeezed into a stretch mini-skirt that showed off slender legs adorned with spiked heels, and metallic top that displayed her ample breasts and a firm belly from which dangled a long diamante belly ring, now hanging precariously from a sliver of rotten skin.

In the Before Time, out on *her* corner for the twelve 'till three lunchtime shift, it had never ceased to amaze just how many office workers needed to fuck in the middle of their working day. Still, it was all good business, especially on alternate Fridays.

When three o'clock came around, the hooker's ingrained routine would drive her back home to her less than salubrious apartment above the Smoke Shop to prepare for regular clients and in-calls.

Even though the Johns didn't seem to come by anymore.

Sure, cars still drove by, but nowhere near the number that used to crawl past in the old days. Back then, there'd been the regulars, the new and the voyeuristic out to catch a glimpse of forbidden flesh with all of the frisson of Victorians espying a well-turned ankle. Cars that did happen by now all maintained a steady speed and had their windows firmly closed; their occupants peering out at the hooker with frightened eyes. And she would faithfully wait out her three-hour shift, no longer caring if anyone was going to stop and ask if she was *doing business*. Things were different now.

One car – silver, German – still happened by every now and then. It would slow down, and she would dip her knees the best she could to catch the driver's gaze. All to no avail as the car would simply race away like a timid animal. Somewhere in the back of the hooker's mind, she *knew* this particular vehicle. It was from the Before Time, but her decaying mind couldn't quite place it.

The reverberating crack of a gun shot barely registered a reaction with the hooker and as she watched with her blank expression, the suited man slumped without ceremony to the sidewalk. Half of his head was gone and the gray-green muck of putrescent brain matter dribbled out of the yawning hole in his skull. He lay there oozing and twitching in a spreading pool of his own slop.

The hooker slunk around the corner and pushed herself hard against the cold, gray brick of the building that had once been a popular nightclub. Experience had taught her that where there were gunshots, there were cops.

And those, she hid from because some things never changed.

A garish red Challenger crawled by. There was a buzz-cut redneck type hanging out of the window with a rifle clutched in his scrawny hands.

"I got him, Olden!" he shouted with undisguised glee to his driver. "Blew his fuckin' brains out first shot! Yeee-ha!" He hollered his war cry as he pumped another couple of bullets into the fat guy's corpse by means of celebration. "One less of them dead fucks to worry about – they should give me a fuckin' medal or sumpthin'!" He flipped off his victim, pulled his denim-clad torso back into the car and his partner floored the gas.

The Challenger was barely a small red spot on the horizon when a blue-and-white cruised by. The uniforms within peered out through the safety of wire-clad windows like curious carrion birds at a kill. Satisfied that the fat guy was well and truly deceased, they sped away. Soon, a black mortuary van would swing by and pick up the businessman's corpse for incineration.

The hooker skulked in the shadows until the cop car was gone. She knew that she couldn't afford to be seen by the Exterminators or the cops otherwise she, too, would end her days oozing gunk onto the sidewalk.

Being a prostitute *and* being one of the undead was definitely not a good combination in these troubled times.

With the suit guy already forgotten, the girl crept out from the shadows and began walking.

It was three PM – time to go home.

TWO

August S Phillips adjusted his silver-plate cufflinks a third time, twisted the crisp, white shirt sleeve around his thick wrist. He paced back and forth in his cramped living room and studied his reflection in the faux-Viennese mirror that hung above the mantel. He'd been presented with the cuff-links two years ago in recognition of twenty years' loyal service to the United States Postal Service; they'd even put on a champagne reception with an array of nibbles, some of which he'd never even heard of.

That had been a proud day.

A mailman's life suited August to a tee. He was a man who enjoyed his own company and he got to work pretty much alone. He had the chance to play the extrovert on his route with a nod and a smile and the occasional light banter to those he had gotten to know over the years. Then he could retreat back to the sanctuary of his tiny home and go back to avoiding the social contact that had always made him feel awkward.

It wasn't that he didn't like his colleagues at the USPS. They were a friendly bunch and some of them had even called around to the house, back in the Before Times. Mom had still been alive then, and she did fuss so when they called him *Augie*. She hated that nickname, said it made him sound like a fucking retard. And she'd pronounce it *reeeeeetard* in her inimitable Southern drawl.

Always a quick one with the expletives was Mother. A pure heart and a foul mouth, the Reverend had described her when they'd laid her to rest; her final words on God's Green Earth as a coronary destroyed her heart had been *'motherfucking cocksucker'*.

The mail service was only just starting to get back on track after the terrifying events of six months ago. The USPS had paid August for all the time he'd been hunkered down at home with only a shotgun and the emergency radio service for company. August figured that people still needed to get their mail, even through a zombie apocalypse.

That's what they were – *zombies* – and that's what they called them. Call a spade a spade, Mom had always said, and she was never shy when it came to spade-calling. August had always been amused at the folk in those old zombie films who referred to the shuffling antagonists as *those things*, like they didn't know what the dead people who were trying to eat them actually were. Had none of them ever *seen* a zombie film before?

From Day One, they had referred to the reanimated dead as *zombies*, no point beating about the bush in a global crisis, August reckoned. Call them what you will – Walking Dead, Living Dead, the fucking Dead Dead if you prefer – they were just regular people who wouldn't – or couldn't – lie down and stay down. Something cruel and unnatural kept them going, driving their putrefying bodies with an irrepressible urge to feed on the living. So far, no explanation had been offered as to what had caused the unholy plague, although the supermarket tabloids and conspiracy theorists had had plenty to say.

From what August had gleaned, it had all been pretty much Obama's fault.

The whole thing had been a surreal nightmare filled with groaning, decaying people that stank to high heaven and would sink their teeth into your flesh as soon as look at you. No amount of horror movies could have prepared the population for the disgusting reality of the dead preying on the living, it was all too much like some nasty dream.

But it *had* actually happened and August – along with a significant number of others – had gotten through it. And, as they say, life goes on.

What a terribly appropriate phrase that had turned out to be.

August fussed at himself once again. Was the tie right for this shirt? Was this the right shirt for this tie? Did the pants make his ass look fat? Was his hair too shaggy? He stared at himself in the mirror and studied the middle-aged man who stared back at him. It had seemed a mere blink of an eye since he straightened the black bow-tie that he'd proudly tied himself as the finishing flourish to the hired prom suit as he waited for his Limo ride to Haley Johnstone's house to show.

Those had been years brimming with hope, with endless possibilities of the vast world beyond the suburbs of the spreading city. August and his recently graduated classmates had stood with their toes on the threshold of the fantastic adventure that was *LIFE*, poised to embrace and devour everything that it had to offer.

And then college had happened. For everyone except August. Dad was long-gone and Mom was working herself in to an early grave with two jobs just to make the mortgage payments and put food on the table.

And somebody had to take care of Davey.

August glanced at the faux-oak framed photograph of Mom that sat on the mantel below the mirror. Her prematurely aged face smiled out from behind the UVproofed glass, her brown, twinkling eyes surrounded by heavily lined skin. Her frail, liver-spotted scalp was clearly visible through the fine wisps of frost-white hair that looked windswept no matter how much she brushed it.

Next to the photograph was Mom's matt black, ceramic urn. It was decorated with gold-leaf angels and on its lid perched the engagement ring Dad had brought back from a business trip to Amsterdam. Dad had not been able to afford a proper ring when he proposed, so he'd surprised her many years later with a belated white gold and diamond ring along with a particularly virulent strain of *Chlamydia* that had almost put paid to her fertility and which she claimed to her dying day was responsible for Davey's *condition*.

Davey was what Mom had called *special*.

Davey was the eldest of the two boys, by three years and change and was so *special* that he'd eat his own shit and scream blue murder all night long like the Devil himself was sticking it up his ass. He'd tear off his clothes and run off down the street and the police would bring him back with sympathetic smiles and platitudes and then Davey would smash up the house and try eating the silverware.

There'd been the days when Davey was catatonic, it brought some welcome peace to the house even though August and his mother had to take turns to wipe the kid's ass when his bowels let go. August struggled to see how not being able to wipe your own goddamned ass was deemed *special*, but there you had it.

August had been nominated Carer-in-Chief the minute he'd graduated high-school. Mom couldn't afford home care for Davey and she would be damned – *God-fucking-damned* – if she was going to stick her eldest son in a state facility.

Haley Johnstone had gone to MIT to do something sciency, and all her promises of keeping in touch and coming home for *every* vacation went quickly by the wayside once she tasted freedom. The handful of friends August had managed to make in school also spread their wings and left the city as quickly as they could – and Ronnie Labouchardiere had travelled to England to major in something scientific under Professor Stephen Hawking.

And there's another special person who can't wipe his own ass.

Naturally, August had never married, never allowed himself close enough to anyone again after Haley's correspondences had dried up. He'd tell everyone – including himself – that he was waiting for the right girl to come along. In reality he knew in his heart that the right girl had already been and gone.

August had put Davey in a private nursing home the day after their mother had passed.

He'd also ignored the old girl's wishes to be buried and gone ahead and had her body cremated; in August's opinion, there was far too much inner city land taken up to accommodate dead folk. And what a marvel that hindsight had been; he would have hated the thought of Mom up and walking around like the rest of the corpses.

He'd paid for Davey's sanatorium out of his own wages, and visited his brother once a month to assuage his guilt at palming off his own flesh and blood to complete strangers.

Davey wasn't a problem anymore. August reminded himself on occasion that he really ought to feel guilty about what had become of his brother, but the harsh truth was that what he did feel was relief. When the dead had resurrected and the fragile fabric that held society together began to shred, Davey, along with life's other unfortunates were rounded up and disposed of in hastily-built incineration units around the city. For many of them, it had been a mercy.

Paying for Davey's care had put a large hole in August's finances, effectively tying him to the small house in which he had grown up and inherited. It also meant that he had to watch every penny and save wisely to pay for the companionship that he craved.

Again, with little guilt, August had built himself a cosy routine of saving for his once a month treat – twice when he got his bonus – of female company.

He'd met Danielle, *his* Danielle only a few months before the world as he – as *everyone* – knew it had changed for ever.

August took out his wallet, fished out the picture he had of the two of them together. They'd had it taken in the photo booth next to their favorite coffee shop. They'd fallen into it giggling like a pair of love-struck teenagers and Danielle had sat on his knee. Danielle's happy smile shone out from the small photograph and they looked for all the world like lovers.

August had been feeling extra lonely recently, ever since they had taken Martha-May away. That flea-bitten tortoiseshell cat with the torn ears and one eye had been older than dirt and was the final legacy from his mother. The cat had smelled bad, was cantankerous and a little too quick with her razor claws for his liking, but he missed her. There was always comfort in having another living thing to come home to.

Hot on the heels of the dead folk climbing out of their coffins, all mammalian pets were rounded up and destroyed; cats, dogs, mice, hamsters, rats – even though there had been not a single instance of anything other than humans *turning* and no evidence from what was left of the scientific community that they could, or ever would.

August had considered arguing that point with the people who came to take Martha-May to the incinerators, right up until the soldiers in biohazard suits had pointed ludicrously big, black semi-automatics at his face.

He *had* made a cursory protest, but the soldiers had advised him in calm, gas-mask muffled voices that they really didn't have the time for his bullshit and that they would be more than happy to shoot him should the need arise. There'd been no alternative but to take them at their word on that one, considering the circumstances.

Gazing at the photograph of his happier self, August realized that never in his life had he felt so desperately, utterly alone.

There had been occasions in the recent weeks on which he'd found himself making an excuse to drive by the street corner where he had first met her, although he told himself that it was only to check that she was alright. He'd drive slowly by, heart racing, hoping against hope that she had survived the madness and would still be there. He'd circle the block as slowly as he dared, taking in his old route by the abandoned office buildings, the litter-strewn streets and *their* coffee shop.

The coffee shop was a wreck now; windows smashed, chairs and tables spilled out onto the sidewalk like innards from a gutted carcass. Next to it, the photo booth was just a burned out shell. It saddened August to see it like that; it had been their special place, where pretence became real – if only by the hour. There had been days he'd paid Danielle just to sit, drink the over priced coffee and talk like he imagined a real girlfriend would. There'd be no sex on those occasions, just companionship and at least the façade of affection.

As he spent more time with Danielle, August had become convinced that he saw something in those liquid blue eyes that hinted at something more than just a business transaction. And that had made him incredibly happy.

In his heart, Danielle had been his constant companion throughout the mayhem and chaos and inescapable presence of death. His memories of her had buoyed up his spirits in even the darkest of hours and given him the motivation he needed to stay alive through the hellish carnage. And he missed her so much that it physically hurt.

August had been rewarded with a glimpse or two of Danielle on his latest sorties. She'd been in her usual place on the corner of the street and he'd slowed his car down to a crawl, still too afraid to roll down the dark-tinted windows on his Mercedes, let alone stop. His heart had skipped a beat or two as she bent her knees to peep into his car, and he imagined that their eyes had met for the briefest of moments.

He'd seen enough of her sickly countenance to know the condition she was in, but her eyes were still alive and they sparkled for him.

And then he'd driven on.

August fiddled absently with his car keys and ruminated on the decision he'd finally made; today would be the day.

The city streets were pretty much cleared of zombies now. The cops and licensed exterminator gangs were still out and about shooting the few remaining dead folk on sight but it had been a couple of months since the city had seen a zombie-related death. August thought it would be fun if they put one of those '*xx days with no Zombie killings*' boards up – one with interchangeable numbers.

He'd heard that the dead were becoming less aggressive and that the Government were planning to use the lesser decayed zombies to replace the tradesmen who were gone now. That was good news for sure; you just couldn't get a plumber for love nor money these days and August's garbage disposal had been all screwed up since the electricity came back on and now it barfed chewed crud back up into the sink whenever the dishwasher drained.

Snorting down his nose at the thought of calling in a zombie plumber, August plucked the ring from his mother's urn and headed out.

THREE

The hooker pushed her apartment door. It swung open. No need for locks these days; very little to steal, no one to steal it.

Out of habit, she closed it firmly behind her.

The three flights of concrete stairs that made her apartment block look and echo like some crumbling mental institution had taken their toll on her atrophied legs and she was exhausted; it had taken a full hour and a half to climb them today. And that was a half hour longer than it had taken her yesterday.

The hooker shuffled across the tiny room, her head lolling slightly to the left and arms swinging loosely by her sides. She aimed for the bathroom, missed and stumbled into the nursery in which stood a cheap pinewood crib. The room was no bigger than a walk-in closet, but before she'd died, the hooker had made it nice by painting it eggshell-blue and adhering Disney character stickers to the walls.

Inside the crib, nestled amongst the glassy eyed, stuffed animals lay the remains of her child, its head crushed by the silver stiletto shoe that was embedded in its soft skull.

Her baby boy – Jethro – had been eleven months old when he'd taken ill. He'd been bitten by one of his playmates at the day care center and the incident had been dismissed as nothing more serious than *it's what babies do* and a write-up in the *Boo-Boo Book*. But that was in the time before things really turned to shit.

She'd instinctively known that there was something seriously wrong with her baby, but by then the hospitals had been stretched beyond capacity, the streets too dangerous for her to venture out. She'd watched helplessly on her TV the events unfolding in the City, and then mirrored all over the country as the dead took to walking around and biting chunks out of people.

When, finally the TV played only static as the networks closed down, the hooker had known that her baby was going to die. And even worse than that, she had known that dying wasn't the worse thing that was about to happen to her offspring.

So she'd taken off her shoe and put the mite out of his misery.

The tiny corpse had finished rotting. The last of its fluids had drained out, congealed and dried on the hardwood floor beneath the crib. All that was left now were dried up, mummified remains that looked nothing like the pink, squealing bundle of life that she'd nurtured at her breast.

Before he'd died, little Jethro had bitten a lump out of his mother's cheek.

The hooker's stiff fingers crept up to touch the suppurating hole in her cheek as a vestige of memory maintained the connection between the wound and the tiny corpse in the crib. She made her way out of the grim nursery by homing in on the harsh sunlight that bullied its way through the narrow, filthy window next to her bed.

Instinct buried in the deepest recesses of the hooker's subconscious informed her that now was the time to prepare for the afternoon clientele, although she wasn't quite cognitive enough to register that said clients never actually came calling any more.

She wriggled out of her mini skirt and peeled the halter off over her head. As she did so, she pulled her right nipple away from its sagging mound and it plopped to the floor. She stood in front of her mirror in black panties and heels and contemplated.

Her body was still firm, her breasts remained full if somewhat downward facing, and the left one was still adorned with a large, dark pink nipple. Her stomach was flat and the outline of toned abs descended towards her pussy, interrupted by the thin, white smile of her caesarean scar. She had a few stretch marks here and there from her pregnancy but those were largely masked by the grey pallor of the decaying muscle beneath her skin.

The hooker peered hard at her own face as if trying to recognise it. Her clumsy hands reached for the cluttered array of make-up scattered over the dresser and she padded a soft foundation brush over her face. She grimaced as the bristles sank through the wound on her cheek and tickled her tongue. She pulled the brush out and it made a faint sucking sound as it squelched from face, the bristles glistening wet and clumped together with rot.

Eye shadow next, daubed on in haphazard fashion with poorly coordinated movements and, as hard as she tried, more went onto her forehead than her eyelids. Finally, the lipstick. She picked out a bright red, glossy color that accentuated the scabbed remains of her lips and spread it around her mouth the best she could, and over onto her shallow cheeks.

Satisfied with her makeup, the hooker stepped away from the mirror. She dropped to her knees and they let out a sharp report as tendons snapped. She scrabbled around under the metal-framed bed and her thin, brittle fingers pulled out a half dozen shoe boxes, each one labelled in teen-girlish red sharpie. She picked up the box that read *'A.S.P'* and placed it on the bed.

She'd used the boxes to store the gifts that her regular Johns bought for her, kept deliberately separate so she'd know which one was from which guy. In reality, the gifts tended to be more for the client's benefit than for hers, typically outfits that they paid her to wear. There was fetish stuff – leather, latex, cheap PVC mostly, clichéd, role-play outfits (French maid, Catwoman, schoolgirl – the practically ubiquitous Princess Leia gold bikini), and bizarrely shaped sex toys of all shapes and sizes.

Some of her more thoughtful clients bought her dresses and outfits that were not fetish although they did tend towards the shorter, revealing styles; as expensive as modest wages would allow, clothes they couldn't get their wives to wear.

The box that she tugged open had a rough-edged heart drawn onto the lid in baby pink lipstick, an echo of happier times. She pulled out a small, black dress, struggled to her feet and pulled it on. The soft fabric of the dress scuffed away small clumps of her scalp, which then clung to the shimmering fabric.

The dress clung to the hooker's every curve and accentuated her body with sensual lines. It came to an abrupt end at the curve of her pert bottom, tucking into that sexy crease between thigh and ass. The collar was high and fastened by a small zip at the nape of her neck and the back was simply non-existent; the flimsy material scooped low to expose her entire back and just the slightest hint of buttock cleft.

She had dim, distant memories associated with the dress. Memories that hung around the less decomposed parts of her brain; of smiles and kindness, caring and compassion.

Coffee.

Although the hooker couldn't remember the *why*, she put on this dress at the same time every fourth Wednesday of the month.

The hooker smoothed the dress over her slim frame and her remaining nipple stiffened at the touch of her wasted hands. She sat down on the edge of her bed with her legs outstretched and stared blankly at the disintegrating toes that peeped out from the ends of her shoes.

And she waited.

FOUR

August's palms were moist and he felt the sweat trickling down his back. He genuinely couldn't think of a time when he'd felt more ill at ease. August gulped down deep breaths and told himself that it had been the walk through the apartment block and up three flights of litter-strewn stairs that had made him overheat, and not that he was as nervous as hell.

He'd parked his car a couple of blocks away – old habits die hard, he supposed. Danielle's neighborhood had never been the most pleasant to walk through in the Before Time, and when zombies had become a *real* problem, slums and drug-infested tenements such as this had been the first to be cleaned out by the Army. They'd systematically swept through and shot indiscriminately at anything that moved, living *or* undead. Then, they had rounded up whoever was left, and shot them as well. The resulting corpses were thrown into the back of garbage trucks and carted away to the incinerators and neighborhoods like this had become some of the safest places to be.

August's footsteps echoed in hollow rhythm on the concrete walkways as he walked. Like most places nowadays, the apartment building had succumbed to the smothering, empty silence.

He fiddled absently with the ring in his pocket and felt like a teenager on a first date. After six months of his whole world – *the* whole world – being turned inside out and upside down, August would have thought that any lingering anxiety he might have had of hearing the word '*no*' from a girl would have been diminished. But sadly no, the fear of rejection was as deeply ingrained in him as with any man and although things were different now, there were some things that *never* changed.

One more deep breath and August knocked on the door.

FIVE

Stirred by the timid knock on her door, the hooker struggled from the edge of her bed. She stood up, wobbled as her ankles threatened to give way in her precipitous shoes and steadied herself against the dresser. A cascade of make-up paraphernalia fell to the floor with a plastic clatter. She shuffled towards the door and grasped the handle on her third attempt.

Opened it.

"Hi," August said, feeling awkward and very much like a rain-soaked Hugh Grant on Andi McDowell's doorstep. "It's wonderful to see you again," as polite as his mother had taught him. "You look beautiful."

The hooker stepped aside to allow August in, holding onto the doorframe as she stumbled slightly. August thought that she looked pleased to see him, fancied he saw a smile on her rotting lips. He looked into her eyes, searching for that remnant of the Danielle she had been before. To his absolute delight, August saw that her eyes were still the same iridescent blue that he had fallen in love with, albeit sunken into her skull some and marred by cloudy cataracts.

The rest of her, however, didn't look so good.

Her skin had the sickly bluish-gray sallowness that was common amongst the dead, it was cracked, split and oozed a foul green/brown slime. In places, eruptions of liquid putrescence pushed to the surface and threatened to burst through like miniature, pustulent volcanoes.

Danielle's body seemed far thinner, more angular than when August had last been this close to her and the soft flesh of her prominent cheeks was now peeling away to reveal the yellowing bone beneath. Clumps of his love's red hair were sloughing from her wasted scalp, and stuck in the viscid ooze of her face like ancient creatures in a tar pit.

A stink of rot and decay wafted from the hooker like some gruesome perfume but like all survivors, August had grown used to the pervading stench of death and it barely bothered him.

August noticed that Danielle had on the dress that he'd bought for her to wear during their liaisons – *their* dress – and it gladdened his aching heart. She had been waiting for him. Did he dare hope that this was a sign that she felt the same way as him?

"How have you been?" August's wilted attempt to make small talk was met with a guttural grunt. "I'm sorry I haven't been around for a while. But, you know how crazy things have been lately." He stopped himself short and felt embarrassed at his *faux-pas;* he was babbling again, always did with Danielle, damned nerves.

August clamped his tongue firmly between his front teeth to force himself to stay silent. The last thing he wanted to do right now was to put the gal off with his incessant jibber-jabber. He followed Danielle towards the bed that had been the scene of many trysts.

Unfortunately, it looked a little less inviting than he remembered it, the covers were crumpled in an unruly heap at the foot of the bed to leave the bare mattress exposed and there were ominous-looking stains splashed across the mattress in dried patches that spanned the spectrum between dried blood red and the greenish-black of putrefaction.

Despite the sickening lurch in his gut, August smiled at Danielle and fiddled with the ring in his pocket. The gold felt warm and smooth and the huge diamond dug into his fingertips.

The hooker turned to face her client and something that could easily have been a smile forced itself across her face. She reached both hands behind her neck and plucked at the zipper with uncooperative fingers.

"No." August pulled her arms away. "Leave it on."

SIX

The hooker's lips split open and wept a rust-red fluid beneath the tawdry lip-gloss as her face contorted into some semblance of a seductive smile. Her eyes burned into August's with animal lust and something else quite intangible that he just couldn't quite put a handle on.

She bent forwards to reach beneath the hem of her dress, hooked her bony thumbs through the waistband of her panties and slid them down. As she did so, viscous globs of snot-green slime snaked downwards along her legs and pooled between her feet. Delicate tendrils of the putrescent gloop made translucent strings between her thighs as they slopped noisily to the floor.

It made August think of melted cheese on fresh-from-the-oven pizza.

August undressed himself, taking great care to slip the ring onto his left pinkie finger, diamond facing inwards. Didn't want to ruin any surprises now, did he?

Danielle climbed onto the bed and reclined with her arms above her head to create an illusion of sexy.

August's eyes wandered up along Danielle's legs and peeked beneath her dress. There he saw her ruined vulva; once deliciously pink and slick and inviting, now it glistened with the silvery green of suppurating flesh. Base instinct overrode disgust and August's penis twitched to life.

August climbed onto the reeking bed and lay beside his love. He stroked her body and reacquainted with every line and curve. His hand rose with the twin mounds of her breasts and dipped with the hollow of her flat belly. And then August ventured down towards that special place where he found a slick, inviting wetness into which his fingers sank. And when he pulled his sticky fingers out of her, Danielle delighted him by licking the discolored rot from them.

Danielle rolled August over on to his back and heaved her decaying body on top of him. She straddled him as one would a steer and her stiletto heels dug into the soft meat of his thighs, just how she remembered he liked it. The hooker positioned her dripping sex just so and lowered herself down on to August's penis.

August gasped as he slipped with ease between Danielle's labia and slid deep into her vagina. She was pleasingly wet for him, so much so that her juices drenched his groin and soaked into the mattress under his plump ass. August groaned at the delightful moisture that made their bodies slick, although he understood that it was more the by-product of her putrefaction than of arousal.

But he was happy to pretend for the sake of love.

The hooker ground herself hard against August, using her hands to support herself against the wall above his head. As she made love to him, a cacophony of grunts escaped from her throat and gave the impression that she was truly enjoying their copulation.

August squirmed and bucked his hips as the pressure in his dick built towards an unbearable, almost painful crescendo. It had been an age since he'd done this, and there had been only so much frustration that onanism could alleviate.

August thrust his fingers into Danielle's hair as he came and accidentally dislodged her left ear. It slid down her neck and hit his chest with a *splat*. The hooker clamped his hips tightly with her thighs and grunted with her own orgasm.

SEVEN

It was done.

The hooker looked down at August, his face and torso flushed red in the afterglow, his eyes half closed.

August looked up at his Danielle and for the first time in six months felt entirely at peace. She had always accepted him for who he was; there had never been the need for pretence. In that respect, she was the one who had found his awkwardness *cute*.

"Thank you," he said, forever the consummate gentleman. "You are quite exquisite."

Taking her hands from the wall, Danielle placed one on either side of his chest and lowered her face towards his. She smiled again and her peeling lips parted to display discolored teeth.

"I love you, Danielle," August blurted out, unable to help himself. He then liberated the diamond ring from his sweating finger. "And I was going to ask you if you would –"

A rasping snarl spewed from the hooker's rotting lips and she lunged at August's exposed throat, her teeth bared in an obscene grin, mouth dripping its fetid juice,

August struggled as his lover's teeth sank deep into his neck and he felt some snap off in his flesh. He opened his mouth wide to cry out, but no sound came save a strangled mewling noise as the air whistled through the rip in his windpipe. He tried to push her away but she was too strong and he could feel his life drain away along with the blood that Danielle slurped from his lacerated throat.

August tunnelled his fingers into Danielle's hair and in a macabre emulation of their recent passion, he drew her closer to him.

EIGHT

August S Phillips and Danielle – *his* Danielle – walked along the street hand-in-hand. They had the slow, unsteady gait of the living dead and they looked for all the world like besotted lovers.

He was naked with a scarlet bib of blood covering his chest, she wore spiked heels and the tiny black dress that showed off her shapely legs, clung to her rounded buttocks and exposed the sensuous curve of her spine. The engagement ring hung loosely from the remnants of the fourth finger of her left hand, the diamond glinting in what light remained from the bloated, setting sun.

They shuffled their way towards their favorite coffee shop.

There they would sit amongst the debris and ruins of a world that once was, and wait patiently for someone who would never come to serve them. And neither of them would care all that much, because they were together and in love and because things were very much different now.

What You Wish For

1

Honeymoon DeVries fidgeted in the hard wooden chair, uncomfortable under the judgemental stare of her son's Principal. She fiddled self-consciously with the halter strap of the gold lame top that showed off her breasts and bare midriff and stole a glance downwards at the black lycra mini skirt that barely concealed her endless, toned legs. Honeymoon wished to dear God that she had been wearing something a little less immodest than her work get-up when the Principal's secretary had called; if only she'd not broken her own strict rule and answered the damned call at work.

This had to be even worse, she thought, than all of the innumerable times in her own chequered school career that she had been summoned to the Principal's office. Honeymoon had been a less than exemplary student throughout most of her school days, only just graduating by the skin of her pearly-whites because of a school system that had made it a near-on impossibility for her to fail. She'd been quite proud of that achievement but her Mom had told her at the time that it was most likely that the school had graduated her because they didn't want her trouble-making ass back for another year.

She felt sad, deep down, through to the core sad. She couldn't be sure if her sadness was because sitting here opposite the stern-faced, grey suited man with the unnaturally black hair – dyed, or was that *thing* on his head a hairpiece? – was bringing back memories of her own shortcomings and all of the disappointed looks and tongue-clucking that had followed along in their aftermath, or because this was about Ritchie?

Honeymoon glanced across at her son, who suddenly was looking very much smaller than his ten years, and very afraid. He sat motionless in the blue plastic chair next to hers, his large, brown fawn-eyes looking so incredibly upset.

Right now, as angry as she was at her offspring, all Honeymoon wanted to do was hold him to her overflowing bosom and weep.

"I'm very, very sorry that it has come to this Mrs. DeVries," the Principal said, but his slow voice belied the fact that, in reality, he was not *very, very sorry* in the least.

"Miss," Honeymoon corrected. "It's *Miss* DeVries."

This only seemed to make the man's demeanor worse; nothing like throwing gasoline onto the raging fire of his prejudice.

Where to start, really? Single Mothers? Mothers who get knocked up at seventeen? Black women from the Estates? Black Women in general? Honeymoon was just one great big, fucking cliché.

"I'm sorry. *Miss*," the Principal snorted and peered with derision over the top of his bi-focals. Honeymoon wondered if they were taught that look at Teacher

College and they held it in reserve especially for times such as this.

"As you are aware, this is the third time this semester that Ritchie has been summoned to my office?"

"Yes, Sir, I am," Honeymoon replied. "And I'd just like to say —"

"— and that we have a three-strikes policy at this school?" the Principal interrupted. He shuffled his skinny ass around in his chair like the furniture was too big for him.

"You did mention that the last time," Honeymoon said and her voice hardened some. She could already see full well where this was going; it was kind of like watching *Titanic;* you knew damned well that the ship was going to sink at the end, but you couldn't help but keep on watching.

"Ah yes, the last time." The principal leafed through a fat file with his stubby fingers. The file had her son's name neatly printed on the front cover. "Yes, here it is." He smoothed the report down on his blotter and peered down at it as if it were the most important sheet of paper on the planet.

"Swearing at a teacher, refusing to quit talking when asked, *and* assaulting another student."

"We went through all this before," Honeymoon protested, knowing with a heavy heart that arguing with this officious dickwad would do her — and her son — no good at all. "He was provoked; the other kid called him a n—"

"— and now we have this latest incident." The Principal puffed out his chest, all full of self-importance. As if scaring the living shit out of ten year old boys was the man's one and only delight in life. "Tell me." he leaned forward, lowering his voice to emphasise his gravitas. "Have you considered having Ritchie tested? There are some really good clinics I could recommend."

Honeymoon glowered at the Principal and physically bit down on her tongue until her eyes watered and she had the unmistakable, coppery taste of blood in her mouth. Just what was it with people like him insisting that everyone be *tested* for anything and everything? There was little wonder that the United States was rapidly becoming a country of hypochondriacs and rich Asian doctors! Luckily, common sense prevented Honeymoon from pointing this out to the nasty little man behind the desk; to do so could only have meant one possible outcome, and she still held on to a fragile thread of hope. Honeymoon studied the Principal and would have bet her last welfare check that he'd been bullied at school. Thoughts of wedgies, swirlies and the whole gamut of schoolkid humiliations being inflicted upon the Principal as a child curled the corners of her mouth in the semblance of a wry smile.

"I am sure that you will agree, *Miss* DeVries, that we simply cannot be expected to tolerate this type of disruptive and disrespectful behavior. Not under any circumstances," the Principal droned on. "And that you will understand that I have no alternative than to suspend Ritchie from school until the end of this semester."

Honeymoon felt the bile rising in her throat, choking her with its bitter, acidic tang.

"But that's three weeks," she sputtered, angry with herself for showing her frustration in front of the prick in the suit. "I have to work."

The Principal leaned back in his chair, the faux-leather creaked. "Well, perhaps young Ritchie here should have thought about *that* before exhibiting such deplorable behavior." A look, quite possibly smug, flittered across the man's pallid face. Was it possible that he was *actually* enjoying this?

"But I have to work," Honeymoon said, as if repeating her only remaining protest would make any grain of difference to the man.

It didn't.

"Miss DeVries," the Principal patronized. "We are an elementary school, not a day care facility. And I do have the other students to consider; those who actually do wish to learn." He fidgeted in his seat, becoming acutely aware – and uncomfortable with – Honeymoon's growing anger. He'd been assaulted by pissed-off parents more times than he cared to remember, which was why his finger poised nervously over the panic button he'd had installed on the underside of his desk.

Honeymoon swallowed hard as her brain raced. She'd been in this place so many times with Ritchie during the course of his less than illustrious academic career to date that she wouldn't be surprised if the school district gave her a named parking spot. Different schools, different towns, same old crap.

Of course, she knew that her son's behavior was deplorable, and heaven knows she'd tried to talk to him about it. But for as much as he smiled and told her he was going to get his shit together, Honeymoon knew in her heart that she'd be here again before long – if not in this exact chair, then another chair in another office and facing yet one more Principal who looked down his snooty nose at her whilst informing her that her son, Ritchie was, in effect, a *Bad Apple*.

But suspending a child who clearly didn't want to be in school in the first place? Now, Honeymoon considered that to be just plain stupid. Talk about rewarding bad behavior, or negative reinforcement or whatever labels the school councelors liked to stick to such things. Way to guarantee the boy's future lack of respect once the suspension was over!

Honeymoon glowered at the Principal and hated him for backing her into this corner *and* for judging her as a mother. And above all, she hated him for being right.

"How dare you?" she heard herself saying.

"Pardon me?" the Principal sounded surprised. Honeymoon guessed that the women in the sad little man's life rarely raised their voices to him.

"You sit there in your dumb chair behind your dumb desk and pass judgement on me and my son!" Honeymoon stood up and she towered over the now considerably paler Principal. She couldn't see it, but she guessed that by now that skinny finger of his would be twitching like a dying squirrel over his big red panic button. "You sit there and call my son disrespectful and rude and tell me that I haven't taught him how to behave properly when all *you* can do is try to catch a look up my skirt and cop an eyeful of sideboob!" She pointed an accusing finger at the man, painfully aware that the fake fingernail that adorned it was cracked clean down its center.

"I – I can assure you that I am most certainly not –" the Principal stammered as his faced reddened.

"Save it, asshole!" Honeymoon exploded. She grabbed Ritchie's arm and with a dramatic flourish, dragged her son from the office and took great care to slam the door hard behind her.

The satisfying sound of the frosted glass rattling in its frame echoed in Honeymoon's ears as she marched her errant child down along the hallway. The conflicts that battled in her head made her vision all red and tears of frustration welled up to blur everything. She wanted to protect and mother her son, keep him far away from all the horrible people who made their ill-informed conclusions and treated him like something unpleasant they'd just stepped in on the sidewalk.

And then there was the part of Honeymoon that would quite merrily have drowned her own son in a bucket.

"Nice one, Mom." Ritchie looked up at her with his sad face. He knew better than to complain that his mother's nails were dug deep into the soft flesh of his upper arm. "You sure put that asshole in his place."

"Shut it, Ritchie." Honeymoon cuffed her son hard over his right ear, taking no pleasure at his startled whimper.

"*OWW!* Mom!" Ritchie whined and pulled hard against her grip. "I hate you! I hate it here! I wish I was someplace else!"

And there it was again – the mantra that his Grandpa had taught him to help get him through the rough times, and which was guaranteed without fail to wrench on that special place in the heart where a Mother's love resided. There were times – like this – when Honeymoon imagined she could physically feel her heart breaking, one tiny piece at a time.

"I just don't understand you, Ritchie. You're my own flesh and blood," the words choked in Honeymoon's throat, "but sometimes I feel as if I don't know you even one little bit. I know things are tough for us right now, but I do try my best to be a good mother."

Fat tears drip-dropped down Honeymoon's cheeks now; they splashed onto her son's miserable, upturned face. She felt frustrated and angry and protective all at the same time and it hurt like hell. All she had ever wanted was to be a good Mom and a wife to someone who loved her, and all of this bullshit made Honeymoon feel so terribly alone.

Honeymoon strode towards the exit sign that seemed to be moving away, as if its purpose was to extend the humiliation of the black mom in an almost exclusively white school as she escorted her cliché of a son from the

351

premises. She sensed a myriad eyes staring at her, could sense them straining to catch a glimpse of the *Bad Single Mother* through the narrow slit-windows of every classroom door that she walked past.

Resolute to the bitter end, she kept her eyes faced forward, focussed on the red exit sign above the door that signalled her escape from this hell, determined that she would not be returning any of the stares to add to her observers' petty judgments.

The final classroom door – Room 3B – had a slightly larger window and something inside caught Honeymoon's eye. She turned her head and saw the teacher – a plump, tragically ginger-haired woman – who was pointing at her through the glass. The collective of small, inquisitive faces within the room gawked out at Honeymoon to add to her embarrassment. She could only begin to imagine the unpleasant things that Miss Plump-Ginger was telling the impressionable youngsters; *that's what happens if you don't apply yourself at school, that's what a terrible parent looks like.* Hell, she could even be telling them that Honeymoon and her boy were precisely what happened to kids who didn't eat their damned greens.

But it wasn't the overweight, copper-haired teacher that caught Honeymoon's attention as she hurried by; it was the woman who stood behind her. She had long, blonde hair that was scraped up into a severe bun that perched at the top of her head like some uber-neat bird's nest. She wore a calf-length, cream dress that clung to her curves and pushed up a generous, matronly bosom in a manner that really had no place in a third grade classroom.

And then there was the blonde woman's face – well, there was the strange thing. Although later, Honeymoon would convince herself that it was simply a trick of the fluorescent lights through her own tear-filled eyes, at that moment she would have sworn on her Mother's grave that the woman's face was moving, shifting in some weird, fluid manner as if undecided as to whom it was going to resemble today.

And then, the moment – fleeting as it was – was gone.

Honeymoon finally broke free of the school and its nasty, patronizing Principal and the accusing eyes that had all delighted in her shame. That and the most damned peculiar classroom assistant she thought she'd ever seen.

2

Roxy's Dive Bar – '*Free Pool!!!*' – was hardly the right and proper place for Bring-Your-Suspended-Kid-To-Work Day, but Honeymoon had no other choice but to drag Ritchie along with her directly from their calamitous meeting with the Principal. None of Honeymoon's friends were available at short notice and her Father-In-Law was having his quarterly check-up at the Spinal Injury Clinic.

Dawg, the bar manager, didn't even look up from the porn he was so engrossed in on his smartphone when Honeymoon trooped in late with her boy in tow. All he cared about was her getting down to some serious work to make up the time she'd lost dashing out when her kid's school had called. Honeymoon had at least had the good sense to secrete him in the farthermost reaches of the bar, where the shadows congealed black and inky and little light dared to venture.

The bar was a dingy, dank shithole but it served the best damned wings this side of town. The whole place reeked of stale cigarette smoke because the owners had discovered a loophole in the Anti-Smoking law – in so much that anyone who was in a position to pull Dawg up on the bar's infringement of said law really didn't give a crap what went on at Roxy's. After all, this was a place where women openly sold themselves for sexual favors and it was not uncommon to find human teeth on the sticky tables. In fact, the sickly tobacco stink was actually a welcome barrier to the all-pervasive, cloying stench of stale body odor; the stink of unwashed sweat and desperation.

Dawg peered around the place, sparsely populated as it was, and wondered absently who the odd looking woman hanging around the bathrooms belonged to. She wasn't one of his regular girls, that was for sure; she was dressed far too demure in her calf-length, off-white dress, although Dawg could tell that she had a nice rack on her, should she ever decide to show it off. That and she did seem to have the air of *waiting for someone* about her.

The bar manager snorted his disinterest. It wasn't all that unusual to see a non-working girl in Roxy's, as sometimes Johns would bring their wives or – more commonly – mistresses in to pick up a girl for a three-way. Some couples would venture in to take in the heady, sex-laden atmosphere before heading home for an over aroused, sordid fuck, whilst some of the bored housewives from the rich, gated estates would come in of their own accord looking to pick up some rough pussy to add a little sapphic excitement to their otherwise monotonous afternoons.

Honeymoon glanced over at Ritchie, who sat immersed in some beeping, flashing game or other on his cell and hidden behind a soda and large bag of chips that all but obscured his face. She buried her guilt behind the fakest of fake smiles and turned her attention to the john that sat in eager anticipation upon the bar stool next to her.

He'd told her his name was Sidney Styles, which Honeymoon knew was bullshit because the initials of the shabby brown briefcase he'd absently sat in a pool of stale beer on the bar were 'GD'. His sort did that all the time at Roxy's, as if terrified that the girls would track them down in the throes of unrequited love and beg them for marriage like some schmaltzy scene from *Pretty Woman*. And that thought always made Honeymoon smile.

And besides, Honeymoon had no place to complain about the guy's lack of honesty, since she'd introduced herself to the squat, balding little man as Sylvia.

"So tell me, Sylvia, what is a beautiful gal like you doing working in a place like this?" the cliché spilled from Sidney's fat mouth like saliva from a drooling dog. "I mean, you could be an actress, or a model or something." He fidgeted his extensive ass on the stool, a delicate balancing act as his flabby buttocks flowed either side of the harsh wood. The stools at the bar were designed to be uncomfortable, as that tended to accelerate the whole process of propositioning a girl and getting the punter away from the bar for the next schmuck in line. And it wouldn't be too much longer, Honeymoon predicted, before said proposition would be made; even if it was only so poor, fat old Sidney could get some feeling back in his ass.

"I used to do some modelling," Honeymoon lied. "But I find this job *far* more interesting. I meet the most *fascinating* people in here," she lied again and rested her hand on the man's chubby arm. She felt his goose flesh rise beneath her fingertips, a thousand tiny erections aroused by her touch.

Sidney chuckled, as if he hardly believed that such an exquisite creature as Sylvia could possibly find him of interest. "I think you should go back into the modelling, darlin'," he said. "Pretty thing like you should use what God gave her to every advantage."

"Oh, but I do." Honeymoon executed her well-practiced lean towards the man. One bare knee touched his leg and her bountiful breasts threatened to spill out onto his lap. She maintained eye contact the best she could with the man but his eyes were far too busy crawling over every inch of her exposed ebony skin.

"Mom?" Ritchie interrupted the tender moment. "Mom?" more insistent this time. "Can I have more soda?"

Honeymoon turned to face her son, her countenance one of fury.

"What have I told you –?"

"Hey!" Sidney stammered. "I didn't know there was a kid in on the deal." His eyes flittered to Ritchie, to Honeymoon and then straight to the door of the bar. "That's totally *not* my thing, lady –" and so saying he slid from his stool, groaning loudly as he straightened his fat legs.

"No, no, it's not like that –" Honeymoon sputtered as she caught Dawg's critical eye in her peripheral vision.

"I'm sorry, Miss, but I'm not getting caught up in that kind of scene – not again." Sidney slapped a crumpled twenty on the damp bar, grabbed his beer-soaked briefcase and hurried towards the door.

"You little shit!" Honeymoon snarled at Ritchie and slapped him smartly across the face. The sharp sound of her palm on his tender young skin resounded through Roxy's like a pistol shot.

Ritchie's mouth trembled and his eyes brimmed with the tears that he fought with all his resolve to keep at bay.

"Oh, sweet Baby Jesus, I am *so* sorry, Ritchie." Honeymoon's regret hit her hard – far harder than she had hit her child. "I didn't mean to –"

"I hate you!" Ritchie wailed as immediately he seized the advantage that his mother's guilt afforded. "I wish I was someplace else!" And upon delivering his *coup de grace,* Ritchie turned on his heels and stormed away; damned if he was going to let his mother see him cry.

Honeymoon cradled her face in her hands as she lost her own battle against the tears that welled up as her heart broke into a dozen pieces, and she sobbed.

"I think you should call it a day, darlin'," Dawg leaned over the bar with what could easily have been construed as genuine concern. "'Place's no fit place for a kid anyways," he offered in his inimitable growl. "I've told you that before." He then rested a comforting hand on Honeymoon's bare shoulder as she cried. Sometimes, Dawg mused as he watched Honeymoon's heartache, life could be real shit.

3

Ritchie stared out into the dark of the night that filled his bedroom. Everything he could see was shadows, eerie shades of gray and black, nebulous shapes.

Just how he liked it.

Unlike most of the other kids in his grade, Ritchie actually liked the dark. He found comfort in it, and a solitude that allowed him to pretend that the world he despised so had simply faded away into nothingness and he was all alone.

He could hear Mom through the paper-thin wall that separated their bedrooms and she was making those *noises* again. They were the all-too familiar sounds she always made when she had some guy around for a sleepover and she locked her bedroom door. Ritchie tuned his mind out to the giggles and strange moans, experience had taught him that soon enough the sounds would cease and the guy would leave shortly thereafter.

They always did.

In the periphery of his peripheral vision, Ritchie caught a movement. Something lurked in the blackest of the shadows that seemed to always gather around the battered army chest that served as his closet. The thing – whatever it was – appeared less than something *seen*, he thought, but more of a *feeling* that somebody – something – was there. Something that Ritchie felt he really needn't be seeing. Ritchie stared straight upwards at his low ceiling, his eyes picking out the slow, rhythmical rotation of the dust-laden fan that wobbled precariously beneath the single-bulb light fitting above his bed.

Fighting the urge to pull the comforter over his head and hide, Ritchie forced himself to look into the darkest of the dark shadows. Grandpa had told him on occasions such as this, if you looked directly at the things that skulked like ashamed things in the night shadows they would run away and hide from you. And that was because that was simply the natural order of things – like lions chase gazelle and not the other way around. And Grandpa would know, because, after all, he was The Cap'n.

Ritchie twisted his head around on the lumpy pillow and winced as the fine pricks of the feathers contained within scratched the cheek his Mom had assaulted earlier that day.

Suddenly, a face lurched out from the shadows. Disembodied and silent. She – Ritchie made out that it was feminine despite the liquid swirls and shifting of the features – came to a halt an arm's length from his bed and hovered there in the dark, scrutinising his terrified face.

Ritchie let out a muted, mewling sound and pulled himself under his bed clothes. He screwed up his eyes as tight as he possibly could even though that made everything even darker for him.

He lay still, not daring to move or call out. He'd heard that 'possums play dead and their predators just move on, so he hedged his bets towards that strategy. He daren't call out for his Mom; she'd more than likely beat the tar out of him for disturbing her twice in one day. So Ritchie remained as motionless as was humanly possible, breathing in the warm, stale air and the stink of his own nervous sweat that gathered beneath the covers, and he waited for the cold grasp of claw-hands or the hot, dripping embrace of a tooth-filled maw.

Nothing.

After a while, Ritchie began to doubt what he thought he had seen. A trick of the light – no, a trick of the dark – or a joke played by his over active imagination? Certainly it couldn't really have been a floating woman's head with no discernible, solid features? Now, that really was stupid.

Yet he cowered beneath the safety of the now-unbearably hot comforter – because, as every ten-year-old-knows, no ghost, ghoul or maniac killer can possibly get through that magical barrier.

Perhaps later, Ritchie though to himself, he would dare to stick his nose out to take in some much-needed cool air, but for now he preferred to err on the side of caution. He knew in his gut that it – *she* – was still out there, hovering over his bed and just waiting for him to come out.

Terrified beyond belief, Ritchie whispered his comforting mantra; the one The Cap'n had taught him especially for times such as this, the one that skewered his mother through the heart every time she heard him say it. "*I wish I was someplace else, I wish I was someplace else...*" he whispered to himself, over and over.

4

"It's grocery day already? I can't believe it's come around so soon." George DeVries – 'Grandpa', or 'The Cap'n' to Ritchie – grinned up at his daughter-in-law. His wheelchair ensured him an uncomfortable position at eye-level with Honeymoon's dark-skinned, tight-toned belly. He'd never been able to understand the younger generation's obsession with sticking holes in their bodies, but even he was forced to admit that he did find the dangling, diamanté jewelry that swung from Honeymoon's navel disturbingly attractive.

"Fridays do keep doing that." Honeymoon smiled a warm smile at the old man. "Pretty much every week, if I remember rightly."

"I can remember when a week lasted a whole seven days, back in the day," the old man said with a grin. "Now it seems more like you only get the four or five days."

"Now now, Dad, we don't have time to go wandering down memory lane right now."

"Memory Lane?" he chuckled. "It's more like Memory Cul-De-Sac for me these days." They both shared the laugh.

The old man loved how Honeymoon and Ritchie filled his lonely, cramped apartment with laughter and their inimitable *joie de vivre*; there was nowhere near enough of that in his life – or the world in general – these days.

Ritchie sat on the faded brown velour sofa, which according to Grandpa should be heralded in the Guinness Record Book as the *World's Most Comfiest Sofa Ever*. He nursed a generic brand cola drink that was rapidly turning warm in Grandpa's un-air-conditioned apartment and watching *Ninja Turtle* reruns on Nickelodeon. Ritchie loved visiting with The Cap'n –

the old man insisted Ritchie call him that – this was his safe place, somewhere where the outside world didn't dare invade; a sanctuary from a reality filled with strange men that visited his Mom in the night, petty minded Principals and weird, faceless things that floated over his bed in the darkest hours of the night.

Honeymoon sat herself down opposite her Father-in-Law. She looked deep into his kind old eyes and fretted a little about that ever-present, grayish tinge to his pale skin. She loved the man as a father, more so in fact than her own pious hypocrite of a father. George DeVries had taken Honeymoon into his heart as his own flesh and blood that very first time his son had brought her home to say hi. And, he had kept her there long after Richard had gotten himself all shot up and killed in those terrible, early days of Afghanistan.

Richard and Honeymoon had been married less than three months when Richard was sent back home in a black Ziploc, and Honeymoon had been six months gone with Ritchie. Her parents had disowned her the minute she'd told them she was pregnant and to this day it was not one hundred percent certain if that was because she was underage by just over twelve months, or that it was that Richard was a white boy. Whatever their reasons, the Good Lord Jesus had informed Honeymoon's folks that they were totally justified in packing up her bags and dumping them and their daughter unceremoniously in the street. And as far as George knew, that was the last time his son's wife had set eyes on either of her parents.

And now the poor girl still faced the prejudice of those that chose to judge her, that were happy to make up their own back stories about the black single mom struggling to give her offspring the best start in life. Probably, if she was to explain the circumstances that had led her to this point in life, they would understand and look a little less down their noses at her?

But, then again, why the hell should she? It was her life, and what was happening therein was none of their damned business.

George had given his son and his new wife a home in the tiny apartment until she and Richard had saved up enough for a place all of their own. The old man had not once judged Honeymoon, never belittled or looked down on her; his love for the gal who stole his only son's heart was as unconditional as it comes.

And now, now it was Honeymoon's turn to give back. She kept the old man's apartment clean, ran the odd errand, and grocery-shopped each Friday for the meager rations he afforded himself. Honeymoon knew that George had little money to his name as his disability didn't stretch too far and the money he'd made from his TV show back in the 1980's was long-gone, courtesy of a poisonous ex-wife and the divorce from hell.

The old man gave Honeymoon a twenty with his shopping list each week, and she knew full well that she would have to spend at least forty. Even so, she'd never said a word to him about that; the extra came out of her own pocket even though she could ill afford it herself. George DeVries was a proud man and she wasn't going to be the one to take that pride away from him. She also knew that it would kill his soul if he ever knew just how she made the money that went towards his provisions.

"I have my list all ready for you, sweetheart," George said with his usual good cheer as he wheeled over to the two-person kitchen table. "If you could pick up my pain-meds prescription from the in-store pharmacy while you're there, I'd be ever so grateful." He handed Honeymoon a twenty dollar bill and a list written on the back of last week's till receipt.

The old man gave Honeymoon his best smile and studied her face as she studied his. He thought she was looking older of late, far older than the twenty-seven that was waiting for her next month. A trouble kid will do that to a person. George figured that Ritchie must have been playing her up again; the tension between the two of them was almost palpable. The kid wasn't a bad'un, he just needed a strong father figure in his life to keep him on the straight and as much as it broke his heart to think it, George wished that Honeymoon would find herself a nice young man to take care of her and the boy. Ten years was a long time to mourn, especially for a bright young thing like Honeymoon.

Of course, the kid worshipped his Grandpa, and he the boy. After all, Ritchie was all that remained of his own son and he was some assurance that the DeVries bloodline would continue for at least another generation.

It made the old man's heart smile that the kid agreed to call him '*The Cap'n*' and bragged to all of his friends that his Grandpa had injured his back doing all his own stunts – upon which he *always* insisted thank you very much – for his TV show, *Captain Magnanimous*, back in the old, old days.

The truth was though, that George DeVries suffered from an inherited degenerative back disease and that had put him in the damned wheelchair. It was a condition that had plagued the men folk of the DeVries family for generations, dating back to some rogue gene that first reared its malignant head in the mid eighteen-hundreds. Now, there was something for young Master DeVries to look forward to in later life.

The *Captain Magnanimous* TV show had run from '81 to '87 on network TV. It had ridden high in those more innocent days when the threat of ultimate evil could easily be dealt with by skilful negotiation and fair play and not ninja moves and fancy laser guns. The

Cap'n's favorite episode – and Ritchie's – was the third in season six when The Cap'n had thwarted an alien invasion with nothing more than intelligent mediation and an extensive pamphlet campaign. The old man liked to think of the show as being a cerebral *McGuyver* for the under-elevens.

And now here he was, a lifetime on from those heady days, reduced to trundling around in a cheap CVS wheelchair and ever more reliant upon his ageing laptop to keep in touch with a world that had become a mystery to his ageing mind. Once, he had harbored hopes of a resurgence of interest in *Captain Magnanimous* along with the nostalgic waves that had given rebirth to *Transformers*, *Batman*, *Ninja Turtles* and *He-Man*. Perhaps one day, his 'phone would ring and there'd be a fat-cheque waved in his face for a cameo in the big-screen Michael Bay version of *Captain Magnanimous*, or at the very least a voice-over for a CGI TV series.

One day.

"You staying with the Cap'n?" George asked Ritchie. The boy glanced up at his mother, desperate to stay in his happy place.

"I'm sorry, Dad, but Ritchie's coming with me today. I need his help getting your groceries up those three flights of stairs." Honeymoon frowned at the old man. "When *are* they going to fix the elevator, Dad? It's been four weeks now!"

Grandpa shrugged his shoulders. Truth is, he really didn't know. He'd not spoken to anyone but his physician, Honeymoon and the kid in months. He saw Ritchie implore him with those big, brown puppy-dog eyes of his from his sanctuary of the comfy sofa.

"Best do as Mom says, Ritchie," Grandpa mediated, "she needs a strong man help her carry all my stuff. And besides, I got some internetting that needs doing. We can chill and hang out when you get back?"

Ritchie shrugged and pulled a face.

"Maybe we can catch up on Season Two of *Captain Magnanimous*?" George suggested, as cheery as he could muster. "We're up to the two-parter where I single-handedly save the Earth from the evil Dr. Narcissus and yet another of his doomsday devices." George's spirits lifted as he saw the boy's disposition visibly lighten, and an unwitting smile twitched the corners of his young mouth. They both loved their man-time and it was pleasing that Ritchie actually enjoyed the crappy effects and formulaic story lines of the show; The Cap'n single-handedly saved the Earth *every* week - if not from arch-nemesis Narcissus, then from some foam-latex clad things from another dimension-slash-galaxy-slash-time.

Ritchie downed the last of the warm, flat soda and with resigned reluctance followed his Mom out of the apartment, mumbling quietly away at his mantra as he kicked at the cigarette butts his feet found along the gray, concrete hallway.

5

"I can't believe they moved the damned things. *Again*," Honeymoon grumbled as she scanned the store's pickle aisle a third time. Every goddamned week, they put the candied – with a 'K' – Jalapenos in a different place. Honeymoon was almost convinced that they did it just to piss her off. "Hey Ritchie, help me look for Grandpa's jalapenos will you? Those ones he likes – with the white lid?"

"Would you be interested in having a professional photographic portrait of your child, Ma'am?" a melodious voice interrupted. Honeymoon spun around to face the young salesgirl who eagerly thrust a bright leaflet in her direction.

"No thank you," Honeymoon replied, startled by the woman's sudden appearance. "I know what the little shit looks like already." It was an attempt at brevity that came out a tad too terse. The salesgirl glowered at Honeymoon like she was Casey Anthony's less pleasant sister and walked away.

Ritchie looked up at his Mom, amused by her obvious embarrassment yet still sporting the sullen face he'd adopted the moment he'd left his Grandpa's apartment. He shrugged his shoulders and gave a cursory glance at the grocery store shelves.

Honeymoon sighed an exasperated sigh. It wasn't for the jalapenos themselves – although Dad did love them – and though they were overly expensive at five bucks a jar, it was more than worth double that to spoil him. It was a sigh from deep down in her troubled soul for her usual frustration; Ritchie. Honeymoon struggled to comprehend just how surly her son had become of late. Surely, with his teens still a few years off, she could have expected to have had her sweet little boy for a little while longer? But no, he was already metamorphosing into the miserable, ungrateful child that she guessed all boys turned into sooner or later.

"Come on, Ritchie, it's for Grandpa. You know they're his favorite."

"I s'pose," Ritchie chuntered and continued his half-assed search for the illusive pickles.

Honeymoon gritted her teeth once more to hold in the temper felt rising up in her throat on a wave of acidic bile that created a nauseous feeling in the pit of her stomach. She did her level best to ignore the sensation and scanned the upper shelf.

"I hate it here," Ritchie grumbled, somewhat predictably. "I wish I was someplace else."

"And right now, Ritchie DeVries, I wish you were someplace else too!" Honeymoon snapped, not giving a flying crap about how many of her fellow shoppers heard her outburst, and deliberately *not* looking down at her son. No way did she want him to see the tears that filled her eyes.

And when Honeymoon did eventually glance down, Ritchie was gone.

"For Christ's sakes, child –" Honeymoon growled. She scanned her eyes over towards the video games department, which was the boy's second most favorite place in the store after the candy aisle. Cursing him beneath her breath, Honeymoon grabbed the cart and pushed it hard towards said candy aisle, damned if she was going to give Ritchie the satisfaction of calling out for him in the middle of the store and soliciting *Bad Mother* stares from all and sundry. She did vow, of course, to tan his damned hide when she did catch up with him.

Ritchie was not in the games department, nor was he on the candy aisle.

Honeymoon abandoned her cart and walked with hastening steps between the aisles, feeling her anger dissolve into that chest-gripping panic that all parents seem destined to go through at least once in their child's life.

"Ritchie?" she raised her voice, ignoring the stares that shot her way. "Ritchie!" again, a little louder.

Nothing.

The foreboding that embraced Honeymoon's heart felt like myriad icy, dead fingers that threatened to claw the very life from her.

"RITCHIE!!!!" she screamed at the top of her voice, all thoughts of other shoppers' judgement dissipating. She ran from aisle to aisle in a blind frenzy, screaming her son's name down each one and imploring the indifferent shoppers to help in her search. Happening upon an elderly store assistant, Honeymoon grabbed his

arm and begged him to lock down the store and put out a Tannoy alert for her son.

Everyone in the grocery store eyed her as if she were some mad woman, but Honeymoon knew deep inside that someone had taken her son.

"RITCHIE!!!!"

Ritchie Devries watched his Mother as she searched for him around the store. He was scared by her growing hysteria and struggled to comprehend what exactly was going on. He could see that Mom was mad because her nostrils always flared like that when she got *real* mad – like the time she'd caught him and Benny Gill playing with matches in the bathroom. It was the *why* that puzzled him.

It made no sense to Ritchie because he was *right there*, literally beneath her nose.

"Mom?" he said with a quiver in his voice, "I'm right here." Had the woman gone blind? Crazy? Both? He watched his Mom as she craned her neck to peer across the store and scream his name one more time.

"I'm here, Mom, please don't get mad at me." Ritchie was scared now; his Mother's rage – albeit incredibly rare – terrified Ritchie. And although she rarely laid a finger on him in anger, there were times when he wished she would strike him instead of giving him that hurt, disappointed look when she got *really really* mad.

Ritchie saw his Mom mutter beneath her breath, looked on helplessly as she grabbed the cart and spun it around, the thing directly aimed at him.

Ritchie felt nothing as the cart – and his mother – went straight through him.

"Mom!" Ritchie called after her. "MOM!" his voice was forced, shrill. Terrified. He reached out to her and his hand pushed against something that felt weird; slightly yielding, yet intangible, like an invisible bubble of some kind. Then the floor beneath his feet began to feel all kinds of wrong, with the hard tiles taking on a spongy feel that sucked at his feet like ravenous mouths to give him the queasy feeling of him being pulled downwards.

"I'M HEEEEEEERE!!!!" Ritchie screamed as loudly as he could, the panic in his voice matching his mother's. Ritchie's heart pounded fast and hard in his chest and his ears roared with a loud, piping tinnitus that drowned out even his Mom's raised voice.

Ritchie began to cry.

"She can't hear you, Ritchie," a soft, soothing voice purred in his ear.

He turned around, startled but with hope in his heart that at least *someone* had acknowledged his existence.

"How –" the words caught in his throat.

It was the woman from his bedroom. The one with the nightmare swirling, ever-changing face. She bent over Ritchie's trembling form, her weird face uncomfortably close to his, and he imagined he saw the semblance of a smiling mouth that shimmered below her twinkling eyes; one of them blue, one the brightest green.

Behind the woman, instead of the store's uniform rows of pickles in all of their guises, Ritchie saw only white.

"You need to come with me, Ritchie," the woman whispered, her voice at once both terrifying and comforting to the boy. She stood up, her tall frame towering above him and the intricate pattern of her cream-colored dress spun and danced before Ritchie's eyes, much as her face had done mere moments before. She reached out a hand for him to hold.

Fighting against everything he had been taught about *Stranger Danger*, Ritchie found his hand grasped by the lady's hand. It felt warm, inviting and held promises of love and belonging and understanding. He glanced over at his mother, watched her pace around the store with tears streaming down her face, and listened to her panicked cries for him to *damn-well answer her right now!* with deepening detachment.

"It's time to go." The woman tugged gently on Ritchie's hand and led him towards the stark whiteness that glowed behind her.

"Where are we going?" he asked.

The strange woman's benign, shifting, smiling features gazed down at Ritchie's upturned face. "To where you've always wanted to be," she replied.

6

Honeymoon slammed the apartment door shut behind her, a final act of *fuck-you* to the outside world that had, that very afternoon, swallowed her son without a trace. She kicked off her shoes and flopped onto the cheap, red vinyl couch that dominated her compact living room.

It was late, well after ten and well past Ritchie's bedtime. On any other day, he'd be safely tucked up in his bed, thinking she couldn't hear his handheld electronic games from under his sheets whilst she pretended not to hear the electronic beeps and explosions.

Tonight was different, the place was entirely silent.

It was that eerie kind of silence that creeps around to smother you with its lonely presence, a still quiet that can only be banished by another living presence. Honeymoon guessed that was why people bought even the dumbest of pets – fish, small birds, lizards, those fat, hairy-assed spiders – just to have something alive around them to break the spell of that terrible, lonely silence.

She closed her eyes and sought comfort in the darkness. Honeymoon was long-since all cried out, she had no more tears to sting her eyes and erode her make-up, and was exhausted of those huge, wracking sobs that made her chest ache.

It had been the store manager – something, something Patel, if she recalled his name badge correctly – who had called in the police. There was a crazy woman disrupting his store and questioning his staff as to what they had done with her son and why the fuck couldn't they lock the doors and she had proved too much for him to handle on his salary. Honeymoon figured she couldn't blame the poor man, she had been pretty much beyond reasoning by the time he'd come down to the shop floor to deal with her. Way beyond his pay grade.

The police, she could have done well without. Of course, they were now out looking for Ritchie, but Honeymoon sure as hell didn't need their accusatory tones and suspicious looks any more than she needed their scrutiny, but what the fuck else could she do? They'd even mentioned her getting a DNA sample from something of his – hair from his brush, his toothbrush – and they very much hoped that it wouldn't come to that but they'd let her know. Shit, something else to prey on her mind, the cops prying around in her secrets. That *really* was the very last thing she needed right now.

We understand that you were observed physically assaulting your son at his school yesterday afternoon, Miss DeVries. Some surly-looking cop in a dark blue suit had told her, as much as accusing her of being a habitually abusive parent. And, the more Honeymoon had explained that she'd merely cuffed the boy around the head, the more she'd been left feeling like the cop thought she'd murdered her own son in the store and hidden his corpse amongst the damned pickle jars.

And what exactly had the cop mean by; *You were heard by several witnesses to be having an argument with Ritchie just before his disappearance?* They thought he'd simply run off? That he was so shit-scared of his own mother that escaping into the Big Bad World beyond the grocery store was preferable to being with her? Just what kind of mother were they making her out to be?

Our records show that you work at Roxy's Bar. Ah yes, there was precisely the kind of mother they were painting her as. *Your employers tell us that you had the boy in the bar with you yesterday afternoon. Is that correct, Miss DeVries?* Fucking Dawg, couldn't keep his goddamned mouth shut to save his worthless life.

And there she'd been for the whole day, and well into the night. Stuck in the stifling, gray-walled interrogation room with some overweight cop with halitosis so damned bad that it reached out to assault her nostrils with almost-visible tendrils. Yep, Honeymoon knew exactly what kind of mother the officious asshole had her pegged as.

A black single Mom who whored herself out in front of a ten-year-old in a dive bar, and worse still, who's then lost said child in a grocery store in broad daylight. And no mention of the struggling widow of a war hero who would do anything to support her child – *including* whore herself out – who's child had obviously been snatched and was at the mercy of Christ only knows who. No mention whatsoever.

Pretty fucking accurate assessment of the whole sorry situation, Honeymoon thought.

Of course, George had been a rock through all of this. From the moment she'd called him from the police station's ancient 'phone, he'd been one hundred percent supportive. No accusations from him at all, no suspicion.

He'd called in a few favors from some of his internet buddies and somehow managed to get himself down to the police station, despite the busted lift at his apartment block. He'd stayed the duration, holding her hand when she needed it, offering words of comfort when she could see that his own heart was breaking. He'd asked her to go home with him, rather than be alone in her – *her and Ritchie's* – apartment, but Honeymoon had wanted to be home for when Ritchie came home.

If.

Jesus H Christ, girl, Honeymoon chastised herself, that's no way at all for you to be thinking right now! Not now, not *ever*. She had come home because that would be where Ritchie *would* come back to, or where the police *would* bring him once they figured where he'd run off to. She had to hold on to that; to be certain that she would see her son again.

7

George DeVries heaved a sigh and hoped against hope that his daughter-in-law wasn't picking up on his misery from her end of the phone line.

"I know this is hard, Honeymoon, but you really must try to stay as positive as you can," he said softly and his heart broke a little more with each one of her sobs. "I'm sure Ritchie will be home safe and well before you know it." In his own heart, George held a small, dark place that told him that no such thing was going to happen.

He'd spent some time on the 'net since he'd returned home with the sour stink of the police station clinging to his clothes. Seeing Honeymoon in her inconsolable state had hit the old man really hard; just how much more of life's bullshit was that poor girl supposed to put up with?

He had done his research – done it too well and regretted his actions the instant he'd done so. Eight hundred thousand kids under the age of eighteen go missing each year. And that was just in North America.

A quarter of those are taken by family members and fifty-eight thousand by non-family members. The remainder? George guessed they simply ran off, had fatal accidents or simply and inexplicably vanished.

Like Ritchie.

The old man listened with patience to Honeymoon's weeping and tried to make out the odd word that she was attempting to form here and there. Short of listening, and just being there for his daughter-in-law, there was little else he felt he could do.

Ninety-seven percent of America's missing kids are recovered, there's some good news right there. The website from which he'd gleaned this particular nugget had glossed over whether they were found alive or otherwise. That much was a mercy, George figured. Some things are better left unknown.

And that left by his math, three percent – *twenty-four thousand* children – who annually, in *one country* just totally vanished without a trace.

"We just sit tight and wait for Ritchie to come home, or for the police to do their job my darlin'," George's voice faltered as he attempted to placate Honeymoon. "You have to be strong, for yourself and for Ritchie." He wanted to say much, much more, but the words refused to come.

It was at that moment that George became aware of something odd in his apartment.

He could *feel* something. It felt to him as if, suddenly he was no longer alone in the tiny, light-starved room. It was like he was being watched.

"Best keep the phone line free, my dear," he told his daughter-in-law. "In case the police …" he trailed off, his attention taken up by trying to locate the source of his unease.

Honeymoon hung up, no doubt to cry herself to sleep. George hoped against hope that he'd been able to offer the girl some comfort in her hour of need, but feared all he'd done was spout hollow words. He knew from personal experience just how deep and painful losing a child was, how it ripped out a huge chunk of your soul that you knew damned well would never grow back. It had been ten years since Richard, and they say that time's a great healer. Like fuck it was.

George wheeled his chair across to the kitchenette, drawn to that particular area of his apartment by the knotted feeling in his gut.

He pulled off his spectacles and ground a knuckle into each eye in turn. The day had rattled his nerves, that much was for sure, and had left him spooked to boot. The gut-churning terror of his grandson's disappearance had resurrected every buried-deep emotion he'd felt the moment his own son's Commanding Officer had knocked on his door, informed him of Richard's brave demise and explained in a cold-yet-kindly manner that no, it wouldn't be possible to view the body.

Not much left to view, apparently.

And now this; the grandson he treasured more than life itself, the last link to his own flesh and blood.

Gone.

And now his tired, emotionally worn-out brain was teasing him with phantom feelings and the paranoid illusion of not being alone when he was feeling more isolated in the world than he had in all his years to date.

"Ritchie?" George asked the tepid, still air. "Is that you?"

8

The shrill, first ring of the 'phone startled the old man and broke him from his reverie.

It was already mid afternoon and the gray clouds that had assembled beyond his window had, as a collective, decided to off-load their harsh, fall rain onto the humid streets below.

George fidgeted around in his wheelchair, fingers tapping idly on the chunky tread of the rubber tires. He stared one more time at the pair of words that were etched in uneven, childish handwriting on the chalkboard by the refrigerator:

LOUBERTHA HAYES

The words had sent a chill through his marrow when he'd first seen them earlier that morning, an icy coldness that had settled deep down in his psyche. Two words – a name, quite obviously – written in a child's shaky, uncertain hand. Two words that meant nothing to George and had certainly not been there yesterday.

"Ritchie," the old man mumbled to himself for what must have been the umpteenth time. He spun on his wheels and trundled over to answer his telephone.

"Mr. DeVries?" a hesitant voice spoke into his ear.

"Yes?" he ventured and his heart raced.

"It's Loubertha," the voice explained. "Loubertha Hayes."

Of course, the first thing George had done upon seeing the name traced in the dust on his chalkboard was to turn to his old, reliable friend the World Wide Web – who wouldn't? She'd taken quite some tracking down, had Loubertha; here was one old lady who didn't want to be found too easily.

She'd written a book twenty years ago – nothing before that, nothing since. The title of the book, '*When A Child Is Gone*' had raised an inappropriate smile in the old man, being as it was quite the deliberate play on the good ol' Johnny Mathis Christmas classic that plagued the airwaves every Yuletide. The subject matter of the book, however, was somewhat light on joy.

Loubertha's story was a true one, and it was about how her daughter had simply disappeared one day.

It had taken a lot of digging by George to find the copyright owner since the book's original publishing house was long since defunct and the title had been out of print for near-on fifteen years. But, the internet will forever be the die-hard's best friend and George managed to follow the bread-crumb trail to Ms. Hayes's retired literary agent who in turn had agreed to contact the author on the understanding that Ms. Hayes would only call *him* should she wish to speak.

Which clearly, she did.

And that filled George with optimism, since she had gotten her child back.

"Ms. Hayes, thank you so much for –"

"Call me Loubertha!" the woman sounded almost jolly and George imagined her as a huge, mountain-breasted lady sitting in a gingham kitchen surrounded by myriad steaming pies and running, squealing, ruddy-faced children. "Nobody calls me *Ms. Hayes* anymore." Was that a laugh?

"I spoke to your agent, did she tell you–?"

"About your grandson? Why else would I call a complete stranger just before Jerry Springer?" Again, a laugh? "You read my book?"

"I'm sorry, I haven't had the chance. I only – er – got hold of your name this morning. I did read the synopsis online, though."

"Then I figure you've read the best of the thing," Loubertha's voice trilled. "Damned publisher said I had to pad the book out to a hundred thousand words or no one would buy it, not that that was ever the goddamned point!"

"Your daughter came back, Ms. Hayes," George interrupted, really in no mood for the small talk.

"Yes, I did get my daughter back, Mr. DeVries, and please, do call me Loubertha."

"I'm sorry – *Loubertha* – my head's all over the place at the moment."

"Been there, sir!" she empathized over the 'phone with a little over enthusiasm. "I didn't know what day of the week it was, or whether I was inside out or right side in when my Ammunique went missing. They say it's every parent's nightmare – losing a child – but it's not, Mr. DeVries. Every parent's nightmare is what their own damned brain does to them when a child is misplaced."

Misplaced, now there was an interesting word. Keys you misplace, your glasses, a wallet. Not a word George ever thought would apply to a child.

"Can you help me?" the coldness in George's voice tripped over his tongue.

"If I can, I will, Mr. DeVries. But you have to understand that not every missing child case is like Ammunique's. Sometimes they're taken by bad people and never come back," her voice faltered. "And sometimes when they come back, you wish they hadn't."

"I want Ritchie back more than anything in the world Ms. – Loubertha," George said.

"Of course you do. You wouldn't be a grandparent – or *human* – if you didn't," the woman replied. "And from what you told my agent, your case does sound one heck of a lot like my daughter's." A pause. "The sudden vanishing, an unhappy child, a mysterious name written out in your kitchen. It all sounds very familiar to me." That weird noise again. Was the old girl chuckling? "Only, it took me a whole lot longer to find *my* person; the Internet's certainly made that whole malarkey a hell of a lot quicker."

"Your *person*?" George was intrigued.

"I didn't just *know* what needed to be done by gut instinct, Mr. DeVries, none of us do." Loubertha turned a little cryptic and then explained things to George as if he were a nine-year-old with learning difficulties. "We all have to find our person, someone who has been in the same predicament and who have had the knowledge of *what to do* passed down to them. It's been handed down through the generations by a long, long line of parents of missing kids. But it does only apply to those who disappear under very specific circumstances."

George could barely even pretend to know what Loubertha was talking in riddles about. "So, you can help me?" this time, notes of desperation crept from the old man's throat.

"I think I can, sir, but you're going to have to listen to me very, very carefully." Loubertha told him, her voice little more than a whisper. "You certainly cannot write any of this down, not one word, and not *ever*. You must promise me that."

At that point in time, George would have promised the old girl that he'd bare his butt in Macy's window if it meant getting Ritchie back. "I promise, Loubertha," he said. And at that point George realized he'd been terribly rude and not offered her *his* Christian name.

9

George carefully studied the bloodied lumps of his own tongue that sizzled and spat on the cooker.

It had been a messy business, all told, and not at all like he'd seen on dozens of movies in which a person's tongue was deftly and so very neatly sliced out from the root with one easy cut. He'd hacked away at the thing with his sharpest vegetable knife for at least twenty minutes and had eventually succeeded in getting most of the organ out of his mouth in three thumb-sized chunks.

Loubertha had told George that, in order to retrieve a family member from the mysterious place that took the children – and she'd emphasised that this could only be done by a blood relative – one had to sacrifice something from one's own body that was held most dear. Loubertha had taken her eyes. She'd scooped the things out of her face with a spoon and thrown them on the open wood burning stove in her kitchen as some form of sick sacrifice. She'd had to dictate the book she'd written to her sister and after that she couldn't be assed to learn Braille. And so Loubertha Hayes had never written another word from that day to this. George made a mental note to track down a copy of the book – should have asked Loubertha for a complimentary copy – and read up on what became of her daughter, Ammunique in the years following her return.

As an erstwhile actor, the old man had figured that his tongue, the key tool of his trade was fair exchange for the safe return of his grandson. It all made perfect sense to him and he just hoped that he'd done enough.

George coughed at the warm blood that trickled down the back of his throat, spattering it across his bloodied shirt and out across the white-tiled kitchenette wall. He mumbled his new mantra as best he could with so little remaining tongue, and the words tumbled out from his ruined mouth like some alien dialect, *"Bing 'm ba fom humpace el. Bing 'm ba fom humpace el. Bing 'm ba –"*

Over and over, George repeated the words that Loubertha had dictated to him, over and over as he gagged on coagulating blood and the sickening stench of his own flesh as it crackled and popped on the stove.

George leaned back in his wheelchair and tipped his head forwards to allow the blood to pour from his quivering lips rather than down his esophagus to further sicken his stomach.. All he could do now was to keep on hoping that he had done enough to bring his grandson back from the God forsaken place Loubertha Hayes had told him about; the place that fair *teemed* with the lost children of generations. And George also hoped that the bleeding in his mouth would stop soon, so that he could see his grandson again and hold the boy tight and never let him go.

As his life ebbed slowly away, George DeVries thought he heard a noise not unlike a bubble bursting.

10

Honeymoon had held her son so tightly to her breast that he had almost suffocated. She'd cried and howled as she clasped him to her body, terrified to let go of him for even one second in case he vanished again.

Her second instinct when Ritchie appeared had been to thrash the living daylights out of the boy for wandering off in the grocery store, but she was so goddamned relieved just to have him back, that it was all she could do to string a few coherent sentences together.

Why did you run off, Ritchie?! Where have you been? Don't you know I've been worried sick-? All of the usual rote, parental chastisements were over-ridden by the absolute relief of having her son back.

He'd seemed tired – understandably so – and full of rambling stories about white rooms and weirdly-dressed kids and strange ladies with odd, *swirly* faces. All that was missing from Ritchie's fantastical tales were a bunch of bug-eyed, gray men and Honeymoon would have herself thinking alien abduction. She scoffed at herself for thinking such bullshit, but at least it prevented her from entertaining the thousand and one alternative scenarios that her brain was doing its very best to torment her with.

Honeymoon had made the decision to call the cops first thing the following morning to inform them of her prodigal's return. She knew that she was being irresponsible, but the boy was so clearly exhausted and they'd want to question him and take their samples and perform the intrusive tests to see if –

And right there was a thought that Honeymoon didn't even want to entertain.

Let the boy rest, he – *both of them* – could face all of that tomorrow with a good night's sleep behind them.

She had tried to call George but he wasn't picking up so Honeymoon left a message to let him know the good news; the trip to the police station had left the old boy pretty whacked so she figured he was probably sleeping it off. She'd take Ritchie over to see his beloved Cap'n after she'd dealt with the cops.

Laying fully clothed on her bed, Honeymoon succumbed to her own exhaustion, her heavy eyelids drooping as a fitful sleep threw its darkness over her. She felt herself relax for the first time in three days and welcomed the luxury of sleep.

She dreamt of the hospital where Ritchie was born. The cold, clinical smell, the cloying stink of disinfectant and sweat and blood. And she dreamt of the second night she'd spent in that vast, soulless place, when baby Ritchie DeVries was not quite two days old and she'd awoken in the small hours to find his body limp and lifeless with blue lips and glassy, staring eyes.

In the depths of her dream, Honeymoon relived the range of chilling emotions that had cascaded over her that night; the grief and panic that was quickly over-ridden by cold, calculating instinct and the numbness that allowed her to do what she knew she had to do as nothing more than an automatic reaction.

The plastic wrist and ankle identification bands had slipped all too easily from her baby's tiny, stiff limbs

382

and onto the sleeping baby in the adjacent crib. That child's, she placed onto her own baby's floppy limbs and then she switched the two new-borns around.

The following morning, Honeymoon had quietly and respectfully packed her – and her baby's – things and checked out of the hospital as the poor lady in the adjacent bed mourned the unexpected passing of what she thought to be her own child.

Honeymoon awoke from her guilt-drenched dreams with a start.

A noise?

She darted to her son's room and threw open the door.

A scream stuck hard in Honeymoon's larynx and all she could do was utter a single, high-pitched squeak as she collapsed to her knees on the threshold of her son's bedroom.

Before her eyes there lay a scene of bloody carnage. Arcs of fresh, dripping blood had decorated every single wall and over and across the ceiling; puddles of the stuff steamed and coagulated around the threadbare rug and scattered globs of shiny pink flesh patterned with tattered shreds of Ritchie's caramel skin glinted in the yellow light that shone from the hallway behind her.

Other than the ragged clumps of skin, there was nothing in the blood soaked room that even vaguely resembled her son.

Nothing.

And when Honeymoon's scream finally did come, it was one of the unimaginable anguish and terror of losing a child for the third and final time.

Honeymoon's cry disturbed the shape that skulked over in the corner by the old army chest that Grandpa had given Ritchie what now seemed a lifetime ago. The shape was a ghostly white that Honeymoon could see straight through and its nebulous conformation moved and quivered like some gargantuan, living smog. It stared directly at Honeymoon and its blood-stained head undulated and shifted to form the vaguest semblance of a face.

It was a feminine face, soft and somehow oddly comforting.

A woman's face that Honeymoon recognized.

Then, with a liquid '*plop*', it was gone.

And Honeymoon thought that the nebulous thing had looked just like a shadow, only in white.

End

The Moroccan Reverberation

The Chinook CH-47 flew fast and close enough to the sea to churn the water's surface into myriad white crested waves with its tandem rotor blades. There was little fear that the 'bird would attract the target's attention as helicopters were a common occurrence in this part of the South China Sea as they patrolled the shipping lanes for drug gangs and pirates out to make a quick – if somewhat hazardous – buck.

Agent Cassandra Webb – Cass to the select few she allowed to get close – stared down from the open door of the helicopter as the wind whipped her shock of red hair like flames around her narrow, handsome face. She studied the choppy sea with calmness, although she could see the dark silhouettes of sharks as they patrolled the azure water below. She touched a steady hand to the shark repellent gun strapped to her thigh and remembered that someone had once told her that if a shark attacks, you just bat 'em on the nose. That said, she much preferred the gun.

She shifted her focus from the ominous shapes that lurked below to the sparkles of light cast by the ascending sun that sat fresh and bloated on the horizon; almost time. They were two hundred nautical miles north of the Straight of Malacca – a long way from land and a long, long way from home.

Her superiors had known before they asked that Agent Webb would not be able to refuse this mission to extract a fellow agent from his own failure; especially as said agent was her ex-partner and someone she'd not set eyes on in three years.

Not since Marrakech.

Now there was one hell of a mess for you; a *clusterfuck,* her commander had called it in a rare outburst of uncharacteristic profanity. He'd actually gone on to apologize for cussing in front of a lady, of course, but he'd been accurate in his assessment of Cass and her erstwhile partner's mission. The whole Marrakech assignment had been a screw up from start to finish, one that had left Cass bleeding almost to death on a grimy street and her partner fleeing for his life. Even now, three years on and a world away from the yellow, choking dust and the mule-kick of the bullets that tore up her body, Cass could hear Agent Holcomb's footsteps as he ran like the devil was on his ass. In leaving her behind, he'd done what he thought was best in the interests of the mission, even though it had left her to bleed out in the street; always a possibility in their line of work.

Cass had worked for the agency for eight years – including her twelve months of rehabilitation post-Marrakech – a secretive, a-national agency without a name or even a catchy acronym; no borders, no boundaries, no rules. She would go as far as to say she *loved* what she did, never more so than when she was out in the field. Although she and her colleagues were more procurers (of information, of people) than spies, in many ways it could be very James Bond at times, only with a hell of a lot more paperwork and nowhere near the plethora of casual sex that most people imagined.

She'd jumped at the chance to take the mission to rescue Agent Holcomb, and to hell with how dangerous they'd said it would be. It would be worth the risk just to see the look on his face; he thought she was dead.

Cass smiled a wry smile at that thought and as she looked up she caught the helicopter pilot staring at her with a puzzled look on his face. She flashed him a toothy grin and he nodded at her.

Time you weren't in the chopper, crazy smiling lady.

Cass pulled the zipper on her matt black wetsuit snug up to her chin, shrugged on her backpack and jumped.

At twenty feet, the drop into the ocean bought Cass the time to recce her target and gulp a lungful of warm air that was tainted with the hot tang of exhaust fumes.

She hit the water feet-first and slipped beneath the agitated waves with barely a splash. And when she surfaced, the helicopter was high above her and heading back to the carrier where it would await her signal.

Cass had been dropped a hundred yards astern of Samuel Delaforce's seventy-foot yacht that bobbed gently on the undulating sea. It was as close as they dared get without breaking cover; she was going to have to swim the rest of the way.

Christened *Aqua Dentata* by the eccentric Delaforce, the yacht was one of Delaforce's smaller vessels but still it cut a beautiful, streamlined outline of gleaming white and polished chrome and mirrored windows that reflected the color of the sea. As pretty a vessel as the *Aqua Dentata* was, the only fact that interested Cass right now was that Delaforce kept a skeleton crew. As someone who bought and sold secrets and acquired the un-acquirable for the highest bidders, Samuel Delaforce was understandably cautious and fewer crew meant less people he had to trust. And that meant that Cass's extraction had a fighting chance of success.

Cass focussed on the glinting steel ladder that dipped into the sea from the stern of the boat, and the six-foot lifeboat on the deck next to it, and she began to swim.

Halfway to her goal, Cass felt something bump on her right calf. She dipped her head beneath the water and saw a tiger shark circling away from her with a nonchalant sweep of its tail. It was no more than a six-footer; a juvenile but still enough *Galeocerdo* to spoil her morning. Cass reached for the repellent as the shark manoeuvred to point its nose towards her. Behind it, she saw a dozen others making lazy circles around her as they sensed an imminent kill and an easy meal.

Cass drew in air, submerged and turned to face the shark; it was twenty yards and closing. She knew that it meant business, the nudge at her leg had been the first stage of the creature's attack plan; a gentle nudge to size her up, followed by a sluggish bite at her thigh or midriff and then retreat. The shark would then fall back to a safe distance and wait for her to bleed to death before eating. It was the perfect behaviour to avoid injury by panicked, flailing prey – they may only be oversized fish, Cass mused as she braced herself for the attack, but sharks hadn't survived four hundred million years by being dumb.

She kept her arms and legs close to her body and moved as little as possible as the shark closed in. As the shark accelerated the final few yards with a powerful thrust of its tail, and all she could see were the uneven rows of pearl-white, serrated triangles in its gaping maw, Cass thrust the repellent gun at the creature's face.

The compressed gas in the gun went off with a muffled *whump* and the shark's nose exploded in a cloud of thick red and the fish veered away from her with a bemused look on what was left of its face. Plumes of scarlet pumped from the ragged wound and attracted the immediate attention of its companions, the bolder of which were already taking tentative nibbles at the dying shark. By serving up an impromptu shark buffet, Cass had bought herself time to swim to Delaforce's yacht.

She reached the yacht's chromed steps in record time – not difficult to beat your personal best with a dozen sharks behind. She shuffled off her backpack and fished out a heavy, conical limpet bomb.

Slipping the backpack over one shoulder, Cass dove downwards and followed the smooth line of the hull. At the bottom, she attached the bomb to the hull by the trio of suckers on its base. She hated the suckers because they would fail if you didn't get the suction just so, but they were the only solution for carbon-fibre hulls. A million dollars and the boat was made of what Cass considered little more than glorified plastic; a variation of the stuff she used to keep her food fresh in the refrigerator.

Once she had the device secured and the timer set for ten minutes, Cass bobbed back to the surface and climbed the steps onto the *Aqua Dentata*.

Cass clambered cautiously aboard, eyes and ears alert; there may only be a token crew on board, but she knew from experience that men like Delaforce were particularly thorough when it came to security.

She squeezed herself into a narrow gap between the lifeboat and the cabin. She shuffled off her backpack, picked out the plastic wrapped gun and laid both at her feet. Cass then slowly and quietly unzipped her wetsuit and slipped out of it like a snake from its skin. She was happy to be free of the suit's restrictions; it was surprising how much movement those things could limit in a crisis.

The cool morning air caressed Cass's skin, invoking gooseflesh along her arms and legs, which made her glad that she'd elected to wear a swimsuit rather than the bikini she usually wore. The swimsuit she had chosen was a black, backless halter – functional yet sexy and precisely the type *he* preferred. Sure, she felt a little exposed but the suit did cover most of the scars she'd earned the hard way in Marrakech and it was cut high enough up in the thigh that Cass was pleased she'd sprung for the Brazilian wax before embarkation.

"Hey!" a voice off to her left.

Cass spun her head and saw a tall, dark-skinned guy dressed in white linen cargo pants and T running towards her, spear gun in his hand. Behind him, another two guys armed with Kalashnikovs, the weapon of choice for terrorists and henchmen alike.

Remaining calm, Cass plucked a leather holster from her backpack and slipped it over her left shoulder. She then liberated the gun from its protective wrap and nestled the weapon in the holster.

She was gone from her hiding place before the guards got there.

"Where'd she go?" Speargun asked his colleagues in his thick Pidgin English. The other two shrugged and he waved a hand at them to go search the boat. His other hand hovered over the walkie-talkie clipped to his belt, a look of reluctance on his face.

Cass lowered herself from the lifeboat and grabbed the guy from behind with steel-strong arms, one hand over his mouth. Surprise paralysed her victim for the split second it took for Cass to position her right hand on his head and snap it round with a sharp twist. His neck gave out a satisfying crackle like pine cones on a winter fire and he fell limp in her arms. His gun ejected its spear, which arced upwards and fell with an impotent clatter on the roof of the cabin.

Cass lowered the guard to the deck and slunk away, the remaining two guards were on their way back to report their lack of success.

"Shit." One of the guards prodded Speargun with his foot. "We'd better let Delaforce know about this." His eyes darted around as he scanned the boat for the silent assassin.

Cass pressed herself against the chill metal of the cabin doorway and listened to the guards. She absently stroked the gun that lay heavy against her ribs but made the call to leave it put; her weapon of choice was her hands, not just for the silence they afforded but because she found that much more...*intimate*.

The guards jogged by and she stepped out behind them.

Her first blow connected with the shortest guard's skull and he hit the deck hard. His compadre spun around, gun toted and sheer terror lighting up his eyes. A skilled, barefooted roundhouse kick from Cass to the guy's larynx both guaranteed his silence and caused him to drop his gun to clutch at his crushed throat. Another kick and the guy flew overboard with a heavy splash.

The short guard scrambled to his feet, machine gun aimed at Cass's chest. She sidestepped and lashed out with a blurred fist into the guard's solar plexus and he bent over double, exposing his vulnerable nape. Acting with ruthless efficiency, Cass obliged with a swift chop of her right fist and down he went for good.

Cass stepped over the guard's body, opened the cabin door and stepped into the boat's air-conditioned interior. She oriented herself and figured that it wouldn't be too hard to find what she was looking for.

All she had to do was follow the screams.

Delaforce barely registered surprise when Cass strode into his inner sanctum like a cock in the henhouse. The room was fitted out in a precise emulation of a dental surgery; complete with posters that depicted the variety of teeth and tooth anatomy. Cass noted the framed certificate of graduation from the University of Pennsylvania Dental School. Hell, Delaforce was even wearing a dentist's smock.

So the rumors *were* true; Delaforce *had* put himself through dental school after he'd made his fortune, and all to sate his renowned tooth fetish. It had made the man more efficient when it came to his favoured method of torture throughout his escalating underworld career.

"You must be Agent Webb?" Delaforce said as with great care he probed a pair of glinting surgical pliers into the mouth of the guy strapped to the dental chair, their progress unhindered thanks to the metal oral speculum that held his victim's mouth agape. "I know you two have met before, so I'll not bother with formalities." Delaforce gripped an incisor and yanked it out with a sickening *CRACK* and Agent Holcomb screamed the best he could.

Cass's ex-partner was strapped into a green, antique iron dental chair, the likes of which she'd seen in medical museums and in an S&M club they had once frequented in Phuket on the weeks before Marrakech. They'd tracked down a fat, greasy lowlife in the back room of the club and all but beaten him to death before he'd given up the information that had led them directly into the ambush that had almost cost Cass her life.

There was a dull thud as the limpet bomb detonated and the boat took a crazy list starboard.

"You blew up my yacht?" Delaforce looked offended, as if the bomb had been a personal insult to his manhood. He stepped away from the chair and Cass saw that at least eight of Holcomb's teeth were missing. Blood dribbled from his gaping mouth and pooled on his bare chest; his tongue was a swollen, dry, twitching thing amongst the bloodied mess and his eyes stared at Cass with disbelief.

"I've come to get you off of the boat," Cass said.

Holcomb strained against his restraints and uttered a gargled noise that sounded like *thank you*.

"Not you, him." Cass nodded towards Delaforce. "You left me for dead, *Agent* Holcomb," she spat the word agent like it felt dirty in her mouth. "This time, *I'm* doing what's best for the mission."

"Did you get what you wanted from him?" this time to Delaforce.

"Sang like a canary." Delaforce smiled at Cass.

"So why are you still pulling his teeth out?"

Delaforce looked a tad sheepish and offered, "Old habits die hard?"

Cass rolled her eyes and urged Delaforce from the room. She paused at the doorway for one final look at Holcomb.

"Now let's see how you like it," she said quietly and pulled the door closed to dull the sound of her ex-partner's screams.

Delaforce's yacht sank much quicker than Cass had anticipated, thanks mostly to that damned plastic hull. She'd barely had time enough to drag her quarry to the lifeboat and launch it before the yacht had completely submerged.

And now they waited and watched the sharks circling.

If she'd gotten her timing right, they'd all be here in two hours, thirty-four minutes; the Russians, the Americans and the Chinese. There'd be the formality of the bidding and the lucky winner would take possession of Delaforce and his secrets and then drop Cass off at the destination of her choice. Cuba, perhaps, or possibly Haiti; she had ex-Khmer Rouge contacts there and she'd be able to live out her premature retirement like royalty.

Cass scanned the horizon and saw the first of the three small dots appear, most likely the Chinese, she thought – they were *always* early.

The irony wasn't lost on Cass, of Delaforce being thrown to auction. He was an individual with a seven figure bounty on his head in all G8 countries, plus the growing number of rogue states who were more than willing to pay for what he knew or to silence him. And now that Holcomb had spilled his guts, the asking price for Delaforce had gone up to eight figures.

Delaforce was telling Cass for the thousandth time that did she know that a shark's skin is made of hundreds of thousands of teeth and that some countries still used it as sandpaper and that if they attack you should just bat 'em on the nose?

And Agent Cassandra Webb ground her teeth and told herself that if the man mentioned the damned sharks one more time she might just forgo her payday and throw the illustrious Mr. Delaforce overboard to see if his Shark's Nose theory actually worked or not.

End

Winning and Losing

Fuck.

There they were. All six of them. I must have checked each and every one of those numbers a thousand times.

Eight. Forty-six. Seventeen. Ten. Thirty-Two. Twenty.

All fucking six of the damned things, each one taunting me from the tattered lottery ticket that I'd been carrying around in the back pocket of my Levis for a week, all but forgotten.

Until now, that is.

Procrastination, it's a writer's thing – and I dare to call myself a writer because that's what I do from time to time – I write. We writers are all guilty of that great crime of procrastination; not for nothing was the activity (or lack thereof) tied with the epithet *Thief of Time* by Charlie Dickens – a fellow writer – see what I mean?

For we wordsmiths, there can be nothing more worthy of avoidance than the keyboard; it can, at times, be almost tangible, something physical that steers us away from our work. It can feel as if the words in our heads are too frightened to come out, as if being committed to the world outside will make them cease to exist as *actual* living, breathing things; which of course, they never were in the first place.

I digress.

I'd been through the usual ritual; emptied the dishwasher and refilled it with last night's dinner dishes, taken out the trash, watered the wilting array of houseplants that we bought only two weeks ago in a fit of optimism that this bunch would avoid the withering death that has plagued our every houseplant, like *ever*. I'd then made my fifth coffee of the morning and perused a little Internet porn – all of which is beginning to look horribly familiar these days; is it possible that I was coming to an end of the porn, that I'd actually seen it all?

Then it was one more check of the e-mail before I got started, then another coffee before the next chapter, a quick inventory of the pantry contents for the grocery shopping list before sitting down at that dreaded keyboard – and half the day had already slipped mysteriously by.

It hadn't always been this way, not so long ago it had been far worse and I'd procrastinated for over half a year so I could accept my moment of boredom, this brief escape from the writer's block that has plagued me since my last drink – six months, two weeks, three days, one hour and thirty-six minutes ago – so I'd made a pact with myself that I'd just check the lottery ticket I'd rediscovered in the pocket of a long-forgotten pair of pants, and *then* get down to some serious word-processing.

And there they were. All six numbers, a perfect match to those on my computer screen. Six numbers that added up to hundreds of millions of dollars. More in fact, than any one man could spend in a lifetime.

I'd won.

In that instant, I was staring into the mouth of no more counting the cents, living hand-to-mouth and worrying about how in God's name we were going to make the next mortgage payment. No more Amy working herself into an early grave at two jobs to give me the opportunity to sit and write – my wife's belief in me and my *'talent'* had been unwavering in the ten years we've been married.

Christ only knows what talent she thinks I have, though, as we've both seen very little of its rewards to date. But, stubborn as she is, she has steadfastly refused to let me go out and get a job, always insisting that stick to what I do best.

Write.

She worked two fucking jobs just for me to string just a few dozen words a day together. I was managing to write just enough to earn a few hundred bucks here and there writing for the myriad independent hack film makers that plague our fair city, along with a little sporadic revenue that could be generated from scribbling lame jokes for lame sitcoms and talk show hosts. But it was nowhere near enough remuneration to provide the lifestyle I'd promised my beloved when I first swept her off of her feet.

Amy is smart, by far the smartest person I know, or have ever known, come to think of it. She could have chosen any career path; doctor, lawyer, musician, pretty much anything she wanted to be, really. Instead, here she was, slogging it out in some dead-end, mind-numbing office job she'd taken on to support me and my writing habit.

That, and her other job.

Ah yes, the *Other Job*. For three evenings a week, my wife is a *companion* to sad faced old men who's own wives disgust them, and who in turn, most likely repulse said spouses. She charges them two hundred fifty bucks an hour for her time as a companion – *companion* is Amy's word for what she does, not mine – and we both know what she really is.

It began innocently enough, as dinner with lonely but ridiculously rich businessmen who just wanted to be with someone attractive who could hold their own in an intelligent conversation. That, in turn lead to her attending corporate events with said gentlemen who wanted to be seen with a vivacious, fun female on their arm; presumably to emphasise their ongoing virility to colleagues who really couldn't care less. *Yeah, the old boy's still got it, alright – just look at the hot babe he's paying to pretend to like him!*

Inevitably, her Johns – again, her word, not mine, I prefer to call 'em clients because that sits easier with my conscience – wanted more from my wife than just her time. And they soon came to expect sexual favors as part of their paid appointments. She and I had had the discussion about it – a loud one, as I recall – and now they all pay handsomely for the privilege of screwing my wife.

It was okay with me for a while, once I kind of got used to the idea, and sometimes I would actually find myself asking her to relate the juicy details of her trysts as part of our lovemaking. But after so long, it began to prey on my mind a little too much and even that lost its frisson.

And sometimes, my wife's clients get a little carried away. There's this one guy who likes to play rough and my poor, sweet Amy will come home dishevelled with scratches on her tits and bruises on her arms and face.

Yet never a word of complaint from that wonderful saint of a woman.

'*Live your dream*', she'd tell me, '*use your talent to be somebody*'.

And now, with this obscene amount of lottery cash, we could live *her* dream. We could take time out to relax, kick our heels, and maybe even have kids. Hell, we could finally take that cruise that she's always nagged me about! An inward shudder; I hate cruises, the main reason for which being that ships do have a tendency to sink – I've seen *Titanic* enough times to know that much at least. And then there's an old joke I heard about a middle-aged couple that went on a six-month around the world cruise;

"*And next year*," they'd said upon their return, "*we want to go somewhere different*."

I mean, just how many cruises, road trips and sightseeing vacations can you take before you're sick to death of them?

And now we could be the ones doing all of that. Amy could quit both of her soul-sucking jobs, and I could quit playing housewife and writing shit jokes for shit sitcoms and concentrate on *proper* writing, full time.

Why?

Now, there's a loaded question for you.

You see, I've always been driven to write, ever since I wrote my first book, aged seven. It had begun as a book about my then favorite topic of stick insects, only to suffer from one of those sudden changes of interest that plagues all young children. Sadly, my '*Guide to Stick Insects and Dinosaurs*' was destined never to grace the shelves of Barnes & Noble, nor make my fortune. My drive as a *creative* writer has always been to seek the success that seemed secreted illusively just around the corner like some murky shadow. And for me, success has always equated to money.

So what would be the point?

Here I was, contemplating riches beyond my wildest dreams and the knowledge that neither of us would ever have to work again.

One fell swoop, one twist of coincidence that had pushed six random numbers together, and my lifetime's reason for existing would be gone. It may just be my imagination, but I could already feel my drive fading as I contemplated the sheer amount of money that would be mine with just one phone call to the nice, no doubt incredibly helpful people on the Texas Lottery switchboard. Was I already beginning to lose that inherent panic that a breadline existence gives a person? Perhaps there *was* some truth after all behind the myth of the starving artist, maybe you have to starve the body in order to feed the creative spirit?

All of that would be gone.

I sat there a long while and contemplated such a future; a life devoid of my one sole purpose, a gaping hole where motivation to create had once lurked, albeit elusively.

Emptiness.

Although, on the other hand, it would be a life free from worry, an existence free from watching the love of my life work – and fuck – herself into a premature hole in the ground.

And such was my dilemma; an empty life free of financial constraint and direction, or a life filled with struggle tempered with that slightest hint of a hope of achieving *the dream*.

I made a decision.

The decision.

I can't say that it was an easy one, but at least I made it with the very best of intentions. It's one that I am going to have to live with for the remainder of my life – no matter how short that is likely to be now.

As I watched the torn-up shreds of lottery ticket swirl down the toilet bowl – a somewhat fitting metaphor, I thought – the time-honoured cliché echoed around my brain: *you're damned if you don't, you're damned if you do*.

So I poured myself another drink. It was the cheapest of Vodkas on the market, not quite the stuff that makes you go blind, but close enough. Vodka was my clandestine drink of choice, my most secretive of friends; Amy would never smell it on my breath, would never guess that I'd fallen off the wagon in a most spectacular fashion. If I was anything in this life, I was a smart alcoholic.

Ah yes, the demon drink. Welcomed back into my life with arms akimbo, it would most likely kill me sooner rather than later. And right about now, that seemed more preferable to living with the enormity of what I had just done.

It's late. My wife has just walked in and she looks damned tired – is that *another* bruise under her eye?

As always, upon returning home, I know she's going to ask me how my day was – my *fucking* day – and I'm going to tell her the same thing I always do.

That my day was just fine, thank you.

An Ordinary Day

It was a day like any other, right up until the hydrogen bomb detonated above the city.

And then *everyone* died.

Waiting for the Call

"He's not an *addict*, he's just a *user*," Mom said.

It was a well-worn phrase of his wife's that Papa had grown weary of hearing over the years. It ranked right along up there with '*he just makes bad choices*' and '*he only smokes the weed*' on the list of things that would never fail to get Papa's goat and cause a heated argument between the two of them – only now he had discovered that it was usually best to keep schtum; a lesson learned the hard way across the yawning darkness of his years dealing with his wife's unfathomable and unerring denial over the Addict they had somehow brought up.

They'd been sitting there on the couch for a considerable amount of time now, by Papa's reckoning. Quite possibly it had been as long as five years, maybe even a month or two beyond that; it was becoming increasingly hard for Papa to tell – and Mom couldn't have cared less in her current state of mind – what with the living room clock's double-A having run bone-dry a good year or so ago.

It had all begun when the Addict had turned thirteen. Something about reaching that golden milestone of teenagedom, along with the new friends he'd made from the rough end of the estate, the constant missing of curfew, the slipping grades at school and the sudden and total loss of interest in his beloved basketball. There'd been interest in their handsome, smart, talented son at county level at one point in time, but now the only county interest he garnered was the variety that came with a bright orange jumpsuit and one of those nifty little grabber things that meant you didn't have to bend over too much when clearing the highway verges.

And then there'd been the smell. That unmistakable, acrid reek of marijuana that clung to the Addict's clothes like – well, like a bad smell. And for as much as the Addict protested that it was merely the scent of his new aftershave – and for all that his mother chose to believe him – there was simply no mistaking that rancid herbal aroma that hovered about the Addict like some ethereal aura. And besides which, Papa had wondered even at the time just what kind of cologne company would make an aftershave that smelled like someone ran over a skunk on a hot, sticky road.

"It's a phase, is all," Mom had said with that nurturing smile of hers when the Addict had invited a bunch of his new friends over to the house for an impromptu hot tub party. "He'll grow out of it soon enough, like he did with eating the Lego's," she'd mused whilst watching a dozen gangly, acne-riddled teenagers lazing in the tub with fat reefers dangling from the corners of their mouths and trying their utmost to blow smoke-rings with the thick, grey fumes. She said she'd thought it made them all look like extras in a James Dean movie, but Papa thought they looked like a bunch of jailbirds just biding their time 'till a cell was made ready for them.

Of course, Papa had known best to keep his lips firmly zipped on that particular observation too. Just like he had the night the cops had brought the Addict home at three in the damned morning.

"They should have thrown his sorry ass in jail," Papa had said to Mom once the fresh-faced, squeaky voice lady cop had climbed back into her car.

"Jail is no place for a fifteen year old!" Mom had chastised her husband as if he were the absolute worst parent on the face of God's green earth. She'd then ushered the Addict inside to the warm comfort of their home with soothing promises of hot cocoa and chocolate chip cookies – his favorite in the entire world.

"And neither is the central verge of the freeway," Papa had countered, feeling rather proud of his segue.

"It wasn't the *freeway*, it was the two-way through Glendale Forest," Mom had been quick to defend her boy, who looked suitably sorry for himself, if somewhat high; he was still unable to string a coherent sentence together and he seemed unable to help himself smacking his dirt-dry mouth open and closed in a sorry attempt to alleviate the cotton mouth that was sticking his tongue to his arid palate.

"What kind of lesson is he going to learn from this?" Papa had felt his blood pressure rising, his cheeks flushed hot, the all-too familiar seaside *whoosh* of blood in his ears. "He gets caught sleeping rough with half a pack of cigarettes and an ounce of weed on him and the goddamned cops don't even give him a caution!"

Mom was – as always – was quick to jump to the Addict's defence. "He's just a child, Papa!" she'd cried. "He's learned his lesson, and he won't be doing it again, will you, son?"

"No, Mom," the Addict groaned. His own tears flowed freely now, their salty progress leaving track marks of clean down the boy's grimy cheeks.

Papa recalled an article he'd read once about how crocodiles would appear to cry when they ate their prey. And for many ignorant centuries, people thought that this was in some kind of reptilian remorse over having killed some poor, defenceless creature so they could have dinner. In fact, the tears flowed from the heinous reptile's eyes simply because they had no hard bone separating their eye sockets from the roof of their mouth; it was the pressure of the still-warm – and often kicking – flesh sliding down the vile creature's throat that made them weep.

The Addict's tears against his mother's sobbing bosom reminded Papa of the disingenuously lachrymose crocodile – nothing more than an involuntary and unfeeling reaction to having been caught by the police.

And so the inept cop had driven away in her shiny black-and-white, no doubt to regale her colleagues back at the Precinct with the humorous story of how she'd picked up a teenaged boy who was so damned high he could barely remember his own name, let alone what street he lived on. And, no doubt, she would then light up one of the Addict's joints and pass it around the police rec' room and they'd all have a good old laugh about it.

Papa looked down at the telephone.

It was an old style phone, one of those made from shiny black Bakelite and with the rotary dial – only the Bakelite had dulled with age and only gleamed around the rotary dial where fingers had worn it smooth over the years. The 'phone had a long, straight cord that snaked away beneath Papa and Mom to plug into the socket in the wall behind the small wooden table that skulked by the arm of the couch, and a curly black one that attached the receiver to its cradle. The telephone snuggled there between Papa and Mom like a small, mute child; its presence on the centre cushion serving as an uncanny metaphor to the yawning chasm that had slowly but surely encroached upon their once deliriously happy marriage.

Even the telemarketers had quit calling; maybe word had gotten around the numerous call centers that the householders on this particular number were a morose, untalkative pair who were never likely to buy anything from the chirpy-voiced salespeople who at one time used to call three, four, sometimes five times a day. Instead, the thing just sat there, dull and lifeless. And every couple of days or so, Mom would pick up the clammy plastic receiver and hold up close to her ear, just to make sure the thing hadn't been disconnected.

"Still working," she'd say with nary a glimmer of a smile. Then she'd listen intently for a while to the dull monotone of the 'phone's connection, as if by doing so she could reach out through the myriad wires of the network and somehow connect with the Addict.

*

The Addict was happy.

He'd not given so much as a passing thought to his parents, nor to the fact that they had remained sitting upon the old couch back home with the million-year-old 'phone between them since he'd decided it was best for all concerned that he leave home for good.

Yep, he was as happy as the proverbial sandboy – the drugs took care of that, thank you very much!

In his drug-fuelled haze, the Addict didn't take much note of his surroundings; they came in a poor second alongside getting high. He'd kind of slipped in recent months from the heady club scene – the thudding noise, the endless supply of nefarious substances with which to pollute his willing young body, the countless eager females willing to do just about *anything* for a hit, or for cold, hard cash to score a hit – and now he spent most of his time holed up in the squalid motel room he shared with a dozen or so others of his ilk. His deadened senses had long since grown immune to the sharp tang of smoked chemicals and unwashed bodies, the earthy reek of bodily functions and the overflowing slop bucket they had in the corner – the toilet had long ago blocked up and who the hell was going to complain to the management when they were months behind on the rent and the place looked like a shit-hole?

Yes indeed, the cocktail of malignant substances the Addict pumped into his system – smoked, swallowed, injected, hell, he'd even stuck some of it up his own ass on occasion to get a quicker high – served incredibly well to block out all of the unpleasantness of the motel room, and of his life in general; when the Addict was high, it didn't matter to him that his life was a complete and utter mess, that he'd dropped out of his education to devote one hundred percent of his time in the pursuit of chemical oblivion, that the police and numerous bondsmen were hunting for him for skipping bail, and that he'd pretty much destroyed his parent's lives to boot.

But when the Addict came down from those increasingly hard-to-come-by euphoric moments, boy, howdy were things grim! Those were the times of the severest introspection at which the Addict well and truly despised himself, hated what he had become, and was terrified beyond his frazzled wits of what his future held – if indeed he held any future at all.

And still the young man refused to think of himself as an *addict* in any way – his mother's mantra had stuck so resolutely in his adolescent mind and taken firm root there; like a festering tooth in a rotten jawbone, it putrefied in his subconscious and infected everything around it – that he was simply a user having good ol' party times in his formative years.

Marijuana, cocaine, crack-cocaine, heroin, DMT, GHB, Ketamine, Khat, LSD, MDMA, crystal meth' PCP, amyl nitrite, nitrous oxide, solvents, barbiturates, benzodiazepines, oxydodone, fentanyl, DXM, Amphetamines – and not to forget those traditional old stalwarts of addiction, alcohol and nicotine.

Not at all bad for *just a user*, eh?

Right now, the Addict was high; his mind all but detached from his body and afloat on a surreal sea of chemically induced stupor, all thoughts of ruined lives and life-altering mistakes had miraculously dissolved away into a swirling, nebulous nothingness. Here he could truly fly, soar untold miles above all of the problems and responsibilities that real life harbored for him down below. Here he was an eagle, or a condor, or maybe even a bat...

*

Mom glanced at the phone again.

Papa saw her eyes twitch in *that* direction and vowed to himself that if she did it again, he'd throttle the living daylights out of her with his own bare hands.

But of course, Papa wouldn't ever do that. He'd made the vow to himself a thousand times over the passing years, and – obviously enough – he hadn't actually followed through with the threat. The sad truth was that Papa had neither the motivation nor the intestinal fortitude to strangle his wife to death, no matter how many times she glanced at that confounded lifeless chunk of plastic that perched on the couch between them. And perhaps the saddest thing of all was that Papa knew that should he ever get around to it, if he suddenly and finally snapped one cold, grim afternoon, his poor, empty wife really couldn't have cared less.

"He's probably at a party with his new friends," Mom broke the pregnant silence between them. Her voice was monotone, flat like it was when she used to read the words from the back of a cereal packet at the breakfast table.

Did you know that this product contains more than one third of your daily recommended intake of riboflavin?

Papa felt a pang in his gut, an empty, gnawing hole in the pit of his stomach, the unmistakably desolate feeling of loss for the perfect life they'd once enjoyed.

And he remembered.

It had been five years ago – maybe a month or so more – when he'd awoken to the screech of smoke alarms and bitter tang of thick, creeping smoke. He'd awoken Mom and he'd raced to the bottom of the stairs, only to be beaten back by the billowing black smoke and fierce heat.

Papa had still been attempting to battle his way upstairs when the fire fighters hauled him out of the house. They'd ignored his cries and wild, sobbing pleas to be let back in, and he'd barely noticed the Addict standing in the driveway, his arm in the sling the EMT had given him, one side of his face grazed from the concrete he'd landed upon having leapt from his bedroom window. They say that God looks out for the stupid and the drunk – and it would seem that He extends that generous courtesy to crack-addicts too.

It had transpired, quite predictably that the fire had been started by the Addict falling asleep with a fat joint in his mouth. Papa wondered if he'd looked all that much like an extra from a James Dean movie when the thing had fallen from his mouth and his bedclothes had caught alight.

"He's promised not to smoke in his bedroom," Mom had defended when Papa had previously and with great reluctance allowed the Addict back into the house after having caught him stealing from his wallet – and having sold the family's game console and guest-room TV for drugs money. "So quit getting on his case," she'd said. "If he's promised, he's promised, and let that be an end to it."

Of course Mom believed every word that came out of the Addict's crack-blistered mouth – she always did – her devout and unerring belief in their hopelessly addicted son was the very worst kind of enabling possible; had there been just one grain of doubt in that woman, things may well have turned out to be so very different.

The entire upper storey of the house had been destroyed by the ensuing fire – along with the Addict's little brother and sister.

Seven and four, respectively, they'd died screaming in their beds whilst Papa and the Fire department had attempted to save them. They'd succumbed to smoke inhalation in the end. The irony of this sad fact was not lost on Papa.

Papa and Mom spent the more than generous insurance money not on repairs to their home, but on the third – and final as things worked out – stint in rehab for the Addict; after which he'd gone straight back on the illicit substances the second he'd gotten out. Still, it didn't matter to Papa and Mom that the upstairs to their once beautiful family home was now uninhabitable, since there was no reason to go up there any more – their own bedroom was on the ground floor and upstairs had been very much the kid's realm. Even the little one's goldfish had died a week or so after the fire – there were no longer those doting little fingers to sprinkle a pinch of fish flakes on top of the water at bedtime.

And Papa thought of the Addict at the party that Mom imagined him to be at, his eyes rolled to the back of his head, the acrid stench of his drug of choice – still Papa couldn't bring himself to say the word *crack*, even in his head – clinging to him like a thick, hazy shroud, and Papa hoped that the Addict was having a really good time.

*

The Addict was happy.

Tonight they were going to party.

Okay, it was still just a party in their filthy, needle-strewn motel room, but it was a party nonetheless. One member of their motley group – a tousle-haired, fat girl who went by the unfortunate name of *Bike* due to her propensity to allow anyone to mount her corpulent body in return for a hit of whatever happened to be the substance of the day – had robbed some little old lady of her pension at knife point earlier that afternoon. Bike had then proceeded to blow the entire contents of the old dear's purse – the princely sum of sixty-five dollars and thirteen cents – on a half dozen bottles of Spec's low-cost, dirt-cheap vodka (not quite the stuff that'll make you go blind, but near enough) and a couple of fistfuls of assorted drugs from the local dealer. She'd blown the guy – an odd looking character they all knew as Goofy because of his long, lank hair and improbably prominent buck teeth – just for good measure and had gotten a wrap of pretty decent grade heroin for her trouble.

The Addict was still coming down from the hit of crack he'd taken just before Bike had returned from her immoral hunter-gathering and to him the room and everyone it contained had a kind of cosy, bluish glow about it. His mind wandered freely across the drug-addled landscape of its own disease, with all thoughts of the family he'd left behind him little more than a nebulous cloud that hovered over his conscience.

Mom loved him, of that the Addict could be certain.

Mom was the one who sent him money every month, pushing to the back of her mind that he'd most likely be spending it on drugs – her rationale being that she'd much rather he got it from her than steal it from others. Having said that, the Addict did both anyways.

Ever the expert enabler was Mom.

She was also the one who lapped up his every word when he promised her on his life that all he ever took was weed – even after his stints in rehab when he'd been forced to confess to shovelling a veritable laundry list of illicit substances into his young, vulnerable body. The Addict had decided that he could forgive Mom for having dragged him kicking and screaming – literally – to his very first stay in rehab, for taking him away from his beloved drugs for seven long weeks that had seemed at the time to be a geological age.

But Papa.

Papa was evil.

Papa was the one who *didn't* believe the Addict whenever he'd protest his innocence; like when he flatly denied smoking weed *and* crack in his bedroom, even though the sour stench would permeate the entire upper floor of the house and circulate around the air-conditioning system to pollute the bedrooms of his younger siblings. And it was Papa who rooted through the Addict's bedroom, digging up the discarded drug paraphernalia that the Addict had gone to no trouble whatsoever to conceal. Hell, Papa had even texted a picture of the Addict's crack pipe to Mom – who resolutely refused to even enter her son's room; out of sight, and all that – in an attempt to break her naive circle of denial, the conniving old bastard.

There'd been clashes, of course. And although the Addict knew that Papa was no fool, the boy was canny enough to know how to play the old man off of Mom, how to stir up trouble between the two in order to deflect attention from himself.

A cunning lot are the addicts; there's just something about the hold their chosen substances have over them; whilst addiction had stunted the Addict's mental and social development, it had provided a heightened level of intelligence that was solely focussed upon obtaining that next, much-needed high, whether it be by fair means or foul. And along with that, throughout the course of his drug-taking career, the Addict had managed to shed his sense of decency and conscience, much like a snake sloughs off its old, unwanted skin.

*

"You're over reacting," Mom had said when Papa told her that the Addict had pulled a gun on him. "It wasn't even a real gun, it's just his BB gun," she'd chastised her ever so foolish and melodramatic husband.

"How was I supposed to know that?" Papa had defended himself, the sick feeling back in the pit of his stomach. "The cops will shoot kids brandishing BB guns," he'd argued, "why do they have to make them to look so much like the real thing?"

The truth was that when the Addict had waved the gun at Papa for catching him taking a hit from his beloved glass pipe in the upstairs restroom, Papa had genuinely feared for his life. Forget that a metal BB shot from such close proximity could take out an eye, pierce the skin, or even kill should it hit something internal and vital; at that particular moment in time, Papa had perceived that gun to be as real as the Glock he kept in the tiny thumb-print secured safe beneath his own bed.

He'd thrown the Addict out that night – having given him the choice to leave of his own volition or with assistance from the local Sheriff's department. The Addict had shoved a few clothes – along with his treasured drugs and associated accoutrements – into his backpack and disappeared into the night.

Mom never did forgive Papa for chasing away her sweet little angel, and Papa felt bad because of that; even though he knew in his heart that he should have thrown the boy out several months earlier, when he'd brandished the hunting knife during some stupid argument over laundry.

And Papa would forever regret giving in to his wife's tearful pleading to allow the Addict back into their home after that, to give their son *one last chance*. And, as irony would have it, it did actually turn out to be the Addict's last chance of all – for there'd be no more opportunities for him to destroy their home and stand in the rain whilst his little brother and sister were lowered into their tiny graves.

*

"Try this," Bike said to the Addict. "It's fucking awesome." She pressed her flabby body close up to the boy, her voluminous breasts overflowing her inadequate tank top that had long ago ceased to be anything close to its original white. She took a long, deep draw on the reefer one of the guys had passed over and then wiggled a tiny baggie of white powder in front of the Addict's nose, teasing him with the reprehensible delights contained within.

"What is it?" the Addict asked. In reality he cared no more about the given name of the wonderfully white powder than he did about the filthy hypodermic that Bike had plucked from the floor; worries about hepatitis, AIDS, sepsis and the whole host of other unpleasant diseases that were so easily caught from shared needles were so long ago in the Addict's past that he'd all but forgotten about them. All that mattered to him right here, right now was the promise of that next glorious hit.

"Goofy told me it's his very best H'" Bike told him, the tops of her huge, liquid breasts quivering like pink, fleshy Jell-O as she spoke. "It's been a long time since we chased the dragon together," she said this with the tone of a hopeless romantic suggesting an anniversary return to a favorite restaurant. "Perhaps we could fuck on it, too?"

And they say that romance is dead.

The Addict reached out and plucked the small plastic bag from the girl's fat fingers. He held it a few inches from his face to examine the fine, white powder that nestled within. "Looks like good stuff," he declared grandly as if by merely staring at the heroin through the clear plastic he could tell. "What did you have to do to get this?" He gave Bike a knowing smile.

"The usual," Bike shrugged her not inconsiderable shoulders and offered the Addict a smile of her own. "It was no big deal."

The Addict was forced to agree with Bike on that one, a good ol' suck-and-spit for quality gear like this was more than a decent transaction in his book. After all, *he* was fully prepared to screw the fat girl for a taste of the powder – hell, he'd go down on her if it came to that, as much as the thought of having his head buried between her obese, pasty thighs and in proximity to her foul, unwashed privates revolted him. "You got a lighter?" he grunted at Bike, his attention fixed firmly upon the baggie.

"And a spoon." Bike presented said items for the Addict's inspection.

The Addict grinned like a madman. Partly because he was delighted that Bike had been fully prepared for their evening's delectations and partly because she'd actually remembered to procure a metal spoon this time. The time before, she'd tried to heat up the H in one of those cheap, white spoons they dish out for free at roadside services. Of course the thing had almost instantly melted into a fat, charred lump of plastic that had plopped onto the carpet and smouldered there until someone had the foresight to tip half a bottle of warm beer onto it. The addict had thrown a fit; the waste of a good high always rankled and he'd ranted at poor Bike that she had come damned close to burning the place down and how could she be so *fucking careless*!?

And all without even a hint of irony, it has to be said.

Without ceremony or further ado, Bike had the contents of the baggie carefully emptied out onto the spoon – the girl was surprisingly nimble with those thick, sausage fingers of hers when she needed to be – and had the red *Zippo* flickering beneath the tarnished metal.

The Addict sniffed hungrily at the tiny wisps of white smoke that curled up from the head of the spoon like miniature ghost fingers; and if the delicious tang that assaulted his nostrils was anything to go by, this held the Devil's own promise of being one hell of a hit.

*

The old-style telephone stubbornly held its silence, just as it had done so for so long now. This time it was Papa's turn to eye the thing's stolid, unblinking face. He wished that he had the strength to swipe the hellish thing from the couch and toss it into the trash where it could no longer exert its cruel, paralyzing power over what little remained of their lives. Perhaps with the 'phone gone he and Mom could start anew, rebuild their home and their lives – even if it was not necessarily together. Anything had to be better than this; the endless waiting, hoping, praying and wishing for the thing to ring out, yet dreading that one day when inevitably it would.

Yet Papa knew that Mom would never allow him to

do so. The telephone was her one lifeline, her emotional crutch, an imaginary umbilical to the son she refused to accept she had already lost to addiction. If Papa so much as laid a hand on the thing, she would most likely kill him for his trouble.

So Papa just sat there and maintained his own silence – the time had been and gone when he and Mom had had anything much to say to one another – as if he were caught up in some nefarious war of attrition with the telephone; the first one to make a sound loses. One day he hoped that he would find the courage to pick up the cursed thing and hurl it as far away as he could, and to hell with the consequences. But Papa knew that day was most likely a ways off, and that he wasn't ready yet to hurt the woman he still loved so very deeply.

Not just yet, anyhow.

*

The Addict whined like a little bitch when Bike stuck the needle into his arm. Sure, she'd had to force the thing through the soft skin of his forearm to pierce the bulging blue vein below because the needle's tip had become blunted with so much use. Even so, that was no reason in her book for him to bleat like a little kid who'd just scraped his knee on the sidewalk.

"Quit wriggling, you big baby," Bike admonished as she held the needle steady in the addict's arm and struggled to pull up the plunger a tad as her sweating, chubby fingers let her down somewhat.

"It fucking hurts, you fat bitch," the Addict cried out, caring as much about the girl's feelings as he did about his own welfare. Truth was he was not used to injecting, that was the simple fact here; the Addict preferred to take his pleasures through his lungs, nose and stomach. Oh yeah, and not forgetting about his flirtation with the

418

suppository method of obtaining that ever-elusive high.

The Addict forced himself still and watched, mesmerized as a tiny trickle of blood – *his* blood! – puffed up into the clear liquid contained behind the fading, gradated markings on the syringe. The blood swirled and dispersed throughout the thick fluid to render the mixture a surreal yet beautiful, cloudy pink.

And then it was all gone.

Bike pushed down the plunger and in an instant the hypodermic sticking out of the Addict's arm was empty. She slipped the needle out of the Addict's vein, tossed it back onto the grimy carpet and looked on in stoned fascination as a thin trickle of blood oozed out from the hole she'd made in the Addict's smooth skin. She then watched as the Addict eased himself backwards on the grubby couch, his eyes closing in eager anticipation of the high that she knew would be racing towards him like an unstoppable freight train.

After what seemed to him to be a disappointing *forever*, the scorching hit of the heroin ploughed into the Addict's brain with an almighty *whoosh*. The euphoria it brought in its wake felt to him like the world's fastest, most vertiginous rollercoaster coupled with the biggest, most mind-blowing orgasm all rolled into one unspeakably intense blast of pleasure. His racing brain fired off what seemed to the Addict to be every single neuron it possessed in absolute and perfect synchronicity – he could actually *see* for himself the bright, white sparks shooting off like sparkling, dazzling fireworks behind his tight shut eyes.

The Addict held on to the sticky arm of the filthy couch with one hand, his other gripping a fistful of Bike's flabby thigh as if to ground himself as his conscious soared high above his own body whilst at the same time burrowing deep inside his own psyche. In his heaving chest, his heart thumped hard and loud, as if doing its level best to burst out through his ribs and join in with the party. The Addict wished at that moment that he could share how he was feeling with someone – *anyone* – that there was someway he could express in words just how alive he felt, how incredibly *aware*; that *this* was what everything in life was all about, and *this* was why he had chosen the path that he had, the pursuit of such incredible, drug-induced enlightenment. And the Addict knew that if he could ever share this moment with Mom and Papa, then they would get where he was coming from and all would be right with them.

They would finally *understand*.

The Addict actually felt the very moment that his heart stopped.

It startled him at first, the sudden cessation of that one constant sound that had accompanied him through each and every day of his twenty-three years of life. For it to just suddenly and simply be no longer there took the Addict a moment or two to comprehend within the swirls and blur of his rushing mind.

The Addict was experiencing a silence so complete, the likes of which he'd never known before, not even in his highest highs or lowest of drug-induced unconsciousness. The sounds of the motel room drugs party were gone, and there was no longer the comfort of that familiar rush of blood through his ears, nor was the lifelong companionship of the *lub-dub-lub-dup-lub-dup* of his heartbeat to break that terrible, deathly silence.

Yet, enraptured in his high, the Addict didn't much care, couldn't even begin to comprehend the gravity that the eerie quiet signified. The Addict was everywhere yet nowhere, his mind racing through its own thoughts and scattered fragments of memories like a puppy chasing butterflies in a warm, spring meadow. It was dark behind his eyelids – pleasantly so – and so wonderfully still and hushed in that beautifully enlightened world that the drug conspired with his dying brain to create.

And at that moment, the Addict quite simply, just *knew*.

*

Mom and Papa sat there in their own silence, the stale waft of ancient smoke and scorched things creeping quietly around them, the dulled black plastic telephone perched between them like an angry, brooding creature of the night. Just another night amongst the endless others, waiting for the infernal thing to ring, yet hoping against hope that it would not.

Their clothes had long since rotted away and hung from their bodies in fetid, tattered strips – neither one possessed much of a desire to change – and Mom and Papa's naked flesh had melded to the faux-leather of the couch that had been their home for quite possibly five years, maybe even a month or two beyond that. Their bodies had atrophied through idleness along the years, their limbs now little more than withered, skin covered bones, and their buttocks spread out beneath protruding femurs and pelvic bones like sickly, melted lard, pallid skin joined as one to the seeping plastic of the couch.

The flesh of the couple's backs had long since worn away through their endless years of just sitting, the eroded skin and muscle having soaked away over time between the worn cushions, and the knobbed bone of Mom and Papa's spines dug into the faux-leather to fix them in that erect, stoic position that looked for all the world as if they were attending some make-believe class in advanced deportment.

Along with their wilting bodies, Mom and Papa's minds had also crumbled; what fragile grasp either of them had ever had on reality following the fire and the Addict's departure from the family home had worn ever more flimsy and paper-thin until finally, one day long forgotten now, it had dissolved completely.

But still they sat and waited; their one companion that hideous, ancient telephone, the resonant echoes of hope swirling desperately around in what remained of their sanity as they stared down at the one thing that so maliciously held wide the abyss between them.

And then, quite unexpectedly – yet somehow most *expectedly* – the telephone began to ring.

The sound was shrill, like the clanging of bells on those old-style fire engines so often portrayed in the old black-and-white movies Papa had so loved to watch in years gone by. The incessant and infernal ringing shattered the silence of the ruined house with its demanding voice, its chimes seemingly ever more urgent.

Mom and Papa stared down at the telephone, their eyes fixed with a look of horror, neither of them making a move to pick up that dulled, Bakelite receiver.

For after having waited so long for the call, neither of them wished to answer it.

End

First Impressions

Nurse Jessica's First Night.

It was dark outside.

It was always fucking dark outside when Rusty Deakins finished his shift. In fact, the orderly couldn't rightly remember the last time he'd walked out of the loony-bin and felt the warmth of the sun on his face. Rusty clocked off with a scowl and shuffled his weary body towards the exit, feeling around in his pocket for the half pack of smokes he'd been craving since lunch.

With barely a downwards glance he stepped around a patient – one of that week's newest intakes – who squatted down on her haunches and looked for all the world like she was taking a pee. The woman's skinny frame, clad in green/blue institution-scrubs rocked back and forth and she paused occasionally to thump her head with a balled fist, before repeating the pattern – as she had done all damn day. It looked to Rusty as if she was trying her best to beat out whatever it was inside her head that had landed her in this hellhole in the first place.

Sometimes, in his more reflective moments, Rusty

would try to imagine what it must be like for the patients under his care in the psychiatric hospital, to try empathise a little with the tortured thoughts that he figured must echo around in their tormented heads day and night.

But, most of the time, like the rest of the staff here, Rusty really didn't give all that much of a shit.

"Yo, Rusty!" a gruff voice split his reverie. Rusty glanced over to see his night-shift contemporary storming in through the main doors.

"Oh, hi, Jebediah," he mumbled. Rusty didn't much care for Jebediah; much too loud and all-up-in-your-business for his liking. Still, it was nice to have the occasional interaction with somebody who wasn't in the asylum because of a court order. "How's it hanging, dude?"

"Straight down the fuckin' middle, same as always!" Jebediah hollered across the hallway, oblivious to the fact that it was eleven at night and most of the patients were sleeping. "How 'bout you?"

"Much the same, Jeb; better now I'm outta this place," Rusty said. "Gonna sink a few cold ones before I go home to the Missus."

Distracted from the squatting patient, Rusty didn't see the thick-set nurse with a smiling face and dancing eyes grab the woman by a fistful of hair and drag her roughly into one of the bedrooms. Job done, the nurse stepped out of the room, closed the door gently behind her and bustled towards the vacant nurses' station.

Jeb laughed. It was a loud, exaggerated laugh which never ceased to grate on Rusty's nerves; nothing was ever *that* funny.

"Gotta love how ya still call ya Mom *The Missus*!" Jeb hooted.

Rusty curled his lip. "Yeah, that's exactly what it is." *Prick*. Rusty hurled the mental insult at Jeb.

Both orderlies shared a laugh, Rusty's a little more forced than Jeb's, and their voices carried down the stark, white hallway, echoed from the stippled walls. A doctor and one of the day shift nurses hurried by, pulling on coats in anticipation of the chill, autumnal night that skulked beyond the door, eager to be gone and on their way.

Behind them, an inmate – Rusty found it impossible to think of the patients here as anything other than *inmates* – made his slow, shuffling way towards him, a thick, yellow phonebook clutched tight to his chest.

"Say, man," Rusty asked Jeb, "how come you're still doing the night shift? You know you could have transferred off at the end of last month?"

"Yeah, I know." Jeb smiled. "It has its attractions." He nodded towards the nurses' station, where the voluptuous Nurse Christobel – she of the dancing eyes – was settling in for her own night shift. Jeb cast a lascivious smile her way and she winked back at him.

"I get ya." Rusty grinned, ever the one to live his sex life vicariously through Jeb. All he had to look forward to going home to was the wretched stink of soiled diapers and disappointment. Still it was Halloween in a few days and he had the older neighborhood girls in their slutty costumes to look forward to. "We're gonna have to crack a few beers sometime soon and ya can tell me all about it."

Rusty glanced at a patient who was approaching with his fat, yellow phone book that was tattered and dog eared through months of obsessive reading and he decided to bid his farewells before he found himself engaged in yet another meaningless conversation with a certified lunatic.

"Anyhoo, gotta be going, Jeb, have yourself a great night." Rusty walked away. "And don't do anything I wouldn't do!" A laugh as he pushed the double doors open and the night air chilled his face and his breath plumed out into the dark.

"No chance of that, good buddy," Jeb mumbled to himself, "no fuckin' chance at all." And at that, he allowed himself a hearty chuckle.

Suddenly, the patient with the phonebook grabbed Jeb's arm and spun him around to face crazy, twitching eyes.

"Phonebook!" Jeb beamed. "How the *fuck* are you this fine evening?" He greeted the patient with a hearty slap on the shoulder. Phonebook towered over Jeb, an easy six-four/six-five, beanpole thin with rarely washed, greasy hair that lay plastered to his scalp. And not forgetting those crazy, staring eyes.

"The space antelopes are going to eat our spleens." Phonebook informed Jeb with gravitas, his voice lowered and paranoid eyes darting like fish trapped in a bowl. "They're on their way to Earth as we speak; travelling over twenty million light-miles from their home planet, *Antelopia*."

"Don't ya mean twenty million light *years*?" Jeb corrected.

"Don't be stupid," Phonebook chastised Jeb as one would an errant pre-schooler in remedial science class. "*Light years* is a measure of time, not distance. *Everybody* knows that."

"And they're coming all that way –" Jeb played along. He enjoyed the rare moments of interaction he got with the more lucid and entertaining of the patients. "– just to eat our spleens? You sure about that, buddy? Last night it was the hedgehogs that live in the Earth's core coming to harvest our pineal glands?"

Phonebook glanced around, and once he was happy that no one was eavesdropping, "That's what they *wanted* you to think," he whispered. "It's the *Gummint*, they're in cahoots with 'em. Why do you think we can survive without our spleens, Jebediah?"

"Beats me, bud." Jeb was growing tired of baiting the crazy person and yearned for the sanctuary of the supplies cupboard – his bolt-hole from all the craziness on offer at the madhouse.

"It's because we don't need *em!"* Phonebook's voice exploded and he drew startled stares from the handful of staff who were well on their way to vacating the premises. "It's obvious! Don't you see! We're being bred for our spleens! To feed the space antelopes! It all makes perfect sense!"

"Come along, Phonebook, you should be in your room and asleep by now." Nurse Christobel materialized as if out of nowhere. Jeb was startled by his main girl's sudden appearance; damned if she didn't possess the uncanny ability to sneak up on folk like she was some kind of phantom. He'd worked with Christobel for two years know – had gotten to know her in quite the intimate fashion – yet her ability to move around in such a silent manner still creeped him out to hell and back. The gal sure was a whole lot of fun and a damned fine lay though, and Jeb was prepared to overlook most things for that.

"Come on now, off you go." Christobel ushered Phonebook on his way and her soft soled, flat shoes *squish-squashed* softly on the white tiled floor as she walked alongside the crazy guy. Phonebook mumbled under his breath and scuttled away. "And *you* should know better than to encourage him," he buxom nurse chided Jeb. There was a distinct sparkle in her eye as it reflected the fluorescent lights.

"Christobel." Jeb nodded and played it cool. He looked the gal's body up and down, and thought that she looked particularly fuckable this evening, what with that crisp, white uniform clinging to her petite-yet-voluptuous outline like some viscose second skin. And

Jeb particularly admired the way the uniform's buttons puckered at the front over Christobel's bountiful bosom as if her delectable breasts were straining for liberty. Nurse Christobel's shoulder-length jet-black hair shone that fresh-washed shine and provided the perfect frame for her round face – it hid the angry eruptions of acne that marred her forehead, which, despite her heavy application of foundation, she couldn't fully conceal. The nurse smiled at Jeb, her full, red-glossed lips parted and pearly teeth glinted.

Jeb revelled in being in such close proximity to Christobel, and his dick stiffened; damned if the woman didn't just ooze sexuality from each and every one of her thoroughly cleansed pores. Even the way she chewed stale gum with her mouth open turned him on.

"I hear ya got a new one starting tonight," Jeb said, keen to break the silence. He was all too aware that he was standing slack-jawed and staring for a tad longer than was actually flattering.

"Yeah, I hope she lasts longer than the last one." Christobel forced a smile. "I don't want to have to go through the whole induction bullshit three times in one month – *three fuckin' times*!" She chewed on her gum and Jeb could smell just the faintest trace of mint on her breath.

"I suppose *I'm* going to have to show her the ropes – if she ever fuckin' gets here – let her know how we do things around here." Christobel threw Jeb a wink and his dick stiffened some more.

"Rather you than me, Ma'am, sounds too much like hard work."

"It is," Christobel agreed. "But the new ones always make for the best footage." She grinned as she plucked her smartphone from a pocket. She waved the thing in Jeb's face whilst glancing over his shoulder. "Why, here she is now."

Christobel waved across at the new nurse who had just walked in amidst a chilled breeze and a flurry of something that looked like it could be the beginnings of snow. Christobel turned on her heels and hurried over to greet the new arrival, switching on her phone's built-in video camera as she walked.

"Say hi to the camera!" Nurse Christobel thrust her cell phone towards Jessica's face, and the new nurse immediately felt uncomfortable. As she talked, Christobel's mouth made wet, smacking sounds as it fought to contain a gray wad of stale gum, which Jessica thought most common. Nonetheless, she forced a limp wave and strained her thin lips into some semblance of a smile.

"Hi," she said.

Christobel smiled down at Jessica and her full, red-glossed lips parted to show perfect teeth.

"Come on, don't be shy!" Christobel grinned at her new charge.

Jessica's mouth creased at the corners as she gave a disarming smile. In contrast to Christobel, Jessica was a slim, slip of a girl, her body practically straight up and down. However, she did take pride in her honey brown, flawless complexion and full-bodied, auburn hair that she kept trimmed into a smooth, tidy bob.

"Come along, let's get you started." Christobel ushered Jessica towards the nurses' station, her legs taking long, purposeful strides that had Jessica struggling to keep up.

Jessica glanced nervously around at the stark, white walls and empty hallways of the psychiatric hospital, and clutched tight onto the brown paper lunch sack, paperback novel and DVD she'd brought along, as if for security.

"So, tell us about yourself," Christobel said as she pulled the camera back from Jessica's face and played

Leno.

"I'm Jessica," Jessica offered. "The agency sent me. I was told to report to the reception desk at eleven."

"And here you are!" Christobel laughed and put down the phone. "Welcome to Bedlam." She stuck out a hand for the shaking.

Jessica followed suit. "Bedlam?"

Christobel grinned and studied the hand clasped in her own. Jessica was a nail-biter, she noted; another Nervous Nelly who likely wouldn't last above a couple of nights. As she shook the girl's clammy hand, Christobel smiled and absently wondered if they would get this one to pee in her pants like the girl before last. "It's what we call this place, unofficially of course. The Management prefers to call it a *psychiatric facility*." She frowned at Jessica's blank face. "Bedlam was a famous English asylum from back in the old days," Christobel explained with a wry grin. "They used to organise tours so the rich folk could gawk at the lunatics." She stared at Jessica and sighed. "Do they teach you guys *nothing* at nurses' college?" she laughed.

"You're unlucky they've started you off on night shift." Christobel lowered her voice to a whisper, "it's where nurses' dreams come to die." Christobel smirked at the disconcerted look on Jessica's face. "I see you came prepared for the boredom," deftly changing the subject, she nodded at the paperback and DVD tucked snug under Jessica's arm.

The nights were indeed long and monotonous, and it was hard to keep a brain busy once silence smothered the hallways in the small hours; which was precisely why Christobel made her own entertainment.

"Here, take a look at this." She presented the phone to Jessica, screen-first this time.

Jessica recoiled at the image that appeared on the tiny screen. A guy wearing blue scrubs and a scraggy beard was standing over a distressed, mewling patient who lay on the floor in what was unmistakably a puddle of her own urine. In one hand the guy held an old, battered teddy bear; in the other, a cruel-looking cattle prod. He dangled the bear in front of the patient's face and when she reached up for it, he jammed the prod hard into her side. The patient flopped around on the tiled floor with a shrill, keening sound and soiled herself. From the background came the unmistakeable sound of Christobel's voice, egging the guy on and giggling with delight when the guy stuck the prod into the patient's genitals and she simultaneously screamed, peed and puked. Jessica wrinkled her nose as she realised she was exactly on the spot at which the film had been shot.

"Fun with loonies dot com?" Jessica read the web address from the screen.

"Cool, yeah?" Christobel beamed.

"This is your website?"

"Yep." Christobel leaned closer and dropped her voice to a conspiratorial whisper, "My boyfriend writes websites. He made this one so I can upload movies directly from my cell phone." She looked pleased with herself. "Look, over two million hits!"

Christobel slipped the phone back into her pocket and took Jessica's arm, guiding her around to the business side of the utilitarian nurses' station.

"You *are* allowed to be on this side of the desk – you're part of the team!" Christobel's voice was back to full volume. She relieved Jessica of her belongings and placed them neatly on the desk beneath a flickering CCTV monitor. "I say *team*; I mean me – and you, of course – and there's an orderly around somewhere. And that's it. There used to be six of us on night shift but what with all the cost cutting, it's down to three."

"What happens if there's an emergency?" Jessica asked.

Christobel laughed. "We haven't had one of those in a while. The crazies are drugged up to keep 'em docile and their rooms are on lock-down. Ain't any of 'em going nowhere!" She could see from the disappointment in Jessica's face that the nurse had clearly taken the job with over-inflated dreams of helping the crazy fuck-ups.

Welcome to the night shift, *Toots*.

"All *we* have to do is watch 'em on this for a couple of bucks above minimum wage." She waved a finger at a monochrome CCTV monitor. "Not exactly the career I had in mind when I signed up for nursing college either, but what can ya do?" Christobel forced a laugh.

The monitor, held to the wall by a precarious, peeling metal bracket had a screen split four ways. Each segment displayed a sparse room in which a sleeping patient could be seen as a shapeless mound in their bed.

All but one.

In Room Three, a young, female patient sat in the center of the room watching an old-style cathode ray TV. As if she knew that she was being watched, the girl's head snapped around to face the camera and her eyes met briefly with Jessica's. Then, the screen jumped and four different rooms were displayed in glorious black and white.

"And this here's the panic button," Christobel continued, poking a scarlet fingernail at a large red button beneath the desk. "It's for just in cases, but I've not had to hit it in the eight years I've been here." She sighed, a big sigh. "If the loonies ever get unruly, we just stick 'em with one of these." Christobel plucked a fat syringe that sported the thickest of needles out from her pocket. "This'll put 'em straight back out. Hell, this stuff'd knock an elephant out in five seconds flat!" Again, that smile. "I'll get you yours after I've finished showing you around."

Jessica nodded her appreciation; it was good to know

that there were sensible precautionary measures being taken, despite outward appearances.

"Ya know," Christobel went on, "I guess the most exciting thing that happens is when we lose one."

"I thought you said they were all locked in their rooms?"

"I meant *lose* one." Christobel made a sawing motion with a hand over her wrist. "Knotted bed sheets are particularly popular in this facility, that and the flatware they steal from the canteen. You'd be surprised at the damage a plastic Spork can do." Christobel pulled a disgusted face.

Although the suicide rate was pretty low at this *psychiatric facility* compared with some other institutions Christobel had heard about, they were still guaranteed five or six a year. Truth be told, that particular rate was way too low for Christobel's liking; there was nothing like a good ol' suicide to cut through the boredom. She did wish they'd stick to hanging themselves though, because cleaning up after a slit-wrister was hard, messy work.

"And sometimes I bang the morgue guys when they come to pick up the stiffs." Christobel's chest heaved with a lascivious giggle. "There was this one time when I'd *literally* just finished fucking the morgue guy in the Dead Room –"

"Dead Room?"

"It's where we put the recently-not-living-no-mores," Christobel teased.

"Ah, I get it. Sorry." Jessica's face reddened.

"Anyhoo, this guy – can't remember his name, not really important – had just finished up doing the nasty when the deceased's family turned up." Christobel sniggered. "I was rummaging around in the dark, trying to get my clothes back on and the morgue guy was pulling up his pants – all the while the family were knocking on the door to come pay their respects." She bent close to Jessica's ear. "And I'd totally lost my panties and had to greet the family with this humongous damp patch on the ass of my uniform." She stage-whispered, "And I can tell ya', there's nothing quite like a freshly laundered uniform for showing up the jizz!" Christobel's guffaw resounded along the hallway.

"*Eww*, you didn't use a condom?" Jessica asked, ever the practical one.

"Nah. Those guys work night shift for the City Morgue," Christobel giggled, "who the fuck else are they gonna screw?"

Jessica played along with the woman's sly laugh.

"Say, ya wanna go see the Dead Room?" Christobel's face straightened. "We got a stiff in there right now; sliced the crap out of his wrists this afternoon. Apparently the M.E. *and* the police came; I really wish I'd been here to see that – I just *love* me a guy in uniform." She swivelled her hips suggestively like some cheap Elvis impersonator. "We just need him picking up before he starts stinking." She stepped out from behind the desk. "I'll show you where the restrooms are on the way – ya need to pee?"

Jessica told Christobel no thank you; she did not need to pee, and trotted along after the nurse like a faithful puppy dog.

The main hallway right-angled about a hundred fifty feet down, and the hallway that led from that was badly lit and had long, fuzzy shadows that made it seem all the more foreboding. At the junction between the two there was a plain white door, indistinguishable from all of the others save for the name plate; '*ROOM 3: JANE DOE*'.

"While we're here, I'll introduce you to Emily," Christobel said.

"Emily?"

"She can't tell us her real name, so we christened her

Emily," Christobel explained. "Because she *emmalates* people off the TV."

Jessica considered correcting Christobel but her inherent good sense advised that course of action would win her no favors.

Christobel stabbed at four of the numbers on a panel beside the door and waited for the loud click as the door unlocked. She pushed it open

"Hey, Emily!" Christobel called out as if the room were a thousand feet square and not the statuary fifteen by twelve. "Say hi to Nurse Jessica!"

Jessica peered into the room. It was illuminated by the severe light from the tube-style TV which was topped by a thin, black DVD player and Jessica immediately recognized the occupant as the one she'd seen earlier on the nurse's station CCTV monitor. The girl – *Emily* – sat in the center of the room, cross-legged like a first grader at story time. Jessica could see that she was slightly built, although most of her small frame was hidden beneath the shapeless hospital nightgown. Her pale, pinched face and startlingly emerald green eyes were partially obscured by long, straggly hair and Jessica guessed Emily to be early to mid-twenties.

"Watchya doin' disturbing me?! Ya know I'm, like, friggin' pregnant!" the girl broke the awkward silence. She turned around to face the nurses, her face contorted. "And my tits are, like, Niagara friggin' falls."

"She's pregnant?" Jessica asked.

"Nah, she's been watching *Jersey Shore* reruns again," Christobel said.

"I'm gonna call my kid *Darquetanyan* and get me a friggin' sponsorship deal!" Emily threw back her head and let rip with a raucous, nasal laugh.

"She sounds just like Snooki, yeah?" Christobel grinned.

Jessica nodded. There really was no escaping the fact

that Emily *did* sound uncannily like the vacuous reality TV chick.

"She just sits there all day and night and copies what she hears on the TV," Christobel told her. "I don't think she ever actually sleeps." She smiled. "She's also the most watched crazy-fuck on my website." Christobel stepped into the room, bent down and snatched the TV remote from Emily's hand. She prodded at the rubber buttons and the DVD player whirred into action.

"Lions and tigers and bears! Oh My!" Emily exclaimed, a perfect impersonation of the gingham-clad Garland. "Oh, Toto, I wish I were back in Kansas with Aunty Em' again, I wish -"

And then Emily sang the opening lines of a voice-perfect *Somewhere Over The Rainbow* that made the hairs stand up on Jessica's arms and tears well up in her eyes.

It was beautiful.

Christobel switched back to the TV channel with a frustrated poke at the remote. "I can't stand it when she sings; gets to ya after so long," she grumbled.

"Wow," Jessica gasped. "That was awesome. She sounded just like -"

"Judy fuckin' Garland. Yeah, I know." Christobel eyed her patient with disdain; she was once again presented with the back of the girl's head.

Christobel gave an inward shudder, *a goose just walked across your grave,* as her Grandmother would have called it. Emily tended to have that effect on people who crossed her path; there was just something about the way she copied things that just plain creeped folk out. Sometimes it was the accuracy of the voices, and sometimes it was because Emily not only sounded like the people she impersonated, but she actually *looked* like them. It was subtle, nothing you could take a picture of, but somehow her gaunt face would take on enough of the person's characteristics that you'd swear to Holy Mary, Mother of God that she was actually *becoming* them. Christobel had even seen Emily do it on occasion with cartoon characters – and just how fucked-up was that?

"And that's all she does?" Jessica asked.

"Yep – never said a word of her own – not fuckin' one!"

"That's really sad."

"Sad?" Christobel spat. "It's fucking creepy, is what it is." She smacked the gray gum wad around in her mouth in contemplation. "I read a book once – well, I followed this link off *Wikipedia* – and it was all about Demons that *emmalate* people – Mimic Demons they call 'em –"

"And, you think that Emily is one of those?" Jessica suppressed a grin.

"Nah," Christobel laughed, "she's just loony tunes like the rest of the crazy fucks in here!" She slapped Jessica's arm again, and they both laughed and stepped back into the hallway. Christobel pulled Emily's door closed behind them.

"Now, are ya sure you're not gonna get spooked?" Christobel asked as she led Jessica across the hallway. "We've got us a real live dead 'un in here." They paused by the door to the Dead Room, which bore the more palatable epithet, *'Chapel of Repose'* on a small, brass plaque.

"I *have* seen corpses before," Jessica told her, although she did much prefer her charges alive.

"But this one's a suicide," Christobel whispered. "Which means that his spirit may still be hanging around. Because heaven won't let him in or some such."

"You're *trying* to spook me?" Jessica asked.

"Yep!" Christobel's eyes twinkled as she laughed her gum-slurping cackle and flecks of stale-mint spit escaped from her mouth. She keyed in the pass code and swung open the door.

Jessica followed her inside and immediately felt the hairs on her arms stand to attention; the temperature in the *Chapel* being deliberately cooler in order to slow the decomposition of the deceased. The room itself was dingy and somewhat foreboding, lit only by the subtle, subdued lighting recessed in the Styrofoam ceiling tiles, and empty save a small desk in one corner and a gurney in the center. And on the gurney lay a body covered by a white sheet upon which were dark splashes of dried blood in the proximity of the corpse's wrists.

"Ta-da!" Christobel's loud, cheerful tone was highly inappropriate and hung in the air like a sour stench. "Welcome to the Dead Room!" She stepped back to let Jessica all the way in and the door *swooshed* closed behind them. "Also known as the bang room because it's where we come to -"

"I get it, thank you," Jessica interrupted, wrinkling her nose at the death-stink that permeated the room. A body lets go of its gasses once the muscles are no longer capable of holding them in, and there's just something about dead people's farts that is – *different* – from regular farts; maybe because putrefaction begins within an hour or so of death and all of those busy-bee bacteria let off their own flatulence to add to a corpse's final humiliation. Jessica had smelled that stink many times before, but always masked by a hospital's disinfectant smells or the formaldehyde aroma of an undertakers. This one smelled most decidedly *odd*.

"We gotta have somewhere to go to have fun – and the occupants don't seem to mind too much," Christobel defended with a giggle. "Hell, their ghosts may even get off watching us earthly folk making with the sex!" She ground her hips against some imaginary partner for emphasis.

Jessica did her best to disguise her disgust at Christobel – and failed miserably.

"Look, I hate to be indelicate, especially in the presence of the recently departed an' all," Christobel announced with faux-reverence. "But I gotta go drop a deuce. I'll be right back." And with that, she flounced from the room.

Jessica was unsure about what she should do next; should she go back to the Nurses' Station and appear rude, or stay put and do her best to ignore the death-smell? Best stay put, she decided, didn't want to alienate her one and only peer on the first night. Jessica stepped towards the gurney, more than a little curious now as to how this patient had torn their wrists out and she couldn't help but wonder just how long the poor soul had taken to die.

In that instant, the corpse on the gurney sat up and let out a banshee wail.

Heart pounding, Jessica shrieked and stumbled back towards the door in a blind panic, a scream jammed in her throat as she clawed for the doorknob, which seemed a million miles away.

The body swung its legs over the side of the gurney, the movement making the wheels squeak out their complaints. Then the sheet fell away and revealed crazy, staring eyes and that terrible, screaming mouth.

The door opened behind Jessica and she all but fell backwards through it. The lights flicked on and in marched Christobel, filming on her cell phone.

"You should see your face!" Christobel laughed at Jessica. "Another home run, Jebediah!" She high-fived the corpse, who then hopped off the gurney with a loud grunt.

A nervous laugh escaped Jessica's throat, her body flushed through with adrenaline as she fought the subconscious reaction to run.

Jebediah threw the bloodied sheet back onto the gurney and manoeuvred his lanky frame over to say hi.

"Nurse Jessica, meet Jebediah – we call him Jeb. Jeb, meet Nurse Jessica," Christobel introduced.

"Pleased to make your acquaintance, Ma'am." The orderly stroked his unkempt beard and held out a hand that had impossibly long fingers. He smiled a wide smile as he shook Jessica's hand and tipped Christobel a sly wink.

Nurse Jessica's Second Night.

Christobel sat back in her chair, feet casually slung up on the desk. She gave a cursory glance at the monitor above her head as she fiddled with her cell phone. There was little time for the patients who were all mostly sleeping, crying or masturbating at this late hour, for she was working diligently to upload her latest cinematographic opus; she'd entitled it '*New Nurse Gets The S**t Scared Out Of Her*'.

"Good evening, Nurse Christobel." Jeb appeared, as usual, as if from nowhere. He was too damned good at that, Christobel thought; Jeb's silent appearances made her as nervous as hers made him. "Don't tell me we scared off another one?" He grinned and his eyes darted downwards to Christobel's ever-present, bountifully ample cleavage.

"Nah, she's been visiting with Miss Emily since she signed in," Christobel said with contempt.

"Well, ya did tell her we have to make our own entertainment." Jeb snorted. "And Miss Emily *is* entertaining alright."

"You ain't wrong there, Jeb." Christobel chewed loudly and serenaded Jeb with the familiar waft of stale mint. "And speaking of which, ya' want to shoot some movies tonight?"

An eager countenance lit up Jeb's face. "Sure thing, doll." He grinned. "You pick us out a good 'un while I go finish up in the laundry room and we'll make ourselves an Academy Award winner!" Jeb jangled his circle of keys as he hurried away along the hallway and raised a hand above his head by means of a *see-ya-later*.

*

Jessica sat, crossed-legged, on Emily's bed, her feet beginning to tingle with pins and needles. She looked down at the fragile girl who sat in the spot that was obviously a favorite, spindly legs tightly crossed.

"I'd like to put a movie on for you," Jessica coaxed, "it's one of my favorites."

Emily turned to face the nurse. "*Ozzy*! Ozzy, you arsehole!" Her features contorted as Sharron Osborne's dulcet English tones stuttered out. "What the bloody hell –?"

Used to the girl's non sequitur outbursts, Jessica ignored Emily and clicked on the DVD she'd previously slipped into the player and Emily's attention returned once more to the TV.

"It's '*Lady Sings The Blues*'," Jessica explained as the opening titles rolled.

Emily, transfixed by the TV screen, began to sing; her voice at once melodious and heart-wrenching. It was a song that Jessica knew well, it was her Mother's favorite – *That Old Devil Called Love* – and it sent shivers along the nurse's spine.

Jessica stared, dumbfounded as Emily sang and two things occurred to her; one, the song had not yet appeared on the movie; and two, Emily's voice was a pitch-perfect copy of Diana Ross *impersonating* Billie Holiday. And, although she was only seeing the girl's face in profile, Jessica was damned if Emily didn't look like some freakish emulation of Diana Ross.

Suddenly, Emily jumped to her feet, eyes wide and bright and with a broad, toothy grin cracking her face.

"It's sweatin' time!" she exclaimed, Ross/Holiday instantly forgotten. "Come on! Get that body going! Oh yeah! Come dance with me!"

Richard Simmons?

Jessica shook her head; she absolutely hated the infuriating little man. His campy voice and endlessly cheerful attitude never failed to make her skin crawl. Nonetheless, when Emily extended a bony hand in invitation, Jessica jumped off the bed and joined in with the routine.

"*Oh yeah!* That's it! Five, six, seven, eight and double touch – now walk the floor!"

Emily and Jessica recreated the moves that had helped myriad homely housewives across the decades feel a fraction more desirable for their bored, disinterested husbands.

"And exhale! One, two three and four! *Step higher!*"

A metallic, clattering noise from across the hallway broke the spell. Emily dropped to the floor and resumed staring at the TV with that blank face of hers. Jessica cocked an ear at the clattering and thought she heard Christobel's cacophonous laughter in amongst all the ruckus.

Jessica cracked open the door and peered across the hallway. She saw that the door catty-cornered from Emily's was open, and the sounds that had interrupted her *sweatin' time* were coming from within.

"I'll be right back," she whispered.

*

Jessica stormed into Room Four. "What the hell are

you doing?!" she shouted, her voice cracking just a tad.

"Hey, Jessica!" Christobel was startled by the other nurse's intrusion. "Me 'n Jeb thought you were busy, otherwise we'd have invited you over."

Somewhat out of place, an aluminium trash can stood in the corner of the room, and Jessica spotted a fluffy mess of green hair poking out from beneath the lid. As she watched, the lid began to rise up and a pair of wide, terrified eyes peered out. There came a loud clatter as Jeb hit the side of the can with a long, metal crutch "Keep your goddamned head down 'till I tell ya to come up, ya fuckin' *retard!*" he snarled and the green hair retreated back into the darkness. "We're havin' some fun with Trashcan," Jeb explained.

"This patient should be asleep," Jessica snapped.

"We woke him up for playtime," Christobel said. "Which was easy 'cause it looks like he *accidentally* missed his meds!" She actually seemed to be incredibly proud of herself at this revelation. "Lighten up, Jess; it's only a bit of fun." Christobel gave a dismissive shrug, happy in her justifications. "Get him to pop up again, Jeb!" she directed and pointed her cell phone once more at the trash can.

Jeb crashed the crutch into the side of the can once more and the metallic clatter reverberated through the room and spilled out to disrupt the quiet beyond the door.

"Up ya come, ya crazy fuck!" Jeb yelled and grinned like a disturbed child tormenting its first puppy.

The patient jumped up, eyes glaring with terror. He let out a tortured wail from the gaping, toothless mouth that nestled in the middle of his thick-bush beard. Jeb dug the metal crutch hard into the patient's ribs and the guy let out another shrill cry.

They'd spray-painted his entire head green.

"It's Oscar the Grouch!" Christobel cried out with glee and moved in for a tighter shot. "He looks just like

Oscar the fucking Grouch!"

Jeb clapped his hands as he basked in Christobel's delight. Damned if he wasn't guaranteed a BJ at the very least after this particular triumph.

"This is gonna look *so* awesome!" Christobel enthused and threw Jeb one of her especially dirty smiles. She then turned to Jessica. "Look! He looks just like Oscar –"

"– the Grouch, yeah, you said." Jessica didn't try to hide her disapproval. "Well done – both of you." She gave Christobel and Jeb her sternest look, although she doubted that it would have any lasting effect on either conscience. "*You* should be at the front desk, *Nurse* Christobel."

Jessica spun on her heels and bustled out of the room, fully aware that she had just crossed a line or two; after all she was still very much the new kid on the block and she'd spoken to her colleagues like they were errant nine year olds. So now was perhaps a very good time to retreat.

"Pay no attention to her," Christobel reassured Jeb as Jessica stomped off down the hallway. His face was a picture of concern, but then he always was the worrywart of the pair. "I'll talk to her when she's calmed down," she said. "She's not gonna say nothing to nobody."

*

Jessica returned to Emily's room, her heart still jackhammer-thumping against her ribs. She saw that Emily had removed the DVD from the player and had the TV remote in her hand, flicking aimlessly through the channels.

"This whole place is crazy," Jessica said. "I'm sorry, I didn't mean – what I *meant* is that I'm not sure who's the craziest in here; you patients, or those two."

"Oh Peter, what have you done?" Emily's Lois Griffin voice was faultless. "This is just like the time you had the *Enola Gay* over to cook dinner for the kids," and so saying, Emily jumped to her feet and danced once more to her imaginary music.

"One two, one two – and three! Point those toes!" It was Simmons again. Then it was Christina Aguilera's voice that flowed out from the young girl's mouth, "*You're beautiful –*" and then, "what are you freakin' looking at?" Snooki's irritating nasal whine at once blended seamlessly to an emotionally slurred, "I am not an animal." And it was as if John Merrick was standing right there in the room.

"*Help me, please help me,*" Emily whispered quietly.

Jessica grasped Emily's hands and looked directly into the girl's strange, haunted eyes. She imagined she caught a faint glimmer of the trapped consciousness that flickered behind that ethereal, blank expression.

"That was *you*?" Jessica gasped.

Emily stared at her, lips pursed.

Jessica felt excitement rise up in her chest. "I'll go get the others – they have got to see this!"

Jessica opened the door and with a sinking heart, saw Christobel and Jeb making their way down the hallway to the Dead Room. They were giggling like horny teenagers and Jeb's hand had hoisted up the back of Christobel's skirt to snake down into her leopard print panties.

Jessica came back to Emily who was back to her spot on the floor with, her thumb working overtime on the TV remote. "Never mind them, this can be our secret for now," she said with a low, conspiratorial whisper.

Nurse Jessica's Third Night

Painfully aware that she was fifteen minutes late, Jessica scurried along the hallway, her progress punctuated by the *squeak-squeak* of her wet shoes; the drizzle outside had soaked them all the way through to her feet. She'd managed to keep her paperback, DVD and lunch bag dry by secreting them beneath her coat; another five minutes out there and, they too would have succumbed to the relentless precipitation.

She saw that the day shift had made an effort to get into the mood of the day; they'd put up a sparse collection of Halloween decorations – paper chains of skulls, small, plastic witches straddling plastic brooms and dangling from the ceiling on the thinnest of strings, a brace of tiny glow in the dark skeletons hanging from the door to the treatment room, and a large sparkly banner that declared *Happy Halloween!* – it was all little more than a token gesture really, pretty much the kind of stuff one would expect to see in a kindergarten since this was one place where it didn't pay to scare the residents *too* much.

As she approached the deserted nurses' station, a sudden movement on the CCTV monitor caught Jessica's eye. "Sweet Jesus, no!" she gasped. Without even taking the time to remove her sodden coat and still clutching her belongings, Jessica ran as fast as she could down the hallway and towards Emily's room.

The awful quality of the porn film that played on Emily's DVD player was no more enhanced by the cheesy music and badly dubbed, fake moans of its sound track than by the gaudy images of ugly tan lines and wet, glistening genitalia.

"Come on, Emily!" Christobel goaded. "You're supposed to be making like Linda Lovelace!" She held her cell phone aloft to best capture the shot of the shirtless Jeb standing over the naked, cowering patient.

"Make her suck it, Jeb!" Christobel directed.

Jeb unbuckled his pants, let them slide down and his dick sprung out of his boxers like some thick, blue-veined Jack-in-the-box. "I been lookin' forward to seein' ya copy *this* particular movie for quite some time, little girl," Jeb said with a lascivious grunt. "Now why don't ya git your *purdy* little mouth around this and show ya cousin Jeb what ya can do!"

Christobel pulled a face. "Cousin?"

"Don't you go judgin' me, Christobel; you got your fantasies, I got mine," Jeb growled before returning his attention to Emily who sat with her back pressed tight into the corner of her room as if attempting to will herself through the wall. Clearly terrified, she hugged her knees tight to her chest to protect her small, pointy breasts and the sparse, blonde tuft of hair that peeked out from between her legs. Stripped of her gown, Emily's body looked wasted and vulnerable; her ribs prominent, arms and legs practically devoid of muscle, her elbows and knees bony, sharp and pointed.

Jeb grasped his overly long penis in one hand and slapped Emily's face hard with it. He then pressed it against her lips, but Emily kept her mouth clamped tight.

"Stop it!" Jessica burst in, her face flushed.

Jeb's turned to face the unwelcome intrusion. "Hey! Looks like I'm gonna have me a threesome!" he said with a lascivious lick of the lips for the benefit of Christobel's camera.

"Leave her alone!" Jessica screamed, her fists balled like she meant to use them. "And turn that filth off!" She pointed at the TV.

"Now looky here, *nursey*." Christobel squared up to her subordinate. "You seem to be forgetting who's the temporary one here!"

"*Temporary* doesn't mean I have to stand by while you rape the patients!" Jessica stood her ground.

"It's not rape, Jessie-baby, these 'uns don't count on account of 'em not being of sound mind," Jeb offered, and genuinely appeared to believe that he was making a sound point. He looked down, dismayed at his wilting dick. "It's probably in the constitution of the United States." His laugh was a nervous one.

Jessica looked at Jeb with disdain. "What's wrong with you, Jebediah?" she growled. "Is your dick not big enough to satisfy a sane woman?"

The jibe prickled Jeb to his core; if there was one thing in life that he could be proud of, it was his pecker. Surely the stupid nurse could see for herself just how impressive the thing was, even in its current half-flaccid state. "There ain't nothin' wrong with my dick, bitch!" Jeb faced Jessica and wiggled the offending organ in her direction. "And when I've finished up with Emily, I just might show you *precisely* what I can do with it!"

Jessica's face glowed hot and she could hear the raging *thump-thump-thump* of blood as it pounded in her ears. "Don't you *dare* threaten me, you asshole!" she screamed at Jeb. "And will *you* quit filming me!?" She turned in the blink of an eye on Christobel.

Christobel lowered her cell.

"I'm reporting you both to Management, and *then* I'm calling the police. You sick bastards shouldn't be allowed anywhere near people like her." Jessica pointed at Emily who quivered, blank-faced and painfully naked in the corner.

Jeb fumbled his rapidly diminishing erection back into his boxers where it strained outwards against the tartan material. "Now, there's no need to be hasty –" There was fear in his eyes. He glanced over at Christobel; this was all her fucking fault, playing him along with her dirty smile and easy-access pussy.

"There's *every* need to be hasty," Jessica snarled and her temper flared again. "You are sick people!" At this,

Jessica threw her lunch, paperback and DVD at Jeb and ran from the room.

Jeb shuffled forwards in a clumsy penguin walk to follow Jessica, his pants still crumpled around his ankles.

Christobel put a calming hand on his arm. "Stay put, Jebediah," she instructed. "I'll deal with Jessica; make her see things *our* way." She smiled sweetly at Jeb, jaw working hard on her gum. She tucked her cell phone into a pocket and headed for the door. "And pull your fucking pants up!" she barked.

*

Shaking, Jessica steadied herself against the desk at the nurses' station. She shrugged off her coat and it dropped with a wet *schlop* on the floor.

"Jessica!" Christobel raced along the hallway.

"Stay away from me!" Jessica spat.

"I'm sorry." Christobel held out her arms in a submissive gesture. "What more can I say?" She looked genuinely saddened, although that had more to do with getting caught than at her actions. "You have to understand, we just get so *bored*."

"That doesn't give you the right to assault the patients," Jessica said.

"They don't know any different," Christobel countered. "You can't think of 'em like normal people. For all we know, they probably *enjoy* the attention." Christobel really wasn't helping her cause.

"You really are a nasty piece of work, aren't you?" Jessica growled. "You're supposed to be taking care of the patients, not tormenting them for your stupid website."

"Please try to understand –"

"Emily spoke to me," Jessica interrupted. "In her own voice. She's trapped in her own head and I'm positive she's aware of what's going on. So now tell me they don't know any better."

A movement on the CCTV monitor went unnoticed by the two nurses. A monochrome Jeb walking across the room, casually looking at a DVD case held loosely in his hand. Suddenly, he dropped from view as if his legs had simply quit working. Jeb's silent, screaming face upturned to the camera for a split-second before it was obscured by a dark, bulky shape. Then the screen went blank.

"I really doubt that," Christobel lowered her voice. "She's never said *anything* she's not copied from the TV."

"I heard it." Jessica stood firm. "There's *definitely* something behind all of her voices and nonsense. And you and your pervert boyfriend have been molesting her."

Christobel took a deep breath. To loose her cool now would potentially mean losing her job, gaining a criminal record – and quite possibly worse. "Look, why don't you go outside, take a smoke break and calm yourself down?"

"I don't smoke."

Christobel fished around in her pocket and then forced a cigarette and a lighter into Jessica's hand. "Well, now would be the perfect time to start, don't you think?" The attempted brevity and fake smile were met with a stony face. "Just go smoke this – or don't. Think long and hard about how getting being involved in any of this will affect your future career." Christobel locked eyes with Jessica. "And if you still think that the management needs to know about this, I'll make the fucking phone call myself." Christobel was encouraged by a softening in Jessica's expression. "I'll take care of Emily and find Jebediah something to do in the laundry room."

"No more?"

"I promise." Christobel crossed her heart and hoped to die.

Jessica glanced down at the coat that lay in an untidy, damp heap at her feet and decided against wearing it. She made her way along the hallway to the main doors with Christobel's peace offering. Maybe tonight *was* a good night to pick up a new habit.

Christobel watched her go with a sly grin. Another dumb-ass temp' duly placated. The next order of business would be to get rid of the stupid girl completely; should be a walk in the park after tonight.

"Now, where were we?" Christobel plucked the cell phone from her pocket and walked with purpose back to Emily's room.

The door to Room Three was cracked slightly open; the only light within was that which crept in from the hallway – there was not even the flickering glow of the TV. Christobel pushed open the door. "Jeb?" she asked the darkness. "Quit foolin' around; we ain't got time for your dumb Halloween shenanigans, we gotta finish up before Nursey McPerfect comes back."

Something inside the room stirred and Christobel heard the shuffle of slow, deliberate footsteps. "I'm not in the mood for horsin' around, Jeb." She stepped in to the gloom.

A crackling, plastic crunch startled Christobel, made her jump a little. She looked down at her feet and saw that she'd stepped on the DVD case that Jessica had thrown at Jeb earlier. It appeared to be empty and splashed with something dark and glistening that resembled blood.

"Very funny, Jeb." Christobel giggled. "Jessica was right, you really are an asshole." Another movement in the dark and the TV burst into life, the white static of its screen illuminating the room and the horror the shadows had concealed.

Christobel choked on a scream and staggered backwards until the knobbles of her spine pressed hard to the wall, her hand held to her mouth in a faithful imitation of the terrified, scantily-clad girl on the cover of the DVD.

The scene laid out before Christobel was one of total and absolute carnage. Great swathes of blood had sprayed across the tiny room. It spattered every wall, as well as up to and across the ceiling from where it dripped down in thick, glinting stalactites. Clumps of raw meat and shreds of bloodied skin were scattered across the floor, stuck to the bed sheets and clinging to the TV, and what remained of Jeb lay in one corner, his shredded corpse spread out like a human platter, his head thrown back as if in a hearty laugh.

Christobel saw that Jeb's throat had been torn out with such voracity that she could make out the white points of vertebrae that protruded through the gore. Jeb's belly and chest had been ripped wide apart and ragged flesh hung limp around the gaping cavity like raw, bleeding meat on a butcher's slab. And adding insult to injury, Jeb's viscera had been ripped out from larynx to pubic bone and spread decoratively around the room.

Christobel willed her feet to take her away from the bloodbath and its sickening, cloying stench but they simply refused. She released a sob along with the breath she'd been holding and her bladder let go of its load. The heat of her pee felt perversely comforting as it trickled down her thighs to pool at her feet and the nauseating, ammonia stink of her waste infused with that of Jeb's innards. Christobel couldn't help but notice that Jeb's crotch was gone; it looked to her as if the contents had been scooped out with some oversized, cruelly jagged melon baller. The magnificent member that she had enjoyed so many times in her mouth, her pussy, her ass and between her breasts was gripped tightly in Jebediah's hand and it looked like he'd been trying to stick it back in place even as he'd died. Jeb's penis was still half erect and blood oozed out from its ragged stump as it gradually deflated like a kid's punctured pool toy.

Finally, Christobel forced herself to move, although her feet agreed only to tiny steps, and she focussed on getting the fuck out of the tiny room.

Too late.

A guttural snarl, a whiff of foul, coppery breath was followed by a force of inhuman strength that shoved Christobel to the floor. She hit the tiles hard, her head bounced with a loud, nauseating crack and a hot, metallic taste poured down the back of her throat that reminded her of her of the nosebleeds that had so plagued her childhood. She heard a breathy *whoosh* like a swooping night owl and the swipe of a hot, sticky something almost knocked her head from her shoulders. It took out Christobel's eyes, rending one completely from its socket and ripping away the front of the other and it dribbled warm, viscous liquid down her cheek.

And then Christobel's assailant was upon her, forcing her down with its crushing weight, ripping, tearing with razor claws and keen teeth that dug deep and vicious into her flesh. She wriggled and screamed and flailed and instinctively Christobel threw up her arms to protect what remained of her face from the frenzied attack, only to have the flesh stripped from her bones. The hot, panting body pressed down hard and forced the air from Christobel's lungs, rubbing coarse fur against her shredded skin and she felt the rigid grating of teeth on bone as her attacker ripped away her cheeks and guzzled up the remains of her eye.

The nurse pushed out with her feet to maneuver her pain wracked body towards the door, but the weight of the thing that pinned her to the floor, along with the spilled, slippery body fluids on the tiles prevented her escape. Instead, Christobel's flailing feet slipped and slid in a tragic, horizontal dance as the thing eviscerated her.

A world beyond pain now, awash with adrenaline, Christobel experienced a peculiar *drawing* sensation as her bowels were dragged out and chewed upon; the rip and shred of muscle, the feeling her own bones made as they crunched between powerful jaws. Vicious claws dug into her chest and forced her rib cage apart. The splintering of ribs and the sense of being pulled asunder finally proved more than Christobel's mind could handle and it began to close down. And when her heart was wrenched out and eaten, Nurse Christobel died.

*

Jessica flicked on the light and walked in. The bulb that dangled from the ceiling was splashed with blood and lit up Emily's room with an eerie, reddish glow. She surveyed the butchery with a wrinkle of her nose and *tut-tutted* to herself.

The remains of Jeb and his slutty nurse girlfriend lay scattered and homogenised in pools of dark, congealing blood. Puddles of dark, clotting blood congealed and glinted underfoot and as she stepped through the room, Jessica took great pains to avoid them; they were quite deep and would ruin her shoes.

Quietly watching her TV, amidst what now resembled a gruesome homage to Tom Savini, sat the girl they'd named Emily. She was naked and drenched in blood from straggly hair to thin, pointed toes and her eyes shone out through the gore, bright and malevolent. Relaxed, Emily rested back on her elbows, legs spread wide, as if offering her vagina to the TV.

"I knew it had to be you," Jessica said softly as she

knelt beside Emily. She stroked the girl's crimson-soaked hair, tucked it behind an ear to reveal the pretty face beneath, saw the residual lupine features – fading fast by now – and the hint of honed, carnivorous teeth that glinted between the girl's bloodied lips.

"Do you have any idea just how many crappy jobs in depressing mental institutions I've taken just to track you down?" Jessica laughed and it was a light, warm chuckle. "Nah, I guess you don't."

Emily turned to face the nurse and made eye contact for the very first time.

"And then I saw on the Internet this patient and her crazy voices - and here you were!" Jessica said. "Which is why I brought you this." She plucked the cracked DVD case from the gore-strewn tiles and wiped away the blood. *Werewolf Terror from Hell IV* - the title was written in that clichéd, dripping-blood font that was so incredibly popular in the nineteen-eighties. Beneath the title, a werewolf wearing a sports jacket was terrorizing a screaming, semi-naked and unfeasibly large-breasted cheerleader. The movie itself was strictly low-budget, straight-to-video crap, but had nonetheless served Jessica's purpose rather effectively.

Jessica pulled out a syringe from her pocket, one with a ludicrously fat needle. "I have just the right buyer for someone of your quality," she soothed as she popped the protective plastic cap from the needle. "And he's going to pay me so much money that I'll never have to set foot in one of these hellholes again." She smiled at Emily and saw what she imagined to be a glimmer of understanding in those deep, *brown* eyes – the transformation back to human was not quite as complete as she'd first thought. "You'll be so much happier with your own kind," the nurse said.

Jessica eased the needle into the girl's neck and depressed the plunger. Her eyes stayed with Emily's and

Jessica was positive that she saw the faintest traces of the mimic demon that skulked behind them.

As Emily departed consciousness, she slumped limp and lifeless into the nurse's arms and Jessica cradled her newest acquisition for a while.

END

To watch the award winning short movie of *First Impressions*, please pop in to www.jameslongmore.com

About Your Author

James hails originally from Yorkshire, England having relocated with his family to Houston, Texas in 2010. He has an honors degree in Zoology and a background in sales, marketing and business. Relatively new to the writing arena, his writing style and story telling have already been compared to Stephen King, Dan Brown and Robert Ludlum.

An Affiliate Member of the Horror Writer's Association, James has to date five novels published, with another due in 2017 – in addition to three novellas and eight short stories dotted about in various anthologies.

James also writes screenplays and currently has three under option (a spine-chilling horror, a Tarantino-esque crime caper and an animated family movie). In 2014 he was commissioned by Spectra Records to write a biopic feature on the early life of Bob Marley, and in 2015 was writer for hire on the Kenyan sitcom '*The Samaritans*'.

As if that weren't enough, James has written and directed a bunch of short movies, winning Best Director in the 2013 *Splatterfest* film competition and Remi awards at Houston's *Worldfest* Film Festival in 2012, 2014 and 2015.

In his spare time, James pens and performs stand-up comedy on the Houston comedy circuit.

James' writing style has been described as

uncompromising, unique and entertaining; he combines highly original ideas with brilliant vocabulary and highly effective yarn spinning in which the story always comes first! Be warned, his work does have a tendency towards the dark side – usually with a rich vein of humor – and there is *always* that delicious twist at the end!

www.jameslongmore.com

Also by James H Longmore

'Pede
Flanagan
And Then You Die
Buds
The Erotic Odyssey of Colton Forshay
Feeder/I Am Joe's Unwanted Penis
Tenebrion

Other HellBound Books Titles

Worship Me

Something is listening to the prayers of St. Paul's United Church, but it's not the god they asked for; it's something much, much older.

A quiet Sunday service turns into a living hell when this ancient entity descends upon the house of worship and claims the congregation for its own. The terrified churchgoers must now prove their loyalty to their new god by giving it one of their children or in two days time it will return and destroy them all.

As fear rips the congregation apart, it becomes clear that if they're to survive this untold horror, the faithful must become the faithless and enter into a battle against God itself. But as time runs out, they discover that true monsters come not from heaven or hell… …they come from within.

No Rest ForThe Wicked

A modern day ghost story with its skeletons buried firmly in the past.

From beyond the grave, a murderous wife seeks to complete her revenge on those who betrayed her in life; a powerless domestic still fears for her immortal soul while trying to scare off anyone who comes too close; and the former plantation master - a sadistic doctor who puts more faith in the teachings of de Sade than the Bible

When Eric and Grace McLaughlin purchase Greenbrier Plantation, their dreams are just as big as those who have tried to tame the place before them. But, the doctor has learned a thing or two over his many years in the afterlife, is putting those new skills to the test, and will go to great lengths in order to gain the upper hand. While Grace digs into the death-filled history of her new home, Eric soon becomes a pawn of the doctor's unsavory desires and rapidly growing power, and is hell-bent on stopping her.

Sángre: The Color of Dying

Carlos Colón's first published novel is the story of Nicky Negrón, a Puerto Rican salesman in New York City who is turned into foul-mouthed, urban vampire with a taste for the undesirables of society such as sexual predators, domestic abusers and drug dealers.

A tragic anti-hero, Nicky is haunted by profound loss. When his life is cut short due to an unforeseen event at the Ritz-Carlton, it results in a public sex scandal for his surviving family. He then rises from the dead to become a night stalker with a genetic resistance that enables him to retain his humanity, still valuing his family whilst also struggling to somehow maintain a sense of normalcy.

Simultaneously described as haunting, hilarious, horrifying and heartbreaking, Sángre: The Color of Dying is a breathtakingly fun read.

Demons, Devils & Denizens of Hell Volume I

A hellish collection of short stories from some of the best in the business - compiled by the award-winning author P. Mattern.

Featuring tales from the darkest pits of hades by, Tania Hagan, Lily Luchesi, Jay Michael Wright II, Ken Goldman, Sergio "ente per ente" Palumbo, Emery LeeAnn, Crystal Barnard, James H Longmore, Toneye Eyenot, James Richardson, Lori Fontanez, Marcus Mattern, Lance Tuck, L. Ashby, P. Mattern, Elizabeth Cash, Bryan A. Tann, Elizabeth Zemlicka, Michael Sutton, Thomas S. Gunther, Feind Gottes, and the incomparable Nik Kerry

The Big Book of Bootleg Horror

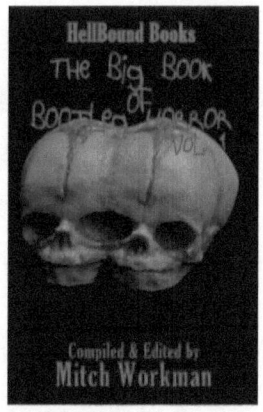

Twenty tales of terror, darkness, the truly macabre and things most unpleasant from a delectably eclectic bunch of the very best independent horror authors on the scene today:
S.E. Rise, Kevin Wetmore, Paul Stansfield, Craig Stwewart, Shaun Avery, Jeff Meyers, Marc DeWit, Timothy Wilkie, Quinn Cunningham, Melanie Waghorne, Marc E. Fitch, Stanley B. Webb, Tim J. Finn, Ken Goldman, Ralph Greco Jr, Roger Leatherwood, Vincent Treewell, David Owain Hughes, J.J. Smith and the inimitable James H. Longmore

In this superlative tome, HellBound Books have embraced the taboo, gone all-out to horrify and have broken the flimsy boundaries of good taste to make The Big Book of Bootleg Horror the perfect anthology for those who take their horror like we take our coffee - insidiously dark and most definitely unsweetened.

Shopping List

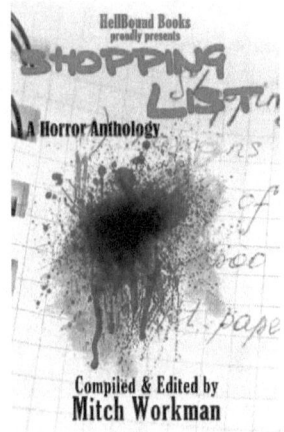

A simply superlative collection of spine-tingling horror from the very best minds in the business!

We decided upon the shopping list theme for this particular volume as an antithesis to those wildly successful writers (they know who they are) of whom it is often said *'we would read their damned shopping list if they published it!'*.

Well, we have given twenty-one of the hottest authors in the independent horror scene the unique opportunity to have their own shopping lists read by you - along with their most terrifying tales of course!

Stories of gut-wrenching terror from:

Kathy Dinisi, Robert Over, Christopher O'Halloran, Eric W. Burgin, Russ Gartz, Mark Slada, Jeff Baker, Tim Miller, Nick Swain, JC Raye, Jovan Jones, Ben Stevens, David F. Gray, Brandon Cracraft, M.S. Swift, Kevin Holton, David Owain Hughes, Bertram Allan Mullin, Jeff C. Stevenson, Sebastian Crow and S.E. Rise

James H Longmore

A HellBound Books LLC Publication

http://www.hellboundbookspublishing.com

Printed in the United States of America

465

www.ingramcontent.com/pod-product-compliance
Lightning Source LLC
Chambersburg PA
CBHW030645120726
47905CB00001B/62